Resounding praise for the miraculous debut novel by
KAREN TRAVISS
CITY OF PEARL

"[A] satisfyingly complex tale of human/alien interaction on a
colony planet which, at times, evokes the earlier moral fables
of Le Guin . . . at other times the revisionist critique of
expanding human empires . . . and at times the union
of romance with SF that we see in the work of Catherine
Asaro or Lois McMaster Bujold. The fact that Traviss manages
to keep these sometimes conflicting modes in balance, mostly
through her strong sense of character, suggests that she's a
writer worth watching."
Locus

"In Shan Frankland, Karen Traviss has created a tough,
interesting, believable character . . . *City of Pearl* is
science fiction with teeth."
Gregory Frost, author of *Fitcher's Brides*

"A fascinating cast of characters involved in a richly
complex situation . . . Her people are convincingly
real . . . Traviss has created a vivid assortment of alien races,
each with distinctive characteristics and agendas . . . She
brings a rare combination of insight and experience that will
greatly contribute to our field."
James Alan Gardner, author of *Expendable*

Books by
Karen Traviss

CROSSING THE LINE
CITY OF PEARL

CROSSING THE LINE

KAREN TRAVISS

An Imprint of HarperCollins*Publishers*

EOS
An Imprint of HarperCollins*Publishers*
10 East 53rd Street
New York, New York 10022-5299

Copyright © 2004 by Karen Traviss
ISBN: 0-06-054170-9
www.eosbooks.com

First Eos paperback printing: November 2004

HarperCollins® and Eos® are trademarks of HarperCollins Publishers Inc.

Printed in the U. S. A.

10 9 8 7 6 5 4 3 2 1

For Richard D. Ryder, Andrew Linzey, and all those who question where we have drawn the line.

Acknowledgments

Thanks go to Charlie Allery, Debbie Button, Bryan Boult and Chris "TK" Evans, for thorough and critical reading; to Dr. Ian Tregillis and Mark Allery for technical advice; to Dr. Farah Mendlesohn for cheerleading; to my editor, Diana Gill, never fazed by wild plot changes; and to my father, George, who taught me the value of thorough preparation.

ACKNOWLEDGMENTS

CROSSING THE LINE

Prologue

It was much, much worse at night.

Night cut you off from any reference, any reassurance, and nights here on Bezer'ej were far blacker than any Shan Frankland had seen on light-polluted Earth.

Once the lights that danced in the blackness were the product of her optic nerve playing electrical tricks. But these lights were real.

They were coming from her hands.

The display was mainly blue and violet, flashing occasionally from her fingertips. It was almost as bad as her claws. And it wasn't something any human should have had, but Shan wasn't any human, not any more.

Don't think of it as a parasite, Aras told her. *Think of it as a beneficial relationship. It can be.*

Aras had five hundred years to get used to carrying *c'naatat*, being *c'naatat*, living with all that *c'naatat* meant; and she had been infected for a matter of months. He meant well. He did it to save her life. But it was hard waking up to a new body every day.

She studied the pattern of lights again and wondered if there was language within it, as there was for the native bezeri. She also wondered if her *c'naatat* had done it to teach her a lesson for hubris, for her contempt for the organic illuminated computer screens grown into the hands of combat troops.

You'll never put one of those bloody things in me.

But here she was, with that and plenty more. The symbionts had almost certainly scavenged the component genes at random, unaware of her beliefs and her guilt. She was just an environment to be preserved with whatever came to hand. If they had purpose beyond that, she wasn't sure that she wanted to know about it.

Shan put her fingers to her head and felt through the hair. There wasn't the slightest trace of unevenness in the bone, no evidence that her skull had been shattered by an alien weapon. *C'naatat* was efficient. It seemed to enjoy doing a tidy job.

Small wonder that some of her former crewmates from *Thetis* thought she was a paid mule for manufactured alien biotech. The truth was messy and unconvincing, but truth often was, and it didn't matter. The crew knew the broad detail, and so did the colonists of Constantine who gave her asylum, and it would only be a matter of time before the matriarchs of Wess'ej found out what Aras had done to save her.

And then all hell would break loose.

She buried her head under her blanket and tried to sleep, but the lights persisted, and she fell into dreams of drowning in a locked room that was scented like a forest.

1

There are countless constellations, suns, and planets: we see only the suns because they give light; the planets remain invisible, for they are small and dark. There are also numberless earths circling around their suns, no worse and no less than this globe of ours.

GIORDANO BRUNO,
Dominican monk and philosopher,
burned at the stake by the Inquisition
in February 1600

"Is it true?"

Eddie Michallat concentrated on the features of the duty news editor twenty-five light-years away, courtesy of CSV *Actaeon*'s comms center. The man was real and it was happening *now,* in every sense of the word.

For nearly a year he had been beyond BBChan's reach on Bezer'ej. But the glorious isolation was over. Isenj instantaneous communications technology meant there was now no escape from the scrutiny of News Desk. In the way of journalists, they had already given it an acronym, as noun, verb and adjective—ITX.

"Poodle-in-the-microwave job," Eddie said dismissively. "Urban myth. People talk the most incredible crap when they're under stress."

He waited a few seconds for the reply. The borrowed isenj communications relay was half a million miles from Earth, and that meant the last leg in the link was at light speed, the best human technology could manage. The problem with the delay was that it gave Eddie more time to stoke his irritation.

"That never stopped you filing a story before."

How the hell would he know? This man—this *boy*, for that was all he appeared to be—had probably been born fifty years after *Thetis* had first left Earth. Eddie enjoyed mounting the occasional high horse. He saddled up.

"BBChan used to be the responsible face of netbroadcast," he said. "You know—stand up a story properly before you run it? But maybe that's out of fashion these days."

One, two, three, four, five. The boy-editor persisted with the blind focus of a missile. "Look, you're sitting on a completely fucking shit-hot twenty-four carat story. Biotech, lost tribes, mutiny, murder, aliens. Is there anything I've left out?"

"There wasn't a mutiny and Shan Frankland didn't murder anyone." *She's just a good copper*, Eddie wanted to say, but it was hardly the time. "And the biotech is pure speculation." *My speculation. Me and my big mouth.* "We don't know what it is. We don't know if it makes you invulnerable. But you got the aliens about right. That's something."

"The *Thetis* crew was saying that Frankland's carrying this biotech and that she's pretty well invulnerable to injury and disease, and—"

Eddie maintained his dismissive expression with some difficulty, a child again, cowering at the sound of a grown-ups' row: *it's all my fault.* He always worried that it was. "Oh God, don't give me the undead routine, will you? I don't do infotainment."

"And I don't do the word 'no.' Stand up that story."

The kid was actually trying to get tough with him. It wasn't easy having a row with someone when you had time to count to five each time. But Eddie was more afraid of the consequences of this rumor than the wrath of a stranger, even one who employed him.

"Son, listen to me," he said. "You're twenty-five years away as the very, *very* fast crow flies, so I don't think you're in any position to tell me to do *sod all*." He leaned forward, arms folded on the console, and hoped the cam was picking up a shot that gave him the appearance of looming over the kid. "I'm the only journalist in 150 trillion miles of nothing. *Anything* I file is exclusive. And I decide what I file. Now run along and finish your homework."

Eddie flicked the link closed without waiting for a response and reassured himself that there really was nothing that 'Desk could do to him any more. He was *here*. *Actaeon* had no embeds embarked. BBChan could sack him, and every network on Earth would be offering him alternative employment. It wasn't bravado. It was career development.

Ironically, the stories he had filed months ago were still on their way home at plain old light speed: the stories he would file now, would ITX, would beat them by years. He was scooping himself and it felt wonderful. It struck him as the journalistic equivalent of masturbation.

"I wish I could get away with that," said the young lieutenant on comms duty. He hovered just on the edge of Eddie's field of vision. "Why didn't you tell him you were on your way to see the isenj?"

"Because all news editors are tossers," Eddie said. He felt around in his pockets for the bee-cam and his comms kit. "If you tell them what story you're chasing, they decide in their own minds how it's going to turn out. Then they bollock you for not coming back with the story they imagined. So you don't tell them anything until you're ready to file. Saves a lot of grief."

"Wise counsel," said the lieutenant, as if he understood.

From *Actaeon*'s bridge, Eddie could still see the dwindling star that was EFS *Thetis*, heading back to Earth with the remnant of the Constantine mission, a party of isenj delegates and their ussissi interpreters. So vessels weren't titled European Federal Ship these days, then. A nice bland CSV, a harmless Combined Service Vessel, purged of any reference to territory to avoid offending the recent multinational alliance between Europe and the Sinostates. He had seventy-five years left to amaze the viewing public with the latest in alien contact before the real thing showed up on their doorstep. *Thetis* was a much older, slower ship than the *Actaeon*.

And *Thetis* had been the state of the art just over a year ago. Time was flying obscenely and confusingly fast.

"It's not like he can send someone out to relieve you of duty, is it?" said the lieutenant. He seemed to have badged Eddie as a maverick hero, an understandable reaction for a young man enmeshed in the strict hierarchies of navy life. No, there was nothing News Desk could do out here: Shan Frankland had taught him that. When you were on your own, without backup, you had to make your own decisions and stand by them. "Is Frankland really as bad as they say? Did she really sell you out? Did she let people die?"

"Who's saying?"

"Commander Neville."

"Look, the commander's been through a lot lately. I'd take some of her observations with a pinch of salt. You can't lose your kid without losing some sanity too." *I'm just an observer.* No, he wasn't. He was involved in this. He had been involved in it right from the time he had decided there were some stories about Shan that he was never going to file. "Lindsay had a sickly, premature kid. That's what you get if you're not used to low oxygen. You've got to remember the colony's medical facilities are pretty primitive."

A pause. "But presumably Frankland's aren't."

"Are you trying to interrogate me, son?"

"Just making conversation."

"Word of advice. Never try to get information out of a hack. We wrote the book on wheedling. I can't give you any information on Frankland because I don't have any." *Well, technically, I don't.* It suddenly struck him that he was calling all younger males *son*, just as Shan did, a copper's kind patronage with its edge of threat. "No, Frankland probably saved a lot of lives. But maybe she's proof that it isn't what's true that makes historical record, it's who gets their story in first."

A blood sample from Shan here, and a cell culture there, and maybe David Neville might have survived more than a few weeks. But releasing that biotech into the human population was a price Shan Frankland refused to pay, regardless of what it cost her. Eddie knew that now.

And he still felt guilty that he believed, however briefly, that she had been carrying the biotech for money. He wondered whether he would have made the same choice if placed in the same dilemma.

"Come on," he said to the young officer, who was hanging on his pronouncements like a disciple. "Take me down to the shuttle bay. I'm going to have tea with the isenj foreign minister."

Aras crunched down to the cliffs on a paper-thin crust of light snow. He still worried when Shan was out after nightfall. But she could come to no harm. She couldn't freeze to death, and she couldn't drown, and she couldn't die even if she fell and broke her neck.

And neither could he.

But she was uneasy. He could smell that even from a hundred meters away. She was where he had hoped to find her, sitting near the cliff edge again, looking down at the glittering darkness of a sea half illuminated by Wess'ej in its gibbous phase.

He concentrated, willing his visual range to expand. A human would hardly have spotted her. A wess'har's low-light vision would have picked her out. But on top of that, Aras had his infrared sensitivity, gleaned from the isenj by his *c'naatat*, and Shan was at that moment a shimmering golden ghost of bright-hot exposed skin and darker, cooler garments.

The *c'naatat* produced a fever during its active phases. He could see it. She wouldn't be feeling the cold at all.

"Time to eat," he said quietly. "Still watching for the bezeri?"

She smiled, a brief flash of hotter, whiter light flaring in a mask of amber. "I wanted to wave to them." She peeled off her gloves, held out her hands and flexed them. Brilliant violet lights flickered briefly under the skin. "I think I can guess where I picked that up."

She was bothered by it. She feigned calm well enough to fool a human but not enough to evade a wess'har sense of smell. Her expression, her posture, her voice; all said she was fine. But her scent said otherwise.

"It might not be from the bezeri," he said, as if that made a difference. "*C'naatat* is often unpredictable. I've been around bezeri for many years and never absorbed any of their characteristics."

"As far as you know, of course. Well, could be worse. At least it's not their tentacles, eh?" She flexed her fingers again and stared at them. The lights, as intense now as anything the bezeri emitted, added to her illuminated image. "Shouldn't I talk to them? I feel I owe them an explanation."

Aras thought the bezeri probably had all the explanation they needed or wanted. However much Shan thought she could protect them, however ashamed she was of her own species' short history on Bezer'ej, the bezeri themselves were still raw from losing an infant to human violence. Aras wondered how the humans—the *gethes*, the carrion-eaters—who flew into violent outrage themselves at the harming of a child could think another species would behave any differently.

It was just as well that the bezeri were soft-bodied, confined to the sea, and without real weapons beyond their piercing mouth-parts. Shan's apologies would mean little to them.

He held his hand out to her. "Here. They're not coming. They haven't been near the surface for weeks. Let's eat."

It was like watching a child who was scarred by a fire of your making, a constant rebuke to your carelessness, except that he had done this deliberately. She was trying to cope with her *c'naatat* and finding it hard. *What choice did I have? She would have died if I hadn't infected her.* But he knew how it felt to wake wondering what alterations that the microscopic symbiont was making to your body. He had seen *c'naatat* develop in others, and no two experienced exactly the same changes.

That was the least of her problems. In time—and she would

have plenty of that—she would have to cope with the lonely reality of having everyone she knew age and die, leaving her
alone, except for him. He knew where his duty lay. He owed her
that much.

But she was right. It could have been worse.

She could have found herself reliving other beings' memories.

"I'm starving," she said. *C'naatat* demanded a lot of energy
while it was rearranging the genetic furniture. "I could murder
some nice thick lentil soup. And some of those little rolls with
the walnut bits in."

"We'll see what the refectory has to offer."

They walked back to Constantine across a plain that was
starting to push blue-gray grass through the snow. Usually Aras
managed to see only what was truly there: tonight, once again,
the images of what had once been were intruding on the present.

Shan walked through wilderness. But Aras walked along the
vanished perimeter of an isenj city called Mjat and down what
had been a main thoroughfare flanked by homes. There was less
than nothing left, but he remembered exactly where it had been.
He hadn't needed to see the *gethes'* clever geophys images of
the ghost of a civilization to recall those roads, because he had
mapped them.

And he had destroyed them.

He had washed the cities with fire and cut down isenj and set
loose the reclamation nanites that devoured the deserted
homes. It had been five hundred years ago by the Constantine
calendar, but he remembered it all, and not only from his own
viewpoint. Back then he had had no idea that isenj had genetic
memory.

"I'm sorry," he said. "But I had to do it."

Shan seemed to think he was talking to her. "Stop apologizing." She thrust her arm through his. "It's okay."

Apart from a brief, violent escape of contained rage when
she had found out she was infected, she had shown neither self-

pity nor recrimination. He admired that about her. It was very wess'har. It would make it far easier for her to adapt to her new world.

Could be worse.

Aras walked the invisible central plaza of Mjat. *Worse* could have been genetic memory, and that was perhaps worst of all, worse than claws or vestigial wings or a million other scraps of genetic material that *c'naatat* had picked up, tried on for size, and then sometimes discarded.

Now he was clear of Mjat and back in the small world of humans, his home for the best part of two centuries. Wess'ej, the planet where he had been born, hung in the sky as a huge crescent moon, and he didn't miss it at all.

The biobarrier crackled slightly as they passed through into Constantine's shielded, controlled environment. Aras trod carefully to avoid the overwintering kale that was shrouded in snowlike sculptures.

Wess'har had no sculpture, no poetry, no music. He almost understood those concepts now, but not entirely. There was a great deal of human DNA in him: *c'naatat* had probably found it in shed skin cells and bacteria and taken a fancy to it, but it had not helped him grasp the human fondness for what was clearly unreal. He had often wondered why the symbiont had devoted so much energy to altering his appearance and fashioning a makeshift human out of him.

It took him some time to realize that it had given him yet another refinement to help him—its world—survive. It was trying to help him to fit into human society. It seemed to know he was outcast from his own forever.

It knew how badly he needed to belong.

Malcolm Okurt had not signed up for this. He told Lindsay Neville so. He took it as a personal slight, he said, and it was bad enough having to crew a vessel with *civilians* without getting dragged into *politics* as well. He was the only person Lindsay knew who could spit the words out like that. At chill-down, his orders were to follow up the *Thetis* mission. Nobody mentioned anything about aliens, especially not four separate civilizations.

"I thought you'd want to get out of here as fast as you could," he said.

Lindsay paused, and not for effect. "I've got unfinished business. I lost my kid here."

Okurt knew that well enough. She just wanted to remind him that she needed a wide berth at times. She didn't feel the pain at all, not right then. She made sure she didn't because if she did then she would fall apart, and as she told Okurt, she had a task to complete.

She steadied herself and glanced at her bioscreen, the living battlefield computer display grown into the palm of her hand. She couldn't switch off the light, but she had disabled the monitor functions because it depressed her to see the unchanging bio signs of her comrades in chill-sleep. It made them look as if they were dead.

Okurt must have been watching her gaze. "They phased those out years ago," he said. "Unreliable."

So nobody had them any more, nobody except her and a few Royal Marines who were on their way home. She turned her hand palm down on the table.

When Okurt was agitated he had a habit of spinning his coffee cup in its saucer, and he was doing it now. "We might have been able to help, had we been allowed access."

"I know." She was drawing parallel lines on the pad in front of her, darker and deeper and harder with each stroke. "Do you have current orders regarding Frankland?"

"We're backing off for the time being. No point getting into a pissing match with the wess'har, not if we want to do business with them. If she's got what you say she's got, there'll be other ways to acquire it. I've got enough on my plate trying to keep the isenj sweet without the wess'har noticing we're kissing both their arses."

"I can't help thinking this double game is going to be the proverbial hiding to nothing."

"It's diplomacy. Evenhandedness. Like arming both sides in a war."

"The wess'har don't deal in gray areas."

"Well, they'll get fed up with the isenj taking pot shots at them sooner or later and then an offer of assistance might be appreciated."

"And who's going to negotiate with them?"

"I pulled the winning ticket."

"Oh. I take it the isenj aren't privy to this."

"Of course not. And it wasn't my idea. Thanks to the bloody EP or ITX or whatever they're calling it today, I don't have the luxury of making my own decisions. I've got politicians and chiefs of staff second-guessing me a comms call away. I might as well be a bloody glove-puppet. And don't tell me ITX is a boon to mankind. It's a pain in the arse."

Lindsay wondered how different things would have been if *Thetis* had been able to get instant messages and instructions back from Earth. It might have made matters worse. She wondered if it would have saved Surendra Parekh: somehow she doubted it. Somewhere there was a bezeri parent who had lost a child because of the biologist's arrogant curiosity about cephalopods, and for a split second she felt every shade of that alien pain.

No, she was content that Shan had let the wess'har execute the woman.

But that didn't excuse her allowing David to die. She took the rising bubble of pain and crushed it into herself again.

"At least we'll probably go down as the most economically viable mission in history," said Okurt. "Instant comms, new territory, maybe even immortality in a bottle. That's what exploration's really about. Unless Frankland's already acquired the biotech for a specific corporation, of course."

"She said she wasn't paid to get the tech. I'm inclined to believe her. She's not like that."

"Come on, *everybody's* like that sooner or later."

"Not her. She's EnHaz. An environmental protection officer. As far as she's concerned, she's on a personal mission to cleanse the bloody universe. And she loathes corporations, believe me. Enough to let terrorists loose on them. Enough to *be* a terrorist."

"Well, whatever EnHaz was, I've got my orders—detain her, as and when, for unauthorized killing of a civilian and for being a potential biohazard. That'll do for now."

Despite her hatred, Lindsay fought back an urge to correct Okurt about Frankland's involvement. It might have been her weapon that shot Parekh, but she hadn't fired it, whatever she claimed. The woman would have said anything to protect her pet wess'har, Aras. Lindsay had confronted him once: she had no doubt he would have killed her too without losing a second's sleep over it.

"I want Frankland," she said. "But I want her for the right reasons. This isn't vengeance."

She dug her stylus into the paper. She hadn't written a single word, just black lines. When she caught Okurt staring, she tapped the border of the smartpaper and the surface plumped up into pristine white nothingness again.

"I'm sure it isn't," he said, eyeing her in evident disbelief. She put the stylus back in her breast pocket.

Actaeon's wardroom was comfortable and quiet, with all the refinements that fifty years of further development could make in a ship. You could hardly hear the constant rush of air or feel the vibration of machinery that had permeated *Thetis*. But it was still too small for two commanders. All the security she had once derived from knowing her exact place in the service hierarchy had evaporated. Out of rank, and out of time: she wanted to be busy.

"I can't sit around filing reports forever," she said. "You need an extra pair of hands."

"What I need is to get this base set up on Umeh, and I need people who've had alien contact experience. And I don't mean Eddie bloody Michallat, either. I won't have BBChan running the show, even if they do think they're a government department."

"The isenj like Eddie. He might be your best route to Frankland too. Even she liked him in the end."

It was too painful to say *Shan*. It was the way you referred to a friend.

"She's just one woman," Okurt said. "How much trouble can a disgraced copper be?"

"Find out why she was demoted in the first place before you dismiss her." Lindsay was surprised he hadn't heard the gossip. Buzzes like that usually flew round a ship fast: the antiterrorist officer who went native. Yes, Shan had enjoyed quite a checkered career. "Civvy police dip in and out of uniform discipline as and when it suits them, and she doesn't know the meaning of rules of engagement. So don't give her an inch. She wasn't always in EnHaz—she's ex–Special Branch. You name it, she's done it."

"Get it in perspective. She's just another plod with a few more brain cells. She isn't special forces."

"Don't say I didn't warn you." Lindsay reached in her jacket and pulled out her sidearm. She laid it on the table. Okurt said nothing but his eyes were a study in amazement. "Promise me this. If we're ever in a position to take her, let me do it. I let her walk away once and I regretted it. I won't make that mistake again."

Okurt still stared at the weapon. "Perhaps you should stow that in the armory," he said.

"No thanks." She slipped it back into her jacket. "Trust me. I've never been more controlled. There's only one person who needs to worry about me."

A plod with a few more brain cells.

No, Okurt didn't have a clue about Shan Frankland.

2

To: Foreign Office, Federal European Union
FROM: CDR. MALCOLM OKURT, CSV *Actaeon*

We have been unable to detain Superintendent Frankland as she has been granted protection by the wess'har authorities. The best intelligence we have is that she is still on CS2. Under the circumstances, I believe we have no option but to let the matter rest for the time being: pressing the issue will compromise any later negotiations we might have with the wess'har regarding landings on CS2. The BBChan embed here says that we should start calling the planet by the name Bezer'ej when dealing with the wess'har, and Asht when talking to the isenj, but not CS2 or Cavanagh's Star 2. Apparently it smacks of colonialism and might offend the local population.

It was hard being nothing more than an extra pair of hands.

Shan stabbed the shovel into the frost-hardened ground and turned another spadeful of soil. She made a few rough calculations. Another fifty square meters and she'd be done.

The claws were really getting on her nerves now. She kept catching them on the handle of the spade, snagging her pants, scratching her face. She couldn't quite get the hang of them. Sometimes they were worse than the lights.

But they weren't worse than the nightmares.

The sensations persisted into waking. She was in a room enveloped in a smell like a forest floor. She couldn't see anyone, but she knew somebody was there. The sequence of events was jumbled: but however it manifested, the events were the same—searing loneliness, the wild panic of trying not to breathe and then inhaling a lungful of icy water, followed by agonizing pain between her shoulder blades.

And she had thought she was coping pretty well, all things considered. The dream symbolism was unoriginal except for the smell. *Maybe I'm not as tough as I think*, she decided. An unbroken night's sleep would have been welcome.

And nobody needs a copper out here.

The ground was almost too hard to dig, but she wanted to make an early start, a *manual* start, to prove that she had no intention of freeloading on the Constantine colony's generosity.

And they don't need to learn how to control a riot or secure a crime scene or keep yourself from going barmy with boredom during a month-long surveillance. They don't need me at all.

It was just as well that the wess'har thought she might come in useful one day. Otherwise she was just a mouth that needed feeding, and there were no shops here. If she didn't plant it and grow it, she didn't eat it. Suddenly all those dreams she had once cherished—a patch of soil to cultivate when she turned in her warrant card, a little more time to herself—seemed painfully ironic. She'd got exactly, *literally*, all too bloody generously what she had wished for. She rammed the spade hard into the soil again.

The sun—Cavanagh's Star to humans, Ceret to wess'har— was making little impression on the frost at this time of the morning. Shan stopped and leaned on the shovel. Josh Garrod was making his way towards her, stumbling over the furrows that frozen water had burst and broken.

He was in a hurry. That wasn't encouraging; there was nothing to rush for here. She started towards him, sensing that there was some emergency and responding to ingrained police training, but he waved her back with both hands. He had her grip slung over his shoulder on a strap.

Maybe it was good news that couldn't wait. She doubted it.

When he reached her he was puffing clouds of acrid anxiety. Her altered sense of smell, another little retro-fit provided by her *c'naatat*, confirmed her fears. She had never seen the stoic colony leader in a flat panic before.

"You've got to get out." He pulled the bag off his back and held it out to her to take it. "I'll show you where to go—"

"Whoa, roll this back a bit," she said, but she already knew what he was going to say. "Just tell me why."

"They're here," he said. "They know. They're searching Constantine for you."

"Wess'har?"

"I'm afraid so."

There was the merest kick of adrenaline and then a sudden, cold, alien focus. "Where's Aras?" It had only been a matter of time. There was no monopoly of information. But she had expected a little more breathing space before the matriarchs discovered what Aras had done to her. Now she didn't even have time to wonder how.

"They've taken him. He told me to hide you. I promised him, Shan. Don't make me break that."

"Well, you've done your bit." She took the grip from him and slung it across her shoulder, then started walking back towards Constantine, shovel in hand.

Josh grabbed her shoulder. "You're not going back."

Shan glared at his hand. He withdrew it. "I bloody well am."

"You can hide out—"

"Yeah, 'course I can." Aras didn't deserve this. She owed him. She quickened her pace. "Good idea."

"Shan, they'll execute you. You know that."

"They'll have a job on their hands then, won't they? I'm a bit hard to kill. You might have noticed."

Josh broke into a run to keep up with her. She was a lot taller than the native-born, and now faster on her feet, too. "It's a big planet," he puffed. "They'll never find you."

"You reckon? We found *you*, and we were twenty-five light-years away. Sorry, Josh—I only know one way to deal with this, and that's to go and meet it. If it takes me, fine, and if I take it, that's great too, but I won't spend the rest of my life looking over my shoulder. Because that's going to be a bloody long time."

He didn't know her at all. He should have realized that she would never leave Aras. It was more than the biological links that *c'naatat* had forged between them: it was every bond of loyalty she had known as a police officer, stronger than family, and then—then there was something more besides, something she hadn't felt before. It was primeval, foreign, urgent. It was an overwhelming compulsion to *defend*.

She wondered if it was a remnant of the Suppressed Briefing. Perhaps there was still stuff that the Foreign Office had drug-programmed into her subconscious to be accessed later that she still didn't know about. It was as persistently irritating as a half-forgotten name or song, itching away in the back of her mind but refusing to be remembered clearly.

No, this was *different*.

Josh stumbled after her across the frost-hard ruts of soil, sidestepping planted areas despite his panic. Ahead of them the half-buried skylight domes of Constantine shimmered in the weak sunlight; on the horizon, the idyll of a terrestrial farm was shattered. Beyond the biobarrier the wess'har had erected to contain Constantine's ecology, the silver and blue early spring wilderness of Bezer'ej was a constant reminder that humans were temporary visitors here.

Out of habit, Shan reached behind her back and remembered she'd left her handgun in her room. She felt the fabric of her bag. Her fingers found the comforting outline of a pack of cartridges and a couple of small grenades that she didn't like to leave lying around. But in her mind's eye she could see the gun still sitting on the table beside her bed.

"Shit," she said aloud. She'd assumed you didn't need a weapon when you were digging. It was the sort of mistake she never normally made. *"Shit."*

"I put it inside your grip," Josh said, suddenly revealing that he knew her a lot better than she thought he did. "I thought you might need it."

Neither of them said *gun*. "Good thinking," said Shan.

She had expected to find a full-scale rummage team scouring Constantine. There were certainly enough wess'har troops stationed at the Temporary City on the mainland to provide one. But they were wess'har, and they didn't think like humans and they certainly hadn't read the police manual on apprehending suspects. She was surprised to see just three of them ambling round the underground galleries of the buried colony, giving the impression—an inaccurate one, she knew—that they were lost.

They held lovely gold instruments. Their weapons, like everything else in their functional culture, looked good. Two of the wess'har were males, but the other was a young female, bigger and stronger than her companions, a junior matriarch.

None of them looked at all like Aras.

It was easy to forget he was wess'har too. He was still strikingly alien: nobody would have mistaken him for a human. But his face and body had been resculpted by *c'naatat* with the human genes it had scavenged during his years of contact with the colonists at Constantine. From the relatively slender, pale elegance of a long-muzzled wess'har it had built an approximation of a man—huge and hard, with a face that was at once a beast's and a human's.

But these were pure wess'har, looking for all the world like paramilitary seahorses. She gestured to Josh to leave, and focused on the female walking along the gallery opposite her, high above the main street of Constantine and almost level with the roof of the church of St. Francis. Shan ran up the winding stairway after her, two steps at a time.

"You looking for me?" she called.

The female spun round and froze. It was never a good idea to startle someone who was armed, least of all a wess'har. But the creature cocked her pretty chess piece head to one side and stared.

"Are you the *gethes* Shan Frankland?"

"Who's asking?"

"I don't understand."

"Yeah, I'm Superintendent Frankland." As if her rank might

make a difference: it was simply habit. "And who the fuck are you?"

"I am Nevyan." The junior matriarch blinked rapidly and Shan was momentarily distracted by those unnerving four-lobed pupils set in gold irises. "You will come with us. The matriarchs know you are infected."

"Where's Aras?"

"In the Temporary City."

"I want to see him."

"Ask Mestin."

"I'm asking you."

"Ask Mestin." Nevyan was frozen in that characteristic wess'har wait-and-see reaction. Her irises snapped open and shut again. She smelled intimidated but she was holding her ground pretty well. "She is senior matriarch here."

"Okay, then we'll go to see Mestin." They stood and looked at each other, and Shan took a guess that Nevyan had absolutely no idea about humans, and knew even less about her. "And this has nothing to do with any of the people here. You understand? You leave them out of this."

"I was told to find you and Aras Sar Iussan. I have no orders regarding the colony."

The two males had wandered up behind Nevyan now, watching. Weapons at their sides, they appeared satisfied there was going to be no violence. Shan kept her eyes fixed on Nevyan's until the junior matriarch broke the gaze and began walking towards the ramp that led up and out of the subterranean settlement. Shan fell in behind her. How old was she in human terms? A teenager, a young woman? Shan couldn't tell yet.

One thing was for sure.

She hadn't been around long enough to know that prisoners—even compliant ones—needed searching.

Mestin decided she would hand over command of the Temporary City with not one pang of regret.

The last year had been a hard one. She had not expected it to be so difficult; Bezer'ej was normally a quiet tour of duty, somewhere to contemplate and study while the business of maintaining the cordon around the planet went on unnoticed, carried out by her husbands and children. And four years of her service had been just that, until the new humans came, and the isenj tried to follow them, and the fighting had started.

We will be home soon, she thought. Home, and maybe nothing more arduous to do than making decisions for the city of F'nar and educating her children. *If the* gethes *stay away.*

She sat out in the garden, well-wrapped against the cold with her *dhren* pulled up over her head and shoulders. The opalescent fabric shaped itself obligingly around her jaw to shut out the wind. *The first thing I shall do is walk around the whole perimeter of F'nar, right around the city.* It was not that she disliked Bezer'ej. It was unspoiled and exotic and beautiful, but it was not home, and she needed home very badly right then.

She couldn't take her eyes off the moon, off Wess'ej. Somewhere—right on the limb of the illuminated part, right *there*—was home, F'nar, one of the thousand modest city states of Wess'ej, warm and peaceful and in balance with the world.

Mestin stared at the imagined point until F'nar slipped into the darkness and night fell on it. She had done this every evening, cloud cover allowing, waiting for the time that her tour of duty would be over. She wondered how Aras had managed to spend so many years here without the comfort of fellow wess'har. At least she had all her clan with her, working together.

Aras had nothing.

There was no point putting it off any longer. He was sitting alone in a room in the depths of the Temporary City, under arrest, waiting for her. In another room sat Shan Frankland, the *gethes* matriarch. Mestin didn't know quite what to make of Frankland.

The woman had stayed here before for two days, in hiding from the rest of the humans. The matriarchs on Wess'ej had even held a meeting with her and judged her a useful ally. Yes, a *gethes* had been to Mestin's city while she and her family stayed here fending off isenj attacks. It galled her.

But that was before they realized why her fellow humans wanted her so badly.

So Frankland was now *c'naatat*. It was something the *gethes* found very desirable, in that greedy and desperate way of theirs, and something that *Shan Chail* would apparently not surrender to them. They said she feared what it would do to human society: Mestin wondered if she simply wanted a higher price.

The wind was biting and she felt the peck of ice crystals on her face. Nevyan, her daughter, walked up to her clutching her *dhren* tight around her. It was a nervous tic. The fabric would shape itself to whatever garment Nevyan arranged it to be, and needed no clutching or pinning.

"They're waiting," she said.

"I know."

"They offered no resistance."

"I didn't think Aras would try to avoid facing the consequences. But I'm surprised the *gethes* was so cooperative."

"She was more concerned about Aras." Nevyan said. There was a long pause: Mestin didn't fill it. "It surprises me. And she has just one bag of possessions, like us. She doesn't seem like . . . a *gethes*."

The light from the open hatchway created a pool of yellow illumination across the ground. Mestin stood watching the silver grasses shaking as some creature—probably an *udza*, in this weather—prowled in search of prey driven to ground level by the winds. There was a brief frozen silence, then a sudden *yip* from something that had not escaped the *udza*. Everything here seemed to devour everything else. It was a violent and unforgiving world for all its beauty.

"They'll kill him," Nevyan said. She smelled of agitation: she was competent, promising, but she was still very young and unused to hard decisions. That would have to change. "But how can you kill a *c'naatat*? Didn't they survive terrible—"

"That's not our problem. All we're to do is to take them back to Wess'ej, to F'nar, and let Chayyas decide what happens next. It's her responsibility. Neither mine nor yours."

"But he's the last of the *c'naatat* troops, even if he's been foolish. They saved us."

Mestin hadn't actively disliked humans before the *Thetis* arrived. The small colony that had been allowed to live here since before she was born had proved passive and harmless, a curiosity set on creating a society that honored something called God. But their benign nature had ill-prepared her for the humans who had come in the *Thetis* with their weapons and their greed.

They'll bring another war upon us, she thought. In the end, humans were all *gethes*, all carrion-eaters. Aras Sar Iussan might have found them less repellent, but perhaps he had now become too like them to be objective.

"I'll talk to them now." Mestin threw her *dhren* back and walked down into the Temporary City, Nevyan at her heels.

Aras seemed unrepentant. He sat on the resting ledge cut out of the wall of the room Nevyan had set aside to hold him, smelling of no emotion in particular. His hands were folded in his lap. Mestin wondered if there was anything that could really frighten him any more. Perhaps he was looking forward to the end, having lived alone far too long, because that was surely what would happen to him: Chayyas would have him killed—somehow.

Nevyan was right. He was the last of the *c'naatat* troops, and—war hero or not—the unending problem of isolating the symbiont would die with him. It was for the best. She thought it would be the kindest solution for the *gethes* female too.

Aras looked up at Mestin and said nothing, and carried on saying nothing until she turned and left. What would she have asked him, anyway? Why he had committed such an act of madness? It was irrelevant. Wess'har cared only about what was done, not what was intended. Motivation was a human excuse, a sophistry, a lie. But she could think of no reason why a wess'har who had spent his whole life ensuring that *c'naatat* didn't spread would suddenly give it willingly to an alien.

Outside the room that held Shan Frankland, Mestin hesitated before stepping over the threshold. There was a scent, but she was too unfamiliar with *gethes* to identify a state of mind from it.

This *gethes* had changed. Mestin had seen her when she had been brought in for brief sanctuary, and at the time she had struck her as much taller and more aggressive than the colonists, but a human nonetheless—fidgeting, soft and confused. She didn't match the self-assured picture that conversations with Aras had created. But now she seemed still and purposeful. She was leaning casually against the wall of the room, but she straightened up slowly when Mestin came in and thrust her hands into her garments. Her long black hair was pulled back and tied with a length of rough brown fabric. She didn't seem afraid either.

"This is the only cell I've ever been in that hasn't got a door," Shan said.

"Do you remember me, *Shan Chail*?"

"Mestin. Yes. And that's your daughter? The youngster who brought us in?"

"Nevyan. Yes."

"Where's Aras? Is he all right?"

"He's unharmed."

"What's going to happen to him?"

"Shouldn't you be concerned about what will happen to *you*?"

Shan appeared unmoved and made that quick hunching action with her shoulders. Mestin had seen Aras do the same. "If you have me, then you don't need him, do you?"

"He has committed a foolish act. You're a different matter."

"Meaning?"

"You have uses. You know that. That's why you were allowed to remain."

"How did you find out about me?"

"We can monitor *gethes* voice transmissions between the *Actaeon* and your homeworld. There's been much talk of your condition. Is it true it would give you great status and wealth in your society?"

"You know perfectly well that *Actaeon*'s skipper was ordered to detain me as a biohazard. Does that sound like status to you?"

Mestin still couldn't work out if Shan was afraid. She tried to stare into her gray alien eyes: apparently you could judge a human's condition that way, but she looked and saw only single, empty, black pupils that told her nothing. "You made no attempt to evade us."

"Where would I run? And what would you have done to the colonists if I had? Back home we'd say you had me bang to rights."

Mestin gave up trying to understand and turned towards the door. Chayyas would have to sort it out in the next few days.

"Hey, what happens now?" Shan called after her.

Mestin turned round. "I have no idea," she said. "And I imagine nobody else has either. We have no deviance so we don't know how to punish. And we've never found an alien infected with *c'naatat*—not in our lifetimes."

There was a pause. "Yeah, I think I know what happened the last time you did," said Shan.

"You'd know more about Aras's actions at Mjat than I would."

"Look, he's not going to make a habit of this, is he? Let him go."

All the *gethes* seemed to worry about was Aras. Her protectiveness towards males almost made Mestin warm to her, but she decided to end the debate. She had a suspicion she was being dragged into a bargaining session. "You have been fed, yes? Now do you have everything you need?"

Shan gave her an odd flash of her teeth: no wonder ussissi were wary of humans. She indicated her bag in the corner of the cell, a shapeless dark blue fabric sack with straps that attached to the shoulders very much like a wess'har pack. Nevyan was right. If it contained everything she owned, it was an oddly modest amount for an acquisitive *gethes*.

"I always travel well-equipped," she said, and her occasional blinking had stopped completely. Her eyes were disturbingly pale and liquid. "I've got everything I need."

Mestin held her fixed gaze for a few more seconds and thought for once that she had understood everything the *gethes* had said.

Aras had a dream again, of fire and of hatred and of angry sorrow. It wasn't his own. It wasn't even the inherited memory of the victims of Mjat, because that was a waking recollection, a real event from his captors' experience that he could verify because he had been part of it. This was another sort of fire and emotion altogether.

Dreaming was not a wess'har characteristic and neither were long periods of sleep. But when he dozed briefly, vivid dreams came to him from his altered genome, sometimes the almost-human face of an Earth ape, sometimes a closed door, and sometimes red and gold fire. And the alien emotion that accompanied it all was throat-stopping rage.

This time he was looking through a distorted frame, like a heat haze or clear shallow water, and the fire came towards him in a great arc and filled his field of vision. There was no burning. But a gut-panic almost took his legs from underneath him. Then he woke.

He was leaning against the polished wall of a chamber in Chayyas's home in F'nar, where Mestin had brought him to await the senior matriarch's judgement. The images and feelings were still vivid in his head and his throat. It was the anger that disturbed him most.

This had to be Shan's memories. He was behind her eyes. He had no sense of location, only a vague darkness, but he could feel a great racking sob fighting to be free of his chest and the pressure of something smooth and hard gripped fiercely in his hand—*her* hand—and a painful constriction in his throat and eyes. And then he heard a man's voice.

Are you going to sit there all fucking night or are you going to frigging well go and do something about it?

They were angry, violent words but he had no sense of them being wielded to wound her. Then the pressure in his chest and throat burst and there was a massive rush of cold and energy into his limbs. Then, nothing. It left him feeling as if he had been jerked out of the world and dumped in a void.

Aras had gone through this sequence, waking and sleeping, at least a dozen times since he had contaminated Shan and had in turn been contaminated by her. Whatever else *c'naatat* had snatched from her, it seemed to think this was useful. It was an angry and violent event. It was consistent too, and from what he knew of humans' fluid, inaccurate, ever-rewriting memories, that meant she had replayed it many times to herself.

He hoped he would be able to ask her about the events that had burned it into her. But the chances were that he would not see her again, and the thought left him aching with desolation.

He straightened up and looked out the window onto the terraced slopes of the caldera that cradled F'nar. The sun had not yet risen above the horizon but the nacreous coating on all the deliberately irregular little houses built into the west-facing slope looked luminous.

The City of Pearl, the humans called it; the few colonists from Constantine who had seen F'nar had viewed it through religious eyes and pronounced it a miracle, and named it accordingly after a passage in one of their holy books. But Shan, in her pragmatic way, had called it insect shit, for that was what the coating actually was. He liked her pragmatism.

It was all a matter of perception.

Aras didn't believe in miracles, although if one were about to present itself its timing would have been excellent. He was not afraid of dying. At several points in his artificially long life he had bitterly regretted being unable to die. What he feared most now was loss. He had put Shan in this position without her consent, and now she would be left alone to suffer the same loneliness that he had, and he would lose the one close relationship he had felt able to form in centuries. It was . . . unfair.

Aras paced slowly round the room, measuring the dimensions in footsteps. Whatever happened to him, they would not harm Shan. She was too useful. She would be fine. She would be *safe*. He took some comfort from that, but not much. Would he have to advise Chayyas on how to have him killed? Human explosives might do the job best. Anything less immediate and catastrophic would only give his *c'naatat* time to regroup and keep him alive.

He heard Chayyas coming a full minute before she appeared in the room. He could hear the swish of her long *dhren* against the flagstones and the scrabbling footsteps of the ussissi aide trying to keep pace with her. When she entered the room, she filled it, and not only with her size and presence: she exuded the sharp scent of agitation. A human would have tried to present a controlled façade, but any wess'har could smell another's state of mind. There was no point in putting on a brave face.

"Aras, you put me in an impossible position," she said, without greeting. She shimmered. She had a very fine *dhren*, as luminous as the city itself. "I have no idea what to do with you."

"Is Shan Frankland well? Is she still at Fersanye's home?"

"She has eaten this morning and asks after you repeatedly."

That made him feel much worse. "I didn't plan this."

"Why did you do it, then? Why did you corrupt the order of things? Did you want a companion that badly?"

"She was dying. The isenj fired on her, and that was a conflict of my making so I couldn't stand by and let her die." He paused. It was a cheap shot to raise the matter, but it was relevant. "And it never troubled your forebears to alter the balance when you needed us as soldiers to defend this world."

"What was done in the past isn't a justification for doing it in the present."

"Then you must look at the circumstances," he said. "And I will not plead for my life. Do what you judge best."

"Aras, nobody has ever deliberately harmed the common good. I have no idea whether a penalty is appropriate. But if we were to destroy all traces of *c'naatat*, it would save much harm in the future, and not just for us."

Even now that angered him, although he had a random thought that his anger—his wess'har anger—was mere irritation compared to Shan's inner rage. "I can't accept that. You can destroy me, and you can even destroy *Shan Chail*, but how can you justify wiping out the life-form in its natural place? It's part of Bezer'ej. We have no right to end its existence because it's inconvenient for us. That makes us no better than the isenj. Or the *gethes*."

"Then I would have to weigh one people's welfare against the benefits to all the other species," said Chayyas. "Just as I might have to with the *gethes*."

"And you might want to utilize *c'naatat* again one day—for the benefit of all other species, of course."

Sarcasm was lost on a wess'har. Aras had learned it from humans. There was a part of him, the part gleaned from alien genes, that found it very satisfying. Chayyas took the comment at its literal face value and turned to the ussissi who was shuffling from foot to foot at the entrance to the chamber.

"Fetch Mestin," she said. "Tell her I want to talk to her. I'll go to her if she prefers."

The ussissi shot off without a word. Chayyas appeared pained, and the scent of anxiety had not diminished. If anything, it was more pungent. She turned to go. "Whatever happens, we haven't forgotten what you did for us all, and how much we owe you."

It was the first time in his very long life that anyone had ever thanked Aras for his military service.

"Better late than never," he said, and was more than satisfied with Chayyas's parting expression of incomprehension.

3

I once had difficulty accepting that Satan was as real as God, but now I see what c'naatat brings with it, I'm as sure as I can be that evil is an entity. If this parasite is not the temptation of the Devil, then I don't know what is. It is sin in its every facet. If we knew how, we should destroy it. For the time being we should simply be thankful that the wess'har have the wisdom to control its spread, and that we have our faith to prevent our temptation by this false eternity.

BENJAMIN GARROD,
addressing Constantine Council 2232

It was nicknamed the Burma Road, for reasons nobody could now recall. The passage ran in a complete ellipse through the midsection of *Actaeon*, and at the end of a watch, you had two choices: to join the flow of joggers pounding round it or stay out of the way. Lindsay chose to run.

She hadn't needed to run on Bezer'ej. Heavy mundane work and high gravity had been exercise enough to keep her bones and muscles healthy. But there was little to do on board *Actaeon* that put any physical stress on her. Besides, she needed the boost of endorphins to lift her mood. She concentrated on her breathing and settled into a steady pace in the knot of runners already on their fifth or sixth circuit.

Nobody acknowledged anyone else. They were all in their own separate worlds, rankless in shorts or pants of defiantly nonuniform colors. It didn't feel like running. Lindsay felt as if she was fleeing the ship with a calm and orderly crowd. She wondered if the treadmill in one of the gyms might have been a better idea.

"Your—samples—are still—clear," said a breathless voice right behind her.

Oh, how she hated people who tried to make conversation while they were running. And it was one of the ship's medics, too, Sandhu or something. "What d'you mean?"

"Nothing weird," said Sandhu, and that was it. Lindsay fumed. Then she dropped a stride and drew alongside him. She caught his arm insistently and they dropped out of the pack, leaving the other joggers to disappear around the curve of the Burma Road.

They stared at each other, catching their breath.

"Want to explain that?" Lindsay asked.

"I thought you'd like to know we haven't found anything unusual in your samples."

Everyone had routine tests once a month. It was normal procedure on missions. "Why should there be?"

"Well, you never knew when Frankland acquired her biological extras, did you? And you said she was iffy about physical contact, so let's assume it's transmissible somehow."

"You think I might have picked up a dose, then? Couldn't someone have told me this? Don't I have to consent?"

"Biohaz procedure. Standard."

"Biohaz my arse. Serious money, more like."

"You have no idea how serious," said Sandhu. He adjusted his shorts and jogged off up the Burma Road again, leaving her staring at his wobbling backside.

So they were going to try every avenue to isolate the biotech.

Lindsay pushed herself away from the bulkhead and broke into a jog again. Okurt should have told her they were checking her out. If they had found anything, what would they have done to her? She shuddered and tried to lose herself in physical exertion.

That was the good thing about running: it helped you think things through.

How were they going to get to Shan Frankland?

Lindsay concentrated on each stride. The solution would come to her in its own good time. She thought for a moment how odd it was to see daylight in a windowless, skyless tunnel of metal and composites. The continuous strip of daylight lamp ran above her head like a glimpse of an explosion ripping open the deck above, a detonation frozen in time.

She was one lap short of completion when she ran into the very last person she had ever expected to see again. She ran into him quite literally: he stepped out of a hatchway and she cannoned into him. He steadied himself and smiled, but it wasn't affectionate or friendly or even welcoming.

It was Mohan Rayat.

There were definitely things going on that *nobody* was telling her.

Shan had never been much good at waiting.

She lay on the thin mattress of folded cloth, staring at the open doorway and straining to listen for the sounds of anyone in Fersanye's household who might try to stop her leaving. There was no door handle to try, because there was no door.

The wess'har had taken the hint that she needed her space but they still had no concept of privacy. It was unnerving trying to wash or use the latrine when you couldn't lock a door. The cold water that streamed from the ceiling when she yanked on a chain snatched her breath for a few seconds and then—she imagined—*c'naatat* kicked in and made her breathe normally again. It was still painfully icy. Dream-images of drowning in that dark room crowded in on her and she fought back panic.

There were distant sounds of clattering glass and double-voiced conversations, and she could actually hear the speech patterns clearly now. While she dressed, she pursed her lips and said "wess'har" very quietly, just to try, and was caught out by the sudden emergence of two sounds, word and overtone. *Oh my God.* Even her voice was changing.

Habit made her take her handgun out of her belt and check the clip. *Nevyan, you'll never make a copper. Fancy not searching me.* The 9mm was very old technology, barely changed in centuries, but it worked, and it didn't need recharging. If you maintained it religiously it never broke down. Then she reached in her grip and took out a directional-blast grenade.

Royal Marine Sergeant Adrian Bennett—shy, loyal, but lethal Ade—had shown her how to use one in an idle moment. She had no idea why he'd left her a couple of the devices when the detachment pulled out. Perhaps he knew she might need one, and he'd been proved right. There was no point pissing about now. The only thing that mattered was securing a deal for Aras.

Shan tucked the grenade inside her jacket and went in search of an exit. She passed males and children on the way, but they simply looked at her and let her pass. Perhaps they thought there was nothing a single *gethes* could do on her own in a strange city.

One of the males stepped into her path. "Fersanye offers food," he said, struggling with English.

Shan took it at face value. "I'm going for a walk," she said. "*Sve l'bir.* Okay?"

Outside, an alley lined with ashlars curved away in both directions. The *tem* flies hadn't coated the shaded surfaces. The stone was still honey-gold, dappled in light and dark by the sun piercing a mesh of vines overhead, and therefore probably too cool to attract them.

"Ah well," she muttered, and cast around to decide on a direction. Either way would take her to the end of the terrace, and she could then at least look up and get her bearings. Or she could follow concentrations of noise. Wess'har made plenty of that.

The first noise she latched on to was a *skitter skitter skitter*. She drew her weapon, a pure reflex, and a ussissi came round the curve of the wall and stared up at her, and then at the weapon.

She replaced the gun in the back of her belt, embarrassed at her excess. The ussissi's gaze followed her hand. "I want to see *Chayyas Chail,*" she said, and was surprised to hear herself manage the beginnings of an overtone again. And the language, wess'u, was starting to emerge from nowhere, a word here, a phrase there. "Can you show me her house?"

"Perhaps you should go tomorrow," said the ussissi. "Call her first."

"Thanks, but no. Show me."

It seemed to work: the ussissi must have been accustomed to the imperious direction of females a lot taller than him. He said nothing, turned round again and pattered ahead of her, sounding like a dog scrabbling on tiles.

The belts of scarlet beaded cloth that trailed from his shoulders slapped against the ashlars as he kept close to the walls. He didn't turn round to see if she was keeping up with him. Framed by the light from the window at the head of a flight of stairs, the creature made her think of a white rabbit, and she stopped the analogy right there.

This wasn't some quaint children's fantasy. She was a long way from home and there would be no waking up from curious dreams to transport her back to familiarity. For the first time in her adult life, Shan was surrounded by beings as hard, as ruthless and as intelligent as she was, and maybe even more so. It unsettled her. All her natural advantages were gone.

And nobody deferred to her rank or uniform, either. She was going to have to do this the hard way.

"Are you coping with the facilities here?" asked the ussissi suddenly.

"If you mean the toilets, yes. I'm more agile than I look."

He made a clicking sound and said nothing more. There were windows every few meters along the inner length of the stair wall, and Shan was aware of faces at some of them, long gold and copper wess'har faces, startling flower eyes, all staring. Some might have remembered her from her last visit to the city. All must have known who she was. There weren't that many wess'har-human hybrids around, after all.

She could even pick out some more words. She could hear the patterns emerging, and they seemed far less incomprehensible than they had the previous day. She could hear rhythm, familiarity, and then another recognizable word leaped out, shocking and reassuring at the same time.

G'san. New weapon.

She was picking it up. "And what might that new weapon be?" she asked, smug at her growing skill.

The ussissi didn't even glance back at her. "You," he said.

She drew level with him at the end of a terrace and found herself on the halfway level of the curving walkways that lined the caldera. They were all neatly edged with irregular low walls that made Shan think instantly of accidents. Maybe they did fall down those slopes sometimes. No wess'har would have been looking for anyone to sue, though, even if they had lawyers, which she knew even without asking that they didn't.

The basin was about four kilometers across, and the slope directly opposite them was draped with a faint haze. If the circumstances had been happier, it would have been a perfect summer morning, and if there had been a railing to lean upon, she would have leaned on it and taken it all in. But there was no rail. A couple of wess'har youngsters walked past at a respectful distance from the edge and glanced back at her in silent curiosity before looking away and going about their business.

The children—what little she had seen of them—unsettled her. It was that quiet appraising glance that they all had: they seemed more adult than the adults. She looked down at the ussissi, who was also gazing at the view, although he had surely seen plenty of it before.

He raised an arm. "Across there," he said. "Do you see? Follow the line of the upper terraces and you will see a watercourse. The buildings to the left are Chayyas's rooms."

Shan squinted into the light. The building didn't look like any presidential palace she'd ever seen. It was just a rambling collection of wess'har holes in the rock like all the others, although it was carefully random in its form and so *not* like any of them.

It would take her less than an hour to stroll over for a visit. "Thanks. I think I can find that by myself."

"Tomorrow," the ussissi reminded her. "You should tell her you're coming."

"Of course," Shan lied, and didn't care. If wess'har didn't knock, then neither would she.

Navigating around F'nar was relatively easy. Stand anywhere, and if the heat haze permitted you could see every part of the city. Wess'har didn't plant screens of trees, just as they never had blinds or curtains—or doors. External doors seemed only to be a weather precaution, or a barrier to *tem* flies trying to get inside the house to continue their exquisitely decorative shitting.

Water tinkled around her down glass drainage pipes, their sunward side crusted with pearl. She touched the surface. She found her fingertips smeared with what looked like a shimmering cosmetic. She sniffed. It was fresh *tem* shit, but as shit went, it was remarkably pretty and odorless: somehow, she had almost expected an exotic fragrance. She rinsed her hand under the running water and wiped it on her pants.

The glass pipes were everywhere. Wess'har seemed obsessed with the material. They were a transparent people in every sense, transparent to each other and transparent in language. At least that was something she didn't have to worry about here. She knew she didn't have to brace herself for what she might find behind a locked door.

Every space between the houses and every patch of soil that wasn't filled by a home was crammed with growing things. She almost thought *green* things. But they were purple and red and silver and white. As she walked, planning her confrontation with Chayyas, she saw wess'har tidying the plants and removing leaves and stalks. Ahead of her a male was carefully pressing tufts of brilliant carmine into a narrow strip of red-gold soil that ran along the front of his home.

Shan paused. He looked up at her, all glittering four-pupiled eyes, with an amazement that she could smell. He began trilling and fluting. She recognized the word *gethes*, and she also recognized *c'naatat*, but she couldn't quite pick out the meaning.

He stood up and came up so close to her that she stepped back. They didn't seem to have an idea of personal space; he was way too close for her liking.

She tried a smile to indicate she didn't feel threatened, and then realized he probably didn't understand a display of teeth any better than the ussissi. The trilling followed her as she walked away.

By the time she got to the end of the terrace, marked by a particularly lovely cascade of water fringed by purple-black moss, there were more wess'har waiting for her to pass, making fluting, incomprehensible comments. Christ, she wished she could summon up more of the language. There was the faintest hint of agitation: nothing threatening, just a mild anxiety that was almost excitement.

Shan had no idea what was going on. She paused and looked around at them. Maybe they were holding her responsible for Aras's plight. That terrace really wasn't very wide at all. It was a long way down.

I'd only break bones, she thought. *A few internal injuries. But it'll hurt like hell.*

But still nobody stopped her or searched her.

The wess'har might have been a mighty military presence in the system, capable of destroying civilizations, but they had no idea about security at home. She walked cautiously into the winding passage that led from the entrance to Chayyas's clan home, alert for threats, completely unable even now to override her training. A couple of males—Chayyas's cousins or husbands or sons—simply stared and parted like grain before her as if she had a right to be there.

Yes, they really needed to sharpen up if they were going to resist human incursion. They needed to learn about *locks*.

But then a ussissi trotted up to her. The creature was just chest tall, and she caught it by the ornate chrome-yellow fabric wrap that hung draped across one shoulder. It looked like another male, a little smaller than the females. She drew it to her and leaned down, so close they were almost nose-to-nose.

"You speak English?" she asked. The meerkat-like things all appeared to speak several languages. "You know who I am. Take me to Chayyas."

The ussissi stared into her face. She revised her view that they were covered in amber fur. She could see that his skin was finely divided by thousands of barely visible folds, like crepe paper, like a very minutely detailed Fortuny pleated gown. The needle teeth, though, were exactly what she had taken them for at first sight. Her face was perilously close to them. She held on.

"Chayyas," she said. "*Now.*"

There was a moment's hesitation. "This way," he said. She followed him through three more interconnecting doorways and down a flight of shallow stairs.

"*Chayyas Chail* will be most upset," the ussissi said, his voice like a child's.

"I'm pretty pissed off myself."

"You should ask for audience. I could arrange it. I am Vijissi, the matriarch's . . ." He searched for a word. ". . . diplomat."

"Well, I'm not diplomatic, and I'm not big on patience either. I'll see her now, thanks."

Vijissi stopped at a portal and poked his head round it. He jerked it back. Shan crouched level with the creature, knowing he wouldn't bite a chunk out of her now. He smelled of feathers and clean wildness. "Is she in?"

"She is, *Chail.*"

"Thanks. Now go, please." She didn't want the unfortunate ussissi around if firing started. She felt for the grenade in her jacket. "This is personal."

The ussissi hesitated for a second but scuttled away, and it was the first time she had noticed they had two pairs of legs under those robes. That explained their characteristic scrabbling footsteps. Then she walked into the chamber.

Chayyas stood gazing at moving images of a landscape that seemed to be set in the stone of the wall. The matriarch was long and gold and hippocampine, with that pretty muzzle and tufted mane that Shan was beginning to recognize as highly individual features. They didn't all look the same to her now.

"What are you doing here?" Chayyas looked up, unconcerned. "I didn't summon you."

"You really ought to do something about your security, for a start," Shan said. "I'll tell you that for free. But I've come for Aras."

"Aras is detained."

"I know. But it's me you want. I'm the *gethes*." Shan stepped closer. Chayyas probably didn't know how humans smelled at the best of times. Could the matriarch know she was gambling? More to the point, did *she* know herself whether she was gambling? "Well, I'm here. That solves the problem of the biohazard getting into the human population. Let Aras go."

"We have already neutralized you by confining you to Wess'ej. Why should I make concessions?"

"Because it's the right thing to do. He did it for me. I'm the risk, not him."

"That is the problem. He doesn't behave as a wess'har. He puts personal and individual whims above the common good."

"Okay, let me put it another way. You have one chance to learn what it takes to deal with humankind and I'm it." Shan reached behind her back and down her spine into her waistband the way she had a thousand times before, feeling the body-warmed composite and wrapping her fingers round it. She pulled the gun out in a practiced arc and held it two-handed to Chayyas's left temple. Chayyas didn't move. There was no reason why she should know what a gun looked like.

"You have lights in your skin," said the matriarch.

"It's the gun you need to look at, sweetheart."

"Will that kill me?"

"Indeed it could."

"Why do you want to do that?"

"It's the sort of thing humans do if they want to achieve an end. I want you to let Aras go."

"Or you'll kill me."

"Perhaps."

"My bloodline lives on. I don't fear death."

The safety was off. "Neither do I. But you know you need the intelligence I can provide. Leave Aras out of it and you have my full cooperation. Harm him, and you're going to have to guess your way out of this. You can't even stop me bringing a weapon into your home. How are you going to cope with an army?"

Chayyas's scent began to take on a more acidic note. "I don't bargain with *gethes*."

"I'm the one who might spread this thing to humans. Without me, there's no threat."

Chayyas didn't quite smell of fear. The pupils of her amber eyes were just slits, a faint black cross on a cabochon topaz. "Is that weapon less powerful than the isenj one that struck you?"

"Probably," said Shan, listening to herself as if she were standing outside her own body. *Where the hell am I going with this?* She sat down and put the gun on the table, safety still off, within easy reach. Then she took the grenade from her jacket and turned it round so Chayyas could see it. "But *this* isn't. Once I pull this pin, you have a count of ten to get out of this room before it blows. This will fragment me. You know what that means. Not even *c'naatat* can repair me then. Problem solved."

What the hell am I saying?

Chayyas said nothing and looked at the grenade as if it was just a fascinating toy. *She thinks I'm bluffing.* Shan flicked her thumb under the cap, suddenly struck by the completely irrelevant fact that her claws were looking almost like normal nails now. *Am I?* And bluffing was something she couldn't afford to do, not with a matriarch.

It was all happening too fast. She hadn't planned this at all well.

I have to mean it.

She drew the pin out all the way. "Ten," she said. "Nine." Chayyas still stared. "Eight." Shan shut her eyes. "Seven." And then it seemed that Chayyas suddenly understood, because there was a rush of air and acid and a massively powerful grip closed round her hand and the grenade, pinning both to the table, and almost crushed bone. Shan opened her eyes in shock and pain.

Chayyas held on grimly. "Replace that pin," she said. *"Now."* The matriarch's anger seethed like boiling vinegar in the air. The pain was all-consuming but Shan held her position.

"Let Aras go." *Jesus, I can't hold this thing much longer.* "Let him go."

The matriarch's pupils snapped from flower to cross and back again.

Shan held on and Chayyas held on. Shan hoped her eyes wouldn't start watering from the pain. If her hand went numb and she dropped the damn thing . . .

Chayyas stared at the little dial on the cap of the grenade. "Reset the pin."

"I thought you weren't afraid to die."

"I have *children* in this house."

Chayyas had her eyes fixed on Shan's and Shan didn't break the gaze. The matriarch's grip slackened a fraction, but it still held. And so did Shan's stare.

You look away first—you're dead. Her old sergeant's voice spoke up, unbidden: *don't step aside, don't blink, don't apologize.* Shan had stopped bar brawls just by walking into the room in the right way. But her sergeant hadn't taught her any wisdom that dealt with aliens. She fell back on instinct.

"We could be here a long time," said Chayyas.

"If that's what it takes," said Shan, eyes beginning to water with the effort. Jesus, it hurt. "Punishing Aras won't serve any useful purpose."

And then Chayyas blinked, as if distracted by the mention of Aras. She looked away. Shan felt an exultant surge of animal triumph and pulled both hand and grenade clear. For a second she could have sworn she smelled something like ripe mangoes—both heady-sweet and grassy at once—filling the space between them. It took all the effort she could muster to hold the grenade steady enough to replace the pin. The violet lights rippled, exaggerating the tremor.

"There's no purpose I can think of," said Chayyas.

Shan stood up and pocketed the grenade, hoping that the *c'naatat* would deal quickly with any bruising. She didn't want Chayyas to know how much pain she had put her through. "I want custody of him," she said, nursing her crushed hand in her pocket.

Chayyas, still seated, was staring alternately at the gun and at Shan. She was holding her fingers tip to tip, flexing them: they were all the same length, with three knuckles in each, giving them an arachnid look. "He's your *jurej*. Take him."

"What's that? *Jurej*?"

"Male."

"I'm sorry?"

Chayyas blinked flowers. Shan, in control of the universe for a few brief moments, fell back into the confused world of the visiting alien.

"Neither of you can have another," said Chayyas. "And there are no unmated adults in wess'har society. He's your responsibility."

"Hang on, I'm not sure I—"

Chayyas was fixed on the gun. "You wanted our asylum. You behave wess'har. Therefore you *are* wess'har." She reached her thin many-jointed hand towards the 9mm and picked it up. "This won't kill you?"

"Steady on," said Shan. "The safety's off."

"Are you afraid?"

The challenge was unintended, she knew, but she couldn't back down. Something foreign and primeval was overriding her common sense. She'd seen it too often in drunks, in flashpoint fights, in murders.

"No," she said, suddenly completely unable to say that

enough was enough and that they should all go about their business.

She had no reason to fear death now. It was life—this out-of-control, alien life—that was starting to scare her.

Chayyas took the gun in her hand, and Shan wondered how she knew how to aim. The she wondered how she knew how to start squeezing the trigger. Something said *you're okay, it's only pain*, and despite all her hard-wired instinct to fling herself to the floor, Shan managed to brace herself before a point-blank shot deafened her.

She fell.

The isenj city of Jejeno, capital of the Ebj landmass, was all that there was.

From the time that Eddie Michallat looked out of the shuttle hatch when the vessel landed on Umeh to the time he reached the center of the city, he saw nothing—*nothing*—but buildings speckled with pinpricks of light that were winking out as the sun came up.

The complete absence of any open space disoriented him. He had grown used to unbroken horizons on Bezer'ej even in a year. It spoke to something primeval in him; he *wanted* to miss the wilderness.

He let his bee-cam capture it all. It danced close to his head as he leaned out of the open door of the ground transport, because there were no windows. Isenj didn't appear to like watching the scenery go by. Maybe it was too depressingly monotonous for them.

Still, they were enough like humans to need light when it got dark, and to make buildings, and to use a language. And that was close enough.

The isenj did indeed like Eddie. He made sure of it. Eddie listened to them politely and didn't dismiss them. He relayed what they said and felt, no more, no less. He didn't stare at them as if they were monsters, and they responded by letting him visit their world and see what they'd built, the first civilian to set foot on Umeh after the *Actaeon* advance party had landed.

They even let him file a live piece at the shuttleport to record the moment. It was the first rule of journalism: look after your contacts, and they'd look after you. He applied it with relish.

Jejeno boiled with isenj. They parted in front of the transport like shoals of fish and closed again behind it, apparently unconcerned and intent on whatever business they were about. As Eddie watched, one of them tripped and fell, and a small depression opened in the living sea for just a second; then it was filled again. He never saw the isenj get up. He never saw any other isenj take any notice either. Maybe he was mistaken.

He craned his neck as far as he could, until the imagined point in the crowd was far behind him and the ussissi interpreter, Serrimissani, tugged on his sleeve.

"It happens," she said. "Concentrate on your task."

Eddie wished himself into a state of belief that the fallen isenj had picked itself up and carried on walking, but something told him that was not the case. *Forget it. This isn't Earth.* He adjusted his respirator and wondered if he was wasting the bee-cam's memory on this unchanging vista. Just how much cityscape did people need to see?

But it was all there was. Viewers needed to know that. On the other hand, it might have been rush hour, or Mardi Gras, and he had no way of knowing if these crowds were a permanent event or not. All he knew was that he felt suffocated.

He pulled back from the open door and turned to Serrimissani, who looked for all the world like a malevolent Riki-Tiki-Tavi.

"Crowded," said Eddie. It was a gross understatement. "Where do they grow their food?"

"Everywhere they can," said the ussissi. Her voice was muffled by the mask she was wearing over her snout. It looked like a piece of clear plastic and reminded Eddie rather too much of the various transparent carnivores of Bezer'ej, sheets of clear film that would fall on you from the sky, or drag you down into water, and digest you. "In buildings. Revolting."

"Vegetables?"

"Growths. Fungus."

She might have meant truffles, Eddie thought, trying to put the visit in the brightest context. He had a feeling she didn't. He settled for nutritional yeast.

The buildings pressing in on him gradually changed from low-rises to tower blocks, a fact he took as an indication that he was getting closer to the center of the city. It was a dangerous assumption to make in an alien culture, but building high meant some sort of priority: it certainly wasn't a matter of getting a prettier view of the landscape.

The tight-packed crowds moved past him at a more sedate pace, slow enough for isenj to stop and stare in at him, and he waved and then wondered if the gesture had another meaning here. Their piranha-spider faces betrayed nothing. Looking past them, he could recognize nothing in the built environment that suggested shops or offices. There were just façades intricately decorated with symbols and patterns, carved and painted.

In front of one of the buildings there was an island in the river of streaming isenj: some appeared to be standing still, pressed together and waiting by a doorway. It was closed. He turned to the interpreter.

"Queuing for food," said Serrimissani, without waiting for his question. "There's sufficient, but the logistics of distribution are unwieldy."

"What do the isenj make of humans?"

Serrimissani fixed him with a predator's expressionless black eyes. He could almost see her digging for scorpions and crunching them up between those needle teeth. "They can see kinship with you. They enjoy complex organizations."

"What do *you* think of them?"

"They honor their debts."

"How much do you get paid for interpreting? Sorry. Is that a rude question?"

"They do not employ me. I have food and somewhere to rest, just as I have on Wess'ej."

"You work both sides of the line? And the isenj trust you to be here?"

"What could I do that they would not trust? This is not a conflict of knowledge, so I cannot spy. Nor is it a war where the wess'har take the conflict into their enemies' territory. So I do my job and threaten no one. How do you get paid?"

It was a good question. Eddie hadn't had a raise in seventy-six years, and it still irritated him that the BBChan personnel department had decided that he wasn't entitled to service increments because he'd been in cryosuspension for most of that time. Hell, he'd worked with people who seemed to spend their whole career in comas and they still got raises.

But then he hadn't been around to spend his pay, and it had earned plenty of interest. He was surprised how little it suddenly meant to him. Perhaps that was how rich people felt all the time. His stomach felt oddly displaced. "I get tokens that I can exchange for food and other things that I need."

"Want."

"Sorry?"

"Humans want many things but they need much less than they think," said the ussissi. "I accept the philosophy of Targassat, having lived among the wess'har. Beware acquisitiveness, Mr. Michallat. It will take you hostage."

Eddie savored the moment of being lectured in asceticism by a mongoose. It almost dispelled the aching bewilderment at realizing he was rich and none the better for it. The transport came to a halt.

Serrimissani turned her head very slowly. There was no wet gloss to her eyes; they looked matte as velvet, sinister, utterly void. "Are you ready?"

Eddie caught the bee-cam and pocketed it. "I've interviewed Minister Ual before. I'm ready."

The ministry—and Eddie had no other word for it—was

conspicuous in the unbroken wall of buildings by the fact that it was very, very plain. There were no extravagant designs, either painted or carved. As he walked through the door and into the reception hall, the first thing that struck him was that it was *empty*. It was also vast. It was at least twelve meters high and lined with smooth aquamarine stone, a stark and cool contrast to the hot rusts and ambers and purples outside.

There seemed to be nobody around. Then he heard movement, and Serrimissani tugged at his sleeve and bobbed her head in the direction of one of the archways off to one side. An isenj appeared. There was an exchange of high-pitched sounds.

Eddie occupied himself by letting the bee-cam wander around the hall. So status bought you space, did it? Yes, isenj were a lot like humans.

"Ual is ready to see you and asks if you would like refreshment," Serrimissani said.

"Not the fungus."

"Water flavored with something that the *Actaeon* provided."

"God, I hope it's coffee."

There were moments when Eddie knew he had touched common ground with the isenj. It was easy to expect them to be utterly alien because they looked unlike anything he'd ever imagined. But their attitudes seemed much less alien than those of the wess'har.

He sat and waited. A thought struck him. *What about snakes?* What about jellyfish? Here he was mentally arguing the finer points of difference with himself: but he was talking, yes *talking*, with aliens who had communal lives and built cities and had wars over concepts he understood. The only reason he could even begin to misunderstand them was that they were so very similar to him and that they could exist in an environment so like his own in universal terms as to be identical. So he had no chance of even starting to grasp the nature of other forms of alien life. And he was suddenly gripped with sadness at his own limitations.

Serrimissani nudged him irritably. "You are distracted," she said. "Ual is waiting."

Eddie struggled to regain excitement. *Chin up. You're talking to your third species of alien interviewee. Be glad.*

"Sorry," he said. "A tear for all the things that are beyond me." And he ached to recall who said that. It defined humanity.

An isenj aide showed them into another polished water-colored chamber, and Minister Ual was seated on a dais in the center of it, as if to emphasize the luxurious, privileged distance around him. Eddie was ushered to a box covered with layers of something soft and yielding; as near, he thought, as they could get to a chair. He smiled at Ual.

Isenj were as appealing as only spiders with piranha faces could be. But they were sociable and polite and generous. Minister Ual was enjoying a cup of something fluid, lapping it from a shallow vessel with the ease of a Mandarin potentate. His ovoid bulk glittered with hundreds of smooth, transparent green beads strung on quill-like projections from his body, and he rattled like a chandelier when he moved. Eddie hoped the noise wouldn't play hell with the mike.

Ual had one other characteristic that Eddie could not ignore. He had a vague scent of the woods, like a forest floor after rain. It was not unpleasant, but neither was it a fragrance that Eddie associated with government ministers.

Serrimissani wasn't needed. Ual had made speaking English his priority, despite the effort it took to control his breathing enough to force out recognizable English words. The ussissi stayed in the room nonetheless, watching the bee-cam wander round the interviewee, and Eddie tried to crush the fear that she might pounce on it and crunch it up. She reminded him too much of snakes and Kipling. He looked back at Ual. There were no eyes that he could see to make contact with.

"The enclosed environment outside Jejeno is small, but I believe it will be more comfortable for your fellows than living on board *Actaeon* indefinitely," Ual said. There was a rhythmic gulping between every word, like someone learning to speak again after a crude laryngectomy. Eddie struggled silently for him with every syllable. "Once it is established, the environment will be cooler, more moist and more breathable. It will be soothing for you, and we will learn a great deal about biospheres into the bargain."

"Is that how you see the human-isenj relationship developing?"

"Mutual aid is a good basis for any bargain. You will benefit from improved communications. We're open to ideas for improved food production and we want to learn about terraforming. You've now seen our most pressing problem for yourself, in every street."

Eddie hesitated before asking the next question, but it had to be asked. The bee-cam responded to his discreet hand signal for a close-up of Ual's face. "Is population control not an option?"

"It's more complex than that. No two states can agree upon a common policy for fear of being overrun by their neighbor. There's a psychological element to this, you see, as well as a biological one. The more overcrowded we became, the higher the death rate. The higher the death rate, the more fertile we become and the more reluctant people are to limit their families, in case their line should die out."

"Improved food production won't solve that."

"Not long-term. But resettlement will. It will reduce the collective anxiety."

"You colonized your moon—Tasir Ve?"

"Tasir Var."

"Did that work?"

"Evidently not. We hope you'll help us restore its ecology too."

"So what was behind the drive to settle on Bezer'ej?"

"I think we've learned a great deal since we overexploited Tasir Var. The next world will be more carefully planned, more managed."

"You've got deep-space capability. Why not look further afield than this system and avoid conflict with the wess'har?"

"We *had* deep-space capability, but it's a resource-intensive project to maintain. We're fortunate that you may soon be in a position to help us maintain our more remote instant communications relays because we can no longer reach them ourselves. Food and environmental cleansing are our priorities now. It's another area where we might find mutual advantage in cooperation."

"Joint missions?"

"You have a similar drive to expand. Why else would you all be here? And you think you're eternal. It's hard to imagine your whole species and history being trapped on a world that will eventually be destroyed by its own sun. No, Mr. Michallat, I do believe humans and isenj will be partners, and both will benefit." Ual tapped a limb on the glassy surface of the low table between them, indicating the cup and the bowl. A little fragment of quill fell to his lap and he reached down to sweep it aside. Eddie wondered what happened when a bead-bearing quill broke off.

Serrimissani stared at Ual, and Eddie saw the concept of disdain expressed as perfectly as any adept Indian *kathkali* dancer could ever mime. After an eloquent delay, she trotted forward to fill both vessels from their respective jugs. She did not look amused. He could see her little teeth glittering between slightly parted lips.

"Let us drink up, Mr. Michallat. Will you be transmitting this interview soon?"

Eddie nodded and drained his coffee, which was tepid by now. And it wasn't wardroom quality. "As soon as I edit it."

"You'll cut out parts? It was very short."

"Actually, I probably won't omit any detail. I just have to package it with some attractive shots. Would you mind if I traveled a little further and recorded some different images?"

"If you can find any," Ual said.

Eddie loved him instantly and totally for his candor. He would swap Ual for a human politician any day. On the way back to the shuttle, he replayed the footage on the smartpaper the *Actaeon* had given him and marked appropriate sequences. Ual was right. It all looked much the same to him. No wonder they called those shots wallpaper.

"Ah well," he said. He could only report what he saw.

Serrimissani watched his fingers moving across the smart-paper. "Are you going to make a habit of this?"

"I have to. It's called a series."

"I think you have already recorded all you need to know."

"I do believe you're right," said Eddie. That was what worried him. "Look at it this way: I don't see it as my job to interpret the isenj to Earth audiences, but there aren't any other hacks around to tell a different side of the story, so that means I have to be doubly careful that I don't just tell mine. I'll be a window, nothing more, as far as I can be."

The ussissi gave him a look that might have been sympathy or pity: he only knew that it made him feel like a scorpion, a snack-size one.

"A window should ask more open questions," she said.

Shan's world was silent except for the numb ringing in her own ears.

Faces—wess'har and ussissi—that were clustered in a circle above her jerked back and parted.

For a few moments all she could see was their mouths opening and closing erratically. Her eardrums felt as if someone had shoved a rod through them. A few moments later the sound suddenly rushed back in.

"Li sevadke!" said a reedy child-animal voice with its own echo. *"Ur, jes'ha ur!"*

Shan struggled to sit up. She could see properly now: Vijissi, Chayyas, and a wess'har male she didn't know, and they were giving her plenty of space. Chayyas was shaking her head occasionally, as if trying to dislodge something: the close-quarters discharge must have hurt her ears too.

Shan tried to put her hands back behind her to prop herself

up but fell back on one elbow. The back of her head hurt like
hell. She reached around, expecting to feel an exit wound,
sticky blood, gritty bone: but it was all in place.

Chayyas had put a bullet in her. Shan just couldn't quite work
out *where* yet. That was the problem with custom-enhanced
hollow-tip rounds: terrific stopping power, the very best she
could get made. She just hadn't planned on one stopping *her*.

"Can you hear us?" Vijissi asked. "You hit your head when
you fell back."

That explained a lot. Her left shoulder hurt too. She fumbled, feeling for wounds, and realized the shot had penetrated
her upper chest. It had probably clipped her lung, judging by
the taste of blood: she'd seen enough bodies in postmortem to
work that out.

But *c'naatat* was practiced at injuries. It had played this
game before, when an isenj round had penetrated her skull and
Aras had bled his hand into her open wound to repair her. This
was just meat, nothing as complex as a brain injury. *Easy peasy.*
The symbiont flaunted its skill. It was patching her up before
their eyes.

"I can hear you," Shan said at last. She tried to stand up but
thought better of it. Her audience rustled further away from her.
Chayyas smelled scared, but she didn't say anything. Shan
turned her head with painful difficulty.

It was a scene she'd seen many times before as a police officer. But it had always been someone else's blood sprayed over a
wall, never hers. She stared at the spatters: the matriarch and
her diplomat stared too.

So they were afraid of her blood.

Vijissi edged round her, bobbing his head, apparently staring
at her jacket as if he didn't quite believe what was going on beneath it.

"So it *is* true," he said, then looked away. "I mean no offense. But it's one thing to know this can happen and another to
see it with your own eyes."

Shan scrambled onto all fours and her sense of balance

kicked in. All she had now was a headache, a stiff neck, and a strange smell of dust in her nostrils. Her gun was on the table. She reached for it and shoved it back in her waistband. And her jacket was ruined; *that* pissed her off. She could repair herself, but she couldn't get a new jacket out here.

Chayyas kept her distance, shutter pupils snapping from open petals to slits. "An astonishing thing," she said at last, very quiet, almost distracted. "Extraordinary."

"Yeah, terrific. It's my party trick." If Chayyas was testing the efficiency of her *c'naatat*, it was a bloody stupid way to do it. But it had shaken her, that was clear. Shan examined the singed hole in her jacket for a few moments then gave up. She stared at her hands: there were no flickering lights. "Had your fun now? Can I go?"

"I had to see."

"You've seen." She gestured at the wall, suddenly more concerned whether the bioluminescence had stopped for good than the events of the last few minutes. "Are you going to clean this up, or do you expect me to do it?"

Vijissi kept looking towards Chayyas as if he were expecting some action from her. Shan had a feeling there was something else going on, something she didn't quite understand, and Chayyas seemed subdued. Maybe she'd never seen anyone's body parts splattered across the furnishings. It did tend to spoil your day.

Chayyas went to the door. A brief blast of double-song at painful volume made Shan's ears ring again. Then there was the sound of many rapid footsteps fading down the passage, and Chayyas stalked back into the chamber. She could understand *get the fuck out of here* in any language. She also knew she had Chayyas's reluctant but undivided attention.

"I hope you understand your side of the deal," Chayyas said. "Because we'll hold you to it. You are wess'har now. You'll help us fight if need be. You'll do your duty as a matriarch. We expect a great deal from you, Shan Frankland—possibly more than you are capable of giving."

Chayyas had suddenly become very still, not just at rest as a relaxed human might be, but utterly immobile. Shan had seen Aras do that a few times when he had been taken aback or alarmed. It was a strange thing to see. It was the small detail that made them more alien.

I can do it, Shan thought. *I can bloody well do anything right now*. The relief of being in one piece was flooding her with elation and confidence, and she was ashamed of that. It was weakness. She shouldn't have been afraid. "I'll take Aras if I may." Take him where? She had no idea, but it felt like time to stalk out having won the argument.

Vijissi tugged on her sleeve. "I think the phrase is '*quit while you are ahead*,'" he whispered, and pulled her sleeve meaningfully in the direction of the door.

She followed Vijissi deeper into the maze of rooms that made up Chayyas's residence, feeling as if she were walking a heaving deck, and wondering how she would recount the events to Aras. And her jacket—shit, how was she going to get that repaired? There were suddenly a lot of wess'har about, mostly males, but also some females. They stared at her. She thought the novelty of seeing her alien face might have worn thin by now.

Vijissi peered round doors and jerked his head back, chittering to himself, until he found a room that appeared to suit his needs and he beckoned Shan in.

It was empty. Three connecting doors led off deeper into Chayyas's maze, one of them covered with a vine-patterned damask-like fabric in peacock and royal blues. Vijissi sat her down on a ledge cut into the wall and made a semblance of a stop gesture with both paws.

Hands, she reminded herself. *Not paws*. Shan sniffed hard, trying to get rid of the rasping smell and dappled shape of dust. Scents now felt like textures and looked like colors, and colors had flavors and texture and sound. She had noticed a growing synesthesia over the past months; it didn't appear to be a wess'har characteristic.

"You wait here until I find Aras," said Vijissi. "I would not be proud that you forced Chayyas to back down." Shan couldn't tell from his tone if he was being spiteful or simply helping her through the uncertain territory of wess'har politics. "You have made a very dangerous move."

"Oh, because she'll have my arse some day?" She was back on familiar ground for a few moments. So someone new had her on their bugger-about list. So what? "She can come and have a go if she thinks she's hard enough."

"I thought you might have understood what you were doing."

"I did. I was bargaining for Aras."

"We can smell it, you know. They can *all* smell it." Vijissi sniffed in a rapid staccato like a little machine gun. Shan tried too, but the rasping dusty odor seemed to have temporarily numbed her newly acquired wess'har sense of smell. "That was very foolish indeed, but maybe you are more ambitious than we thought."

"What, for Chrissakes?"

"You have deposed her. Chayyas has surrendered her authority."

4

Wess'har politics and governance would leave a human politician speechless. Political office isn't sought. It's imposed on the most dominant and able females—without votes, without campaigns, without structure, and without parties. The ruling group of matriarchs that appears to evolve in each city state has the task of ensuring that the day-to-day decisions made by households—all run by females, who are outnumbered five to one by males—are reflected in the wider domains of international relations and major infrastructure projects. There is no economy or constitution as we understand them. Consensus appears to take place by osmosis. And woe betide the leader who seriously fails in her duty: she's likely to be killed.

EDDIE MICHALLAT, BBChan,
From Our Extrasolar Correspondent

"Look, I didn't know. I had no bloody idea. Will you *listen* to me, for Chrissakes?"

Shan had a habit of pacing around that now annoyed Mestin very much. Her rooms were small and the woman took up a lot of ground: she would have to learn to be still. Shan paused in front of Nevyan, fists on hips, shaking her head occasionally, no doubt astonished at her own foolish actions. Mestin decided she would make it a priority to find alternative accommodation for her. A few months ago she might have cuffed her. But this was now neither subordinate female nor *gethes*. This was a dominant matriarch, whatever her external appearance.

"How many times do we have to tell you that what you intend is of no consequence?" said Mestin. "You've challenged Chayyas and she has ceded dominance. That's all there is to know."

"Just because I faced her down over the grenade?"

"It's pheromonal. She can't help her reaction." Mestin was aware of Nevyan beside her: she was staring at Shan, utterly mesmerized. "You said yourself that you noticed your own scent when it happened."

"Jesus H. Christ," said Shan. "Just because I got stroppy with her? So what are you going to do when a human army shows up and gives you a frosty look? Surrender?"

"They are wholly human and so we have no biochemistry in common. You, however, are not."

The reminder seemed to silence Shan. She dropped her arms to her sides and sat down on the bench that Nevyan had piled with *dhren* fabric to make it comfortable for her. "I take it an apology would be out of the question?"

"The reaction has taken place. Chayyas has lost her hormonal dominance. Intended or not, you're now senior matriarch in F'nar."

Shan held up both hands, palms out. The claws were gone, Mestin noted. *C'naatat* was even more bizarre than she had realized. "No," Shan said. "Abso-bloody-lutely *not*. I'll have a crack at most things, but not politics. And I don't have the right to do it, let alone the training."

"Then you leave us in temporary disarray, and you have no right to do that either."

"Then give me a solution."

"Where's your grenade?"

"Aras took it off me for safekeeping. What about you? Don't you want the job?"

Shan still knew far less about wess'har than Mestin had imagined. She was still ascribing human motivation to them. "Nobody seeks seniority. It is a duty, not a prize."

"Okay, will you do it?"

"If necessary."

"What do we do, then? Slug it out?"

"You can simply ask me."

"Why didn't you tell me that earlier?"

"You misunderstand our ways. You would have thought I was seeking an advantage."

"Very well, Mestin—please will you take over in place of Chayyas? There. Is that it?"

Mestin cocked her head in deference and felt both relief that she had stopped an unpredictable alien from shaping F'nar's future and dread that she had taken on a task she felt barely able to handle. Nevyan would smell that at once. She wondered if Shan had enough of a command of her rapidly changing hybrid senses to know that too.

"I'll announce the decision." Mestin stood up and trilled at the top of her voices for Aras to come and join them. He loomed in the open doorway, far too big for a male and far too alien, Vijissi behind him. He had a little blue glass bowl of *netun jay* in one hand and an expectant scent; that was inevitable, she accepted. Whatever form he had taken, Aras was still enough of a wess'har male to find a strong and aggressive female completely irresistible.

His eyes never left Shan.

Neither did Nevyan's. Mestin was beginning to feel invisible. She was also concerned that her daughter, who was hers to educate, was settling on a *gethes* as a role model.

"Thanks," said Shan, and took the *netun jay* from Aras. She smiled at him, all teeth, completely distracted for a brief moment while her gaze went from his hips up to his face. Then she seemed to realize she was doing it and looked away, her expression suddenly neutral. "You okay?"

"Of course," he said.

Mestin interrupted. "You'll still need to stay on Wess'ej for your own protection. And you have utility for us. You did agree to serve this world without reservation."

"Yeah, I did." Shan bit cautiously into one of the cakes and then ate the rest of it in one mouthful. She was still glancing occasionally at Aras, and it was a very different eye movement from the one she used when she looked at Mestin. It didn't bode well. "Am I under house arrest?"

"I have no idea what that is, but you're free to go where you please on the planet. Where you'll live is another matter. I have empty rooms—"

"I have rooms too," said Aras.

"Make what arrangements you wish." Mestin didn't know quite what *c'naatat* could do between species, but the warning had to be given. Shan was paying Aras too much attention. "But please don't breed. I know it's cruel to say that, but you both know the dangers."

"Whoa, what—" Shan began.

Aras cut her off. "We understand the burden we carry," he said.

Shan simply looked at him and her lips pursed as if she was about to speak, but in the end she said nothing. Mestin guessed that Shan had little idea what was happening to her and that she had—for once—been surprised into silence. The two *c'naatat* exchanged glances. Mestin could detect nothing beyond Aras's agitation and arousal.

It was unimportant. As long as they were bonded, she cared little how they felt about it. Two unmated adults would create unrest in F'nar society, *c'naatat* or not. She watched them go and turned to Vijissi.

"I would like you to look after *Shan Chail* when she appears to require it," she said. "And whether she welcomes that aid or not."

Vijissi paused, bit on a *netun* with a dramatic snap of his teeth, and hissed like escaping steam.

"I shall," he said.

Utility. Aras considered the word. *Without reservation.* There was a time when he had been told that too—several lifetimes ago, and not quite in those words, but it had been just as unqualified, and equally simple to accept. Difficult times made those decisions easy.

He thought of Cimesiat and all the other *c'naatat* troops who had made the honorable decision to end their abnormal lives, and wondered if he would have agreed so readily if he were asked to serve again today.

Shan was subdued. She walked a little way behind him. As they passed along the pearl-walled terraces to his old home, wess'har paused to greet him with trills, pointing him out to their children. *C'naatat* troops had been heroes. Nobody here forgot that.

And he was the last of them.

"You're really angry with me, aren't you?" Shan said.

"No. Not at all." He glanced over his shoulder: she smelled very good indeed, wess'har good, and that was a fragrance that had not beckoned him in centuries. He tried to ignore it. It wasn't fair on her. "But you've been here less than sixty hours and you've already destabilized the city government and ousted a senior matriarch. I dread to think what you could achieve in a season."

"Is that a joke?"

"Yes." Maybe he could sit her down and explain things to her. Perhaps Nevyan might. "Why did you confront Chayyas?"

Shan made that puffing noise of annoyance. "To stop her frying you, of course. Did I have an alternative?"

"Perhaps *waiting* to see what would happen?"

"Yeah, and it was *me* she put a hole through." There was a slight tremor in her voice. "I made the choice and I'll live with it."

Silence. But her anger only made her more powerfully appealing. They carried on their way around the caldera, a progress slowed by more wess'har stopping Aras to say how *significant*, how *wonderful*, it was to see him. Most had never actually seen a *c'naatat* before, let alone one as extraordinarily different as Aras. Their hero-worship stopped short of actually touching him.

His rooms were at the far end of the top terrace and looked out not only on F'nar but also to the arid bronze landscape outside the caldera. It had taken him years to cut it out of the escarpment a little at a time and line it with stone fragments.

When he pushed on the entrance door, thick with the deceptive glamor of undisturbed *tem* deposits, he half expected to see a family in residence. But he suspected nobody would occupy a *c'naatat's* home, however long it had been abandoned.

It was empty. It was also completely clean and smelled of freshness and water. Someone had been in to prepare it for him. There were *evem* tubers on the open shelves and a variety of boxes beside them.

Shan followed him in. "How long did you say you'd been away?" she asked.

He calculated briefly. "Just over a hundred and twelve years."

"You've certainly got a loyal home help."

"I don't know who did this and I probably never will."

Shan seemed overtaken by delighted surprise. "Humans break into empty houses and loot them. Wess'har break in, do the housework and leave groceries." She laughed, a totally artless peal of laughter. It was rare to hear her do that. "You lot are going to put the likes of me out of work. *Amazing*."

"We have a sense of communal responsibility."

She wasn't mocking them, he knew. But she still had a lot to get used to. He slung his pack onto the hip-high chest that served as a table and pulled out a knife, glad that she had brightened for the moment.

"I'll cook dinner and then we'll talk, yes?"

Shan watched him warily. "Yeah. I do have a few questions."

F'nar was not Aras's home. He wondered if he should have headed north, to Iussan on the Baral plain, where he had been born—born *normal*—and where people hid their homes as carefully as he had hidden Constantine from view. It was devout Targassati country; or at least it had been, centuries ago, before he left for the last time. F'nar society was less rigorous and more conspicuous in its habits. It was soft. You didn't have to look hard for evidence of its existence. But it was probably a more sensible choice of home for humans easing their way into wess'har life.

Shan appeared to have worked out that there were few rooms by human standards. While he sliced the *evem*, she paced from room to room as if calculating something. He had excavated only as much space as he needed, and that meant a main room where the living and cooking and reading was done, a cleansing room, and a small alcove for storage.

"Mmm," said Shan, looking round with a carefully blank expression. "Studio living. Nice."

It was a warm evening and he was already missing the crisp winter in Constantine. He left Shan to examine the vegetables and fruit and went to clean himself in the washroom while the *evem* soaked in broth. When he came back out, squeezing the water from his long braid, she was attempting to make sense of the foods in the crate. It was clear that being helpless wasn't something she was used to. She couldn't even activate the cooking range: she peered at it from every angle and her face became flushed.

"I have a hell of a lot to learn," she said. "And not just wess'u."

"You serve those raw," he said helpfully, and took a bunch of green bulbs from her. "Why not watch me?"

"I should be making myself useful."

Aras prised her fingers off the cooking implements and steered her towards one of the benches. "Sit and watch."

"I know you're pissed off with me. I can't do more than apologize."

"I am *not* angry with you." It wasn't anger she could smell, but he had to pick his moment to explain that to her. This wasn't it. "My actions brought us to this point. Not yours."

He was ashamed of chiding her for impatience. She had been willing to trade her life for his, however foolish that was. And he had been a fool too: he had robbed her of normality and peace and home when he thought he was saving her life.

"But you came for me," he said.

"Eh?"

"You didn't abandon me. You were as good as your word."

Shan looked down at nothing in particular. She did that to disguise the times her eyes betrayed her apparent calm. She wasn't very good at it, although *gethes* might have been fooled. It was the same look she had when he had first told her about being a prisoner of war, a kind of painful embarrassment. "Yeah, well, I never could stay out of a fight, could I?"

"It was a very dangerous and foolish thing to do."

"You're welcome. Glad I could help."

"Why do you take such risks for me?"

"You're a good man, Aras. You're also my only friend."

He watched the *evem* as it simmered and rolled slowly in the currents of the yellow-stained water. He recalled sitting on a plain on Bezer'ej telling Shan about the *c'naatat* parasite for the first time, ready to cut her throat with his *tilgir* if she looked likely to betray the knowledge to the scientists of *Thetis*.

She never knew the thought had crossed his mind. She had trusted him. Not confessing that to her carved a constant pain in his chest.

He glanced back at her. Her normal don't-piss-me-about expression, as Eddie called it—set jaw, unblinking gaze—melted for a few seconds into a slight smile.

Why her? Why save *her*? Mestin had asked him, and he wasn't sure until that moment. Now he knew. She filled almost every void in his distorted life: his instinctive needs, so long suppressed, were being met. She was a little girl, an *isanket*, in need of care and education; she was an equal, a house-brother who could provide comradeship; and she was—whether she knew it or not—an *isan*, a physically powerful matriarch who was the source of protection and life in the family.

And she knew what it was to be isolated and alone. It was a heady combination.

Aras struggled not to dwell on the idea. "Chayyas would have exacted a very high price from you," he said. "Mestin's will be even higher."

"I expect I'll get my money's worth out of her, too. Both of us are in over our heads. Level playing field. I find that reassuring." She made an impatient gesture towards the range. "Come on, dinnertime. *Isan's* orders."

Ah. He would have to discuss it. "You don't have to be *isan* if you don't want to."

"I'm happy to cook."

"*Isans* don't cook."

"What are these responsibilities Mestin says I have, then?"

"To make decisions for the household, to participate in the running of the city, and to protect your males." Mestin seemed to think they had already coupled: it had been the usual way of transmitting *c'naatat*. "The other matters need not bother you."

"Why?"

"They are of a sexual nature."

Shan made a noncommittal sound and looked away. He wasn't sure how to interpret that. He was also sure he wasn't going to ask. She watched him prepare the vegetables and tubers, repeating the name of each in wess'u as best she could, and she was an *isanket* again and he stopped thinking of what couldn't be.

Bezer'ej was in its full phase that night, a wonderful pale blue and terra-cotta moon streaked with silver. After dinner, Aras spent a long time on the terrace staring at it and wondering what Josh and his family were doing now. He hoped they would all understand why he had left. He longed to return, but Shan was here, and all his instincts anchored him to where she was.

He tried not to think of Mestin's household, of Chayyas's household, full of children and love and normality, and it hurt. On Bezer'ej there were no reminders of what he had sacrificed. He needed to go back.

Aras went back inside the house. Shan had settled down on a pile of *sek* covers in the corner of the room with her jacket rolled up under her head, one hand gripping it as if she thought someone might snatch it from her while she slept. He could see no lights and no claws: *c'naatat* had tired of the changes for its own inexplicable reasons. Her hands were human again.

Her boots—very clean, shiny from constant buffing, black—were standing neatly against the wall. If she hadn't been resting on the jacket, he would have tried to repair it before she woke. She set great store by being neatly dressed. The bullet hole in the jacket bothered her.

Aras listened to her rhythmic breathing for a while and studied the lines of the muscles that ran over her shoulder and down her arm. Maybe he would work out what to say to her by the morning. A few strands of her hair had escaped from the fabric tie that held it in a tail, and he thought better of smoothing it back from her face.

"Teh chail, henit has teney?" he said quietly. No, he had no idea how they were going to work this out. "Do you really think of me as a man? Or am I one of your helpless animals like the gorilla?"

He almost wished she hadn't told him that story. But he would have discovered it anyway, along with the flames and the sickened rage that were already surfacing alongside his own memories. The more traumatic and significant the event, the more likely it was to filter through. Failing to help the primate had definitely gouged a permanent scar in her mind.

Shan looked exhausted rather than peaceful. She twitched occasionally in her sleep, making small sounds of nothing in particular.

He wondered if she were having the same dreams as him.

5

I really quite like humans. They understand the need for mutually beneficial agreements. I have no doubt that they will benefit enormously from our communications technology—access to which we will of course control—and we will be grateful for their assistance in resuming deep space travel. If they are offended by being treated as a means of transport, then they don't show it. Are we allying with a dangerous power? I think not. When we have their technology, when we fully understand terraforming, when we have relieved our resource pressures enough to resume our own exploration program, then we are free to end our agreements with them.

PAR PARAL UAL,
addressing fellow state leaders at
the Northern Isenj Nations Assembly

Lindsay fastened the belt on her fatigues and tidied her hair, relying on the distorted reflection in the console screen to check that everything was in order. She felt as she thought she looked: an aeon older.

It was the most useful thing she could do with the screen at the moment. The recreation network terminal was down again, a consequence of her trying to dock her personal unit with it. Life in space certainly wasn't like it was in the movies. There was never a handy universal computing platform around when you needed one.

There were two more serious matters that she couldn't get out of her mind. One was the first cogent thought that consumed her three seconds after waking each day, and that was that David was dead; and the other was that Rayat was back. He was supposed to be on board *Thetis*, on his way home with the rest of the payload, six Royal Marines and the isenj party. He wasn't. He was *here*, and she wanted to know who else was now embarked in *Actaeon*, and why.

She wanted to go and seek him out. But her natural caution told her to establish more facts before she went plunging in. Eddie might know something. He could wheedle information out of anybody, even information Okurt thought he might be keeping to himself. She tried activating the bioscreen but she was still getting flat lines; it looked as if her marine detachment was still on board *Thetis*, long out of range.

Detachment. There were only six of them. But they were still a detachment, and six Royal Marines—six *Booties*—were a considerable asset.

Eddie appeared to have adapted perfectly well to life on board *Actaeon*. The man settled into spaces as easily and smugly as a cat. He was wandering down the main passage that ran the whole port side of *Actaeon*'s main section when she saw him, pausing at every network niche to slot his datacard forlornly into the port. She wondered if she'd crashed the whole rec network.

"Did you know Rayat was on board?" she said without preamble.

Either Eddie wasn't much of a poker player or he was covering a lie. He registered surprise with a frown. "But he was chilled down on *Thetis*. He should be . . . er . . ." He stared blankly at the bulkhead for a few seconds, flipping his card over and over between his fingers, but the maths had clearly defeated him. "Well, a few months down the road home now."

"I thought so too. I saw him about an hour ago."

"I hear a lot of things on this ship, but not that. Did he say why?"

"We're not exactly chummy. He said hi and he walked away."

"And you didn't ask him why he was back? Is it all of the payload? The marines? What?"

"Like I said, he just said hi and walked off."

"You'd make a poxy journalist, doll."

"I was caught off guard." She had the feeling that Eddie had delivered the worst insult he could muster. He was the sort of man who'd interview his doctor on his deathbed. She struggled to regain his respect. "I'm seeing Okurt shortly and I intend to ask. If they've brought anyone inboard, one of us should know about it, and it's not me."

"Paranoia is healthy. Makes you think creatively. So what's he here for?"

"Because they're getting obsessed with that biotech Shan's carrying. He's come back for that, I reckon."

Eddie looked visibly pained. "Oh shit."

"You know more about this than you're telling me, don't you?"

"I doubt it. Are you telling me everything *you* know?"

"I don't know who to tell what these days." She gripped Eddie's forearm discreetly, not sure herself if it were a friendly gesture or one of desperation. "Are you giving samples to the doc?"

"Always do."

"Well, they're checking for Shan's biohaz."

Eddie still wore his I'm-your-chum smile, but it was thinning away to transparency. "And if you found you had it, what would you do?"

"Run, I think. Run like hell." She was starting to wonder if there was anybody who could be trusted with it. She hadn't got quite as far as asking herself how far she would go to stop it falling into the wrong hands—and there were plenty of those grasping around. "If you hear anything, promise me you'll tell me."

"If that works both ways, I will."

She just gave him a blank look and went on her way. She didn't find it easy to lie. If he knew what she had in mind for Shan, she had no doubt he would get word to her. He admired the woman: he made no secret of it.

Lindsay settled in the corner of the wardroom for the morning briefing and thought it was an informally sloppy place to do business. But this wasn't her ship; it was Okurt's. She decided to aim for invisibility, a hard task in her out-of-date uniform.

She didn't even speak the way the rest of the crew did. Two or three generations of separation from mainstream human culture were audible as well as visible.

And there was the other problem, of course. Nobody knew what to say to a woman who had lost her baby anyway.

Okurt seemed excited. He was spinning his coffee cup in its saucer again and Lindsay wanted to slap his hand away from it. But he stopped of his own accord when his staff of a dozen officers filed in.

Two of them sat either side of her, a little too close for comfort. She found it hard to brush hips with strangers now. She tried to shrink.

"We've received instructions to attempt to reopen negotiations with the wess'har authorities," said Okurt.

There was silence. None of them were trained in diplomacy, Lindsay thought, and diplomacy as humans understood it wouldn't work on wess'har. She'd dealt with them just enough to know that.

"They don't negotiate," she said.

"I know it's not going to be easy."

"How are the isenj going to take this?"

"They're not privy to this."

Lindsay went back to staring at her hands. There was quite a lot the isenj weren't privy to. There were times in life when alarm bells started ringing insistently in your head and wouldn't stop. She wondered if anyone else could hear them like she did then. Okurt certainly did, but she knew he would follow the orders of politicians who were 150 trillion miles away from the fallout.

"I plan to make contact with F'nar in the next few weeks," he said. "I have no idea how their political hierarchies operate or even what their geopolitical structures are. Could you help out, Commander?"

Lindsay looked up. "They might prefer to talk to a woman. It's a matriarchal society."

"Are you volunteering?"

There was a chance it would get her close enough to Shan. She stifled her excitement and paused a beat before saying, "Okay." Again, she was conscious of Okurt's gaze resting just a suspicious second too long on her and she clung to a facade of professional calm.

I'm going to have the bitch.

The prospect almost outweighed the reappearance of Rayat, but not quite. The briefing seemed longer and slower than usual. She caught herself carving her stylus into the smart-paper again and made a deliberate effort to take notes until the meeting broke up and she and Okurt were alone in the ward-room.

"Is there something you want to tell me, Malcolm?"

His bemusement looked genuine enough. "Something on your mind?"

"Why is Dr. Mohan Rayat here and not in the fridge in *Thetis*?"

Okurt didn't turn a hair. "We were instructed to retrieve the whole team plus the detachment. Everyone who had any contact with Frankland, just in case they had any contamination."

It threw her. She really hadn't guessed. She fought the urge to check her bioscreen. "For their own well-being, of course."

"You know damn well why."

"Ah, a word from our sponsors, eh?"

"As far as they're concerned, we're just cooperating with their requests. Don't push it." He glanced over his shoulder, casual, apparently unconcerned, and then lowered his voice. "And if I had the slightest suspicion that they were carrying this thing, I wouldn't be letting the commercial medical team crawl all over them."

"I'm not with you."

"If you were chief of staff, what precautions would you take here?"

"Defensive?"

"Political."

Lindsay didn't need to think that long. "I'd probably want to look at that biotech for our own military purposes before we handed it over."

"I'm glad to see your strategic common sense is alive and well."

Lindsay felt she had at least judged Okurt about right. For all his grumbling and cynicism, he was at his core a sailor, an officer, a man who put his ship's company first and looked after his own. So here was another agenda. She wondered how many more there might be, and if Okurt was aware of them all.

"Are those your real orders?" she asked. *No, not that. Don't let Shan be right.* "Cut-and-come-again troops?"

"I still answer to the Defense Discipline Act. Not shareholders." His almost constant half smile evaporated for a few moments: the lines around his mouth collapsed into worry, into concern, but he snapped them back into place again. "And whatever we do with it, it'll be in the hands of our federal interests, not hawked round the international marketplace by multinationals. That stays within this wardroom. Okay?"

"Okay."

"We'll take her. Don't worry."

He didn't need to say who *her* was. Lindsay feigned casual indifference. "Want me to get to work on that?"

"You know how I feel about your involvement."

"I can get to her. I know better than anyone how to do it."

Okurt looked into her eyes for a while, no doubt scouring for signs of crazed vengeance. She made sure he didn't find any.

"Okay," he said. "This place is a sieve. So only you and I know, and that's it. Understood?"

"Never heard you mention a thing," she said.

"And maybe you're not ideal for diplomatic contact."

"Fair enough."

It didn't make her feel brave or clever. She was deceiving a good man. But however decent, sensible, and deserving of loyalty Okurt might be, Shan Frankland had the edge on him: she'd been *right*.

Lindsay knew that if she was going to get to Shan, she'd have to go through Okurt sooner or later. She needed his trust.

"Is the whole payload thawed out?"

"All of them. The only life on *Thetis* now is the isenj and their ussissi support team, and they're still out cold."

So she had her Royal Marines back on board, and she had Eddie, and Eddie could find out God's unlisted number if he put his mind to it.

Both Eddie and Shan had taught Lindsay a valuable technique common to both journalists and detectives. If you had enough individual pieces of the model—however small, however innocuous, however incomprehensible on their own—you could recreate the picture on the box.

She had a feeling she had been handed the solution to all her problems in kit form, minus the instructions and any idea of what she was making.

It was no problem. She had time.

"Go on," said Eddie. Back in the reserve turbine room, they were a hundred meters away from curious ears. The bridge repeater panels flickered and danced, projecting a rainbow of colors onto the lad's face. "Can't do any harm, can it?"

The young lieutenant—Barry Yun—was that most cherished of finds, a bloke in the know who wanted to be helpful. Yun was bored and he thought Eddie had lived a glamorous and exciting life. It was amazing what you could achieve just by being able to tell a good yarn.

"All right," said Yun. "They retrieved the *Thetis* crew. The thing's so slow we could catch up and board her."

"Why?"

"System failure. Safety."

"Unsafe for humans but safe for isenj and ussissi?"

Yun's lips moved silently for a second. Eddie felt a warm glow of triumph. *Make 'em think you already know the lot.* A couple of real facts, just the right degree of a smile, and a bit of timing, and they usually supplied the rest.

"Okay," Yun said. "I thought it was a stupid story too. Reliable buzz says it's this biotech. Do you know what some people are offering for this stuff?"

"No. Amaze me."

"I had to patch the CEO of Holbein through to the boss on his scramble line, not that it's secure on ITX, of course. He wasn't asking what the weather was like on Umeh either."

"All this on a rumor?"

"Pretty strong rumor if you listen. They're scouring everyone who's been in contact with Frankland. Even you."

Eddie held out his palms. "Look. No hair."

"They even unzipped the body bags. No stone left unturned. They were talking about how they could get access to the colonists."

"And who's *they*?"

"The R and D consortium team."

"And you know this how, exactly?"

"I cover a lot of comms watches. Plus they're not too careful what they say in front of the stewards, and I'm always nice to the stewards."

I know, thought Eddie. "You're a man after my own heart," he grinned.

Yun proved it. "So what really happened to the two in the body bags, then?"

"Okay . . . Parekh was executed for killing an alien kid. Dissected it, counter to all orders not to touch specimens. And Galvin went off-camp against express orders too and got caught in the cross fire with the isenj. So the moral of the story out here is to do as you're told."

"I hope *Hereward*'s well cannoned up when she arrives, then. If any of us are still left."

The thought *don't react* flashed through Eddie instantly. "I thought *Hereward* was a survey ship," he lied, knowing the vessel hadn't even been on the CAD screen when he'd left Earth.

"Look, we have big spaceships and small spaceships. There isn't enough of a space navy to build specialized hulls like the domestic fleet. They just strap on more armaments to whatever's flying. We're lucky they haven't sent a sodding submarine."

"I just hope they've told the isenj that she's coming."

Yun just raised his eyebrows. "Classified," he said.

It was so classified that Lindsay hadn't thought to mention it. Maybe she hadn't been told either. It was a massively provocative act to launch another vessel into a disputed area. These species had been at each other for centuries: did the FEU really think another twenty-five years would see them kiss and make up? And a ship called *Hereward* suggested Albion had fallen out with the Alliance des Galles again. The FEU had never been a happy family.

But he didn't think the wess'har—or the isenj, come to that—would give a damn which European tribe was in the ascendant. They'd just lock and load.

"I wouldn't mind seeing my old mates," Eddie said, trying not to look too interested in the *Hereward* even though it was burning holes in him. "Or is that classified too?"

"They should be out of quarantine on Thursday. I imagine they'll gravitate towards the wardroom, seeing as there's beer available."

But Rayat was already out. That told Eddie something, but he wasn't sure what. He decided not to push his luck. He'd gleaned plenty from Yun for the time being.

He rather wished he hadn't. The shitty thing about knowing stuff out here was that it *mattered,* whereas on Earth you knew you were a cog, a nothing, a player in the game. You weren't actually responsible for the sequelae of information that was awkward and had consequences—not unless you were doing an investigative piece, and then it was up to the Shan Franklands of the world to go and take action on the strength of your allegations. You could go down the pub for a beer and start on something new and interesting the next day. Nobody really got hurt.

Out here he wasn't a cog. He was the entirety of the media: he was the populace: and he was society. He was all the people who weren't wearing a uniform, military or corporate. The information he gathered had real, immediate consequences beyond embarrassing headlines and calls for ministerial resignation.

That meant he had to be very careful how he used it.

"Barry, are we carrying much in the way of armament?" he asked.

"Depends what you mean by much."

"More than just demolition ordnance and a bit of close-in protection."

Yun's eyebrows danced briefly again. "Oh, plenty more. We can't exactly nip back and pick up anything we've forgotten to pack."

"Shit," said Eddie.

If he rose early enough, Aras could tend to his crops before anyone else was about in the fields. He could see well enough in the pre-dawn light to hoe safely around young plants. It was also cooler and more like Bezer'ej at that hour.

He was missing Bezer'ej. On Bezer'ej, he had no reminders of his enforced celibacy.

At the entrance of one home he passed, a young father was leaning against the doorway, savoring the breeze, a child clutched to his chest. Aras could hear him humming a single note under his breath, the sound Shan called *purring*, distracted by his thoughts as he suckled the baby. When he saw Aras he simply nodded acknowledgment.

Aras felt a stab of sorrow but returned the nod and hurried on. It was another reason he was going to find the time in F'nar hard to pass. The human infants in Constantine triggered no instinct in him. All he could detect was their frustration and rage. He didn't like them much: raw, unshaped *gethes*, all demand and self-absorption, barely tolerable until they learned that they had to fit in with the rest of the world.

No wonder so many humans never managed that.

Aras took the hoe from his pack and assembled it with its narrowest blade. There was ripe yellow-leaf to be harvested. He squeezed the top of the leaf in his hand and it crumpled like soft fabric. The foliage had softened and turned from red to gold, all its toxins safely drained back to its roots. It was ready to eat.

Toxins didn't trouble him but he harvested at the appointed time. There was more yellow-leaf to pick today than he needed, so he would take it back to the food stores at the Exchange of Surplus Things. That was the way it worked. The Christians in Constantine had also operated a communal food system, but theirs seemed to require that someone tallied all the produce and checked that everyone was contributing their share and not consuming more than they were entitled to.

I thought I understood them.

He had lived in the company of humans longer than he had his own kind. His body housed human genes gleaned from bacteria, viruses and skin cells. But the blood-to-blood contact with Shan had brought with it a far more fundamental experience of what it was to be human, and it was shocking.

I never understood them at all.

Aras hefted the hoe. The handle felt like . . . felt like a weapon, a stick of some kind. Not his: *hers.* When he squeezed it he could feel outrage, horror, a sense of knowing something that had changed her world forever.

He abandoned the hoeing and concentrated on recalling the memory. Whatever it was, he needed to know what had marked her so much that it surfaced above the images of waterfalls of fire and the pleading ape.

Human genetic memories didn't feel at all like isenj ones. Eddie had once shown him how moving pictures were assembled, and Aras found parallels between that technology and the assorted memories that had lodged in his brain. Isenj memories were complete, accurate, real-time sequences; humans' were snatched and distorted, like spooling through scraps of spliced footage at high speed and having both blank sections and sudden vivid freeze-frames.

And isenj memories felt like the past. Shan's felt like *now.*

He concentrated.

Sitting in the dark on a hard bench, a heavy baton in hand. It was Shan. There was an overwhelming sense of disbelief and shock. *Do something about it. Balance the score a bit. A door swings open in a sudden shaft of yellow light and it's someone she knows, someone she respects, telling her to sort it. A massive cold surge of adrenaline and then a blank and that baton feels part of her arm, all sweet animal rage. There's a man's face, and he grins but then he stops smiling and—*

Aras felt the repeated downward swings of the baton so vividly that it was all he could do to hold onto the hoe. Then he dropped it. Relief as intense as quenched thirst flooded him. He fell to his knees and struggled to find his own thoughts again. No, this was nothing like the mind of an isenj.

Whoever Shan had beaten, she had savored every moment of it.

It disturbed him. He didn't want to think of his *isan*—and he admitted to himself that he saw her as that now—as a torturer. It was an unpleasant thought for anyone: it was especially unbearable for him. He busied himself piling the yellow-leaf into a rolling crate and wheeled it down into the network of passages that moved items around the city and to other settlements. The pipework above his head throbbed with the intermittent flow of water to the irrigation systems.

There was one barge resting at the loading point, already partly filled with *evem*, and he laid his bundle of yellow-leaf on top of it before pulling down the cover and inspecting the route information displayed on the top, a few glyphs fingered into the soft surface. *Iussan, Baral.* So the weather was dry enough back home to start digging up last year's *evem* early.

Why had Shan delighted in breaking a man's bones with her baton?

Aras climbed back to the top of the entrance shaft and found three children—an *isanket* and two boys—standing and staring at his collection of terrestrial crops. One boy kept putting his arm through the prickling biobarrier and inspecting his skin. The other two were much more interested in the plants, but they acknowledged Aras with sober nods like adults would. He thought of Josh's daughter Rachel, all giggles and carefree silliness.

"Aras Sar Iussan, this is new," said the *isanket,* pointing.

"It's called *tea,*" he said. "Humans dry the leaves and make an infusion from it for drinking. Its closest relatives are grown for their beauty, but the tea plant has both qualities, so Targassat would approve of it."

"Is it pleasant?"

"You would find it bitter. Humans enjoy it. This is for *Shan Chail.*"

The *isanket* looked hard at the glossy leaves as if absorbing every detail of them, which she was. Then she tipped her head politely and walked off, the two boys trailing obediently behind her as they would throughout the rest of their lives.

Aras tried to recall his first *isan*'s face and failed. He felt no guilt at that: Askiniyas had been dead nearly five hundred years, one more *c'naatat* host who had decided it was better to return to the cycle by her own hand. Sometimes, when people talked of the sacrifices of *c'naatat* troops, they often forgot the matriarchs who had transmitted the symbiont to their males out of duty, some unaware of the true nature of *c'naatat*, others not.

Askiniyas hadn't known. Nor had his house-brothers until his infection traveled through them all.

I started it. It was my fault.

Ben Garrod might have been right. Josh's ancestor claimed there were punishments meted out by the unseen being called God, and if there was a punishment for infecting your entire family through copulation, then Aras felt he had truly been punished by his endless celibacy.

It was time to be getting back. He dismantled the hoe and put it in his pack, reluctant to hold the handle tightly again in case he relived the moment when Shan began breaking bones and gloried in it.

Whatever had driven her to torture rather than kill, her explosive, vengeful anger was now within his very cells.

He would have to handle it carefully.

6

I care not for a man's religion whose dog and cat are not the better for it.

ABRAHAM LINCOLN

Shan sat on the toilet with her chin resting in her hands, savoring a moment of privacy.

It wasn't a perfect lavatory bowl and there wasn't a seat to speak of, but it was hers, and it worked, and it required no special technique or physical agility to make use of it as a wess'har latrine did. She'd had enough of going native. She was determined to be a good wess'har citizen but she drew the line at their plumbing and their furniture. She had her toilet: and now there was a half-built settee out on the terrace, which she would finish when she sorted out how to make proper mitered corners. Then she'd make a bed, a nice comfy bed.

She heard the front door open and close.

"Shan?"

"In here, Aras."

A pause. She hoped he hadn't taken it to mean *come in.* "I have yellow-leaf. Lots of it."

"Lovely. Great."

"Are you unwell?"

"I'm fine."

"Are you—"

"Look, I'm fine," she said. "I won't be long. Give me a few minutes."

Poor sod: it wasn't his fault. She felt bad about wanting a few moments to herself, but . . . her *flash-to-bang time*, as Ade Bennett called it, was perilously short these days. Josh had probably averted her meltdown by sending specs for a Constantine-style toilet bowl to an obliging wess'har craftsman.

The bowl the *jurej* had fashioned was ice-clear aquamarine glass, and too disturbingly transparent to be ideal for a toilet. But she learned to look away. And now she had a real toilet door too, and suddenly she felt a lot less like rounding on Aras and snarling at him.

Poor sod.

The nightmares weren't helping her mood either. She was still drowning, still being jerked awake by a searing pain in her back and a devastating sense of abandonment.

"You were up early," said Aras. He sounded as if he were moving around the room. "Are you still having problems sleeping?"

Oh, please. Just a couple of minutes. "It's probably *c'naatat* shaking down." She stood up and took a deep breath. She could always retreat here again. "Bound to be a few glitches."

When she opened the door, Aras was standing at the spigot, peering into the bunch of yellow-leaf he was rinsing. He placed a finger carefully into the soft crumpled leaves, lifted something out with his claw and set it on the windowsill. "Just a *banic*," he said. "It'll go about its business when it dries out."

He seemed preoccupied. It was mainly the silence that told her so. In the few weeks they had been sharing a single, suffocating room, partitioned by curtains, silence had been one thing he wasn't good at. Aras liked talking. He had been through five hundred years of solitary, relatively speaking, and now he had a listener who was just like him, except that he was from a species that needed to huddle and chatter, and she liked her own company.

You can't imagine what he's been through, she told herself. *Patience. Just a bit of patience.*

She found herself staring at his broad back and noting how nicely it tapered into his waist. The sudden realization that it wasn't just xeno-anatomical curiosity made her face burn. She thought of Mestin warning her not to breed, and wondered if the matriarch had spotted what she had only just discovered.

Oh no. Not that. Get a grip, you silly bitch.

"You don't look well, *isan.*"

She reminded herself how much she despised Lindsay Neville for getting pregnant in a careless moment. "I'd rather you called me *Shan,*" she said.

"Very well." Aras put the bowl of yellow-leaf on the table and picked up his hoe from the corner. He hefted it in his hand, staring down the length of the handle as if something terrible were crawling up it towards him. "I need to ask you a question."

"Okay."

"When I grip this," he said, "I have vivid recall of an incident. You had a weapon like this."

Shan nodded. Of course she did. "My baton," she said. "A truncheon. I've still got one in my kit."

"You beat someone with it."

"Well, that doesn't narrow it down much." She was about to make a joke of it but Aras didn't smell amused. He reeked of agitation. She tried again. "Yes, I used a baton, and I used it a lot. If you're churning up my memories, you'll know that."

"I see this one over and over again. You were very upset and a man was shouting at you to do something about it, and then you were looking at another man and you started beating him with the baton. You broke his bones. I heard it. He wasn't armed."

It sounded like a rebuke. And it was an indictment of her approach to policing that she was genuinely having trouble pinning down what he was recalling, but she was embarrassed to say so. She struggled. "Sorry, I don't recognize what you've remembered. Lots of blokes have shouted at me over the years. And I've smacked quite a few of them. Hard."

"But I keep picking up pieces of it."

"Sorry."

"You were sitting on a bench in the dark when a man came in and told you not to sit there *all fucking night.*"

For a few more seconds it was as much of a puzzle as before: and then it flooded back with a sickening wave of adrenaline.

Shan knew exactly where she was, but she didn't *want* to know.

She'd battled to come to terms with the images from that night. After a few years of seeing them behind every locked door and trying to stop them crowding into her mind between the time she closed her eyes and the time she fell asleep, she had succeeded in burying the detail.

The pervading dread of doors had never left her, though. Like all terrible things she had seen and couldn't then erase, they became more persistent the more she tried to stop thinking of them.

"I need to know . . . Shan." Aras's voice was quiet and almost apologetic now. "I need to know what marked you so, and I also need to know why you tortured a man. It bothers me. I find it hard to accommodate."

It was a shabby slate-blue door that had previously been dark green because she could see where the paint had flaked off. There were some doors you could kick in, cheap doors with fragile locks; there were others you needed a dynamic ram or a couple of plastic rounds to tackle. She preferred a good kick. It psyched you up for what followed.

"I don't think you're in any position to judge me, Aras."

"Perhaps not, but I must know."

The lock took one all-out kick. The detective inspector with her said he was impressed that she could do the physical stuff as well as a bloke. He let her go ahead.

She couldn't see what was happening at first. It took her a few seconds to look down on the floor at what one of the two middle-aged men was recording on a top-of-the-line camera. It took another second to register what she was looking at and then she lost all professional control and slammed one of the men into the wall, face first.

It was the wrong house. No credit and ID cloning kit, just fucking weirdo porn, said the DI. He was pissed off. It was a fucking bum tip, he said, but they might as well nick the lot of them, not that it would be worth the paperwork for the sentences they'd get. He looked into her face, and she didn't want him to see the tears in her eyes. "Don't be such a fucking girl," he said. "You'll see a lot worse."

But she never had.

Now Aras was staring into her face. "What's wrong?" he asked. "You look—"

"You've got no other memories of this? Nothing at all?"

Aras was going to wring it out of her. She couldn't even manage the words, not even twenty years later. She was as ever torn between unbearable pain and anger, and she chose anger because she knew how to wield that without crumbling. Her sympathetic sergeant, the man who'd found her sitting on the shaking edge of tears in the darkened locker room, knew that much about her. *Go on,* he'd said. *Do something about it if you feel that strongly. It's not as if it was a kid or anything, He'll only get six months' suspended, tops.*

Even the score.

She did. She had never exhausted herself beating the shit out of someone before or since. She didn't care if she was suspended, charged, sacked: all she cared about was *justice.* But nobody saw anything, even if the desk sergeant kept wandering by the holding cell to check that she was coping. The guy was decitizenized anyway. Unpleasant things could happen to people with sufficient criminal record. They'd offended once too often and their rights were formally abrogated. Nobody was going to stop her. No lawyer would take it on.

Aras was still staring into her face, bewildered. If she looked anything like she did that night, he would be seeing her anew.

"Here." She handed him her swiss. He knew how to use it. She gathered herself up into the woman everyone seemed to think she was, the one who could cope because she didn't have feelings like the rest of them. It was self-pitying, she knew, but she wanted Aras to understand she had her limits of endurance as well. "Read for yourself. Look up *snuff* and *squish*. I don't imagine Josh kept material like that in his bloody little Eden, did he? I didn't think so. Okay, here's your primer in human depravity. There are humans who are entertained and aroused by watching children and animals tortured and killed, so they make movies of it. It's quite an industry. Take a look at my files."

Aras said nothing. He held the swiss flat on his palm, and she had no doubt he would read it: wess'har weren't squeamish. Perhaps he understood the very worst about humans anyway.

"You wanted to know," she said. "And I didn't torture him. I *crippled* him, and I did it as efficiently as I could without killing him, because I wanted him to have plenty of time to think about it. And I'd do it again in an instant, just as you did at Mjat, because it needed doing. Now read those fucking files, and never mention it to me again."

Shan shut the front door behind her a little too hard, sending flakes of pearl shivering to the ground, and walked down onto the terraces. Mindless physical displacement sometimes helped put her back together again. A couple of wess'har nodded politely to her as she passed and she tried to smile back, but her scent must have told them she was in turmoil. *Yeah, don't be such a fucking girl.* It was a lifetime ago.

And it wasn't Aras's fault. Nothing was. He was just a bystander with her memories playing out in his head, when God only knew what pain of his own was already there. She wondered when some of that was going to well up unbidden in her. She wondered if it would be worse than the images that were resurrected and fresh in her mind now, and whether it would replace them and so in a way erase them, bury them, make them go away again.

She got as far as the fields and busied herself inspecting the swelling peppers and the tops of the sweet potatoes. It wasn't necessary to go to all this trouble. She could survive on just about anything, and knowing Aras had put so much effort into trying to provide her with familiar foods simply made her feel all the worse for taking out her frustrations on him.

She squatted down. The smell of wet soil put her back in her recurring nightmare, the water flooding into her mouth and nose. She shook it off.

No, she wasn't losing it. She was *adjusting*. It was a life, a body, a future no human had ever had to face, and she was doing just *fine*, all things considered.

"Chail, neretse?" said a double-voice behind her. *Have you seen this?* A wess'har male—one of Fersanye's neighbors, she thought—beckoned to her. She was starting to recognize them all now. He led her over to another patch of soil a little distance away. Aras tended scattered plots everywhere, wess'har style, to make the planting look more random, less obtrusive. The biobarrier crackled against her skin as she stepped through the invisible bulwark between Wess'ej and a little piece of Earth.

This plot was dotted with sapling bushes with glossy, emerald-green serrated leaves. They looked like camellias. She didn't think Aras would grow anything as irrelevant as decorative flowers.

The male—Tlasias? Tasilas?—was fascinated. "What is *tea*?" he asked.

"It's a drink," she said.

Her wess'u was serviceably fluent now. Tlasias appeared to understand her. He touched the leaves and inspected them. "But how? You extract the juices?"

"You make . . ." She searched for a word for infusion. She didn't know one yet. "A solution from the dried leaves."

Then the penny dropped. She was looking at tea plants. *Camellia sinensis.* Aras was growing tea for her, and he hadn't told her. It was a surprise. Tlasias, like every other wess'har, had no concept of giving people surprises. He'd blown it.

It didn't diminish the pleasure one bit. She almost winced at the extra weight of guilt it placed on her, because she had not only given Aras a hard time for reminding her of her demons, but she had also bitched at him while he was making extraordinary efforts to please her. He knew how much she loved tea. She had enough left from Constantine to make a dozen more pots. She was eking it out, saving it for special occasions.

She took a deep breath. "The Chinese say that it's better to be deprived of food for three days than of tea for one. That's how much *gethes* enjoy it." She used the word almost without thinking. There was no wess'u alternative for *human*. It was the generic name they gave all things that ate carrion, a verb, a reflection of their world view that you were what you did, not what you believed or intended or looked like. "And it's kind of Aras to grow it for me."

Tlasias gathered his tools and walked off towards the city. Shan brushed her hands against the leaves of the tea plants, disappointed that they didn't emit that elusive, tarry perfume of the fermented leaf. She could wait. It was a singularly thoughtful gift.

Guilt had never been a defining emotion for her, except for the gorilla and all the other victims she couldn't—no, *hadn't*—saved. She'd never felt guilty about anything she had done. It was things not done that ate away at her.

She felt guilty now. She was guilty of impatience with Aras and of taking miracles for granted. There wasn't a human being alive—or dead—who cared about her well-being as much as one misfit alien with a stack of problems of his own.

When she walked back up the winding terraces to the house the sun was nearly overhead, and ferociously hot. Wess'har going about their business stopped to splash themselves with water from the open conduits that ran everywhere from terrace to terrace. Then they shook themselves unselfconsciously like dogs, spraying water everywhere and attracting a cloud of *tem* flies to the fresh puddles. The flies, for all their magnificent droppings, were insignificant, drab gray things with dull wing membranes. It didn't seem right somehow.

Shan didn't think she could do that canine shake, but the cold water looked like a good idea. She stopped and stuck her head under the torrent. For the merest fraction of a second it was bliss.

Then it was a dark room and every moment of misery and fear she had dreamed and half remembered on waking for the past few months. And she knew suddenly what it was.

Like those optical illusions that only formed an image out of a random pattern when you stopped trying to focus on them, she could now see her newly inherited memories. She was in an isenj prison as clearly as if she had been there herself. Although she was aware it wasn't happening to her, she was being held head down in water, trying not to gulp it into her lungs but unable to resist succumbing to the reflex to *breathe*.

She knew what was coming next. She put her hands flat on the burning pearl wall to stop herself pitching forward as a ripping sensation tore up her back and forced a surprised cry from her.

They said you couldn't recreate pain in your memory. They were wrong.

Someone stopped to trill concern at her but she waved them away without looking up. It took her a long time to draw herself together sufficiently to carry on walking. She couldn't understand why she hadn't made sense of it before. It was everything in Eddie's interview, the material he cut and kept for her alone, except it was detailed and personal. She knew now exactly what the isenj had done to Aras while he was their prisoner.

Her first instinct was to find the bastard who did it and sort them. But that bastard would be long dead by now. The second wave of emotion was to go to Aras and crush him to her chest and promise she'd make it right for him, just as she'd wanted to make it right for the mutilated rabbits and the kitten she'd stumbled on in that house behind the shabby blue door. But it was too late for them. And the unimaginable time stretching ahead of her was suddenly something she would have gladly traded for time stretching back to change the past.

If she forgot the caged gorilla signing a mute plea for help and the house with the blue door and a thousand other things she had seen, then she wasn't Shan Frankland any longer. It was time to come to terms with them. But it was hard. She wondered how Aras was going to handle the shit churning up from the mud in her memories. It wasn't as if he didn't have enough of his own.

F'nar looked incongruously glamorous through the filter of her nightmare. It was full of unforgiving creatures who would wipe out a planet without debate but she knew that there was nothing to fear behind the few doors they had. The relief of that thought was so sudden and intense that it felt like finding something precious you were sure had been lost for good.

Shit. Aras had her swiss. It was the first time it had left her hand or pocket in nearly thirty years except for repairs. It was like letting him browse through her soul, but he could do that anyway whether he wanted to or not, the poor sod. She'd make him a good strong cup of tea and get him to talk about his experiences. After five hundred years he probably needed catharsis more than she ever would.

It was a bugger how things stuck in your mind. *Don't be such a fucking girl. You'll see a lot worse.*

But she never had. She was sure of that.

Lindsay didn't need to look at the bioscreen in her palm to see that some of her Royal Marine detachment were up and about on board *Actaeon.*

Adrian Bennett was standing at the back of the huddle of officers chatting over their drinks at the wardroom bar, trying to catch the steward's attention. He was a sergeant. Sergeants, even Extreme Environment Warfare Cadre commandos like Bennett, did *not* drink in the commissioned officers' wardroom. The *Thetis* party had been barred from the other messes to slow the rumor machine, and his discomfort at being on unfamiliar social terrain showed as he shuffled his boots and folded and unfolded his arms.

Lindsay wanted to rush up and hug him. He was familiar and safe and reliable. He was from her world. Instead, she paused long enough to think what Shan Frankland might have done, and then stepped forward through the braying group of lieutenants and lieutenant commanders, who should have had the plain bloody good manners to clear the service area.

"Steward," she said loudly over their heads. The man looked up, startled. She had never used her three gold rings as imperiously before. "Would you get Sergeant Bennett a beer? And one for me please." No movement from the junior officers at the bar: she stared at one of them, a victim picked at random. "I'd write for you all too, but you're obviously just finishing your drinks."

There was a second's silence. It took them a while to understand. Then the officers parted as if a downdraft had hit them and left.

"Yes, ma'am," said the steward. For a brief and glorious moment Lindsay understood what it was to be Shan, to have *presence,* and it felt good.

She reached out for the glasses on the mock-mahogany bar and put one in Bennett's hand. "I can't tell you how good it is to see you."

"They told us we were restricted to the wardroom and Juliet deck."

"You don't have to explain yourself. Get that beer down you."

He raised the glass, looking bemused. "Cheers, Boss."

The informal title caught her off guard. Bennett didn't use it when addressing her very often: she was normally *ma'am.* But he called Shan Frankland *Boss* all the time, even though she was a civilian and had no authority over him other than the flimsy mandate handed to her by a politician too many years in the past.

Lindsay responded anyway.

"Cheers, Ade." It wasn't the done thing to address a noncommissioned rank by first name, but she didn't care. This wasn't her navy any longer. He was one of seven people in the universe who she could almost regard as a friend. There could have been eight, but she put that idea out of her mind. "I never got the chance to thank you for stopping me getting myself killed."

Bennett looked blank. "Not with you, Boss."

"You didn't start a firefight when the wess'har kicked us off Bezer'ej."

"Prudence." It wasn't a word he normally used. She wondered if he were raising his verbal game to fit better into the wardroom. "No point dying when you can wait and fight another day."

"I didn't think you were bottling out of a fight. Really I didn't."

Bennett just gave her a nervous half smile and busied himself with his beer. "They'd have torn us up for arse-paper anyway," he said quietly.

That was one of Shan's eloquent assessments of threat. Lindsay wondered if that was where Bennett had picked up the phrase; he'd taken a lot of ribbing from the detachment about his obvious affection for Shan. But she doubted it had gone further than a thought. Shan was too focused and too unforgiving to do anything as messy or weakly human as screwing a subordinate.

No personal discipline. That was Shan's verdict when she found out Lindsay was unexpectedly pregnant. The comment still hurt.

"So you're not immortal, then," Lindsay said. Bennett's expression was blank. She tried again. "You haven't picked up Frankland's biotech."

"None of us have."

"They're not leaving any stone unturned."

"I thought as much." Suddenly his expression wasn't I'm-a-simple-soldier, the studied lack of political art that he normally wore. Faint lines creased the bridge of his nose. "So you're coming back to Bezer'ej with us."

"Sorry?"

"I wasn't told *not* to tell you, Boss."

Shan dropped that sort of oblique information a lot better.

But Bennett had made his point, however inelegantly. It was clear he didn't like keeping things from her, and Lindsay struggled to think of some way to repay that loyalty. He'd answer a direct question from a superior officer.

"Okay, what return trip to Bezer'ej, Ade?"

"We've been tasked to find a backdoor route back to the surface if the front door approach doesn't work."

"To do what, exactly?"

"Retrieve samples."

"What samples? And if you manage to get down to the surface without being blown to kingdom come, how are you going to get off again?"

"Haven't got down to that level of detail yet, and I'm not sure that extracting us features in the CO's plans."

"Let's talk about the samples. What? Where?"

"Colony."

"Jesus, you can't just walk into Constantine and ask them for specimens, Ade. You'll have wess'har all over you like a rash. The colonists don't want us there either, remember."

Bennett said nothing. He looked embarrassed and stared down into his beer. He might have had a modest education, but he was no fool.

Oh God. He's trying to tell me something.

She waited for him to look up again and reveal what he was struggling with, but he just kept his eyes down.

He said colony, not colonists.

"Spit it out, Ade."

"Exhumation," he said.

It was another word she never thought he used. He probably thought it was a kind way to say it.

There was only one body buried at Constantine; the colonists preferred to leave their dead for consumption by rock-velvets, the slow and beautiful black sheets of plush tissue that lived on carrion. She hadn't wanted that end for David. Aras had made a stained glass memorial to stand at her son's grave.

"I'm sorry, Boss," said Bennett. "I thought you ought to know."

The harder Lindsay tried not to hear, the less she could see of the black and yellow chevrons of a fire escape hatch on which she had fixed her gaze. She couldn't feel her stomach or legs. What little progress she had made through her grief was now reversed and she was staring over a precipice.

"Why?" She wasn't sure if she had actually said the words aloud. "Why dig up my baby? For God's sake, can't they—"

"They're just checking everyone they can get to who might have been contaminated," said Bennett kindly. "Honestly, they really haven't a clue what it is or where they can find it, other than Superintendent Frankland and maybe Aras. Neither of them is going to hand out samples."

The chevrons assumed a more normal focus but Lindsay was still fixed on them. She had to control this. She could *not* fall apart now.

"They seem convinced about accidental contamination as a vector," she said. She fell back on dispassionate words to buffer the pain. "Come on. Let's work this through. What do we know?"

"Hugel says she called it a plague. And nobody who knows Shan would buy the idea that she'd carry biotech for money."

He'd slipped and called her Shan. Lindsay noticed, but she was more preoccupied with replaying the painful memory of the last time she had seen Shan. She'd been screaming at her, demanding to know why she hadn't used whatever she had to save David, to help. And Shan's refusal came back to her—measured, detached, the words of a copper giving a relative the bad news.

I have an infection. It would run riot in the general population.

Shan might just have been lying, of course, but Lindsay doubted it. If she had set up anything, she would have also set up a route to hand over the biotech or whatever it was to her masters. She wasn't a woman who left things to chance. But she was stranded, in exile among aliens. No, she hadn't planned this.

Lindsay shook herself out of it. She forced a smile. It hurt so much she thought Bennett might hear her tearing apart inside. "Let's have another beer, Ade."

"I'm so sorry. I really am. It's sick. We could refuse, Boss, really we could."

"No, we'll do it," she said. The pain fell away: the shivering ice in her gut was starting to feel like a comfort, a beacon. "We'll do more than that. We'll actually find whatever this is. And when we do, we won't be handing it over to any corporation. This isn't a recreational drug. This is a *weapon*."

Bennett hadn't finished his beer. He liked his beer, she knew, so he wasn't enjoying being the bearer of bad news. "Commander Okurt will rip me a new one for telling you."

"You leave me to worry about him." She gave his arm a squeeze, another little familiarity that wasn't allowed between ranks. He stared at her hand as if it had burned him. "One way or another, he's letting me in on this."

Lindsay managed to maintain her collected façade until she got back to the cabin she shared with the civilian engineer overseeing the construction of the habitat at Jejeno. Natalie Cho wasn't there. She heaved herself onto her bunk, pulled down the soundproofed shutter, and let go of the sobbing that had been threatening to overwhelm her for the last half hour.

The cabin was the only available accommodation for a woman, short of putting her in with the female ratings, and they would have liked that even less than she would. Natalie wasn't all that enthusiastic about sharing either. The two women retreated to the privacy of the sealed bunks if they happened to have downtime that coincided.

Pulling down the shutter felt like sealing the lid on her own coffin. She put her palm against the bulkhead to reassure herself that it wasn't pressing down on her, and the aftershock of Ade Bennett's revelation struck her yet again. They were so desperate for this bloody biotech that they would even dig up her son's body, just in case. They would dig him up without even telling her. *Her baby.*

Lindsay tried to stifle the sobs. But nobody could hear her behind that shutter anyway. She wondered whether Shan wept in private too, or whether her police duties had numbed her emotions so much that she had no tears left for anyone, even behind closed doors. Lindsay could picture her in any number of situations; but she could never conjure up an image of Shan grieving or consumed by fear or even overwhelmed by love.

And that was what *she* would have to emulate. She would have to be Shan, and put aside normal humanity, and just get the job done.

A switch had been thrown somewhere inside Lindsay. The biotech had at first seemed wonderful, capable of being harnessed for its medical benefits. Then it had quickly grown into a commodity she resented pursuing; and now it had emerged as a monstrous threat that made men and women—*normal* people—abandon all decency.

The wess'har seemed to be able to take breathtaking technology in their stride without taking Pandora's box, upending it, and shaking every last woe and demon out of it. She'd hoped humanity might have grown up too, but it hadn't.

It was a weapon, a costly privilege, a bringer of social chaos. It was everything Shan had said it was. Lindsay understood why Shan wouldn't hand it over, not even for a child's life. It didn't lessen the grief or the pain one bit, but she finally understood that it was the only choice the woman had.

Lindsay wondered whether Shan had agonized over the decision or acted without a single flicker of emotion. It didn't matter. Lindsay almost sympathized now.

But that didn't matter either. It simply meant that now—even more than ever—she had to kill and destroy Shan Frankland.

The construction of the biosphere at Jejeno had given Eddie a break from endless shots of isenj buildings. News Desk had really liked the urban dystopia theme because it was alien:

alien was big at the moment, apparently. The viewing figures were at an all-time high. Nobody cared why as long as they stayed that way.

He let the bee-cam wander round the construction site getting charming shots of isenj laborers and suited humans working together to lay foundations. He wondered how many isenj had been displaced to create this free space in a city where space was the scarcest resource.

"Several thousand," said Serrimissani, translating the bubbling and chittering of an isenj worker. "And all happy to move, because humans will be valuable friends."

Move where? Eddie mentally conjured up the shot of Umeh from the orbital station and could recall only a few patches on the planet that looked unpopulated. They were deserts and ice plains. But then isenj were as physically adaptable as cockroaches—

He wished he hadn't thought that, not in those terms. Not *cockroaches*. It was biologically true and ethically unacceptable.

"Can I talk to the site foreman about materials?" he said, and shook himself out of his liberal guilt. He ambushed a civilian steering a loader laden with bales of translucent green rope at a sedate pace along a path where the foundations had already set hard. "Hey, is this the plumbing?"

The bee-cam danced attendance round the driver's head. She was making a valiant effort not to look directly at it. "It's the deckhead," she said, bobbing her head slightly as if dodging imaginary bullets. "The roof. We web the lines across the framework and apply some chemical and current, and bang, it spreads out in a film and seals the dome."

"When's that due to happen? Can I get some shots of that?"

The driver pointed towards a man in a vivid orange coverall. "Ask the foreman," she said. Then she leaned a little further towards him. "Look, this biotech thing that woman's carrying. Is it true that it makes you live forever?"

"I wouldn't know," Eddie replied, rather too fast. "And if it did, the likes of us wouldn't be able to afford it, would we?"

"Yeah," said the driver. But her expression said that she thought it might be worth saving up for.

Eddie shook off the dull burn in his gut that mention of Shan's little refinements always seemed to give him lately. It was one more weight on the scale of burdensome knowledge that was disturbing his sleep: he hadn't yet mentioned *Hereward* to Lindsay. If she knew about it, then she hadn't traded information with him as they'd both agreed they would. But if she hadn't known about Rayat, then it was possible that she might have been out of the loop completely. He'd give her the benefit of the doubt for the time being.

Eddie concentrated on being busy. A full schedule of filming for the next few days always made him feel purposeful and alive. Not that he cared if News Desk thought he was slacking, of course. Boy Editor was no longer pressing him on biotech stories: Eddie had heard that there were people who really, really wanted knowledge of it to stay off the air until they had managed to secure it for themselves. Time was when nobody, not even governments, could get away with leaning on BBChan. Times had obviously changed.

He cadged a lift back to the back to the grounded shuttle and sweet-talked the pilot into letting him have a comms channel to watch the news. *His* news.

"You see your own material when you edit it," she said, as if she were going to put up a verbal fight. "Why'd you want to see it broadcast as well?"

"It's more real when it's broadcast."

"Yeah."

"And I want to see if they've hacked it about."

She considered him carefully. "Okay."

Eddie tended to lose track of Earth time zones even though he had several clock displays set on the editing screen he carried with him. He unrolled it to check: he was early for the evening European bulletin. The pilot made a "wow" noise at the sight of the near obsolete tech and peered at it as if it were a valuable antique, which—when he finally got home—it probably would be, if it hadn't had PROPERTY OF BBCHAN coded into every component.

Eddie caught the tail end of a call-in debate instead. A man in a suit (and they never changed with time, he noted) was being interrupted by an angry taxpayer.

"They're going to overrun us," said the caller, his irate face framed in an insert in the corner of the screen. "You've seen the reports on the news. Just take a look at what their own planet's like. And you're letting them land here?"

"I can assure you—" the suit began, but he was shouted down by the studio audience. Global comms or not, nothing could equal the collective anger of humans in the same room within sniffing range of each other's pheromones. Eddie was glad to see that some old TV formulas had survived. The interviewer struggled to restore some sort of order, but even with the bee-mikes in the studio silenced, Eddie could still pick up the clamor of voices. The trails for upcoming shows were already running in the icon slot on the screen.

"I think they were talking about our generous hosts," said the pilot.

"I think you're right," said Eddie. "I don't need to see the news now, thanks."

He rolled up his screen and slipped it into his pocket. He was experiencing the first few seconds after a car crash, when something had been done that could not be undone, however much it wasn't your fault, and however strongly you willed time to run back.

"Window," he said, and the pilot looked at him as if he were mad.

7

This isn't an issue solely for the European and Sinostates governments. Who consulted the people of the Pacific Rim, or the Americas, or Africa when the invitation was made to the isenj? In exchange for the bauble of instant communications over stellar distances, one arrogant alliance may have handed over the Earth. They attempt to shame us into silence by accusing us of xenophobia: but sometimes you have to say, "My people come first, and I will not apologize for that."

JEAN ARLENE,
President, African Assembly

Asajin was dead. Mestin hadn't known her well but she noted her disposal with regret. Her four *jurej've* walked through the fields carrying the *dhren*-wrapped body on a pallet and Mestin's heart went out to them. Other wess'har who were harvesting yellow-leaf stopped and glanced before going about their business.

Mestin was managing F'nar the only way she knew, by walking about the city, seeing what was happening and what people were saying, with Nevyan and Siyyas at her heels. She was conscious that it was a theoretical hierarchy and that there was no true hormonal dominance to warrant the two junior matriarchs bothering to defer to her: she was only dominant because a *gethes*—unpredictable, unfathomable Shan Frankland—had ceded her rights. The common good would hold a consensus together, but Mestin worried that she would lack the *jask*, the ferociously protective decisiveness, to make the right choices in a true crisis.

She was not afraid of her peers turning on her. She was afraid of failure. Failure was something she felt Wess'ej would not be able to afford in the coming years.

Mestin stared after the sad little party disappearing into the shimmering amber heat haze. The males would leave their dead *isan* out on the plain for the real *gethes,* the many native species that ate dead flesh, and come back to face an uncertain future.

"Who will take them?" she asked. Asajin had died earlier that morning and it was high time other matriarchs came forward to give homes to the children and *oursan* to the males. Nobody liked splitting up a family. It was a difficult calculation to work out which male would fit in best to which household. Once they were mated again, it would be all harmony and contentment but there was a brief, awkward time when matriarchs would ponder over which genetic qualities they might add to the family mix.

Mestin thought they had better be quick about it. The males looked in poor condition, dull-skinned and lacking a decent sheen to their hair. Asajin had been ill for some time; her *jurej've* had not had the frequency of *oursan* they needed to stay fit. The youngest one, still suckling a child, looked worst of all.

"I will," said Nevyan.

Mestin thought of stopping and arguing with her daughter but decided against it. "What's in them that you would add to the clan, then?"

"It's more that they're in need of an *isan,*" Nevyan said. "And if I'm to follow you one day, then I must learn duty."

Nevyan had never shown signs of bonding with any junior male in particular, and there had been much speculation about what she was looking for in a *jurej*. Mestin had always thought another shot of genes from the confident Fersanye clan would have done the line no end of good, as well as cementing a clan bond. But Nevyan had to make her own choices.

Siyyas said nothing. There was no scent at all to add a silent comment on the conversation; and Siyyas was not the *isan* her sharp-minded, perceptive aunt the matriarch-historian Siyyas Bur was. So much for genetics, Mestin thought.

"Most considerate, not to break up a family," said Mestin. However warmly the males and their children would be welcomed into new clans, separating house-brothers was painful. Establishing a household anew with an unmated *isan* was a pragmatic and compassionate move. It wasn't what she had wanted for Nevyan, but she was proud of her. Nevyan would one day make far better choices for F'nar than she ever could.

"I can join them in Asajin's home," Nevyan said. "There's no purpose in taking them from the environment they know. What will Shan make of this? It would be good for her to learn how things are done here."

Mestin did then stop and turn. Her daughter was leaving home, in a sentence, in a decision taken as they strolled around the city. She was accepting four new husbands and their children, males she hardly knew. But that was irrelevant because once they had mated and the *oursan* bond had been formed, wess'har biochemistry would ensure that they would be what she wanted and would defend against all threats. And they would consider her their perfect *isan* for the rest of their lives.

From what Mestin knew of *gethes,* she didn't think Shan Frankland would understand it at all.

"Why does it matter to you what Shan Frankland thinks?" It wasn't a challenge: Mestin was genuinely curious. Nevyan had given the woman a *dhren,* but that wouldn't make a matriarch out of a *gethes.* "Do you need her approval?"

"She has characteristics we'll all need in the years to come," said Nevyan.

"You can't acquire them by *oursan.*"

"Then I'll learn them by observation."

The thought of Frankland becoming a cousin-by-mating wasn't as distasteful as Mestin imagined. She couldn't think of any of her *jurej've* who would agree to the act of *oursan* with an alien, with or without *c'naatat,* but the human definitely had an edge that spoke of a capacity for survival.

It was a pity not to be able to absorb those genes into the clans.

They waited in silence, watching for the return of the former *jurej've* of Asanjin Selit Giyadas, who would be surprised to find themselves accepted wholesale into the household of Nevyan Tan Mestin but would accept it and—eventually—be completely happy with the arrangement. The males came back into view, almost appearing to reform into solidity from fragments shattered by the mirage of hot summer air. They were walking faster now. One carried the pallet; another clutched the *dhren* and other fabric.

There was no point wasting good textiles. Even the colonists of Constantine spared the rockvelvets the extra task of digesting the clothes of their dead. They had that much in common.

Nevyan suddenly exuded a cloud of anxiety. Mestin wanted to hold her and comfort her, but the uncertainty was something her child had to face. *And now she becomes an* isan. She wouldn't be coming home tonight. It was a cause for rejoicing. By the morning, she wouldn't miss her family. She would be immersed in a new reality.

Mestin thought humans would all have been a lot happier if their copulation resulted in the stable bond that *oursan* ensured wess'har. Fersanye, who was more scientifically minded, said their promiscuity was a consequence of their need to propagate their genes through offspring. Mestin decided it was part of their innate greed to always have something extra, and preferably something that belonged to someone else.

She wondered if Shan Frankland had some of that sexual acquisitiveness in her. *C'naatat* would be a hard lesson for her if she had.

Marine Ismat Qureshi had rigged a temporary securing bar across the hatch that separated the Kilo deck cargo area from rest of *Actaeon*.

It made Lindsay feel better. There was no indication on any safety repeater or state-board to say that the hatch was locked. The bar simply stopped anyone walking in on them. She wanted to brainstorm this plan to infiltrate Bezer'ej in private, without observers, and without Okurt realizing she was maneuvering into a position where he had to allow her to lead the mission.

She stared at the flaccid bag of fabric on the deck and tried to get the idea straight in her mind. And the Royal Marines were all staring at her: Barencoin, Bennett, Qureshi, Chahal, Webster and Becken, all Extreme Environment Warfare Cadre, all relaxed, all apparently unconcerned by the nightmare lying at her feet.

"Dear God," she said. She prodded it with her boot. It was a white, man-sized quilt: it looked like fabric, but it acted like a gel pack. When the fabric moved, the surface rippled with embedded softglass, throwing up slow billows of black like oil welling through milk. There was one totally black area that showed small currents of white when she kicked it gently. It reminded her rather unpleasantly of a bull's-eye target.

It certainly didn't look much like transport.

Qureshi, leaning against the hatch as if her slight weight would add to the bar's effectiveness, folded her arms. "We never said it was comfortable, ma'am."

It was a Once-Only suit.

Lindsay knew how they worked, more or less, but she had hoped never to test one. There were far better ways to escape a stricken vessel and far more efficient lifeboats, but ships kept a few of the suits stowed away on board just in case. And it really was the absolute, final, *last* of last resorts. It was bailout when all else failed.

Its design dated from the first days of manned space flight. Even the name was borrowed from another primitive emergency escape suit that mariners had used centuries before.

And it *looked* it.

"So you just zip yourself into this bag."

"No, you put your spacesuit on before you get in. Then you pull the pin and the insulating foam fills the inner skin."

"Oh, that's totally reassuring. And *then* I plummet towards the planet?"

"We like to think of it as guided descent," said Bennett. "You can steer and orientate."

"Forgive me, but I'm still thinking of it as getting into a glorified sleeping bag and dropping into empty space from orbit. *High* orbit."

"You've done your pilot training," said Qureshi. "If you've parachuted and ejected, this isn't that much worse. Not really."

"Have you *done* this?"

Qureshi nodded, looking bemused, as if everyone did a spot of free-fall through a planet's atmosphere now and then. Extreme environment commandos did. "We've all done it from a hundred kay, anyway. It doesn't make you feel any more sick than a spacewalk. More or less."

"I seem to recall something about reaching supersonic velocity," said Lindsay.

"Correct," said Chahal. "And we're all alive to tell the tale."

Lindsay chewed her lip thoughtfully. "I don't need to point out that this thing doesn't take off again, do I?"

"That's why they call it a Once-Only," said Bennett, and Lindsay wasn't sure if he was being stolidly literal or sarcastic. "But I have an idea for that too."

"Go ahead."

"The colony ship. *Christopher.* They said they mothballed it, remember?"

"You reckon it's feasible?"

"Maybe not the vessel itself, not without a lot of prep, but it's still got a couple of tillies." It was an odd archaic word for a runabout vehicle, and Bennett was the only one who used it to mean shuttles. "And they're built to start first time. So we land, do the biz, and shoot through. Job done."

"Provided we don't land looking like barbecue briquettes."

Bennett joined in the ritual boot-prodding of the crumpled suit. "I know it looks like liquid, ma'am, but once it's activated, it's a heat-shield—all that black and white stuff automatically positions itself where you need it, black stuff to burn off at the hot-spots, white stuff to deflect all round. As long as you get shot of it as fast as you can once you land, it's as safe as houses."

Lindsay's image was of houses falling down in disrepair,

then hard landings in a soft suit. "Why do you need to dump the shield?"

"Because it goes on getting hotter after you've landed, ma'am." Bennett's expression was silent wonder at how she ever made commander. "A *lot* hotter. Remember you're coming in through atmosphere."

"Oh," said Lindsay. She thought of the suit moving patches of black and white *stuff* around, unbidden. "At least I'll plunge to my doom looking like art."

Wherever they were planning to land, whatever their task at the end of it, the Once-Only was the most stealthy system they had. *Actaeon* hadn't come equipped for covert missions. But she *had* come with plenty of ordnance, even if she hadn't been expecting to deal with a massively equipped wess'har defense force.

The armory held a lot of what Chahal called "insurance ordnance"—tactical nukes, neuts, emergency BNOs, chems, FAEs, and even ultra-yield conventionals, and plenty of interesting modes to deploy them together. On Earth that made you a world power; out here it would just irritate the wess'har for a few hours. And there were no resupply chains twenty-five light-years from home.

Lindsay rubbed her forehead. "Okay. You do this all the time. I don't."

Bennett appeared to be watching her calculate the odds. "If we were going to land, ma'am, that's our *only* way past their defnet. It's the smallest possible profile." He was trying hard to convince her. "We've removed all the survival kit to make room for—well, whatever we tool up with."

"I prefer to work backwards from objectives," Lindsay said. She knew damn well what her objectives were now. The problem was what objectives she would have to feign to get the hardware, personnel and access she needed to get within killing range of Shan.

There was also the small matter of what it would actually take to kill the woman. She had no idea. It wasn't a bullet, silver or otherwise. If the miraculous survival of Shan's alien friend was anything to go by, it wasn't a serious crash either.

"I can see one small snag," said Lindsay.

"What?" asked Bennett.

"How do we get into orbit around Bezer'ej for the drop without triggering the wess'har defnet? It's going to take a shuttle, and the shuttle is bigger than the isenj fighters. That means they *will* see us coming."

"Thought of that," said Webster. *"Maiale."*

"I'm lost now."

"Chariots. Means pig in Italian. Um . . . 1939 to 1945 World War? Ring any bells, ma'am?"

"Bennett's the history man, not me."

"They were like torpedoes, one- or two-man submarine transport to ferry diver commandos around. They sat astride them. Quicker than swimming to the target." Webster was an inventive woman. "So we use a powered tow to take us the final leg from the shuttle to the point where we use the suits' systems to descend. That gives us longer on oxygen before we're drawing on the suit's supply. We can adapt one of the small cargo tugs to pull us in, maybe with extra O_2. We're talking a total load of maybe two to three thousand kilos. That's doable. Chaz and I have modeled it a few times."

They all called each other by harmless kids' nicknames: Chaz, Izzy, Barkers. They weren't harmless at all. Lindsay tried to visualize speeds and distances. "Well that sounds like even more fun. And if we land, and achieve our objective, how do we get out through the defnet again?"

"It's a gamble," said Chahal. "But I suspect it looks for incoming, not outgoing, and if these vessels were allowed to land on Bezer'ej in the first place, chances are it's tagged them as friendly anyway."

"And if you're wrong?"

"Then we're fucked, ma'am, but at least we won't know much about it."

This was my idea, Lindsay thought. *I must be out of my skull*. "If you're all up for it—"

The hatch juddered against the metal bar Qureshi had jammed across it. Then there was silence.

"Who is it?" Lindsay yelled. The marines gathered up the Once-Only suit with smooth efficiency and bundled it into the nearest locker. Lindsay walked slowly up to the hatch and nodded at Qureshi to release the magnetic clamp.

The hatch swung open. It was Mohan Rayat.

There were things you thought you would say when you caught up with someone like Rayat. Lindsay hadn't rehearsed them quite as often as she had various denouements with Shan, but she thought she'd have a line. She didn't.

"Dr. Rayat," she said. "Anything we can do for you?"

She had always wanted him to look like a weasel caught in headlights, but he didn't. He could meet her eyes, which she thought was the confidence of a man at ease with being a total shit.

"I think we can do something for each other," he said. "Am I interrupting something?"

"Training," she said.

The marines stood around in that I'm-relaxed-but-I-could-turn-nasty pose that Rayat seemed to provoke. Qureshi looked especially hostile. Maybe her leg was playing her up, and she still blamed Rayat for causing the skirmish where she acquired the wound. Rayat didn't look as if he was leaving of his own accord.

"If you have a point to make, then make it," said Lindsay. "We're busy."

Rayat stared pointedly at Qureshi. "It's a confidential matter."

"There's nothing I keep from the detachment," said Lindsay, and knew it was an empty gesture. "If I can hear it, so can they."

"All right, we have a mutual objective."

"I don't think so."

"Based on what premise?"

"You work for a pharmaceutical corporation and we work for our country. No mutuality there, I suspect."

Rayat shrugged. "Actually, I'm paid by the Federal European Treasury."

"You work for Warrenders."

"I imagine they think so too. Anyway, Warrenders ceased trading about ten years ago. Takeover by Holbein."

Lindsay wished once again that she had Shan's quick, savage tongue. "I wouldn't believe you if you told me what time it was," she managed. But he had been revived for a reason, and before the others: she doubted if it was for health screening. They could have done that without reviving anybody at all, she was certain. Whatever it was, Rayat needed to be conscious for it, and the rest of the party had been revived to preserve the story or . . . she wasn't sure what else. She almost didn't want to imagine.

"I'm sure you're capable of carrying out security checks," Rayat said calmly. "Confirm what I've said and then get back to me. We both want to secure whatever Frankland's carrying for our own government, and I need the means of access, and you need my technical expertise."

"Why would we need a pharmacologist, exactly?"

"That's not my only area of expertise."

It was very easy to say absolutely nothing while Rayat turned and stepped back through the hatch. She couldn't think of a single damned word. Qureshi barred the hatch behind him again.

The *Treasury*? What the hell would the Treasury want with that biotech, let alone Rayat?

"Do you know, I wouldn't even like that bloke as pet food," said Becken. "You believe him, ma'am?"

"I'll check," said Lindsay.

"How did he know what we've been tasked with?" asked Qureshi.

There's no such thing as confidential. Another fragment of Shan's rough-and-ready political analysis surfaced in Lindsay's memory. "Either Warrenders or Holbein or whoever are better informed than we think, or the Defense Ministry is talking to the Treasury."

"Yes, but are they telling each other the truth?" said Bennett.

There were always divisions within governments, between departments, onion-skinned and Byzantine, sometimes openly hostile and sometimes waging covert cold wars with each other. If Rayat was telling the truth about his paymaster, Lindsay still couldn't assume they were all on the same side.

She went back to her cabin to barricade herself in her bunk and ponder the missing elements of her puzzle. *Treasury?* It had to be a patents thing. The biotech would be a massively profitable commodity. Governments needed revenue: there was only so much tax you could levy on an aging population and companies that could up sticks and move to a cheaper tax zone at will, leaving more unemployment in their wake.

But they could have secured ownership through the Defense Ministry. Why did they need Rayat? Why wasn't he talking directly to Okurt instead of her? It had to be another of his scams.

It was the sort of puzzle that Shan Frankland would have shaken apart in no time at all. It was a complete sod, as Becken would say, that Lindsay couldn't ask her to help her plan her own destruction.

The little red swiss sat on the table and Aras wondered if he dared pick it up again.

He didn't know humans at all. He was certain of that now.

Shan always carried the instrument even though it couldn't link with any of the data devices on Wess'ej. She said its blades, probes and various devices were still useful. Aras suspected she carried it much as little Rachel Garrod had clutched a frayed piece of her baby blanket until she was five, and nobody could part her from it. Given the material that was stored in the swiss, he found Shan's attachment to it disturbing. He would have wanted to throw it as far from him as possible and never look into it again.

It wasn't just the file on the men who made entertainment of suffering women, children and animals. There was more deviance and misery in Shan's files than he could take in at one sitting. There were people who tortured their own children to death, or raped them; there were those who mutilated total strangers for unfathomable reasons; and there were so many different forms of murder that he simply stopped running the files long before he got to the robberies and thefts and frauds and something called *public disorder.*

Shan had done many different things in her career. She told him they moved police officers from department to department frequently, because there were some duties that could destroy you in time. Aras wondered if it was already too late for her. He laid the swiss down on the table.

He knew humans did most of those things. But crime had been historic generality in Constantine's archives. It hadn't been the personal and detailed experience of a woman he knew and cared about. He thought of Mjat, and although that had been a terrible time, it was exceptional: it was also necessary. He hadn't done it for amusement or because he had abdicated responsibility for his actions. The wess'har in him said motive didn't matter, but his human influence said it mattered very much indeed.

Eventually he picked up the swiss again and opened files at random on its fragile bubble screen. There was very little in there that told him anything personal about Shan Frankland. He found some music and a few images of what appeared to be comrades of hers in dark uniforms, laughing and shouting, brandishing glasses of yellow foaming liquid at whoever was recording the image. There was nothing that looked like family or lovers. There were a lot of lists too: lists of tasks to complete, and lists of names and numbers.

Then it struck him that it told him exactly what she was. What wasn't in there hadn't happened, or hadn't mattered to her.

Aras now knew what the flames in his dreams were. *Riots.* He was astonished that she and others had to deal with them face-to-face, with only a transparent shield and small weapons.

It was war: the obvious response was to wipe out the source population completely and stop the threat for all time. But humans seemed not to want to find absolute ends to their problems.

Shan's footsteps outside grew louder, distinctive and unlike anyone else's in F'nar. He put the swiss down and waited for her to open the door. She had stormed out angry, and he expected her to return in the same state because she seemed to be perpetually irritated lately. An angry *isan* was something that still made him cower. Whatever *c'naatat* had made of him, he would always be at his core a wess'har male, a provider and a carer and a seeker of approval, nothing without an *isan* to focus upon.

The door made a slight sigh of air as it opened. Shan came up behind him, smelling of no emotion in particular—just pleasantly female—and put her hands on his shoulders and squeezed gently. He held his breath. It wasn't the sort of gesture he had come to expect from her at all.

"Sorry," she said quietly. "I don't normally lose my rag like that."

No anger, then. Aras had no idea whether to reach up and clasp her hands or just sit very, very still. Eventually he slid one hand up from his lap and placed it over hers. She didn't react.

"You've seen some very ugly things," he said. "I think I understand your reaction."

She made a small puff of contempt. "Why didn't you tell me what happened to you as a POW?" She pronounced it pee-oh-double-you, a phrase he had never heard said aloud, but he knew what it meant. "I've got your memories. They're . . . well . . ."

"I tried. You were preoccupied with *c'naatat* at the time."

"I'm sorry. Really I am. I had no idea. I would have handled things a bit more sensitively."

"I have your memories too. Riots. You were truly frightened of the petrol bombs."

"Yeah." She shifted slightly. "That's the problem with a

transparent shield. You see the flames hit. However many times it happened, I never lost the feeling I was going to shit myself. I suppose the most vivid memories surface first." Suddenly she slid her hand free of his and stepped back, as if she'd woken up to something she was doing in a dream. "I'm sorry if I've added to your problems."

"I think we're even. Is that the right phrase?"

"Very apt. What else is bubbling up?"

"I find lot of regret and anger. And violence, much of which you *don't* regret."

"Now you know me for what I am, then."

"I have no difficulties with that. Do you?"

"It's what I had to do," she said. "Come on. Cup of tea. That'll sort *anything* out." She took her precious supply of dried tea from the shelf and put some water to boil on the range. "Kind of you to plant the tea bushes, by the way. Some bloke down in the fields showed them to me. I don't think he meant to spoil the surprise."

"There are some things you seem to need in order to be happy. I'll obtain them for you if I can."

"Are *you* happy, Aras?"

"I find F'nar a difficult place to be."

Shan paused with the jug in one hand and the glass jar of broken dead leaves in the other. She looked unusually soft and sad for once. For a moment he thought he might ask the one question that had been on his mind, whether he liked it or not, for the last few weeks. *No.* It wasn't fair. She couldn't even tell what she was picking up on his scent. She mistook it for anxiety.

"How do wess'har react when you tell them what happened to you?" she asked.

"I've never told them. Not the details."

"Why not?"

"Embarrassment. Shame."

"Have you never told *anyone*?"

"No. There are too many things I wouldn't want them to know."

"That's not very wess'har."

"Neither am I."

"Look, I'm going to live out most of it in my head anyway, aren't I? You need to get it out of your system. Tell me."

"I did shameful things." It wasn't that he didn't want her to know. He didn't want to hear himself say it. "Things I regret."

"We all have. Jesus, you *know* what I've done. We can swap horror stories later. Come on. I need to hear everything."

She said everything, and so he took her at her word. Wess'har were nothing if not literal. He glanced at her swiss, still propped on the table, and noted the time when he started. Shan seemed to be struggling to keep her eyes focused on his and from time to time she blinked rapidly. She was still holding the jar in one hand.

The isenj were not especially inventive torturers compared to humans but they made up for a lack of originality with persistence. Aras described flayings and brandings and beatings. He described broken bones and asphyxiation and freezing. It was random and angry violence rather than a strategy calculated to achieve an end, just outpourings of communal rage concentrated on one man, the destroyer of Mjat, because they couldn't get at the whole wess'har race. But she had seen it, and experienced it, and that somehow made it far easier to pour out a history he had kept secret for generations.

He didn't break down until he described his attempts at hunger strikes and how they'd force-fed him.

"They made me eat flesh," he said. His throat was closing, tightening, thinning out the overtones from his voice. He envied humans their ability to surrender totally to sobbing, but wess'har couldn't weep.

"Is that what hurt you most?" said Shan. Her voice was hoarse. "Is that your shame, Aras?"

"Yes."

"Wess'har flesh?"

"No."

It had been meat—animal meat. It was only a small concern

to *gethes*, but not to wess'har. He raised his eyes from the swiss, where he had been focusing his concentration, and looked at Shan.

Their combined scents of agitation were too overwhelming for him to pick out any cues and all he had to go by was her facial expression. But she just looked surprised. He wondered if it was shared revulsion, but it wasn't; she simply could not see why that had gnawed at his conscience for so many years.

It wounded him. Surely she of all humans would understand why it was a terrible, disgusting thing to live with. Any wess'har would. It was why he could never tell them.

He checked the chronometer on the swiss. He had been talking without pause for nearly two hours.

"You didn't have a choice," she said. No, there was no revulsion there at all. She might have been exceptional, but her instincts were still *gethes*. "You didn't kill to eat, and you didn't give the isenj information. There's nothing to be ashamed of." She put down the jar and took his hands in hers. "What do you need to hear, Aras?"

"I don't understand."

"What would you most like to have someone say to you now, and mean it, to make you feel better about yourself?"

His jaw worked uncertainly. And there was Ben Garrod in his head again, Josh's first ancestor, talking of *sin* and *repentance* and *forgiveness*. Ben said Aras needed to repent for things like Mjat, but he thought of the bezeri and couldn't find that in himself at all. But there was a vivid taste of death in his mouth, not from Mjat so much as the anonymous being whose flesh had been forced into his mouth.

"I want to be forgiven," he said at last. "Ben Garrod said his god could do that."

"I don't think his god's going to be able to get back to you any time soon," she said quietly. "So I'll do it. I forgive you, Aras Sar Iussan. Now let it go." She tidied his hair back from his face where a few strands had worked loose from his braid. "Where I come from, you'd be a hero."

"Not being able to die isn't heroism. And I had no information to give the isenj, so there's no glory in that." He felt a little better now. "Anyway, as you might say, the things they did to me made me stronger. They tried to drown me, and my *c'naatat* adapted me, and now I can walk under water with the bezeri."

"Did your people try to rescue you?"

"No. The isenj liked to say that even savages like them went back for their own."

That revelation really did appear to distress her. Her pupils grew wide and black. "God, you people have an incredibly ruthless streak. Even by my standards."

"Perhaps now you understand why I wish you hadn't made yourself available to the matriarchs. You'll be used."

"Hey, I've worked for politicians before. Twenty-four-carat grade A liars and megalomaniacs. You think your matriarchs can top that? Piece of piss, believe me."

"No, it won't be." He'd worked out that dismissal of difficulty from its context. "And I know you dislike being told you don't understand, but you really don't. Perhaps as more of my memories filter through, you'll regret volunteering for slavery."

Shan had that pained-patience look that he had seen her adopt when Lindsay Neville had made errors. "Aras, when you start getting more of *my* memories bubbling to the surface, you'll know what fuels me and why I had no other option." She paused, jaw muscles twitching, as if she were reluctant to let the words escape. "And it's not just because I'm attached to you, although God knows that was near the top of the list. It's responsibility. I can't walk away when I know I can do something, because I'd tear myself apart afterwards. I don't have another option."

Yes, he'd known that early on, even before the *c'naatat* had snatched components from her blood and brain and bone and buried them in him. He knew she was angry and trying very, very hard to be perfect and put the world right for somebody. Who? He didn't know.

She smelled good. What would happen if she put the world

right for him? Would she fall apart without her impossible objective, or would she become satisfied with life, undriven, alive for the moment? *No*. He needed to stop thinking that way.

"This is depressing," he said, and stood up. "Work it off, that's what you say, isn't it? Stay busy."

They went out to the terrace to inspect the half-finished sofa. Shan shook out the blue material, *ahhing* in delight at the color. "Wonderful peacock blue," she said. To an unaltered human it would have looked white. "Is this the same stuff *dhrens* are made from?"

"No, it won't automatically shape or clean itself. It's just inert fabric."

"That's the best thing about having some wess'har genes. Every shade of blue looks more amazing." She gave him a sad smile, the sort that said she was remembering something else she regretted. "Yeah, I went completely ballistic when I found my eyesight had changed, didn't I? I'm really sorry I tore into you."

"I should have told you that I'd infected you instead of letting you find out for yourself."

"It doesn't matter any more. Don't even think about it."

They worked on the sofa together. It was a very unwess'har thing, a sofa, but Shan insisted she would adopt any custom they asked except put up with their hard, unforgiving furniture. The next item on her list was a mattress. They stretched the fabric taut over the layers of *sek* wadding and pinned it to the frame, then stood back to admire it.

"Chippendale might be spinning in his grave," she said. "But my arse will be the judge of quality." She sank down into the cushioned seat and let her head loll back on the padded backboard, eyes shut. It was as if they had never discussed torture and their shared nightmares. "Oh. Bliss. This, and a cup of tea, and a good movie. Heaven."

Aras wasn't sure where he could acquire a good movie. They sat side by side on the sofa and stared out across the basin of F'nar, dazzled by the pearl roofs and hazy gold walls. There was the tinkle of water from the irrigation conduits.

"Lovely," said Shan. She slipped her arm through his.

"Lovely," Aras echoed, and wondered what it was like to be able to eat other beings and not be scarred by it.

8

Why have the humans abandoned our comrades and the isenj on their ship Thetis? *They have not admitted they have done this, but we know. We fear they plan to harm us, whether by neglect or active violence. Shall we tell the matriarchs? And if they cannot deal with the humans, shall we ask the World Before for their aid? The humans must learn that if you harm one ussissi, you harm us all, and we will fight.*

CALITISSATI,
interpreter to Jejeno consulate,
to F'nar ussissi colony

The cabin hatch swung open and Lindsay's smartpapers fluttered briefly against the bulkhead where she had tacked them. She was close enough to reach out and tap the privacy icon just in time to stop Natalie Cho seeing what she'd written. Detailed options for assassination weren't the sort of thing that made people comfortable about sharing cabin space with you.

"Am I interrupting?" Cho asked.

"Not at all," said Lindsay, and decided these things might be better done in one of the engineering deck lobbies. If she took the notes down now and scurried away with them, she would look even more secretive. She forced a smile and carried on staring at the progression of scribbled ideas that marched across each sheet. They were literally for her eyes alone: the smartpaper would activate its pixels only in direct line of sight to a pair of retinas that it recognized. If Cho cared to look, she would only see a white sheet unless she was right on Lindsay's shoulder. The security setting still said *mind your own business*, of course, but not so provocatively.

"Are you okay?" Cho asked. "I'm not prying, but if you need to talk—"

She wanted to scream that she didn't need counseling or sympathy, but she thought of Shan and appropriated her resolve. She had to look all business if she was going to get access to the hardware she needed.

"I appreciate your concern," she said. "I'll be okay."

No, she wouldn't be. She knew that. *I haven't even got a picture of David.* There was just a task ahead to complete, because if she didn't do it she had no idea where the spiral would end. She peeled her notes off the wall with slow deliberation so as not to look defensive and went in search of sanctuary.

The heads weren't comfortable, but Lindsay could guarantee no visitors. She tacked the smartpaper sheets across three bulkheads and sat on the lid of the toilet bowl, one boot braced against the door even though it was locked. She kept running her eyes over the scrawled words and arrows, right to left, then left to right, then up and down again. It was just absorption. Something would leap out—a solution, or a gap to fill.

Shan: PLAGUE.

She said it was a disease. Lindsay remembered that very clearly. She told Hugel it was a plague.

Who else?

Diseases spread. So who else had it?

She could have been lying. No. She was telling the truth because she was so mightily confident of her authority that she couldn't even be bothered to lie. So she had a disease, and she must have caught it somewhere between Constantine, the wess'har homeworld and the wess'har garrison, the Temporary City.

Someone went into a nearby cubicle, locked the door noisily and coughed. Lindsay fixed on the smartpaper.

Plague.

No, that was a distraction. It didn't matter a damn where Shan caught it or even what it was. What mattered was finding her and destroying the asset. Everyone in *Actaeon* believed she was the source,. and that was what they would pursue, so she needed access to Shan somewhere she could use a weapon of such force that it could kill her.

Where was she?

Wess'ej was out of the question. Nobody had enough data on the terrain to plan any sort of extraction operation even if *Actaeon* had the muscle to take on the matriarchs. They had a chance on Bezer'ej, though, and especially on the island where Constantine was located.

And if Shan wasn't there, she would need to get her there.

There wasn't enough data to take it any further. Lindsay took out her stylus and wrote *Background* on one of the sheets. She'd retrace her steps. She would go back to the origins of the Constantine mission and run from the first telemetry right through their mission data to whatever she could get out of the isenj. Eddie would come in handy there. They liked him; Shan liked him too.

"How long are you going to sit there?" said a voice above her.

She jumped to her feet, a pure reflex of panic. Her stylus clattered to the deck.

"You *bastard,*" she said.

Mohan Rayat peered over the gap at the top of the cubicle. It didn't look at all comical. "Two heads are better than one. Share your problem."

Lindsay peeled the sheets quickly from the bulkheads, cheeks burning. "If you ever do that again, I swear I'll kill you. Get out."

"Why don't you drop the sorry attempt to emulate Frankland and talk to me sensibly? You'll want to hear what I've got to say."

"Sod off."

"Well, listen anyway. I have something you're going to need on that little trip of yours."

Lindsay's stomach leapt with sudden panic. "What trip?"

"Please, cut the crap. What was it our absent dominatrix used to say? 'There's no monopoly of information.' The logistics of landing on a planet do tend to leak out."

"My marines don't discuss operational matters with civilians."

"*Your* marines have to remove kit from pusser's store. The Supply Branch isn't so tight-lipped, and neither are the inventory tags that track matériel around the system."

"It's a shame you weren't standing where Galvin was when the shooting started."

"What, so I'd take two stray rounds from your god-almighty Booties?"

Lindsay knew she wasn't well. She also knew that sleepless night after sleepless night marred your judgment. Judgment suitably suspended, she flung open her cubicle door and slammed open Rayat's. Maybe he wasn't expecting a fifty-kilo woman to ram him and knock him off his vantage point on the toilet seat. He certainly didn't seem to be expecting her to press the barrel of her sidearm so hard into his temple that she could see the skin around it turn white.

"Shut it," she hissed.

Rayat was wedged where he had slipped, one leg behind the pipework and the other at a painfully awkward angle across the toilet seat. "Whoa. It's okay. *It's okay.*"

Lindsay could feel a tremor running up her arm, but it wasn't emanating from Rayat. She could see her own hand, index finger curled against the trigger. It almost didn't belong to her. Her ears hurt from the pounding pulse.

"Do you bloody well know what this has cost me?" She jabbed the barrel harder into his skin. "Do you?"

"I'm sorry. Let's . . . let's just calm down and talk this through."

Shan would have pulled the trigger. Shan wouldn't have lost her temper in the first place. But she wasn't Shan. She couldn't do it. Rayat's eyes said he wasn't sure if she would or not.

"If I put one through you, what do you think they'd do to me? What do you think I've got left to lose?"

"What do you want me to do?"

"Stay out of my way."

Rayat put his hand up to his temple, very slowly, very deliberately, and gradually eased the weapon away from his head with his index and middle fingers. Lindsay let him because she hadn't a clue how to climb down from the situation. It must have showed on her face. She still held her aim level with his head, but she needed both hands to keep it steady.

"I'll tell you," he said. "But this isn't for Okurt, okay?"

Lindsay didn't nod. She didn't want to look cooperative. She let Rayat go on.

"Lindsay, we both have our reasons for wanting to take Frankland. I can't get to her alone."

He'd never called her by her first name. "So why is that my problem?"

"We both need a solution that doesn't involve handing over her tissues to commercial interests." Rayat actually looked alarmed. He might have risked deflecting her weapon, but his tone was quiet and soothing. It dawned on her that while he clearly didn't consider her a hard bastard like Shan, he definitely seemed to think she was unstable. That was fine. She could do barking mad very well. "You're not a fool. You know it's a dangerous technology in the wrong hands."

Lindsay let the pistol dip a little. Rayat's eyes followed it. She braced her arm again and he blinked.

"And whose hands are the right hands?"

"Do you want it to become standard issue for the military?"

"Depends if I was front-line infantry or not." *Barking mad. Play unpredictable.* Lindsay shoved the gun into her side pocket and squatted down so close to Rayat that he couldn't move from where he had fallen. "But I can't see us strolling in and lifting wess'har biotech without an argument, and if Shan's with the matriarchs, she's as good as gone."

Rayat closed his eyes for a second and swallowed. "I don't think it's that simple."

"I know someone will be stupid enough one day to go after her."

"I meant that it's . . . look, I have reason to think there's another source."

"Yes, a bloody enormous psycho wess'har war criminal who's going to be impossible to take."

"No. Not him, and not there."

Rayat stopped. Lindsay was going to take out her gun again and ask *where*, but the hatch to the heads swung open.

"Oh, excuse *me*." One of the civilian stewards stared down at them, clearly interpreting the scene in a highly original way. "Get a room, for goodness' sake." He turned and stalked out.

Lindsay had lost the moment. She shook her head at Rayat. "Oh, great. I think we could do without *that* rumor starting." She stood back and let him get to his feet. "D'you know, Doctor, you really don't sound like a pharmacologist or a Treasury officer at all."

"I think you know what I am."

"Traditionally, my kind don't like your kind very much."

"We both serve our state. I just don't happen to enjoy dressing up like a pox-doctor's clerk and talking like Hornblower."

"You tell me exactly what we're dealing with, and I'll tell you if I'm willing to help you."

Lindsay waited a few seconds. Rayat seemed to be considering the offer but said nothing. She shrugged, collected her papers from the floor of the adjacent cubicle and walked out.

Nobody in uniform ever believed they were told the whole truth. You took your orders, but with a pinch of salt; and you looked after yourself and your comrades, and then maybe your country. That was the trouble with spooks like Rayat.

They never seemed to have any comrades.

Mestin's most junior husband, Sevaor, held out a perfectly amethyst glass bowl as if he expected Shan to take it.

"Mestin will come to you soon," he said. "Drink this while you wait."

Shan took the cup and peered in. The liquid in it was speckled with small brown fragments. Whatever it was, it couldn't poison her and it made sense to accept hospitality.

"An infusion," said Sevaor. He was enchantingly gold, glittering, wood-scented. "*Gethes* like infusions."

"As do I," said Shan, and instantly regretted her sarcasm. "Thank you."

She sipped. It tasted like turpentine. Sevaor was standing way too close for her comfort, and she stepped back discreetly. He closed the gap. She stepped back again.

Wess'har had evolved from burrow-dwelling creatures, and they didn't just tolerate being crammed together—they seemed to crave it. Combined with their eye-watering candor, it made them challenging neighbors.

Shan finished her turpentine tea and stood waiting for Mestin. They weren't big on seating either. The house rang with the double-voiced noise of youngsters and adults. She put the glass bowl on the perilously uneven window ledge and admired the exquisite pools of lavender light that it cast on the floor. Like the buried colony of Constantine, the warren of rooms and alleys that made up the terraced city of F'nar were somehow illuminated by natural light. She still hadn't found out how they did it.

Mestin strolled in to the lobby with the rolling gait of an overconfident sailor. All the females seemed to walk like that. "We go down," she said abruptly, and beckoned Shan to follow her.

And she *meant* down, too. Shan followed Mestin down a corridor that ran from the Exchange of Surplus Things deep into the ground beneath the city, on another field trip that Mestin assured her would help her fully understand what her new responsibilities were.

She tried to link the tunneling habit to a species mind-set. Once you knew that humans were monkeys, things fell into place. Perhaps she'd get a better insight into the wess'har psyche from picking the right animal parallel.

Maybe badgers, she thought. *Blennies. Kakapo.* No, they were all endearing, appealing. Wess'har were aesthetically attractive, but they weren't any more cute than the needle-teethed ussissi. *Trapdoor spiders.* Yes, that was more like it. *Scorpions.*

Mestin's Spartan helmet of hair was silhouetted against the faint light filtering up from the tunnel ahead. Shan followed her step for step. The lighting rose gently like a sudden sunrise as they walked through a modest doorway.

"Jesus," said Shan.

Above her head, to both sides of her, and as far as her eye could see, there were racks and tunnels and recesses. A few were filled with machinery. For a brief moment she lost her up-down orientation, like standing in an Escher engraving. She felt cocooned by a felt-lined silence. There were no echoes at all when she spoke.

Some of the warehoused machines were clearly fighter craft, the kind she had seen on Bezer'ej, and some appeared industrial. Others made no sense to her at all. They were simply organic shapes of differing colors with detail worked into them that could have been controls. She could read wess'har script now, and that was no easy task for a human used to orderly lines of characters. The curved side of one machine bore the apparently random swirls and patches of text, ideograms strung out in fishbone diagrams and flowcharts. It made sense—eventually.

The inscription read TEMPLATE CRAFT.

"Each wess'har city has something like this," said Mestin. "I think you would call it insurance. And I felt you needed to see it to understand why we're so alarmed by the *gethes.*"

The underground hangars almost explained how an apparently agricultural society managed to mount such an impressive reinforcement of the garrison on Bezer'ej, the Temporary City.

"Where's your industrial capacity? I've seen nothing but agriculture." Shan reached out and put her hand on the blue-gray hull nearest to her. It was as clean and impressive as an exhibit in a military museum. "This takes scale and urbanization."

"You ask interesting questions for a police officer."

"I was planning to be an economist before I was drafted into the police. Manpower shortage, you see. But I sort of stayed. Where does this all come from?"

"The World Before."

"I don't understand."

"Our ancestors came to this planet ten thousand years ago. We did not arrive empty-handed."

If you could ever get used to shocks, then Shan was becoming accustomed to them. Just as she thought she had a complete picture of the wess'har, just as she was confident she had the measure of them, *knew* them, they would drop a bombshell into the conversation.

"You never told me you weren't native to this planet," she said.

"You never told me you were the descendants of apes."

"It just didn't occur to me."

"Nor me. I brought you down here to show you the limited defenses at our disposal, not to give you a history lesson." Mestin walked ahead, glancing from side to side as if she were in a market doing her shopping. There were enough cans of serious beans here to make somebody very uncomfortable indeed. "I realize you're not a soldier, but you can understand force as well as anyone."

"But where do you build these ships?"

"*Grow* is probably the more accurate description. Many came with our ancestors and we have modified them. This is the same base technology as *dhren*. But it isn't inexhaustible."

Shan thought of the first time she had met Aras. It hadn't been a happy meeting: her military support team had managed to shoot down his craft. But he had walked away from the crash—her first clue that he had an extraordinary physiology. And when she went to inspect the wrecked metal airframe the next day, it had crumbled and scattered like dust beneath her boots. It was a rare instance of a pilot being repaired and the aircraft dying and decomposing. *Smart metals.*

And there was *Actaeon*, knocking herself out to get hold of *c'naatat* when there were these industrial riches to be plundered.

Mestin looked as if she was scanning Shan's face for a reaction. *And?* Shan took the hint.

"Are you telling me that you're running out of kit?"

"Correct," said Mestin. "But we can adapt what we still have to counter the isenj. They're limited by their population problems. We're limited by the inverse—we are too few. But if you add an extra enemy to that, you can see our dilemma."

Shan thought of the annihilated, erased, utterly destroyed city of Mjat that had once stood coast-to-coast on the wilderness of an island that now housed Constantine. And these machines—or their originals, anyway—were older than the first human cities. "You're not doing too badly for your size," she said.

"We will be too thinly stretched if *gethes* come in large numbers."

"Well, they won't." *They?* Assimilation had ambushed Shan and it hadn't met much resistance. "Economics meets physics. Too far, too expensive, and too bloody hard for that much heavy lift. But a few with a foothold in this system could expand over the years, and you do think long-term, don't you?"

"Bloody." In Mestin's mouth, the word was softened by a chord of multiple notes. *"Bloody."*

"And then there's the Sarajevo factor. It can take just one human to destabilize local politics."

"We noticed." Mestin might have been capable of irony, or she might not. Either way, it stung. "What is Sarajevo?"

"Forget it," said Shan. She felt for a moment that the whole situation was her fault. If only she had—no, that was stupid. The real damage had been done two centuries ago when Constantine was settled; and contact with the isenj had happened seventy-five years after she left Earth. Whatever she'd done or hadn't done, it couldn't have prevented this moment. The two women now stood staring at the smoothly curved fuselage of a craft that was so gently blue, so much like the skin of a grape, that Shan imagined it would feel moist and velvety to her touch.

"So what else can you do?" she asked. "Reclamation nanites,

biobarriers—that implies you have some sort of biological engineering capability."

Mestin inclined her maned head and looked even more disturbingly like a Spartan soldier; and Shan now knew that the two cultures also shared an unforgiving attitude to warfare as well as their mutual frugality and iron discipline. "Yes, our ancestors were skilled at bioweapons. We have never used the technology in that capacity. Not yet."

"Ah," said Shan, mindful of the word *yet,* and feeling that she had found the snake in Eden that Josh always talked about. "But you could."

"Potentially," said Mestin.

They walked a little further down the passage in silence. Shan reasoned that even snakes were entitled to defend themselves. But bioweapons went beyond her all-encompassing view that it didn't matter much how you died in battle. Bioweapons smacked of secret labs and all the terrible things she knew went on behind locked doors.

It disturbed her; Mestin must have smelled that, because she froze.

"Doesn't sound very wess'har, creating bioweapons," said Shan. "The ultimate interference with the natural order."

"A weapon of last resort," said Mestin, wafting citrus. Shan had to remind herself that she was still the ranking female, hormonally speaking. Mestin seemed to be finding it hard not to defer to her. "The pathogens themselves come to no harm. Just the targets." Wess'har morality had a seductive logic all its own. "Did *gethes* give that much thought to the fate of cavalry horses?"

"I'm not arguing. I'm just trying to make sense of this. So you all left the World Before and came here, then."

"No, some left. Most stayed."

Bang. Another bombshell. Why hadn't she realized that? *Because she hadn't asked.* Because she didn't know the question needed asking. It was probably all sitting in the massive wess'har archive that she was struggling to read. She was working backwards in the timeline, and slowly.

"You're going to have to spell this out," said Shan.

"Spell?"

"Explain in detail. Please."

"We are Targassati. We wanted to lead a simpler life and we no longer wanted to take part in what you call international politics. It was an obligation we did not feel we could justify. So we left."

Shan waited. Mestin just looked at her.

"Come on. And?"

"And?"

"The World Before is still . . . er . . . going strong?"

"Yes."

"So you have contact with them. What do they—"

"No. No contact. The ussissi move between worlds, but we remain separate."

"Hostile?"

"Irrelevant."

"I would have thought they'd be handy reinforcements, at the very least."

Mestin's eyes—darker than Chayyas's, more like amber bead—showed narrowed crosshairs, mere slits of pupil. "If we need to ask for help, there might be a price, as you say. We do not welcome interference or change."

"I understand," said Shan, who had seen more change in fifteen months than was decent, and quite liked the idea of stagnation for a while. She tried to imagine what the World Before might be like if the wess'har here represented the ecowarriors. "Look, if you're short on manpower and arms, conventional warfare isn't sustainable. You know that. That's why you used *c'naatat* troops in the past. I think you might have to look at unpalatable choices again. And I'm not just talking about germ warfare."

"From what you have seen here, do you think we have a problem?"

"I'm not a military analyst, but if you can't replace hardware at the rate you're losing it, then you're stuffed."

"Do you recall Chayyas said more might be asked of you than you were capable of giving?"

"It was a hard conversation to forget."

"Then I'm asking you to help us find an immediate solution to the *gethes* problem."

"Boy, that phrase has an unpleasantly familiar ring to it."

"I don't understand."

"Just as well. Look, this is years away. You have time to come up with some ideas."

"But what would *you* do, Shan? What would you do if you perceived a genuine threat to your world?"

"I'm not the best person to ask. I'd only give you a gut reaction, not a considered political option. I'm not known for my restraint."

"What is war but emotional response backed up by weaponry?"

It wasn't a bad point. Shan started seeing the gaps in the hangar, the places where ships were no longer stored. There were a lot more gaps than there were occupied berths.

She thought about it. "Personally, I'd pop round their house and give them a bloody serious warning. And maybe a demonstration of how very unreasonable I could be if they *really* pissed me off."

"We would wish to deal with the threat directly too. But we have such limited military resources these days. We need to make it impossible for *gethes* to get a foothold in this system."

It seemed a very benign discussion. They were actually talking about killing humans. It didn't feel that much of a chasm to cross. "Come on, you're not going to be able to send a task force to Earth without help from someone, are you?"

"No. The other option is what you would call bioweapons. If we have enough intact human DNA, we can create a barrier weapon. It need only be created and deployed once."

"Poison Earth?"

"Poison Bezer'ej."

"Ah." Shan wondered what was happening to her brain. It was suddenly obvious. "You want my DNA."

"Yes."

"Why didn't you extract it from Aras?"

"*C'naatat.* A dangerous organism to handle, and we have found no way of separating it from its host. If we could have done so, things would be very different now, would they not? We would also have isenj DNA. We would be able to use *c'naatat* at will."

"Well, I'm not exactly a regular human any longer. I'm not sure what help I can be."

"But you *were* normal a matter of a season or so ago. Do you have any material that predates your contamination?"

Now that was science that Shan understood only too well. *Forensic evidence.* Hair, saliva, GSR, semen. She could do as thorough a job on crime scene as any SOCO. "Let's have a look through my grip," she said. "I keep my kit clean but I'd bet there are some hairs hanging around." She hadn't used her cold-weather suit since she first landed on Bezer'ej: they could scour that for cells.

"You give this up easily under the circumstances."

"I'd like to think of it as razor wire. If you don't climb over it, you won't get hurt."

"You're a pragmatic woman."

"And you really don't have any isenj DNA?"

"We don't take prisoners," said Mestin.

"What about asking the ussissi to acquire some?"

"We will not compromise them by asking them to act for us aggressively."

Shan tried to conceive of a society where the entire defense industry could be halted by the desire not to embarrass an ally. The challenge with wess'har was to understand that they had just two settings—completely benign and psychotic—with nothing in between. "It's not how we'd handle things back home."

"The ussissi are neutral."

"God, you really are going to need some help to deal with *gethes,* aren't you? Okay. Count me in." She paused. "What happens to the colonists in Constantine if you flood the planet with antihuman pathogens or whatever?"

Mestin cocked her head a few times. "I would rather remove them *all.*"

It was Josh and Deborah and James and Rachel, not a seething mass of anonymous faces. Shan tried to adjust to her new kinship. *There's no reason why they have to share your morality. Stay out of it.* "What about moving them here? Like you did the gene bank?"

Mestin looked genuinely thoughtful, her long muzzle and sharply tilted head reminding Shan too much of a baffled Afghan hound. "Yes, if they represent a strain of acceptable humans, it might be wise to propagate them. There might be no other *gethes* left in time, after all."

Shan had to think about that last sentence.

She wasn't entirely sure she had understood it. Then she knew she bloody well had, and that small expression of a monumental threat was more chilling than a wess'har battle fleet heaving into view.

"What if they won't move?"

"Then they die," said Mestin, as if Shan would be equally unmoved by the prospect.

Shan could almost smell her own citrussy waft of anxiety. "Maybe I can put the relocation idea to them in due course."

Something told Shan she was going to have trouble explaining this to Aras. It wasn't a topic that had ever cropped up in conversation. He had warned her about the matriarchs and how she would be *enslaved,* but she had taken it as an expression of his bitterness about exile.

For some reason, justifying herself to Aras bothered her more than the fact that she was about to teach an alien race how to be efficient terrorists against her own species.

Shan walked up to the nearest fighter and glanced at Mestin

for approval to climb up on it. As soon as she laid her hand on it, the canopy opened: a faint, single, pure note ran from discomfort below her threshold of hearing up the scale until she could no longer hear it. It made the back of her throat itch. The cockpit was alive with a soft bluish glow.

"How did I do that?" Shan asked.

"You must have more wess'har genes than you thought."

Shan stared down into the cockpit, one continuous surface covered with the diagrammatic writing and points of light. The smell of the materials—harshly grassy, like burning tangerine peel—stopped her dead.

She was perfectly aware of where she was but she was also watching her hands—no, Aras's hands—punching rapidly across the controls while a flare of flame wiped out the landscape that was spinning ever larger in the viewplate. Sick physical panic gripped her. Then she smashed into the plate and everything was blackness and pain and heat and her teeth felt as if they had been driven up into her sinuses.

She straightened up and scrambled down the side of the craft, dropping the last meter and landing on her feet with a thud. Around her it was all orderly, soft-lit calm again. She shut her eyes for a moment, and suddenly the drowning dream and all that went with it was vivid and *now*.

"He crashed," she said at last. "Aras crash-landed in one of those things. I just saw it."

Mestin took her sleeve carefully and steered her away from the fighter. The gesture surprised her. It was an oddly compassionate act for a matriarch.

"I had heard that *c'naatat* can pass on memory," said Mestin. "Is it difficult, coping with that?"

"Not any more," said Shan. No, she could handle it. She prided herself on her professional core of ice. She was the copper who didn't faint at her first autopsy, who never vomited at the smell of decomposition, and who could look at evidence even strong men preferred not to see. It didn't mean she didn't care: it just meant that, after a while, she forgot how to.

She wondered if that was why she hung onto the pain of the gorilla and the blue door, just so she could be in thrall to impotent anger again and reassure herself occasionally that she was alive and feeling.

Shan inhaled deeply through her nose and suppressed the agonizing shock of crashing in enemy territory. "You know what happened to him? What the isenj did to him?"

"No, but I can imagine," said Mestin. "They were brutal times. Even the isenj admit that."

Mestin kept steering her away from the craft, the slightest pressure of her hand on her back. Shan wanted to shrug the touch away but decided it might be provocative. If Mestin could scent that she was bothered by the touch, it had not deterred her.

"You think I'm weak, don't you?" Shan said.

"I do not," said Mestin. "I wonder how I would fare alone in your world. I wonder how I would react to my body being colonized and altered by a parasite. I'm not sure I would acquit myself particularly well." She tapped her hand against the hard shape of the gun that Shan kept tucked into the back of her waistband. "Do you fear us?"

"Habit. No offense meant." Shan reached back under her jacket and adjusted the gun again, embarrassed. She wondered why she couldn't recall the borrowed memory of Aras firing that weapon into the skull of Surendra Parekh. She could certainly remember her own oblique view of the execution. Perhaps it hadn't been traumatic enough for Aras to make the same impression as the other events in his life. "I'm a copper, remember. A police officer."

"I know what police do. And I know what *you* have done. I have seen the record of your conversation with Michallat."

Ah, the unbroadcast interview. Eddie hadn't quite got her to admit she had aided ecoterrorists, but it was a close-run thing. She hoped Mestin hadn't picked up the implication that Minister Perault had perhaps conned her into accepting her mission. "Yeah. I don't piss about."

"I think you are very clever, very persistent and very violent."

Shan almost dropped her gaze. "Whatever it takes to do the job."

"But only if you think the job is worth doing. That is why we like you."

Shan was suddenly uncomfortable. She wasn't used to being patted, not by anybody who valued their teeth, and she wasn't expecting to be told she was *liked*. She felt her scalp prickle. Mestin must have smelled her agitation.

"For a physically fearless person you are easily unsettled by small matters," Mestin said. She sniffed discreetly, as if to say *I know*. "Let me tell you this. If it were not for *c'naatat*, I would be happy for you to be a cousin-by-mating. I trust you. Nevyan respects you greatly."

Shan wasn't sure she had understood the matriarch right. Cousin-by-mating? Ah, *in-law*. Sister-in-law. Some of her best friends were *c'naatat* but she wouldn't want her brother to marry one, so to speak. It wasn't offensive. Shan knew the risks. They were no different for wess'har, except that they could be relied upon to do the sensible thing with the symbiont—most of the time, anyway.

Mestin walked ahead of her, back towards the exit, trilling wordlessly under her breath. Shan followed the matriarch's rustling steps with her eyes fixed on the neat stripe of tufted gold hair down her nape. It was another moment when her world shivered into semifocus: another moment when she knew that she didn't really understand what wess'har were, and what they did when she wasn't around. It made her feel utterly alone. It made her want the comfort of Aras's company.

She tried to make light conversation to jolly herself along. "I think cousin-by-mating is a nice way of describing someone who marries into your family," she said. "Wess'u is a very pragmatic language."

Mestin glanced back at her in a half turn but carried on walking. "It doesn't mean that at all," she said.

"I don't think I understand."

"*Oursan*," she said, as if Shan ought to have known what

that meant. They were back on the surface again, among irregular strips of red and magenta crops. "Nevyan was supposed to be educating you."

"Maybe we haven't got to that page yet," said Shan, feeling unpleasantly embarrassed again but unsure exactly why. There was a niggling awareness at the back of her mind, like a Suppressed Briefing. Whatever scraps of memory were surfacing from Aras, this one was shot with anxiety.

She was pondering the feeling as she walked back up the terraces when she nearly trod on a vine as thick as a ship's cable. It was covered in velvety scales and pink-flushed gold, like a ripe peach. When she crouched to touch it, it shot off at speed and its furred leaves—or what had looked like leaves—scattered in all directions, emitting high-pitched squeals. The surprise made her overbalance onto her backside.

The vine-thing paused at a distance and the leaves scuttled back to it and attached themselves again. She sat in complete humiliation on the flagstones, heart pounding. A male wess'har walked by and stared down at her.

"Genadin," he said, nodding in the direction of the creature. "With babies."

Nothing was obvious here. She sat and gathered her composure for a few moments and started rehearsing how she would tell Aras that she had signed up to help the wess'har war machine.

But it could wait.

She had to sort out her uneasy relationship with him first.

Nobody gave a second glance to Lindsay and Eddie while they chatted in a corner of the hangar deck. They were old mates, isolated and lonely. They had personal issues to discuss. There was nothing sinister about it.

Eddie wasn't so sure. She hadn't said a word to him about *Hereward*, and he was now certain every senior officer would have known about the deployment. Well, if that was the game she was playing, fine. It disappointed him, but at least he was

now on familiar territory and using a fine-honed skill in which
he had complete confidence—pickpocketing the brain of a reluctant interviewee without their feeling a thing.

"You okay?" he asked.

"Bearing up." She kept fiddling with her right shoulder
board, picking invisible specks off the gold braid rings. "Eddie,
I need to ask you something."

He folded his arms. "I'm a journalist. Think of me as your
priest."

"It's serious."

Ah, maybe she was going to come clean. He hoped so. He
didn't like to think of her as prey. "Okay. Ask."

"If I got you transport, would you be willing to ask for access to the wess'har?"

It was the last thing he expected to hear, and no mention of
Hereward. He summoned up all his acting skills. "I'd probably
bite your arm off in the rush."

"We need someone to break the ice. You're neutral."

"They still want to negotiate diplomatic relations with
them, eh?"

"I know. Fat chance. But if we knew how they were thinking,
we might get the approach right."

She was lying her arse off. She was an *amateur*. It wasn't the
first time Eddie had been approached—obliquely, charm-
ingly—to gather data. In a simpler age they called it spying,
and it was the sort of thing that got journalists shot or worse in
unsympathetic foreign countries.

"I think this is bullshit," he said. "It's got nothing to do with
diplomacy. What do you really want?"

Her head dropped and she sighed. If she was acting, it was
convincing. "Okay, I might as well tell you. You started this
biotech rumor running and now I've got to clean up the mess. I
need to make sure the pharmaceutical lads don't get hold of it. I
haven't a clue what we're looking for, but if you hear anything
that would help me keep it out of circulation, I'd be grateful. And
so might human civilization, whether it knows it or not yet."

It hurt. It was true. He wished for the hundredth time that he hadn't gone hunting that story, but it was too late. "Lin, I'm in enough shit as it is. BBChan's under a lot of government and commercial pressure for me to find happy space stories. Seems they hold me responsible for giving people the impression that the Cockroach Cluster is on its way to take over the Earth."

"Okay, it's not fair of me to dump this on you. Forget it."

"Now *that's* not fair. The one thing you can't do to a journalist is let me halfway in. You're waging some interagency feud with the Department of Trade or whoever and you expect me to line up as cannon fodder. You tell me the truth, or you can piss off and do your own dirty work."

"I didn't say this was a departmental power struggle."

Eddie spread his arms and gave her a theatrically slack-jawed look. "A wild guess. Now for Chrissakes tell me." *Come on, say Hereward. You know I'll get it out of you sooner or later.* "I know you're not giving me the full picture."

"Okay, but this is between you and me."

"Whoa. This is where I don't do off-the-record. When people say that, they really want to leak something without taking responsibility for it. And even if I do keep it to myself, once I know something it colors all my decisions from then on, doesn't it? So think hard before you open your mouth."

Lindsay paused three beats. He counted them. "Okay. Rayat claims he's working for the Treasury and he says he wants to prevent access to the biotech as well."

"Really?"

"I checked."

"Makes sense. All we need is a plummeting death rate and we've got an economic crisis that's going to make the pensions collapse of 2136 look like a small overdraft."

Lindsay seemed diverted by the comment for a moment. "I'm telling you the truth."

"Maybe, but isn't there something you left out?"

She fidgeted with her shoulder boards again as if her rank was bothering her. "There's always detail, Eddie."

"Try *Hereward*."

She looked genuinely blank. "I honestly haven't a clue what you mean."

"Really. You're a senior officer here and you didn't know that we've diverted a logistics support vessel, probably armed, to this sector?"

"No, I bloody well didn't." She couldn't fake that reddening face. Okurt was going to get a stream of high-grade vitriol, that much was clear. "How do *you* know?"

"Don't make me say it. It's the one ethic we still hold dear in my trade."

"Bastard," she said, but she was looking away and it was obvious she didn't mean him. "What the hell is he playing at? He didn't bother to tell me he was looking for ways to exhume David's body for research either. You'll forgive me if I have a tantrum at being left out of the loop again."

"You really didn't know, did you?"

"'Course I bloody didn't."

"I don't think the aliens have been told either. Any of them. How to piss off two opposing technologically advanced powers in one go—it's economy of stupidity, anyway. What if they gang up on *us?*"

"*We* might realize that, and I think even Okurt might, but he's not calling the shots, remember. He's on the Foreign Office choke-chain."

"And what are you going to do when the locals find out?"

"How are they going to hear about it?"

"There's no such thing as monopoly of information. Lots of people have to be involved with diverting a ship. Victualling, fueling, canceling other deployments, you name it. It'll leak Earthside through families, and then it'll be on the news, and either the wess'har or the isenj will pick it up off an intercepted feed."

"We'll see."

"I hate to use words like gunboat diplomacy, but surely someone's noticed we're not the most powerful species in the universe any longer?"

"Don't ask me to fathom politicians."

"Okay. If you can get me clearance to visit Wess'ej, I'll see what I can see. But just be aware I'm not working for you or anyone else. I'm doing this for me and I'll make the call based on what I think is right."

Lindsay looked studiously blank. "Shan would be proud of you."

"Call me," he said, and walked away wondering if she had stitched him up. He was damned if he was going to be manipulated. He slid down the ladder to the next deck below, just like a seasoned spacefarer, and caught his hand on a rail. "Bitch," he said, not sure if he was referring to his scraped hand or Lindsay. She had made him feel guilty.

But she was right about one thing. He was neutral, more or less. He liked the isenj and he liked the wess'har and he was hard-wired to attack his own government; but he trusted nobody. Suspicion was a great leveler.

And he pondered on what he had done with information in the past, and what he continued to do with it, and he thought of a little known place called San Carlos Water with a heavy heart.

9

There was a time when wess'har made their soldiers immortal.
They have not done it for many years. But they can do it again,
and that is why you should not underestimate a small army.
Make friends with them while you can.

MINISTER UAL, in an explanatory note
to the FEU Foreign Office.

Something small and wet thudded onto Shan's back like
someone had gobbed on her.

Her hand reached for her gun without her conscious brain
getting involved. The last time someone had spat at her while
she was on duty, she'd rounded on the perpetrator, dragged him
bodily from the crowd and introduced him to the business end
of her truncheon. She hated anyone messing up her uniform;
and she certainly didn't like anyone coming up behind her. But
when she looked back there was nobody, just the empty alley-
way washed and beaded in pearl. She let go of the gun.

She strained to look over her shoulder and pulled up her
shirt to check what had hit her. She couldn't see anything. She
could smell a sweet almondlike scent and wondered if it was
sap from a plant higher up the terraces.

Come on, nobody's going to gob on you here. It was something she was going to have to get used to, and she found it hard
to accustom herself to pleasant things. She was always waiting
for them to peel back their deceptive skins and reveal their teeth.

It was a shame Aras wasn't comfortable in F'nar. He just
seemed to be getting more and more agitated each day. Shan
was starting to like the place, and not just because she had no
choice. She could walk down the terraces and alleys and every-

one acknowledged her: they knew who she was, and why she was there, and she was starting to know them. It was like being the beat bobby in an idyllic village.

The only difference was that she was never going to be called upon to rattle door handles or break up a pub brawl. Apart from their abrupt tone—and that was only unedited frankness—there was nothing personally violent or antisocial about individual wess'har. How they made that sudden leap from peaceful citizen to apparent psychopath still bewildered her.

As she walked round the curve of the caldera, clutching a gift for newlywed Nevyan, she passed two young males utterly engrossed in playing with their children, rumbling and purring as the little ones tried their hand at planting tufts of red grass in the gaps between the paving. The males were taking sporadic bites from chunks of *lurisj,* the closest that wess'har had to a mood-altering narcotic. They were simply relaxed and happy, a world away from human drunks and junkies and all the violence that accompanied them.

Then Shan thought about Mjat, and the whole coast around Constantine scoured clean of isenj, and tried to reconcile the two images. She thought briefly of the ease with which Aras had put two rounds through Parekh's head, and then how he had rescued a tiny *banic* from drowning in the washed vegetables. He was an alien all right.

An alien. And there she was, catching herself looking at him in the way she had once looked at Ade Bennett. It was getting more insistent. It wasn't like her at all.

She was still conscious of moisture on her back and twitching her shoulders involuntarily when she got to Nevyan's new house, a warren of excavated rooms that previously had been Asajin's. She looked down at the woven container of *netun jay* in her hand and took a breath. Wess'har didn't give gifts. But they liked their food, and it seemed as good a way as any to wish Nevyan well in her new life. Besides, she had questions to ask her that she didn't feel she could put to Mestin.

Shan raised her hand to knock on the door, but wess'har didn't knock so neither would she. It didn't feel right, though. You only barged in like that with a warrant, or sometimes without one if you felt like it. *Fit in,* she told herself, and pressed silently on the pearl-encrusted door. It swung open and she walked in.

Her gaze went instinctively to the point in the frozen scene where she least wanted it to go.

"O-oh shit," she said. "*Shit.* Sorry!"

She came out a lot faster than she went in, slammed the door and stood against it with her free hand to her mouth in an involuntary spasm of sheer animal embarrassment. She *really* should have knocked. She shook herself back into a semblance of composure and waited outside.

The door opened again. Nevyan, now in her matriarch's *dhren,* wafted not a trace of agitation and simply cocked her head in that canine gesture of concentration. It was down to the shape of wess'har pupils, Aras said. They did it automatically to get a better focus on the object of their curiosity, and Shan—red-faced and uncharacteristically embarrassed—was apparently worth extra scrutiny.

"What's wrong?" said Nevyan. There was absolutely no indication whatsoever that she was offended by being disturbed during an intimate moment with her new males. *Yeah, and all four of them,* Shan thought. *Jesus H. Christ.*

"I'll knock in future," Shan said, finding it painful to meet her eyes. They were vivid citrine, quite unlike her mother's.

"You're upset. Why?"

"You're not bothered by . . . um . . ."

"By what?" Nevyan was now starting to smell agitated. Shan wasn't sure whether it was because she wanted badly to understand or because Nevyan wanted her approval. She was painfully aware of the kid's deference to her. "Have I done something wrong?"

Shan shook her head rapidly. "No. Don't worry. Human thing. Not your problem." She lapsed into English, because wess'u just didn't have the words for it. She held out the *netun jay.* "I came to wish you well. You know. Wedding?"

Nevyan took the cakes and bobbed her head enthusiastically. "This is kind, this is very kind. I know how important this is to humans."

"You're welcome," Shan said. Nevyan seized her arm and led her back into the house. Her males—her *jurej've*—didn't seem at all offended by being interrupted at a critical moment. It was as if she had walked in while they were watching their favorite TV show, a minor interruption to an entertainment that could be resumed later.

In the kitchen the *jurej've* trilled and fluted as they prepared a meal, no more transfixed by her than the kids were. Time was when she could gather a crowd just by walking along the terraces. *I'm one of the tribe now*, she thought. One looked up. *"Shan g'san,"* he said, cocking his head in amusement. A wess'har joke. It was the first she'd heard, or at least the first she'd understood. She smiled. They now seemed unperturbed by her display of teeth.

But their scent of cedar and sandalwood put her on edge, and she wasn't sure why, although she was damned certain that what she'd seen of their anatomy was alarming enough. One of the males wrapped himself around Nevyan, trilling enthusiastically.

"Later, Lisik," she snapped, and cuffed him. Shan looked away. Nevyan turned back to her. "He'll make a good and useful husband when he calms down."

Shan rapidly revised her estimate that Nevyan was going on seventeen. Wess'har didn't appear to grow up; they switched almost overnight from one life phase to another, and Nevyan was now the complete matriarch. It was disturbing to think of her having husbands who needed a good slap to stop them mounting her in front of house guests. "How unlike the life of our own dear queen," Shan muttered, and sat down at the long table in the kitchen, careful to keep her elbows clear of the exquisite rainbow glass bowls and pots.

Nevyan thrust the basket of cakes towards her. "Eat, then," she said, and placed a couple of *netun* on a plate in front of them. It was a gesture you made to family, and Shan liked the feel of that. She bit into the cake with a careful eye on the new males. Yes, she'd seen too much now to ever think of them as harmless seahorses again.

The *netun* were crisp, and the runny, clove-scented filling escaped down her chin with an audible *pop*. Lisik was at her side immediately, clutching a cloth as if to wipe her face, and she held up her hand defensively.

"Thanks. I can do it myself."

Lisik made a noncommittal *chik* sound and went back to pressing some sticky yellow mixture into flat trays.

Another male was preoccupied with suckling a tiny infant no longer than Shan's hand.

It reminded her of a stick insect. The male had slipped his garment off his shoulders to feed it, and what flesh she could see looked smooth and lightly muscled. The baby was clinging to his skin with those long jointed fingers.

She knew that wess'har males gestated and suckled but she hadn't actually seen it, and that made it very different. Her mouth filled with saliva as if she were going to be sick. Her stomach somersaulted. She had once again been punched hard with the reminder that this was not Earth, and these were not humans, and that what she was seeing was the reality of Aras Sar Iussan, who she had almost thought of as a man.

She wiped her lips and chin carefully, wondering what it was like to sleep with a man who could breast-feed. It was a thought she hadn't invited and didn't want to entertain.

Perhaps Aras couldn't. *C'naatat* had made a lot of changes to him.

Nevyan's husband adjusted his position and ran a careful finger over the infant's head while it suckled, oblivious of Shan's attention. It squirmed closer to him. Shan wondered if she had any real understanding of Aras, whether she had his memories or not. It was amazing how much you couldn't see when you were absolutely determined not to, even in one room.

It was equally hard not to look at these males, even though they had no physical features she found consciously attractive beyond the aesthetic. She inhaled that seductive scent of sandalwood and now cedar, suddenly aware of the pressure of the hard bench against parts of her anatomy that hadn't seen much action in a while. *Seductive*. That was exactly what it was; pheromones.

"Are they bothering you?" Nevyan asked, making a chin-jutting gesture in her husbands' direction. "You seem very upset."

"Not at all," Shan said, and finally accepted that her talent for ducking behind a veneer of disinterested menace was sod all use on Wess'ej. "I need to ask you some questions."

"Police questions?"

"God, no."

"I can't follow all your English. Please—"

"Sorry. It's personal. I need advice."

Nevyan's pupils flashed cross-flower-cross as the penny dropped and she realized she could be helpful to what she regarded as the alpha female. Shan had seen her do exactly the same to Mestin in the past. "Ask, if you think I can be of use."

"Okay. I'm disturbed by changes in my body."

"C'naatat?"

"Specifically, urges."

"To do what?"

"What you were doing when I came in."

"I don't understand why that disturbs you."

"Because Aras is—different. Not my species."

"Then he *didn't* infect you by copulation. My mistake."

"I was unconscious at the time," Shan said stiffly, ambushed by her copper's hard-wired suspicion. "He *told* me he transferred blood from his hand into my wound."

"Then that is what he did," said Nevyan.

Shan fought down a flush of adrenal panic. She was a copper, and she thought the worst before she thought the best. Rape, child abuse, and bestiality: all rapists, nonces and sheep-shaggers wanted hanging, garroting, and gassing, the bastards. But what did that make her, wondering what it would be like to fuck an alien? Where was that nice safe line between human and everything else? *Oh God.*

"I'm not someone who gives in to my body," Shan said. "It does what I tell it. I need to know how to stop these thoughts."

Nevyan made a long, low trilling sound. "Why do you have to?"

"Because it's getting on my nerves and we don't have that sort of relationship. I don't want to worry about offspring and I don't want—" She was going to say *love.* Love was dependence, and dependence weakened you. "We're friends. I think he'd be appalled if he knew."

Nevyan was absolutely immobile. She didn't even blink. Whatever Shan had said, it had put her in that alarmed, uncertain, frozen state.

"What?" said Shan, irritated.

"Mestin explained to you about hormonal dominance. You smell like a wess'har, enough to provoke reaction from us."

"I don't like where this is going."

"I suspect you're reacting to each other. Aras is certainly reacting to you. Everyone knows that."

"Well, I bloody well *didn't.*" Shan folded her arms and remembered just in time that there was no chair back to lean against. "He's agitated and irritable, I know *that.*"

Nevyan looked at Shan and Shan looked back at Nevyan. Shan struggled with the baffled silence, then rolled a *netun* back and forth on the plate with her forefinger like a game of table soccer. She knew the kid wasn't trying to drag an embarrassing admission of further ignorance out of her, but it felt like it.

"I don't even look wess'har," she said at last.

"You behave like us in many ways and you smell like us. How you appear is largely irrelevant, even to Aras, I suspect."

"And how do I smell?"

"Like a dominant *isan.*"

"Do *your* males react to me?"

"No, because they're now bonded to me. But they know you're receptive."

"I'm not some bloody brood mare."

"What's that?"

"Oh, never mind. Is all this obvious to Aras?"

"Yes."

"Oh shit."

Nevyan made that impatient side-to-side head movement. "I don't know why you have so much difficulty with this. Do what you need to do. After that, you will both be perfectly content. Unmated adults don't exist in our society."

Shan would never have tolerated that amount of lip from any human subordinate. Her annoyance must have hit Nevyan's olfactory system pretty hard, because the junior matriarch locked position again. "Is that why you took on Asajin's family?" Shan asked.

"Yes, because they would have died without an *isan*," Nevyan said. Her tilted head rather than her tone told Shan it was the proverbial bleedin' obvious answer. "Do you not understand *oursan*?"

"No."

"Ah." It came out as a forlorn trill on a falling note, like birdsong. *Lrrrrr.* "This is how we are. Males need the genetic material of the female to repair their tissues. I transfer it through cells in my body to theirs, and I take in some of their genes too, and we all share it. It keeps them well. It's also pleasurable."

Shan couldn't imagine having sex with a complete stranger as an act of charity. "You seem okay with all this."

"Why wouldn't I be? That is the nature of *oursan* as well as my duty. We're bonded. It's very nice. It feels very good up here." And she touched her forehead with one many-jointed finger.

Shan felt an urge to giggle but didn't find it at all funny. Nevyan, distracted briefly by the high wavering wail of the infant now fully fed, glanced at her males with such obvious pride and delight that the air around her was filled with the powdery musk of her contentment. Then she looked back at

Shan. Her pupils were just a cross, faint rutilations in yellow quartz.

"You are certainly distressing Aras," she said. "Ask him to explain it to you. You know enough about wess'har males now to understand how hard he finds this."

Shan decided she would rather have faced an armed mob without backup than ask Aras to explain the facts of wess'har life to her. She stood up to go. "Well, that's going to be fun," she said flatly.

Nevyan trilled. She found something amusing. Shan glanced back, instinctively and humanly annoyed.

Nevyan stiffened. "You have an *aumul* on your back," she said. "Let me remove it."

She reached between Shan's shoulder blades and then held her hand where Shan could see it. Nestled in it was a very large red and white striped slug, and it smelled of almonds, and it was making melodic plinking noises like a musical box.

"Is it dangerous?" Shan asked. You could never take anything for granted here, not even musical slugs.

"No."

"What does it do for an encore?"

"It scours the *tem* deposits at night looking for organic waste before it sets hard."

"It eats *shit?*"

"I will learn that word."

Nevyan placed the *aumul* carefully on the flagstones and it shot off across the floor at speed like an Arsenal scarf caught in a high wind. Shan had liked it better when she was totally unfamiliar with this alien world. Being lulled gently into thinking you belonged here made it even more disturbing when you thought you recognized something—and then realized it was absolutely, totally and wholly unlike your expectations.

That was Aras too.

Shan took a slow walk back home, looking for courage on the way.

* * *

There was fish on the menu today and that cheered Lindsay up no end.

It was cod in a garlicky tomato sauce. The culture-grown fillets were a regular portion-controlled shape that no real cod would ever have achieved in nature, as was the way with muscle-protein production systems. But that didn't matter. It was cod. Lindsay tucked in with all the gastronomic enthusiasm that only people cooped up on long deployments in isolated places could fully understand.

Or it might have been the battlefield mood-killers that Sandhu had prescribed for her. David was dead; nothing would make her forget that, except for those few brief seconds on waking each day. But the drugs provided a soothing erasure of grief for the time being. She was sad, but it was—she imagined—as she would be in a few years' time, having come to terms with her loss and the changes it had made in her, but not disabled by it any longer.

The drug had been developed to halt plummeting morale in combat. Lindsay wondered if they ever thought it would be used to help a grieving mother kill a woman who had once been her friend.

She savored the thick tomato sauce. And this time she *did* hear Rayat come up behind her.

He made quite a point of acknowledging people sitting nearby. She felt a pleasant flood of satisfaction: she must have made him think twice about startling an unstable woman with a weapon.

"Mind if I join you?" he said.

"It's a free country."

Rayat sat down opposite her. "Yes, we keep it that way, don't we?" He appeared to have a pile of beans and spinach in a carry-out container. It looked like he was used to eating alone in his cabin. "I was thinking about what you said."

"Um."

"Have *you* been thinking about what might happen if you were successful in cornering this biotech for the military?"

Lindsay shrugged. "Drop the games. Please."

"Have you?"

"I'd be stupid if I hadn't, and I'm not stupid."

"I don't think you like the idea any more than my boss does."

"And I don't want to know who your boss is, thanks."

"I have something to share with you."

"In exchange for what?" She glanced up and Eddie was standing at the servery. He looked back and made a discreet warding gesture at her, the forefinger of each hand overlapping in a cross. *Watch that bastard.* She almost laughed.

"Troops and transport," said Rayat.

"You could ask Okurt."

"Okurt's orders aren't the same as mine."

"Or mine?"

"I think you're rightly terrified by this thing and you can see the threat it represents. You know that's why Frankland did what she did to you."

The cod didn't taste so good now. Lindsay shunted it around her plate and then put the fork down. "Okay. Let's talk about this somewhere else."

"My cabin, ten minutes?"

"You're a charmer," she said, and picked up the fork again. Rayat took his lonely container of beans and left. Eddie was engrossed in a conversation by the salads with Lieutenant Yun. Lindsay cleared her plate and left a decent interval before getting up to leave.

Eddie, engrossed or not, turned his head immediately and caught her eye. *Well?* And she could only think of one response, the gesture that Shan used so often to indicate her low opinion of a colleague. Thumb and forefinger held together in a loose fist, she made a rapid stroking motion. *He's a wanker.* Eddie grinned, but it was the studied camaraderie of a man keeping an eye on her.

She grinned back. But she wasn't planning to share any of this with Eddie.

* * *

Shan felt incompetent for the first time in her life, and it hurt.

When she got back to the one-room house and leaned against the iridescent door, it opened and she almost fell in. It wasn't the entrance she wanted to make. Aras filled the doorway.

"You've been a long time," he said.

"We got talking," she said.

"Are you hungry?"

Shan followed him to the table and looked over the dish of *evem*. "I could do with a cup of tea, please."

Aras shook the jar of tea to indicate the falling level of the leaves. "The bushes will be ready for harvest in four hundred days, and this won't last. I could ask Josh for more supplies."

She ignored him. "Nice and strong, please."

"You're upset."

"Yeah, everyone keeps saying that," she snapped. "It's been a bit of an educational morning."

Aras said nothing and watched the water boil, which was another thing you could do with relative ease if you lived forever. She flopped onto the sofa and tried to frame the words. It took longer than she expected.

She wasn't prepared to spend another day sneaking glances at his extraordinarily appealing man-shaped back and buttocks. And she had no intention of giving in randomly to instincts like Lindsay Neville had done. If she was going to go through with this—and Aras must have been suffering untold misery in his isolation—then she'd do it logically and responsibly.

There were worse ways to spend her time. Aras was a striking, magnificent creature. But tigers and peacocks were beautiful too: it didn't mean it was okay to consider screwing them. She wondered what was happening to her cherished view of nonhuman animals as equals.

"Nevyan seems very happy with her new family," Shan began. She accepted the proffered bowl of tea with relief.

Aras shrugged. "It's natural. They're bonded."

"Yeah, they were bonding pretty well when I walked in." She didn't get a reaction so she carried on. "Is that it? They have a quickie and it's happy ever after?"

Aras seemed to understand *quickie* perfectly well. "I can see why *gethes* find it peculiar. We bond for life. We need no sanction or law to achieve that."

Gethes. Thanks. "So this is *oursan,* is it?"

"Yes. We have cells that exchange our DNA, bond us to our *isan,* and give us pleasure, just as you secrete oxytocin. And you consume methamphetamine. These substances make you feel affectionate and euphoric. The same applies to *oursan.*"

Shan thought back to her drug squad training. It didn't help. "You get an emotional high from screwing?"

"Inelegantly put, but yes."

"Where are the cells?"

"In our genitalia."

Shan felt her hand go involuntarily to her forehead in embarrassment. "I walked in on Nevyan having sex with her new husbands."

Aras looked puzzled. His scent of sandalwood was especially strong right then. "But they all have children."

"So?"

"Males never have sex after they've fathered children. The *sanil* atrophies and forms the gestational pouch."

She could work out what a *sanil* was. She wondered why he didn't just say *penis.* "Aras, *atrophied* isn't the word I'd have used."

This really wasn't going as she'd planned. He looked completely and utterly bewildered. If he had tilted his head any further, she would have thrown a stick for him to fetch. Right then she didn't want any more random images that blurred the line between Aras the man and Aras the animal. "You must be mistaken."

"I know what I saw, for Chrissakes. Do I need to draw a picture? Anyway, they were having it away. End of story."

Aras's head straightened up smartly and there was a definite flash of comprehension. "No," he said, evidently relieved. "That wasn't sex. That was *oursan*."

Shan fought to remain detached. He must have smelled that she was agitated: he was pumping clouds of tension himself. But her stand-back-I'm-a-police-officer persona took over and projected complete, glacial, accidental calm. "Look, I know I don't get out much lately, but if that's not shagging it's doing a bloody good impersonation of it."

"*Oursan*," Aras repeated, as if she were deaf. He paused for a second and then unfastened his long tunic, completely unselfconscious. He took in a deep breath and pointed. "*That* is for *oursan*," he said, "and *this* is for sex."

"Ah," said Shan. "*Ah.*"

She thought she had seen just about everything in the course of her police career but now she knew that she *definitely* hadn't. Her shock must have been tangible. But she couldn't even blink, let alone look away.

Aras must have noticed her oh-my-God expression. "I apologize," he said. "Once I'm back among wess'har, I forget the taboos of humans. I shouldn't have done that."

"I think it made an eloquent point," said Shan hoarsely. *Oh shit. Oh, shit . . .* "It's okay."

"This one is for reproduction, for *sex* as you say. The other is for *oursan*. Horizontal transmission." And he fastened his tunic again.

Shan couldn't quite maintain *glacial*. She tried. She battled another totally humorless urge to giggle and very nearly won. "I've heard it called a few things, but that's a new one on me."

"I can explain it further if you like. Genes transferred from one organism to another, not just from parent to offspring—"

"Draw me a picture." She choked on suppressed laughter. "I'm sorry. This isn't how it looks."

"You're mocking me."

"No, I'm just very embarrassed. I'm sorry—"

Aras dropped his head for a moment and then walked past her and out of the door without a word. He closed it firmly behind him, just one shade short of slamming it.

"*Shit*," said Shan. "Our first fight. Oh, terrific."

Men could rot in hell before she'd run after them. She busied herself trying to make proper right angles on the frame of the new bed, sawing and swearing each time she offered up a piece of *efte* and it still didn't fit. No, men were a pain in the arse: necessary recreation, but not one of them warranted changing your routine, your priorities or your name.

But Aras wasn't a man.

He was an alien who happened to look a lot like a man and even had some human characteristics. He was also an alien who had suffered terrible isolation for an unimaginable time. And despite herself, she cared about him: and she had given up caring about people a lifetime ago. Aras was outside the corrupt circle of humanity, a clean soul despite his wars, an innocent . . . animal. She could forgive an animal anything.

Shan realized that she still wasn't sure how she thought of him, or how that sat with the sensation she experienced when she touched the hard muscle of his back. It felt just like when she touched Ade Bennett. It felt primevally *good*.

But Aras isn't human.

And neither was she. *Not any more.* If you were a sheepshagger, maybe that was okay provided you were also part sheep.

"Oh, fuck it," she said, and swept up the dust and shavings from the floor before going in search of him.

There weren't that many places Aras could have gone. She didn't have to search bars for him—not that she would have, of course—and she didn't have to ring round each of his friends to see if he was sprawled on their sofa with a Scotch in his hand, bemoaning the inconsistencies of women and why they were such rotten heartless bitches.

He wasn't human. But he was terribly alone, and he was her only friend, and she wanted very badly to erase his pain as well as her own.

Aras was working on their patch of allocated land. Shan could see him kneeling among the plants, picking out something and putting it in a pile beside him. He didn't look up as she approached. She knew that he was aware she was there: he could smell her easily at that distance, especially in her current state of mind.

"Okay, sorry," she said. She knelt down beside him. "Are you still talking to me?"

Aras paused, folded his hands in his lap and looked at her, head still slightly lowered.

"*Oursan* is a sensitive subject for me. I don't handle it well these days."

"I've been told I have all the sensitivity of a lump-hammer. You might have noticed I'm not good at girly things."

"You never asked to be put in this position."

"I know, but I am." If she didn't say it now, she never would. "Let's try it. I mean, we can avoid reproducing, right? Regard it as a favor for a friend. A bit of normality."

Normality. She was twenty-five light-years from home, playing house with an invulnerable alien war criminal and carrying a bizarre parasite that tinkered with her genome when the fancy took it. Just over a year ago she'd packed a bag and set off for a few days' duty at Mars Orbital, expecting to be home by the end of the week, her biggest worry being that the supermarket would deliver early and forget to reset her security alarm.

And now she could never go home again. *Normality.*

"It might not make you happy," said Aras. "There are . . . anatomical issues."

"Oh, I noticed. You got a better idea?"

"Knowing you as I do, I fear you will dislike the emotional changes that come with it."

"Maybe by then I won't care."

Shan stood up and held out her hand. He stood and took it. She thought for a brief moment of the gorilla, with its leather-glove hands signing a plea for rescue that she never understood until it was too late. The dividing line between human and nonhuman had always seemed arbitrary to her until now.

Aras was both sides of that line, and it kept moving.

10

There's a time to take chances and a time to consolidate. This medical technology could simply wipe our competitors off the map. It's worth every resource we can spare to find it, isolate it, and develop it.

And then we can sell it. And I know who'll buy at any price.

Holbein CEO HANA SOBOTKA,
to Board of Directors.

If anyone had any doubt about Dr. Mohan Rayat's true calling, his cabin would have dispelled it immediately.

He had commandeered more comms kit and links than a simple Treasury drone or even a pharmacologist would ever need. And he had his own single cabin.

"How did you pass yourself off as a pharmacologist?" said Lindsay. "You fooled the *Thetis* payload pretty damn well."

"I *am* a pharmacologist," said Rayat. "It's easier to train a scientist to be an intelligence officer than vice versa. And believe me, there's plenty for a scientist to do in the intelligence services."

"I'll bet." Lindsay decided she could always explain away her meeting with him as a shipboard affair. Being caught in the heads with him had at least given her a cover story. But it wasn't one she could use on Eddie Michallat. "Come on. What is it?"

"I don't trust easy," said Rayat. "But you're a professional and I'm desperate. Take a look at this."

Lindsay watched the triptych of screens above Rayat's pull-down desk. There was a 3-D chart and two separate cascades of numbers and telemetry. The projection 15cm in front of the central screen was a part-formed globe with latitude and longitude lines. A crust of colored images was forming on it as if an unseen child were coloring the image in a book.

"What am I looking at?"

"The telemetry from both the original pre-colony bot ship that landed on CS2 and from *Christopher*, the manned colonization vessel that followed it a few years later." Rayat leaned across and tapped the center screen to zoom in on the chart. "And this is Bezer'ej. I think you'll recognize this coastline."

It was a chain of islands. There was Constantine, if she could call the whole island that, partway down the chain. There were six in all, and she discovered for the first time that they had names: Constantine, Catherine, Charity, Clare, Chad, and Christopher. *Saints*. It had never occurred to her to ask during the year that they were down there. They had never been allowed to leave the island.

She could see the small cluster of dots that indicated the colony. But there was another dot emerging on Christopher, the southernmost island in the chain. She wondered if it was some aberrant data from the geophys scans, a trace of one of the isenj cities that the wess'har had annihilated.

LANDING SITE appeared on the screen behind the jigsaw section of globe.

Well, that had to be wrong. She knew where the mission vessel had landed, because it was laid up at Constantine. She hadn't seen it, but Josh Garrod had mentioned it and Ade Bennett was counting on it being there.

"I can't guess," she said at last. "Other than the discrepancy between landing sites."

"Got it," said Rayat.

"An error?"

"No, I don't think so. It would have to be a very large, complex error. This telemetry is clearly about two landings in different places." Rayat prodded the image and it melted around his finger and reformed again. "The bot ship landed—here. It should have built the habitat—here. But the *Christopher* ended up—over here."

"Why?"

"There's something there on the island of Christopher. They switched landing sites, or it was switched for them."

Lindsay thought of the ease with which the wess'har had remotely immobilized *Thetis* in orbit when the ship first came to the Cavanagh's Star system. Diverting a vessel would have been simple for them.

"And what do you think *is* on Christopher Island, then?"

Rayat shrugged. "Biotech research facility. Nice and remote, away from the wess'har homeworld in case things go wrong."

"You're making an assumption that they think like we do. Given their rather negative attitude to our attempt at research activities on the planet, I'd say that's highly unlikely."

Rayat was so conciliatory that it alarmed her more than his usual dismissive manner. He lowered his voice and counted points on his fingers. "One, they can manipulate environments. Two, they can wipe away every trace of millions of isenj and their cities. And three—I don't have to remind you about Frankland's astonishing recovery. Trust me, they're quite capable."

Lindsay wasn't convinced. "Assuming you're right, what are we going to do about it? Walk in? This is a level of incursion we can't back up with firepower."

If Rayat was losing patience with her, he was showing no sign of it. He must have needed her assistance badly. She knew damn well he despised her as a weakling, a cocktail-party officer; but she also knew that Okurt's orders were at odds with his. They were all scrambling for a piece of the biotech action and anxious to stop the other getting it.

"It's a jigsaw," Rayat said. "We know, more or less, what it does. We have a good idea of where it is, apart from being in the tissues of our two chums. So every extra piece of the picture counts."

"And you want some help acquiring it."

"Eddie's a resourceful man."

Lindsay tried very hard to lock her expression. Maybe Rayat knew she had already approached Eddie, but she couldn't imagine how. No, he was just thinking the obvious thing. There was nothing like a neutral journalist as a convenient vector for information.

"He won't spy," she said.

"He just has to do his job as normal. You know how excited reporters get about digging. They're like a dog chasing a car— they love the pursuit, not the capture."

"Actually, I think Eddie's a lot smarter than that."

"You're fond of him."

"He's a friend. And he's good at what he does."

"Are you prepared to co-opt him?"

Lindsay felt a small pang of guilt and then felt very, very clever. *Rayat didn't know she'd already tried.*

"He's got the best chance of all of us of being allowed to land on Wess'ej," she said. "What are you putting into the pot, apart from a vague location?"

"You know what I am. Let's just say I'm untrammeled by rules of engagement."

"I think I know what you mean." *No,* I'll *be the one to shoot her,* Lindsay thought. "Let me think about it."

Rayat displayed no sign of triumph. He just nodded a few times, looking at the screen. Then he picked up his carton of beans and speared the contents with staccato stabs of his fork, seeming genuinely hungry.

"This seems an enormous amount of effort to expend on so little hard evidence," said Lindsay, just testing the water.

"You have no idea how much excitement this damn thing has generated," said Rayat. "And sooner or later, it'll be in the public domain. I—we need to get in and put it out of reach of commerce and foreign governments as early as we can. One contamination, one slip, and God only knows where it might end."

Lindsay met his eyes and tried to work out who was actually behind them. She hadn't traded anything in the conversation: he had revealed plenty.

If he was telling the truth, of course. And she didn't have Shan Frankland's police gut-instinct for spotting the lies among the facts. She'd have to take her chances. It meant using Eddie. It might even mean harming Eddie. It also meant colluding with a man she loathed and mistrusted.

"Deal," she said. "Let's do it."

11

MESSAGE TO: EDDIE MICHALLAT, CSV *Actaeon*
SENDER: Duty News Editor, West European Hub

Eddie, this is great stuff. Keep it coming. Nobody's seen this level of public interest in the space program for decades, maybe centuries. And forget that other matter—not considered in the public interest, if you understand me. Someone upstairs got a security notice slapped on their desk.

I'll see what I can do about your performance-related bonus. Let me get this straight: you want it all to go to the World Forest Project?

Mestin got a message she hadn't been expecting. *Actaeon*'s senior male, the one called Okurt, had sent a request for Eddie Michallat to be allowed to visit Wess'ej. Mestin knew of Michallat. He wasn't a soldier and he wasn't a scientist. She had no idea what use he was to the *gethes*.

The governing matriarchs gathered in the communal kitchen just off the main library, chewing *lurisj*. Nevyan sat with one of her newly inherited children, an *isanket,* on her lap: both of them were watching Shan carefully. Shan had a red glass cup in her hand and was staring down into the contents. She looked very unhappy.

"What's a journalist?" asked Fersanye.

Shan still seemed to be contemplating plunging into the cup. "They find out things and tell everyone about them," she said. "Especially when you don't want them to."

Humans had a strange view of information. Mestin tried to engage Shan's interest. "Like the ussissi."

"That's one way of putting it. Facts are known as news. When new things happen, journalists tell the world about them.

They gather and disseminate information, sometimes accurately, sometimes not."

The concept of not being able—or willing—to relay data objectively was a difficult one for wess'har. Mestin wished Shan would look up. "But should we allow Eddie Michallat to come here?"

"Eddie's good at his job," said Shan. "But he can cause problems. Not always intentionally, but you don't care about motive, do you? It was his asking questions about *c'naatat* that made it public knowledge."

"That doesn't matter. Everyone here knows about it."

"Matters to me," said Shan, in English. "You're not the FEU's most wanted."

"Yes or no?" said Nevyan.

Shan glanced up just for a moment as if she were surprised by Nevyan's tone. "Yes, with conditions. You let me talk to him. You don't have any conversations with him without me present, because you can't lie properly. And we control where he goes in F'nar. I reckon he might be useful. I have no doubt Okurt and company had the same thought, hence my caution."

It seemed an odd catalogue of precautions. Michallat was one unarmed *gethes* who needed a ussissi pilot to land him here and another to transfer him to an isenj vessel to get back to his ship. His capacity for threat seemed limited.

"We can kill him and have done with it if anything seems amiss," said Fersanye.

Shan was still intent on the contents of the cup, from which she was not drinking. There was something very wrong with her. From time to time she wiped her palm across her forehead. She looked red-faced and shiny. "You don't understand how *gethes* use information," she said. "We—they conceal things, so they never have a complete picture of a situation. Information is currency. But you don't understand currency either, do you? It has value. If you have it, you have power and you can exchange it for things you want."

"You know how to use it," said Nevyan.

"I do indeed. There's not a lot of difference between detectives and journalists. Just the warrant card, the pension, and the right to use force."

"What's wrong with your beverage?" asked Mestin.

"It's water," said Shan.

"What else would you drink?"

"A nice cup of tea, proper builders' tea that you can stand the spoon up in." It was an incomprehensible reply, but Mestin thought the ambiguity was small price to pay for her general clarity of thought. Shan sat up and made a *never mind* gesture with her hand. "Eddie might be coming simply to make a program about wess'har. He might also be coming to gather military intelligence, willingly or not, because the military are as adept as police are at using journalists for their own purposes."

"Does Michallat know that?"

"Of course he does. It's all part of the game. But we can play that game too. It's called propaganda. What do you want to achieve?"

"For all *gethes* to leave this sector and to stay away," said Mestin.

"Then you do something called *saber-rattling*. You let him see your armaments and you suggest there are plenty more where they came from. The *gethes* already know you don't lie and you don't bluff."

"But we *would* be lying and bluffing," said Nevyan.

"I know. Good, isn't it? Leave it to me."

Nevyan lowered the *isanket*, Giyadas, to the floor. The child walked briskly over to Shan to stand gazing into her face. It was clear that Shan had no idea what to do with the child and no interest in communicating with her.

Giyadas just wanted to take in every detail of the alien: the *isanket* was responding to Nevyan's intense reaction to her. Shan, defeated by the steady stare, just looked increasingly wretched and began fidgeting. Then those violet lights in her hands started up again, without warning, and Giyadas stood riveted. It was a very impressive show. Even Fersanye was fascinated.

"Oh *shit*," said Shan. "Not again." She looked at her hands as if they were covered in filth and then glanced down at Giyadas. "Show's over, kid," she said, and got up and walked out.

"She can't be ill," said Mestin. It was extraordinary: this female seemed to have no interest in children at all. "*C'naatat* don't develop diseases. I'll talk to her. Nevyan, respond to *Actaeon* and tell them Michallat may land here."

Mestin found Shan sitting outside the house beside a water conduit, one hand trailing in the cool water, staring into the distance. Mestin took care to sit down in the exact pose beside her. She had noticed Shan did the same when she was at ease with someone she was talking to, just like a ussissi. She hoped it would soothe her.

"You look unpleasant," Mestin said. "You seem to be very hot for no reason."

"That's what *c'naatat* does when it's messing you around. I'm under construction."

"You don't look very different."

"It seems to target what troubles you most. Aras obviously had a thing about his external appearance. Seems my problems are all internal." She flexed her hands, sparking visibly violet lights even in the strong sunshine. "I'm sorry if I was offensive."

"Will you be able to deal with Michallat when he arrives?"

"Oh yeah. I can handle Eddie. And I've never fouled up yet—not unintentionally, anyway."

"They'll be able to smell your anxiety across the caldera. What's wrong?"

"Just developing my relationship with Aras."

"Ah, he's upset you. Now take my advice, a quick cuff—"

"No, I'll never raise my hand to him. He's had enough for one lifetime. We just have some logistics problems to iron out."

"I don't understand a word you're saying."

"Good." Shan turned to face her, suddenly very earnest, and

there was a faint waft of dominance coming from her. The ussissi said there was a *gethes* fruit that smelled very similar, called *mango*. Mestin wondered whether Shan realized she could walk into any of the city-states scattered across Wess'ej and take over as dominant matriarch on the strength of that dominance signal alone: but either she didn't know, or she didn't care.

"I'm not at my best right now," said Shan. "I just have a few things to iron out. And I really don't mean to come between you and your daughter. I know it *pisses* you off." Shan dropped the word straight into the middle of the wess'u sentence. Mestin had tried to use some of her unique vocabulary herself, but Shan had said it wasn't a good idea. "I'll talk to her about it if you like."

"Nevyan admires you. Her view of the world is nearer yours than mine. She feels the World Before was not entirely wrong, and that Targassat abdicated responsibility through nonintervention."

"She likes to *kick arse*."

"She's very dedicated to ideas."

"I've been reading up on the World Before. There's not a lot of information, is there?"

"Perhaps the ussissi have more. Ask Vijissi."

"Poor little sod seems terrified of me."

"Then ask his pack female. She won't be."

"If your cousins are what you say they are, you really need to think about talking to them again."

"There will be a price, and that will be involvement in their policies."

"It might be worth paying. You're not the only ones with something to lose from human incursion."

Shan eased herself to her feet as if something was hurting her, smiled unconvincingly and walked off down the terrace. Mestin watched her go, noting that oddly rigid human gait of hers. For a *gethes,* she was an impressive figure, all control and purpose, with a complete confidence she had not lost despite being surrounded by taller, stronger females.

Mestin had come to like her. She accepted her responsibilities. It agitated her to see her own daughter fixing on her for a role model, but there were far worse *isan've* to emulate than Shan Frankland.

In the end, she might be all that stood between Wess'ej and the *gethes*.

It hurt like hell.

But it was hurting less each time, and that gave Shan hope that *c'naatat* was getting the idea that she would keep doing the damage until it repaired her properly and permanently.

She eased herself up on her elbow and tried to ignore the sticky warmth of blood beneath her. There wasn't that much now, not really. It was her brand new mattress she was concerned about.

"I hurt you again," said Aras. "I'm sorry."

"It's not going to kill me, is it?" She didn't want to distress him. For a very big creature, he was doing a credible job of trying to disappear into the *dhren* fabric that served as a sheet. He looked as if he was expecting a slap across the face. Then he turned his back to her, and she wondered for a moment if he was crying, but wess'har didn't have tear ducts, not even an altered wess'har like Aras.

She studied his back. The muscles were not quite as a human's: what would have been the lats inserted much higher in the spine. Down his backbone was a thick dark line with finer stripes radiating from it on both sides, like the markings of an okapi in negative. But it was still an impressive back.

"Come on, buck up," she said, and leaned on his shoulder to make him face her again. His skin felt like sueded silk, with a slight drag against her fingertips, and a little cooler than hers. "It's no big deal."

Aras gave her a look of wounded disappointment, like a parent who had caught a much-loved child stealing. "I know how painful it is."

"I overreact sometimes."

"My nervous system connects to yours. I feel what you feel. Don't lie to me."

"No point faking it, then, eh?"

"Sorry?"

"Stupid joke." She eased herself on to one side and squeezed his hand in hers. "Remember what Ade Bennett used to say—it's only pain."

Aras looked dubious. It was exactly the same expression she had seen on Sergeant Bennett's earnest face, under vastly different circumstances.

"This isn't right," he said.

"Hey, we're from different species. It's a miracle we've got enough matching tackle between us to get this far. It's improving, anyway—the bugs have had to reroute a lot of plumbing." She had no intention of giving up on this now. It was a task: it would be completed, no matter what. "Besides—if you can feel it, it means I've got *oursan* cells now, doesn't it?"

"The more you try to be humorous, the more serious the situation. Remember that *c'naatat* need no *oursan*. Our health doesn't depend on it."

"You want to spend another five hundred years taking cold showers?" Aras had been deprived of everything that made him wess'har. Shan was determined to give something of it back to him. She was the only female who ever could, and that meant she was obliged. "I didn't think so. And I don't think I do either."

He kept his eyes fixed on hers as if he were daring her to say *forget it, this is too painful, too difficult, let's just be friends*. But that was all.

"I must tell you something," he said. "Things burden me, things I have thought but never told you."

"Okay." Well, there was plenty she hadn't told him as well, not yet. *Bioweapons*. "What?"

"I was prepared to kill you back on Bezer'ej when I first told you about *c'naatat*. In case you betrayed me."

Shan shrugged. "I'd have done the same in your position."

"You're not upset?"

"Not at all. I suggested you do it, remember? Anything else?"

Aras paused as if he hadn't expected that answer at all and was scrambling for a new thread. "I'd like to be kissed," he said.

It wasn't what she was expecting to hear either.

"Kissed?" said Shan. There. A rebuke for her impersonal technique. "Seriously?"

"Sometimes I'd see Josh and Deborah kiss when they didn't realize I could see them. It seemed very intimate. Wess'har don't kiss."

Shan reassured herself she'd heard right. As requests for sexual favors went, it was shocking only because it was so harmless. She'd shown a few men the door in her time. They got the wrong idea about a tall, strong girl with handcuffs and a short fuse, and she wasn't into that sort of thing.

She was suddenly so touched by his innocence and desperation that she could feel tears threatening to embarrass her. He really needed someone with a heart. But she'd do the job as best she could. He seemed far more in need of simple intimacy than thrills.

"No problem," she said, humbled.

After a while she nodded off. She still slept during darkness, although her wess'har genes were rapidly turning that into naps. Wess'har didn't sleep continuously. Their not-sleeping kept her awake anyway most nights; F'nar was a natural amphitheater, and the enveloping sound of their randomly busy lives and the occasional yawling tremolo of matriarchs declaring their territories made sure her *c'naatat* got on with the job of reworking her melatonin cycles.

She snapped awake. *Completely* awake. These days she never woke with a stiff shoulder or a fuzzy head or a brief failure to recollect if it was the weekend or not. She woke cleanly and instantly, ready to function. It was still dark and Aras was sitting with his chin resting on his hands, reading from the display that occupied a door-sized chunk of one wall.

"Please look at this," he said, not turning to her.

Shan stood behind him and started reading. The fish-bone diagram was a wess'u summary of concerns raised by ussissi in F'nar and one of the other wess'har city-states, Pajatis. The nonlinear structure of the script felt much more natural now, but she still had to consciously translate each word from the vast wess'har vocabulary she was assimilating. Key words didn't yet leap out and sock her in the eye like a casual glance at an English document would.

But there were still a few phrases on the screen that got her attention fast.

One was *retrieved soldiers from* Thetis.

"Oh shit," she said. There were a lot of things the complex wess'u lexicon didn't stretch to, and expletives were most of them. "I hope that's not what I think it is."

The other phrase that added to the sinking sensation in her gut was *concern among the matriarchs of Pajatis.*

Shan was so occupied with F'nar that she hadn't yet thought to ponder on how the rest of the Wess'ej world felt about the *gethes* situation. She was English again, the center of the empire, and foreigners were just a detail of the landscape. Besides, she knew that F'nar was held responsible for dealing with off-world policy.

But if every city-state was full of Mestins and Chayyases, and they now wanted to have their say, things were becoming a little too interesting.

Aras inhaled her anxiety scent pointedly. "Yes, I was worried by that too."

"If they're recalling Royal Marines, it's not because they're short of cooks," said Shan. She read on, tilting her head this way and that. "Oh Christ. *All* the humans? They've extracted the bloody payload as well?"

"It was foolish to leave the ussissi behind with the isenj. Very foolish. They jump to suspicious thoughts quickly."

"They obviously know us well, then. So where's *Thetis?*"

"Still on course for Earth, apparently."

"I think I'm with the ussissi on this one. There's something really odd about this." She read on, struggling with technical terms. "What's *chak velhanan geth'sir?*"

"Human manifestation in moving light."

"Holograms?"

"Television news."

"Oh my God. Let's see that. Come on."

Shan had watched several days' worth of news from *Actaeon*'s intercepted ITX links home when she arrived, but she had tired of it rapidly. She didn't care what was happening on a planet she could never see again, and there were far more pressing things to deal with in her new world. But that had been a mistake. TV news was her only *snout,* the only informant she had out here. She leaned across Aras and touched the areas of screen that would summon the material that had added to the ussissis' anxiety.

There was plenty of it.

It was mainly protests. Protests always looked the same: they certainly did if you were the one behind the riot shield trying to maintain order. People milled around the grand doorways of embassies, consulates and government buildings, some in tropical climates, some in snow, but they were chanting and stamping and raising their fists about one unifying thing. *Aliens.* And they weren't clamoring to be the first to shake their hands.

"There are many stories from Eddie here about the isenj," said Aras. "I think he's upset people." He leaned back, and Shan could have sworn his expression was one of vindication. "I told you that your people were foolish to take the isenj back to Earth, but I had no idea you would tear yourselves apart without their aid."

"Yeah, I don't think there was global consensus on the invitation somehow." Shan could add up. She added two and two and came up with the same total of ten that the ussissi probably had. The isenj delegation wasn't going to be universally welcome: and so the humans had pulled their own kind off the vessel carrying them.

"If we were stupid enough to blow *Thetis* to Kingdom come, how do you think the ussissi would react?" she asked. She thought of their Beatrix Potter dressed-up-animal charm and their little girly voices and their savage, serious teeth.

"They would react very badly indeed," said Aras. "Every single one of them."

12

The isenj are what they are. I just filmed what was there. I wasn't being selective, I wasn't editing for effect and I wasn't filtering in any way. But what was shown was repellent. I was accused of racism and xenophobia because I gathered news—not even news by any definition, just shots we call GVs, general views—that made humans distrust and dislike the isenj. What responsibility did I have? Should I have selected material that showed them in a light that humans thought of as good? Should I even have attempted to? In the end I just pointed the camera. Our culture isn't ready to admit that we can legitimately dislike difference. Rejecting cultural differences that we can't tolerate is the last taboo among those of us who call ourselves liberals, one that we can't even discuss. It's simple: we don't want to share space with the isenj. Personally, I liked them and I still do. They're very human in many ways. But they'll be the end of our way of life, and that's not something I'm prepared to be shamed into giving up.

EDDIE MICHALLAT's Constantine diaries

Eddie had never been used to sleepless nights. These days he was experiencing them more often, and it wasn't the round-the-clock activity that passed his temporary cabin in *Actaeon*. Today his head was buzzing with the insistent fatigue of insomnia.

I could forget about Hereward.

News would get out sooner or later and absolve him of responsibility for doing something. *I'm not scrabbling around for stories any more: I can sit on it.* He repacked his grip for the third time that morning and checked his hair again. The kid in Environmental Controls hadn't made a bad job of cutting it. Eddie refused to have it clipped as short as a marine's, just as he wouldn't affect paramilitary garments like some wannabe war correspondent. Ade Bennett had called it *looking warry*. He was a *reporter*, for Chrissakes. He had to be clear about that.

But you know about Hereward.

That was the trouble with knowledge and information. It didn't heal and it didn't sort itself out, and even doing nothing with it might have consequences.

And you know it's a bad move.

He really did care what happened here. He couldn't root for the home team because he wasn't sure who the home team was any more, not this far out, and not this unwelcome. And he thought about a couple of paragraphs in a history book on journalism in wartime; he remembered a place called San Carlos Water, from a forgotten war between what had been Britain and Argentina, and there and then he made a choice that was personal rather than professional.

It was the problem with getting older in this game. Your conscience grew like your prostate, an inconvenience that woke you up at night but was seldom serious enough to kill you.

It had taken Eddie a week to get clearance for the trip to F'nar. He suspected that he wouldn't have received it at all had Shan not exerted her influence at one end and Lindsay at the other. That alone told him he was being used. Okurt allowed the ussissi shuttle to dock, only the faintest expression of resentment betraying his reluctance.

"Journos are like children," Eddie told the commander cheerfully. "We get away with murder because nobody thinks we're dangerous."

"Oh, *I* think you're dangerous," said Okurt, and personally dogged the hatch closed behind him.

It was a day for staring and being amazed. Eddie set the bee-cam to divert on any significant movement, and just to be on the safe side he dusted off the manual cam and packed that too. The bee-cam had been fine on Bezer'ej. Any movement in the wilderness that caught its attention was worth filming, but in a city there were too many distractions and he didn't want to spend all his time barking orders to bring it to heel. He'd let it roam.

Being searched by the ussissi pilot on boarding reduced him to helpless giggles, and the bee-cam captured it all. Eddie thought it might make a light piece to end today's package. The pilot watched the cam in that same predatory way that Serrimissani did, then gave him a long stare and went forward to the cockpit.

Eddie slid his hand into his holdall to check that the precious cargo was intact. His fingers slid over three real glass bottles of wine, paper-wrapped amber jaggery sugar, a flask of live yeast, six bars of lavender oil soap and a big bag of tea leaves, some of the roving correspondent's universal currencies that could buy you rescue in any country. Cigarettes rated the highest exchange rate, of course, but spacecraft and illegal combustibles never mixed.

The booty wasn't to placate any locals, even if they had any use for the commodities, but gifts for Shan. He'd missed her. She wasn't the most lovable person he'd ever met but he did enjoy her company, and—privately and perversely—he liked people who couldn't be bought, threatened or flattered, especially by him.

The shuttle landed on an anonymous stretch of stony soil devoid of anything Eddie could recognize as an airstrip. It looked like the middle of nowhere, and he had seen plenty of nowheres with more infrastructure than this. A wess'har male was waiting for him. The creature was pacing round a vehicle that looked like a futon wearing a valance. It didn't inspire confidence.

Eddie glanced at the departing ussissi, who was still keeping an eye on the bee-cam. At least he didn't hang around for a tip.

He followed the driver's lead and sat on the futon. It shaped itself up round him: the flapping valance became a rigid hovercraft skirt. He felt better already. The vehicle skimmed alarmingly over rocks and hummocks, and what looked like soft sage-colored moss rolled underneath him in dry waves. There was no road that he could see.

"We go overland because of pictures," the wess'har driver said, like two voices were talking at once. "We build roads underneath, so nothing to picture. Understand?"

"Fine," said Eddie. "Thanks." The bee-cam hovered happily, immune to the swoops and climbs of the vehicle as it swept along in an unnatural quiet. The wess'har's openness took him aback. He'd known too many human minders over the years whose main goal had been to stop him recording anything at all, an aim often reinforced by a gun. "Can I film anything I want?"

"If your eyes can see it, you can make images."

"I love this place already."

They were skimming between larger clumps of vegetation now, not trees but growths that looked like huge yellow bromeliads, gold and fleshy and covered with crawling things that were striped in red and white. The land rose gently ahead. The vehicle slowed to walking pace and then it rested on the ridge.

"You look, *gethes*. Look now."

"Wow. Oh *wow*. Sweet Jesus H. Christ."

The city of F'nar nearly blinded Eddie.

It was beauty made solid. The color and the light and the sheer impossibility of it took his words away and he almost fell out of the passenger seat to stand and stare.

He'd have to redo the soundtrack later. He didn't want to sound like a tourist.

"F'nar," said the driver. "*Shan Chail* said you say *fuck me* when you see it, you be so amazed."

"How long have you been speaking English?"

"Four days."

"Well, I say *fuck me,* then." He checked that the bee-cam was equally riveted by the view and got out the hand cam, just to be doubly sure of getting those first shots. "The City of Pearl indeed."

The vehicle could take Eddie no further than the center of

F'nar. He stood at the bottom of the caldera and stared up at row upon row of terraces dotted with vegetation, an inside-out ziggurat or hanging garden: the pearl coating iced almost every surface. He was fresh out of words. He followed his wess'har minder and started to climb the terraces, trying to nod politely at any wess'har whose disturbing patterned eyes he caught.

It was typical of Shan to be living as far from the center as it was possible to get. Eddie, leg muscles screaming for a rest, paused for breath outside an iridescent door set in a wall of ashlars whose irregular lines were almost obscured by the ubiquitous pearl-pebbled coating. It eased open.

"Eddie," she said. "Just in time for tea."

Shan, filling the doorway, looked well. She looked different somehow, and even more dauntingly athletic than he remembered, but she still looked fundamentally human. Eddie held out his arms to hug her. It was an instinctive gesture, but she didn't move.

"I'm not after any epithelial cells," he said, remembering.

"I'm sure you're not." But she didn't concede even a restrained embrace. He had no doubt he would be screened before departing. If they didn't, he'd ask them to. He didn't want to be the vector for any more catastrophic change in human society. Aras was arranging bowls and food on a table, and gave him a respectful nod. He didn't look happy to see him, but then it was hard to tell with the wess'har. He was a grim, quiet, frighteningly large creature.

Eddie smiled anyway, and opened his holdall and pulled out the *efte* fiber bag of rare gifts. "Look, Shazza—wine, soap, and enough yeast and sugar to get some brew going," he said proudly. "And *tea*."

She didn't smile and he wasn't sure if he'd gone too far by letting one of his many nicknames for her slip out. At least he hadn't called her *Genghis* to her face. Then she grinned, almost girlish. "Thanks. I can't get drunk, but you'll never know how welcome that tea is."

"Ha, you're not pregnant, are you?"

"Not even slightly funny, Eddie."

Whoops. He switched fast. "Nice sofa. Isn't white going to get grubby, though?"

She did laugh then, and Eddie was relieved if puzzled. Aras gave him a sympathetic look. "She'll explain later," he said.

Eddie followed Shan out onto a terrace that wrapped round the cliffside. He forced himself to look away from the dazzling cityscape: how quickly could he get to the main point of his visit? There were ways of imparting sensitive information and Shan could grasp the oblique as well as anyone. He just wanted to get it over with.

"This is just the most amazing view I've ever seen in my entire life."

"Beautiful, isn't it?" She still seemed wary. "It's insect shit."

"Sorry?"

"The nacreous coating. It's a deposit left by little buzzy things. Not real insects, of course, but it's what fills the niche here."

"Shit doesn't look that good on Earth."

"Yeah, I thought that too."

"So you're okay, then."

"Yeah. Great."

"Good." They sat down on the ledge that ran round the terrace and Eddie leaned back against the wall, not caring whether it was feces or the finest creation of Ottoman tile-makers. It stunned him with excitement.

Shan had her arms folded loosely across her chest, sleeves rolled back. Light flickered. He glanced over his shoulder to see what was making the reflection dancing on her hands, and then he realized there was nothing, not even that fabulous city below, that was causing it. The light was *in* her hands, under the skin.

"Oh Christ," he said, and stared.

"It's really handy when you can't find your keys." She looked resigned. "And every copper needs their own blue flashing light, eh?"

"What is it, for God's sake?"

"Bioluminescence."

"Does it go with the recovery from fatal head wounds?"

"All part of the package. But let's not talk about it right now."

He struggled for calm. He had more pressing matters, that was true. "Can we get the interview over with first? Then we can socialize."

"Ask away. Don't be offended if I tell you to sod off." She said it with a smile. "Nothing personal. You're all right, son."

He grabbed the bee-cam out of the air beside him and stuffed it in his pocket to make his point. *I'm not recording this. Trust me.* Her gaze followed his hand. He really didn't want to say out loud that he was doing this as a favor. That would have been amateurish.

"Just one question, Shan. Any comment on the fact that the FEU has diverted the *Hereward* to Cavanagh's Star? I might eventually ask the same question of the isenj, because they're unaware too." He couldn't believe he was sacrificing a story for a second time. He was going soft. But he had made his decision. "I also hear there may be a few more to follow."

Shan closed her eyes. It was a few seconds before she spoke. He sneaked another look at her hands. The lights had stopped.

"If you're pissing me about, Eddie, you know what I'll do, don't you?"

"I've nothing to gain from this."

"You're sure?"

"Unimpeachable source."

"Okurt, maybe?"

"No. Someone much lower down the food chain."

"And why are you telling me?"

"Because I think it's a provocative act and I think it's wrong."

"Shit," she said, and closed her eyes again. He knew it was a hot story, but he hadn't expected her to react quite so strongly. "Fucking idiots. And you want what, exactly?"

"Not to make matters worse than they are."

Shan got up and made as if to pat him on the shoulder, but

stopped short. He had expected bright anger: instead she looked suddenly exhausted. "There goes my retirement again," she said. "You haven't broadcast this yet, have you? We would have heard."

"I'm not sure if I ever will."

"When will you tell the isenj?"

"I have no idea. I hadn't thought that far ahead."

"So what *do* you want in exchange?"

"I'm not trading favors, Shan. I really thought you all had a right to know."

"And I don't know how else to say thanks."

Eddie smiled weakly. It was hard being instrumental in history. But he had blown the secret now. He had to live with the consequences.

"It was the Falklands," he said.

"Eh?"

"Nothing. Nothing at all."

Shan gave him exactly fifteen more seconds and then said, "Excuse me for a while." She disappeared into the house and a few moments later Aras came out with a tray of bowls and cups and sat down pointedly next to Eddie. It was compulsory hospitality: he wasn't going anywhere for the time being.

Aras held out a cup to Eddie with an unfathomable expression. He held it in both hands, and Eddie could see that he had claws. The sun was full in his face: the irises of his otherwise charcoal-black eyes revealed not those weird four-lobed wess'har pupils, but single and almost reassuring oval ones. Eddie had never looked at him that closely before. And he'd never been alone with him, never with the alien between him and the only exit.

"Please, make yourself at home," said the Destroyer of Mjat, and handed him a cup of tea.

From the seat of the hover, the ussissi village looked like a nest of eggs half buried in the soil. The fact that Shan had been told to meet the matriarchs here and not in F'nar told her that they were making some concession to the ussissi. That meant there was trouble brewing.

But as crisis summits went, this was a fine venue for one. Shan could see the perfect Easter eggs of domes as she approached, and they were Fabergé eggs, all brilliant color and intricacy. One flashed turquoise as she passed; another was fuchsia and silver, the next purple and ochre, a mass of swirls and dots and curves like the most extravagant paisley fabric. There were ussissi working on one and she turned to stare.

The creatures stared back. It was now impossible for her to break that meerkat association. They stopped as one, and they stared as one, and then they went back to shaping a new dome, paws—no, hands—working furiously to shape the wet plaster, pushing forward with staccato motions. She had no idea what supported that plaster, but she would find out.

"You don't come from this planet either, do you?" Shan said.

Vijissi was standing on the flatbed of the hover, nose pointed into the breeze with an expression of catlike satisfaction. "No, we also come from the World Before. They have always needed us, and we them. We dig, you see. We still do. Once we dug into hills and they would use the holes we left. Sometimes we would unearth tubers, and they liked those. We coexisted and they kept us safe and found water for us. Agreeable." He snapped his head round and focused on something on the ground. "Ah, we stop."

Vijissi slowed the hover down and stopped short of the row of fantasy eggshells. He leaped down and paddled around in the soil with his hands, then straightened up, clicking enthusiastically.

"Are you doing what I think you're doing?" Shan said. He looked like he had a handful of dates. They didn't grow dates here. And they were struggling.

"It is a courtesy not to do this in front of wess'har. You know how they feel about eating flesh." He paused to palm the handful into his mouth. Now she knew why they had those perfect little needle teeth. "But we have to eat certain proteins, and they do not."

"Lovely," said Shan. "Still, no human's in a position to criticize. At least they're free-range." *I never had to think about this sort of stuff when I was walking a beat.* Travel did broaden the mind.

For all its decorative beauty—and Shan was surprised that the wess'har tolerated that degree of visibility—the village was faintly medieval. There were no hardtop roads: that would have meant paving over lovely, diggable soil as well as disfiguring the natural environment. Vijissi parked the hover under a huge overhang of fleshy plant growth that looked much like an aloe plant that had been overdoing the steroids.

"Not very Targassat," said Shan, nodding in the direction of the vivid collection of roofs.

"Temporary," said Vijissi. "They'll decompose by the end of the summer. Mind your head." He held his arm out rather formally in the direction of an impossibly small opening of a very fine slate-blue egg dome. Shan tried crouching to get in and then gave up and crawled through on her hands and knees. Having four legs allowed ussissi to keep their hands free very easily. She envied them as she got to her feet and found herself walking down into a depression not unlike a Bronze Age roundhouse but with much classier textiles. Domes or not, they were still warren-dwellers like the wess'har.

The smooth vault of ceiling was as exquisitely decorated inside as out, and the floor, studded completely with small colored stones and beads, was dappled with kaleidoscope patterns of light from small perforations in the roof. Apart from the floor cushions and the ubiquitous wess'har console, there was no visible concession to high technology.

Shan thought it all looked like a bugger to clean.

She crawled after Vijissi through another ussissi-height opening and found herself on all fours staring eye-to-eye with F'nar's most senior matriarchs. There were other wess'har females she didn't know and ussissi seated on cushions or kneeling around a table that looked like a bale of scarlet fabric.

Even Chayyas was there. She met Shan's eyes without the

slightest hint that anything had ever passed between them. She seemed almost glad to see her.

"We are very disturbed by your news," said Prelit. Shan had met her before, when she sought asylum in F'nar.

"Well, you've got twenty-five years to mull it over," said Shan, and tried to scramble into a sitting position on the floor with as much dignity as she could. She crossed her legs and they all stared at her. It seemed only humans could do that. "Could we do the introductions?"

"I don't understand."

"Who are you all?"

Mestin indicated *isan've* to either side of her, equally fearsome-looking females but wearing very different clothing—a velvety purplish-black tunic, a heavy beige wrap, a saffron and lemon collection of layered waistcoats. It said they weren't from round here, even if they were still all the same amber chess pieces.

"Imeklit from Iussan, Hachis from Cekul'dnar, and Bur from Pajatis," said Mestin.

"We're concerned about F'nar's handling of this," said Imeklit. Shan had long since given up expecting a how-do-you-do from a wess'har. "We want to be involved in the solution. I don't understand why time is an issue. It is a threat: all threats are now."

"So what do you think's happening?" Shan asked.

The wall of grim and unamused sea horse faces stared back at her. Their heads tilted at different degrees, but all their pupils had synchronized in that four-petaled flower that told her they were trying very hard to take her in. It might have been the lights sparking sporadically from her fingertips. Then again, it might have been fear and mistrust of an alien whose kin looked set on conflict.

"I'm not playing *gethes* word-games with you," Shan said. *Remember, they respect outspokenness.* "I want to know what you think and what information you have, in case I don't have all the facts."

It was one of the ussissi who spoke, a female with a black braided web of belts strung round her. "I'm Bisatilissi." She was leaning slightly forward on her four legs, as if she were going to spring. "Your people have abandoned mine on that ship. We think you have taken yours off so they won't be killed when you destroy us and the isenj. Now you secretly send other ships without asking permission. It's clear that you plan to attack us."

Who's in charge here, Mestin, you or the hired help? Shan didn't think that degree of candor would help matters. "I can see why you'd think that," she said. "First of all, they're not my people. I'm stuck here with you and I have a *jurej* who's one of you. I don't know why they've done what they've done, but I can find out, and then you'll have more information to make your decisions."

"And you're confident you can find things out, are you, *gethes*?" said Bisatilissi. "Why should we believe what you tell us?"

They weren't all diplomatic like Vijissi, then. *Time to raise the game.* It was a damn shame wess'u was so short on profanities. "Oh, I can get answers out of anybody, *sweetheart*," said Shan. "And you don't know a thing about me, so here's the first *fucking* lesson. You call me *gethes* one more time and I will come over there and cause you intense physical pain. Do you understand all the words in that sentence?"

Shan looked at the teeth. It was hard not to. Bisatilissi leaned ever so slightly further onto her front feet, and Shan noted with a sinking heart that every other ussissi in the room had done the same. Too late now: she put her hands on her hips, her right hand ready to draw her gun. *I'll survive. More or less.*

"You are a very confrontational person," the ussissi said, not conceding an inch.

But she didn't say *gethes*. "Yeah, and don't forget I'm *c'naatat* too. Fancy your chances?"

Shan had no idea how ussissi would attack but her instinct told her it would be a character-forming experience if they did. But she didn't care. She would *not* be challenged. She was sud-

denly angry to the point of lashing out. Then wess'har and ussissi alike inhaled as if they had smelled the same thing at the
same time, which of course they had. Shan had outscented them
again without consciously trying.

Bisatilissi settled back slowly on her haunches and the rest
of them followed suit. "If you apply your aggression for
Wess'ej, we will have no argument."

"Count on it," said Shan. "And you can call me Superintendent. I'll go back and see what my human contact has to tell
me. Then I'll relay that to you."

Shan nodded politely and walked out into the compound.
She felt suddenly and completely wonderful. *I'm c'naatat.* She
could do what she had to do and not fear the physical consequences. She had the *time* to do what she wanted to do. She
had the *physiology* to do it. She could make a difference, a real
difference.

And they needed her to do it.

"Whoa, nice one!" she said to herself, smiling at the
thought. "Back in harness again." And she was still savoring the
idea of being thoroughly equipped for her task in life when
Mestin emerged with Vijissi.

"You're starting to realize the power you have," said Mestin,
and smelled irritated. "*You* might not come to any harm, but
think of what might happen to others."

"I've spent my whole career doing that. And I do know about
responsibility."

"Yes, you do. I merely counsel caution."

"Thanks. Point taken."

"I will talk to Eddie Michallat with you."

"You can watch, that's all. I do the interviewing."

"But—"

"Mestin, I do the interviewing. I'm good at it. Okay?"

Mestin said nothing. They got in the hover and Vijissi drove
them back towards F'nar. The spangled and glossed and rainbow-
bright temporary egg domes shrank in the distance.

Shan inhaled the fragrances on the air and realized three

things had happened that day. She had actually started to enjoy *c'naatat:* she had rebuilt her status and reputation anew in an alien society: and she had openly acknowledged Aras as her *jurej.*

She hadn't even thought before saying it. It felt comfortable. It was something she could get used to. She decided to let the bizarre hormonal loyalties of *oursan* make the best of a bad job.

Eddie and Aras were still on the terrace when Shan and Mestin joined them. Eddie seemed completely absorbed by the view of the city. The sun was setting and the pearl coating had taken on a peach luminescence that was exquisite. Shan was getting used to that too.

"Great toilet, Shan," Eddie grinned. There were empty cups standing around: Aras had clearly attempted to placate Eddie with the same substance that he knew worked wonders on her. Eddie's eyes were on Mestin, which wasn't surprising for someone who had never seen a matriarch close up before. She obviously beat the lights in Shan's hands for novelty appeal. "This is just breathtaking."

"Make the most of the lavatory," Shan said. "You won't enjoy the local version." She held her hand out to indicate Mestin. "This is a civic leader of F'nar, Mestin Tliat Jasil." The indefinite article still sounded odd: Shan was used to a fixed hierarchy, *the* leader, *the* chief, *the* Guv'nor. "I thought it might help if she heard what you had to say."

Eddie held out his hand and Mestin actually took it, although she had never seen a handshake and so just gripped his fingers with an intensity that showed on his face. Shan bit back a smile. It was rather sweet. It was just sad that they had to meet under such desperate circumstances.

"I have made a meal," said Aras, with a sigh in his voice that suggested he had been waiting longer than he liked. "Shall we eat now?"

They sat at the table. Aras, familiar with human digestion,

had made two sets of dishes, one with ingredients imported from Constantine and one for wess'har tastes. Shan peered at the bowls and plates, pleased to be able to eat both with impunity. Aras leaned across her to place a bowl in front of her and sniffed audibly.

"You have been in a fight," he said stiffly.

"Yeah, and I won," she said, and grinned up at him. Then she realized Eddie was watching her, and killed the smile in case he thought she was going girly.

"I'd like to wash my hands first," Eddie said, and went to the washroom. The assault of cup after cup of tea was having its impact.

As soon as the sound of running water smothered their voices, they talked in low tones.

"Have you been talking to him, Aras?" asked Shan.

"You told me not to engage in current conversation. So I told him about Mjat. That's long past and has no information he could use."

"Anything else?"

Aras stared at her, and she could have sworn he was hurt. "You told me not to reveal anything current to him, *isan,* and I followed your orders completely."

"That's okay." *Isan.* She'd let it go. "Just asking."

Mestin was watching the flow of conversation between Shan and Aras like a tennis umpire. "Ah, you cuffed him, then," she said.

"No, and I never will," Shan said sharply. Aras didn't break his gaze. "He's my *oppo.* It's not like that at all."

There was no reason why any wess'har should have understood that archaic English word, but it tumbled out and Shan wasn't ashamed. He was her buddy, her partner, the bloke she worked with. There was no stronger attachment, neither love nor even the sexual relationship that had now improved immeasurably. Whatever he was, or she was, he was her complete equal, and she had never found one before in her life. It felt safe. She wasn't alone any more.

Eddie sat down at the table, still bouncing with enthusiasm. He reached for his glass.

"Do you want to get the next bit over with so you can drink the wine without worrying?" said Shan.

"The next bit being?"

"I ask you questions. Don't struggle and it won't hurt."

"I'm all yours."

Eddie knew the game. Shan knew he knew the game. It was just like old times, and she opened with a concession that was also a flush question. "Okay, the ussissi think *Actaeon* took the payload and the Booties off *Thetis* because humans are planning to blow her up with the aliens on board." She had learned to use the feminine gender for ships now. "They're well fucked off about it."

Eddie's face told her all she wanted to know. It was complete lack of comprehension, the tiniest of flash-frowns and a single quick movement of the eyes. "Christ," he said. "That's not it at all. Not what I heard."

"They just made an intuitive leap from the reaction back home to your reports, Eddie." Shan knew him now: she knew him because he had not broadcast her frank admission about involvement with Green Rage, nor the isenj information on *c'naatat*. And he had regretted accusing her of being a paid biotech mule. She knew that he felt guilt. Guilt was sometimes as effective as a good kicking when it came to getting answers, and a lot less trouble. "They're suspicious. Wouldn't you be?"

"Okurt extracted the payload and the marines to see if they'd caught a dose of your disease. What's it called? *C'naatat*. Big bucks, top priority."

"Oh dear," said Shan. She started eating. "And now they'll hear that *Hereward* is steaming this way."

"And it's all my fault?"

Mestin cut in. She should have known better than to interrupt. "You didn't launch the ship. You didn't remove the *gethes*. Others are responsible."

Shan's scalp tightened instantly and she turned her coldest

stare on Mestin, who clearly smelled that the interruption was out of order. She froze. Shan, satisfied that she was still running this interrogation and that Mestin knew her place as bagman, turned back to Eddie.

"As I was saying, they're stoked up and they feel very threatened, and so do the wess'har. They don't react well to threats. Ask the isenj."

"*Hereward* will take twenty-five years to get here. We've got time to talk it out."

"You don't understand how these people think, Eddie. They have one switch. Either they're chilled or they're punching. They have a lovely phrase for it. 'Threat is now.' They react immediately, even if it's a long way off."

"What are you telling me?"

"Serious shit time, Eddie." Shan groped for something smart but fell back on cliché, because clichés were all too often the truth. "It's war."

He made a heroic job of trying to look as if his dish of penne with rocket pesto was far more important than the revelation that humankind had fallen into conflict with a species that erased entire cities and took good care of their friends.

"Me and my big mouth," he said at last.

"You only altered the timing, Eddie. At least there's breathing space."

"You think that I don't give a shit as long as I get a story."

"No, I think you care too much." Shan paused. She almost felt bad doing it to him: he was a good bloke. "And there's one more thing they need to factor in back home. The World Before."

Aras, who knew better than to interrupt his *isan* in full flow, froze too. Both he and Mestin looked like those annoying street mime artists who posed as statues to startle passersby.

"This isn't going to be good news, is it, Shan?" said Eddie.

"No. There's an original wess'har homeworld where they do things a bit differently. The wess'har here are just like the Bible-bashers in Constantine—the harmless dropouts. No, it's not good at all."

Eddie put his twin-tined glass fork down on the table with a sharp *clack*, penne momentarily forgotten and congealing.

"I'm not bluffing," said Shan. "I'll show you some interesting locations later. You're welcome to film."

"I didn't think you were," said Eddie.

"Okurt asked you to share information on your return, no doubt."

"And what are *you* asking for?"

"The same, of course. I'll understand if you won't spy. But it's a matter for you. You know what's at stake."

It was an onion, layer upon layer, both of them aware that the other knew that this was an elaborate game of manipulation, veneer on veneer. The first one to the innermost layer was the winner.

It was Shan.

It always was: except for that one time when a minister's sister had maneuvered her into siding with ecoterrorists and set her on a path that eventually marooned her 150 trillion miles from home.

Eddie returned to his dish of penne.

"Okay," said Eddie. "Show me."

13

TO: *Chancellor's PPS, Central Treasury, Federal European Union*
FROM: Undersecretary, Federal Intelligence

RESTRICTED
Dr. Rayat's priority must be to deny this biological agent both to the commercial concerns on board and to defense personnel. There has been some disagreement over your modeling methods, but all our forecasts confirm that the economic impact of a declining death rate would be felt within two years, initially through pressure on pensions. That presupposes that there is not serious economic fallout in the stock and currency markets were the agent to become commercially available. While we realize the Defense Ministry is not a commercial concern, there is still an unacceptably high risk that the agent would spread into the wider population. Rayat has authorization to take whatever steps he feels are appropriate to prevent this agent from contaminating the human population.

In the Exchange of Surplus Things, sitting on crates of fruit or standing silently against walls, the matriarchs of forty city-states waited for Mestin and Shan to find a place among them and make their case.

Shan stood a little to the front of Mestin with her hands clasped behind her back, head slightly bowed, spectacularly alien in that matte black uniform. Blue and violet lights reflected on the back of her garment from her hands: everyone had heard about her strange *c'naatat* adaptations.

Matriarchs and ussissi stared at her. Her smooth black hair was exotically unusual in a sea of gold and amber, and Mestin heard a distant comment that it was hard to tell the creature's gender by sight. She wore her hair long like a male and she was a head shorter than a female.

If you were within scent range of her, you'd know, thought Mestin. She hoped nobody would provoke Shan to anger and unleash that dominance pheromone of hers again: it would cause chaos, and that was one thing they could not afford right now.

Mestin draped her *dhren* carefully so that it flowed round her arms and formed a long-sleeved tunic. It was curious how Shan admired what she called the *opalescence* of the fabric and yet shied away from wearing it: she said she didn't have the build to carry it off, whatever that meant. Mestin wondered if she herself had the defensive spirit, the *jask*, to carry off a decision to take F'nar—and with it Wess'ej—into a state of war with a new enemy.

She looked around. There were nearly a thousand small cities scattered across the planet, and if their matriarchs were not present, they would be watching and hearing through the communications network anyway.

Vijissi had settled near Shan, sitting back on his haunches. She shifted a little, as if to keep at constant distance: he shuffled a little closer each time. He was taking his instruction to look after her very seriously. Mestin suspected he liked her more than he would admit.

"We will bar Bezer'ej to the *gethes* for all time," Mestin said. "*Shan Chail* has provided sufficient tissue for us to create a biological deterrent that will confine itself to *gethes*. We will seek a similar deterrent for the isenj, because we may now have a source, and then we can remove the Temporary City to leave the bezeri in peace."

In her peripheral vision, Mestin noted that Shan's head had jerked up a fraction and then fallen again. She was surprised by something. Mestin would ask her later.

"What will you do with the *gethes* already on Bezer'ej?" asked Bur of Pajatis.

"We'll offer them a chance to resettle here in a controlled environment," said Shan. "They're harmless."

"And if they refuse?"

Mestin saw that Shan had her fingers meshed tightly behind her back. But there was no scent at all, just the sporadic violet lights. "Then they'll die," she said calmly.

"We offer troops if landings and military action becomes necessary," said Bur. "We all will."

Then they simply began leaving the hall. Shan seemed baffled and turned to Mestin. "Is that it?"

"Did you expect more?"

"I thought a war summit might take more than a few minutes."

"There is consensus," Mestin said. "Beyond detail, there normally is."

"We never get past the detail," said Shan.

They were alone with the surplus produce in the hall, except for a male who was stacking pallets of yellow-leaf. It was a record harvest this year.

"What did I say that surprised you?" Mestin said.

"That you had a source of isenj DNA." She simply didn't smell of anything other than that alien musk, and that was softened by her newly acquired wess'har scent. Her voice seemed tight somehow. Some of the overtones were inaudible.

"I thought you might ask Eddie Michallat, seeing as he has easy access to Umeh."

"Ah." That *gethes* breath of sound that implied anything from amusement to disgust. "*Okay.*"

"Is there a problem?"

"I can't see Eddie agreeing to collect tissue samples, or even how he's going to do it, but I'll ask anyway."

"Have you told Aras about this?"

"Not yet. But if he's on the network, he'll know now, though, and I'm going to have a very difficult conversation with him."

"How are relations between you? He seems content."

"Pretty good," said Shan. "At least they were. I'll know when I get home."

"Why did you not mention it to him?"

"Because I knew he would be concerned about his friends in Constantine, and that he didn't approve of bioweapons, and that he would probably have influenced my decision."

"You don't seem a person who is easily persuaded."

"You don't know how much I want him to be happy," said Shan, and gave Mestin one of those odd, tight-lipped smiles that weren't smiles at all. They were quite the opposite.

She was still flashing sporadic violet light as she walked out of the hall. Mestin could have sworn she saw a faint burst of yellow-green as well.

But she didn't smell of anything at all.

Aras had taken Eddie to the underground bunkers as Shan had told him to, and had also made a great effort to say nothing that might indicate there was not an infinite supply of armaments. Eddie was very satisfied with the pictures he got. The scale and perspective of the tunnels delighted him. He seemed to enjoy making images attractive.

Eddie's bee-cam flitted everywhere, recording the craft and machinery. Shan had said there was nothing on them that could provide the *gethes'* military analysts with the slightest information they could use to defeat them. Aras was not used to wars where enemies didn't know what the opposing force intended, possessed, or thought. He kept his counsel.

"Bloody hell," said Eddie. "Has every city got something like this?"

"Yes," said Aras. It was true. He didn't have to volunteer the fact that they feared it would still not be enough.

"Can you fly these things?"

"That one," said Aras. He put his hand on the airframe of the fighter and the canopy parted.

Eddie made a sharp sucking sound and pressed his fingers against his ears.

"I flew one on Bezer'ej, and I crashed in one, which is how I came to fall into the hands of the isenj."

"I know what they did to you, Aras. I'm sorry. I don't know what to say."

"There's nothing to say."

"They don't seem a sadistic people, but who's to tell?"

"It was five hundred years ago. What were your kind doing to each other then?"

Eddie looked as if he were calculating, eyes focused on an imaginary point above him. "The 1800s." He shrugged. "To be honest, we're still torturing each other now, so it's not a valid question. Do you feel a little more forgiving of them, then?"

Aras had no inclination to forgive. It seemed irrelevant to his wess'har side and undeserved to his human one. He wondered how he could deal with the painful realization that Shan had not told him she had cooperated on bioweapons. "I don't forgive. The isenj might have changed. But I can only judge by their actions, and at the moment, they still breed to destruction, and they will still do the same on Bezer'ej. So I will still kill them to stop them doing so. Was that your question?"

"You don't regret Mjat."

"It was unpleasant, but I would do it again under the same circumstances, just as you would attack those who caused death and suffering to your own allies."

"I'm not judging you, Aras. Just asking."

"Humans always judge." Aras had cut Eddie some slack, as Shan put it, by not calling him *gethes*. He rather liked Eddie, even though he had that flat, bitter odor common to flesh-eating creatures. Perhaps he had started to get in the habit of granting forgiveness where none was deserved.

"What about revenge?" Eddie asked.

"That's not the same as balance."

"A matter of degree?"

"Probably. I think you call it reasonable force."

"There are many humans who would find your force against the isenj unreasonable."

"Then they should talk to the bezeri. They numbered billions before the isenj came. Their population has only recovered to a few hundred thousand or so now. They breed slowly. They spawn in only a few places around the island chain and they won't change that, even though it makes them vulnerable." It was another reason why Parekh had deserved to die: the dead infant was a rare and precious being. He didn't have to justify that to Eddie Michallat. "But don't feel obliged to suppress the story. Your people should be told what we did to the isenj. They need all the facts."

Eddie gave him a careful look, and Aras wondered if he thought he might be indulging in what Shan called *propaganda*. The best translation she could come up with was fact-weapon, or, more probably, lie-weapon. But this was completely true. It was merely the timing that made it effective.

"If the bezeri are that intelligent, why don't they just spawn somewhere else away from landmasses?" Eddie asked.

"They value place," said Aras. "I could have shown you a map made long before I came here, a map of sand compressed between two sheets of *azin* shell. Why do maps matter to them? Because they can only exist in certain parts of the ocean, in certain mineral concentrations. If you can't manipulate your environment, then you must work with it. There are other places they could go, just a few, but these are their spawning grounds and this is where they choose to congregate."

"I just wondered if they could move. It's not very smart, choosing a situation that makes you vulnerable."

"And that would justify their fate?"

"No, but if you can just change your behavior and avoid a lot of grief—"

"I seem to recall humans do stupid things that make them vulnerable every day. They consume things they know will hasten their deaths and they live in places they know are likely to be stricken by disaster. Perhaps that justifies their fate too."

"Now that you put it in those terms, I see my error."

"Don't mock me, Eddie."

"I didn't mean to. It's just very harsh."

"Do you blame *Ailuropoda melanoleuca* for being wholly reliant on bamboo?"

"What?"

"The black and white bear you find so appealing. The panda."

"Not at all. Bloody tragic. We destroyed their habitat. It's not as if they had any choice."

"Actually, they are capable of eating small animals, and do. Nobody blames them for having evolved into a very restricted niche. Perhaps that's because they're pretty and their image makes fine toys, whereas the bezeri remind you of an item on the menu."

"Hey, I didn't make the rules."

"And why *do* humans encourage their children to love other creatures in an iconic form, and then to abuse them in the flesh?"

"You've lost me, mate."

"Animal toys. I remain confused by that habit."

"You ask too many hard questions," said Eddie. "And coming from a journalist, that's high praise."

They walked back up to the surface and wandered through the fields. Eddie tripped over a *genadin* and it fled while he tried to track it with his camera. It was a pleasant evening. *Tem* flies danced over a sun-baked rock, laying another coating of pearl.

"Can I ask you something personal, Aras?"

"And Mjat wasn't?"

"I mean about you and Shan. Are you two an item now?"

"What does that mean?"

"Are you dating?" he smiled. Aras realized he was teasing kindly, innocently. "Playing house?"

"If you are asking if I'm *fucking* her, yes. That's the right word, isn't it? She's my *isan* and I'm bonded to her. And I'm happy to be so."

"Shitty death," said Eddie, face fallen, all shock. "You and *her*?"

"Simple congratulations would suffice. That, or a set of attractive wineglasses, according to Shan."

Eddie looked uncertain whether to laugh or not. Aras enjoyed playing that verbal game with humans. They never knew if he was being naively literal or making a joke at their expense. Sometimes he wasn't sure himself.

"What's this thing you're both carrying, then?"

"A parasite."

"What?"

"Perhaps it's best described as a symbiont."

"Not biotech?"

"We didn't create it, if that's what you mean." He thought of Shan, and what she had done, and judged that a bit of *saber-rattling* was in order whether he liked it or not. He didn't enjoy these mind-games; Shan was a master at it. He did his best, without lying. "We can create biological weapons, but this was not one of them."

"I do fully understand what the risks are if it gets into the human population."

"I think understanding that and not being tempted by it are entirely different states of mind."

"How is Shan coping with it?"

"She was angry. Now she has come to terms with it. It's much easier to accept when there are two of you."

"They're hell-bent on getting hold of it, Aras."

"They can't. It exists in me, and it exists in Shan, and *Actaeon* has access to neither of us. It's an organism native to an isolated part of Bezer'ej—and you have no access there either."

"I hope not," said Eddie. "You know they even wanted to exhume Lin's kid to check him out for it?"

Aras hissed to himself, and then wondered how *Actaeon*'s people imagined they could take on the wess'har defenses and reach the plain outside Constantine where he had set the stained glass headstone to mark David Neville's tiny grave.

The isenj had landed, and he had cut them down. The last landing had nearly cost his *isan* her life.

He had no intention of letting invaders touch the soil of Bezer'ej again. He decided Shan might have felt the same way.

She should still have told him.

Actaeon's armory was aft of the habitat section and Lindsay needed Okurt's security approval to enter it on her own.

He handed the manual key-stick over to her with a sullen expression. "Here," he said. "I've even cleared the weapons technicians out. Rayat's boss's boss has spoken to my boss's boss so I'm playing nice. But let me tell you I think it stinks."

Lindsay wasn't cut out for this *keeny-meeny* stuff, as Becken called it. She was a team player. She liked cooperating with fellow officers and delegating to subordinates and having meetings. She wasn't Shan.

She clenched the key in her hand, and suddenly realized she hadn't thought of David once that day.

"I'll take responsibility for this," she said. "Wess'har seem only to want to punish those directly involved in anything. Executing Parekh saved the *Thetis* mission."

Okurt exploded briefly. "Oh Christ, don't go all frigging Titus Oates on me, Lin." He shook his head. "I'm driving this bloody tub. I don't think that gets me off the hook with the wess'har."

"We have to be ready to do this."

"If you're thinking of using serious ordnance on anyone's planet, we're going to have to get out of here bloody fast afterwards. What about Umeh Station, for Chrissakes?"

Lindsay felt a pang of guilt. Okurt had no idea what he didn't know. Her strategy ended at destruction. His had to take account of the safety of civvy and service personnel, a half-finished base and a ship.

"It's a priority."

"Yeah, that's been made clear to me. Just make sure we get this tech."

"We will. Rayat obviously knows what he's doing."

"Lin, love, you're a good managerial officer but sometimes

you really haven't got a clue." Okurt turned to go, but then he stopped. "What happens if they crack our coded ITX? We can't encrypt."

"Maybe they already have."

He strode off. Lindsay stood in the armory lobby staring out at the space where Okurt had been. When you were stuck halfway up a cliff, all you could hope for was to scramble higher. Wess'har, isenj and ussissi didn't encode, encrypt or play spook games: if they were monitoring all the ITX channels, they would be hearing some nonsensical conversations. She hoped their cultural ignorance of cryptography would buy some confidentiality.

The weapons compartment looked remarkably dull considering that it was Armageddon's supermarket. She waited for Bennett and Rayat to join her.

"Come on, then," said Rayat behind her. He was very good at appearing on cue. Voices carried in passages. "Let's see the kit."

"What are we doing?"

"Assessing our options. For when we have a target."

"To do what?"

"Asset denial." Rayat was consulting his handheld. Then Bennett stepped over the hatch coaming into the lobby. "Let's have your excellent sergeant's view of what we can transport."

Some of the bombs looked like cartoon bombs, with pointed noses and red stripes. And some didn't. Some of the racked ordnance here looked like IT equipment, anonymous and box-shaped. Rayat was messaging rapidly from that handheld and then reading, his lips almost moving. Then he looked up, evidently relieved.

"I want to know if we can get at least six ERDs down to the surface in the Once-Onlies," he said.

Bennett looked at Lindsay for a nod. He got it. Lindsay was trying to recall what ERDs were.

"Yes," said Bennett.

"Expand on that."

"Yes, we can do it. They're about twenty or thirty kilos each. If you're asking should we, I'd say no."

"I'm not asking."

Lindsay finally remembered what ERDs were. She knew them as neutron bombs, not enhanced radiation devices. "Oh no, not *that*," she said. "No."

Rayat walked over to racks with handles that pulled down and out, like mortuary drawers made of steel bars. He pressed the handle and they powered open with a pneumatic *ee-uurrrr* sound.

There were just little things inside, smaller than Lindsay remembered from her weapons engineering ad-qual course. They were about the size of an old-style A-Triple-F fire extinguisher, no more than a meter long, blunt-nosed. They looked exactly the same as the BNO "Beano" bombs, anti-biohaz neutralization ordnance, except for the turquoise-colored bands on the screw-plate. And they *were* the same, except for the BNO's cobalt-salting component. Beanos had been banned for Earthside use, but they were stand-by worst-scenario kit in sealed environments.

It was all deceptively banal. They were stock items and they were ultra-shielded, safe to handle and easy to use. It was just being on the receiving end of one that made them nasty.

"You can't use neutron weapons on Bezer'ej," she said. "Or Beanos."

"Why?" asked Rayat. "If we need to destroy organic material, this is the best way to do it."

Lindsay thought of Shan. She thought of her own agenda of assassination, not retrieval. She had no idea if Shan would succumb to radiation alone. "It's a landlord bomb. Kill the tenants and the woodworm, leave the building standing."

"Ah, that's if you *need* to leave the building standing. We don't. Not necessarily. This is still a damn big bomb with a kiloton yield."

"We can't deploy tacticals and expect the wess'har not to go apeshit."

"And they're *not* going to go apeshit if we trash the place with conventional ordnance like FAEs?" Rayat looked at Bennett as if to tell him to clear off. It wasn't the sort of thing that worked well with Royal Marines. Bennett just stood there, boots planted in the deck.

"You want me to thin out, ma'am?" asked Bennett, looking at Rayat, lips pressed tight.

"Yes, go and have a cuppa," she said. It wasn't fair to burden Bennett with the detail. It put him in the position of having to judge if her orders were reasonable. She was pretty sure they wouldn't be.

She dogged the hatch closed after him.

"What's your problem with this?" said Rayat. "What's the point of getting hold of some of the biotech if you leave the rest where it is?"

"I find nukes a bit extreme. Maybe it's a girl thing."

"Why so squeamish?"

"Well, putting aside the reaction of the Wess'ej armed forces, it's an act of war, whether there's a lab facility on Christopher or not."

"So is landing in someone else's sovereign territory with armed troops."

"And the environmental damage will *really* provoke the matriarchs."

"And you think massively destructive conventional ordnance is more ecofriendly, do you? Ask the German Federation or Vietnam. Or the Afghani Collective." Rayat slapped his palm flat on the dull lovat casing, and Lindsay flinched irrationally. "This is the whole point of ERDs. Localized tactical kill. You wait forty-eight hours and then you can walk in."

"You can't walk in after a BNO's sprayed cobalt all over the place. Not for a few years, if I recall my course notes."

"All we need is a big scouring blast and a big burn and whatever survives that will be cleaned up by the neutron emission. We don't really need Beanos."

"You know a lot about this."

"If you'd worked on biotech projects, you'd want to know the fire drill too. But a straight ERD will do the job just fine."

He must have caught the distaste on her face. "I can do all this. You leave the ordnance to me. We can leave your Royal Marines out of the messy ethics too."

Rayat was right. It was all chilly logic, and Lindsay was kidding herself if she thought that simply removing Shan Frankland was the end of the matter, or that her arrest would not provoke some reaction from the matriarchs. They wouldn't care how it was done. The legal niceties of ethical and unethical weapons were a hypocritical human preoccupation.

If there was a separate source of this contagion, then it had to be destroyed too.

"You sure you know what . . . um . . . Spook HQ is planning to do with your sample of Shan Frankland?" said Lindsay.

Rayat nodded. "Sticking it somewhere safe, in case we ever need it really *badly*."

"That makes sense," said Lindsay. The hell it did: the intelligence services employed no more paragons of virtue than any other large organization.

Rayat could sterilize Bezer'ej, if he was right about the location. But she would eradicate Shan Frankland.

"Okurt's furious," said Lindsay.

"What's your phrase? Face aft and salute. He'll carry out his orders."

"I would have preferred a way of keeping him and *Actaeon* out of this."

"Do you really think the wess'har will give a toss about which monkey did what?"

"Yes," said Lindsay, and she thought of the moment when she dutifully cleared up a surprisingly small pool of blood and body-bagged Surendra Parekh, executed by—no, not by Shan, by *Aras*. Two hollow-tip enhanced 9mm rounds to the head, and that was the end of it. Dissecting a live alien child should have got them all killed. It hadn't. Morality was different out here. "They care about personal responsibility."

She followed Rayat out of the armory and locked the hatch again. They went their separate ways.

Neither of them had discussed the obvious fact: even if the wess'har didn't hold *Actaeon* to account, they would certainly come after Dr. Mohan Rayat and Commander Lindsay Neville. And they would be angrier than anyone had seen them—at least since the erasure of Mjat.

They were his friends.

In Constantine, Aras had seen them born, and he had seen them grow, and he had seen them marry. They had raised families. He had eaten at their tables. And he had also watched them die.

He knew he would watch them die again, and he wondered if it would really matter how that came about, naturally or hastened by conflict.

Eddie was asleep on the sofa that Shan had sacrificed as a temporary bed for him. He still couldn't get used to the idea that Aras and Shan saw the cover as brilliant blue when all he could see was white. Aras stretched out on a *sek* mattress on the terrace, hands meshed behind his head, staring up at the stars and waiting for Shan to return. It had been an unpleasantly challenging day even by comparison with recent events.

The sound of familiar heavy boots carried on the still air and then became slower and softer as Shan walked carefully past Eddie and through the house to the terrace.

"I bet you're bloody angry with me," Shan said. She stood over Aras, hands on hips. "Go ahead. Bawl me out."

He couldn't pick up any scent from her: that was odd, and it threw him for a few seconds. "I can't be angry with *you*," he said. "But I'm angry that you didn't tell me what you were thinking of doing, and only because we have shared so much that I expected you to tell me your plans."

Shan knelt down and kissed his forehead, more like a benevolent parent than a lover. "If I'd told you, and you tried to talk me out of it, I'd have had a very hard time."

"But you would still have done it."

"Sorry, but yes."

"Opposition has never concerned you before."

"Yeah, but you're different." Her lips moved as if she was about to say something, but she paused. It was one of those few times when she looked completely vulnerable. Then she braced her shoulders visibly, composed her expression, and again became someone else entirely. "I'm sorry I didn't tell you what I was doing. Fancy a quickie, then?"

"It might wake Eddie."

"Eddie's been here three nights and I'm getting a bit restless."

"Then we will keep the noise down."

Human ecstasy was a more intense and overwhelming sensation than the wess'har state of *our,* but it was fleeting. It was still a fine experience. Shan fell asleep briefly, head on his shoulder, and he thought about Constantine.

The news would devastate the colonists.

Shan woke with a start. "Bugger. What time is it?"

"You've only been sleeping for a matter of minutes."

She sat up and raked her fingers through her hair before tying it back into a tail. "I'm going to head back to Constantine next week and get them used to the idea that they're leaving."

"I'll do it."

"No, it's my call. You can come too, but I do the business."

"Why?"

"Because they'll hate the person who does it, and that won't even shift the needle for me. But they're your friends. Besides, it was my idea."

Aras let out a long sigh that he had learned more than a century before from Ben Garrod. "They have worked so very hard."

"You can't think that way, sweetheart. This is a long game."

"You seem to be accepting *c'naatat* very well lately."

"Best thing that ever happened to me."

"A change of view."

"It just dawned on me that you were right. The more injury I'm exposed to, the stronger I get." She looked at her hands and flexed them, sending not only blue and violet light sparkling through her fingers, but also reds and greens and golds. "And I can control *this* now." She gave him a big grin, and that wasn't very Shan. "Can you detect any scent from me?"

"Only your female enthusiasm."

"I've got my scent reactions under control too. Makes life a lot easier. I don't accidentally depose matriarchs now. Hey, I might even be able to play poker with Mestin. Can you imagine how much better I would be as a copper these days? Doesn't bear thinking about."

She looked as if she wanted him to share her satisfaction. He had hoped she would say that her delight at being host to the parasite was connected to him, but it seemed it was all about how much more efficient it would make her for her mission in life, whatever that was. She never said what she felt about the inescapably permanent partnership with him.

It was foolish. Wess'har only cared about what was done, not what was intended: and she certainly treated him as if she cared for him, even if her manner was brisk. It was just the nagging little human part of him that wanted reassurance. He tried not to listen to its insecure voice. He knew that the unique biochemical bonds *oursan* generated were as strong for her as they were for him. It was enough.

"If you were on your own, you might feel differently," he said.

"Sorry. I wasn't making light of what you've been through. I just try to make the best of a bad job." She screwed her eyes shut. "That's not a criticism. But isn't that what you're doing too?"

"Making the best of a bad job?"

"Well, you don't have much choice either. I'm the only female *c'naatat* around."

"Did you ever ask *why* you're the only female *c'naatat*? It *was* a choice. I made it."

Shan stared at him and was silent. Not having those scent cues made it hard now to work out what was happening. He fell back on human body language. That didn't help much either.

"I've hurt you and I really didn't mean to," she said. Her

voice was level, her expression neutral. "I'm still working out what I am right now. That's not easy when you're used to being certain about yourself."

"I have experienced this, remember."

"But you didn't enjoy it."

"There were a few compensations, but not many."

"I'm finding it quite invigorating."

"You're a solitary person. I had family and friends and I lost them all. I'm sure it looks very different to you."

"Ouch," said Shan. But she didn't expand on that, and there was still no scent from her at all. She got to her feet, pulled on her clothes and went back into the house.

He regretted offending her. But there was no point apologizing for saying what was true and obvious.

Eddie was scheduled to return to *Actaeon* in the morning. It seemed appropriate to have a final dinner with him: Shan had no idea when—or if—he would ever be back, despite the fact that he seemed remarkably able to talk everyone into allowing him free access.

And she still had a task to set him. She hadn't thought of a way to ask him to collect tissue samples from the isenj, or even how he might do it, but she'd think of something when the time came. There was always the risk that he would be offended and she would lose his goodwill and with it his propaganda: but the stakes were high. A working bio-deterrent against isenj would mean peace for the bezeri without further lives being lost or resources being committed.

And Eddie wasn't the only one whose heart and mind she feared she might risk losing.

Aras wasn't actually ignoring her, but he did seem preoccupied. She knew she'd wounded him. It upset her, but it had been necessary.

Sod it, he was wess'har. He had to be used to females going their own way on things. A year ago he was a miracle of creation's diversity, a rare kindred spirit: now he was a partner who had opinions on how she should do her job and who—to be frank—got on her proverbial tits at times. He was turning into a regular man.

"Are you listening, Shan?" said Eddie, drumming his fingers on the table.

"Sorry. Miles away." She glanced at Aras, who was topping up plates and cups, and caught his eye. There was no hint of anger: he simply gave her a slight smile—the best approximation of a human one that he ever managed—and added a few slices of bread to her plate.

"I was saying that the isenj stand to gain from a human presence on Umeh. They're really interested in terraforming."

"Well, they've fucked their own environment," Shan said. "So why stop there?"

"For them, it isn't actually devastated," Eddie said. "Just overcrowded. They have to spend a lot on maintaining it, but they do manage to feed and breathe with a certain degree of ease."

"They destroyed everything they didn't need for their own use," Aras said suddenly "It's a world that revolves around their needs."

"Well, plenty of humans back home take that view too. But we're only shipping back twenty isenj in *Thetis*. How much of a problem can they cause? I'm still astonished by the reaction. You'd think people would regard it as a miracle, really."

"They breed," said Aras.

"That's plague language."

"I heard that word used on the news too."

Shan didn't join in. She'd had enough of debate. They both knew what she thought and she was still wondering at what point she should ask Eddie to do a little job for her.

"Ual thinks humans have a fixation with vermin," said Eddie.

"Define vermin," said Aras.

"An animal in an environment where it isn't wanted and that can breed in large enough numbers to cause disruption to health, agriculture, or commerce."

"Ah," said Aras, and paused for a heartbeat. "Like humans, then."

Shan stifled a laugh. Aras had the timing of a stand-up comedian. But it wasn't funny. It was true.

"I suppose that's one way of looking at it," said Eddie.

"Every species' way of looking at it, except yours."

"We're not all like that."

"Enough of you are." Aras leaned across the table and Eddie flinched visibly, but all the wess'har did was clasp his hand around the bottle of wine and tip it at an angle, like a sommelier presenting a fine vintage for inspection by a connoisseur. "Wine could well be an icon for your species. No wonder you base societies and ritual upon it. It's the fruit of polluted excess. The yeast colony gorges itself on saccharides until it dies poisoned by its own excretion. It doesn't know how to stop and it consumes itself to death."

"We can learn to do differently," said Eddie.

"Show me the evidence. Show me in a million years where humans have changed."

"Constantine. The colonists."

"Their instinctive greed is controlled by their fear. They recognize they have these instincts, and they believe that by suppressing them they will appease their god, but they still have them. And their greed is for time. They want to live forever."

A strong citrus waft of agitation underlined his words. Had he been human, Shan would have dismissed the argument as too much alcohol over dinner, the sort of embarrassment that you slept off and that none of the other guests mentioned again, at least not in front of you. But he was sober, as he always would be, and she had never heard him voice the slightest criticism of the colonists. It stood in stark contrast to his fears for them the night before.

Eddie seemed to have noted that too. "Do I detect a real anti-human movement here?"

Aras stiffened. "It's not about species. It's what you *do*. Do you know what I despise most about you?" His tone, as ever,

was deceptively even, like a priest giving absolution to a mon-
ster and trying hard not to let his personal revulsion show.
"Your unshakable belief that you're *special,* that somehow all
the callousness and careless violence that your kind hand out to
each other and to other beings can be forgiven because you
have this . . . this great human *spirit.* I have viewed your dramas
and your literature, you see. I have lost count of the times that I
have seen the humans spared by the aliens because, despite humanity's flaws, the alien admires their plucky *spirit* and ability
to strive. Well, I *am* that alien, and I *don't* admire your spirit,
and your capacity to strive is no more than greed. And unlike
your god, I don't love you despite your sins."

Shan leaned over the table between them. "Come on, you
two. Break it up, for Chrissakes." She began gathering the
plates. It cut across the tension. "This isn't the time or the place
for a row. And I'm tired."

Aras took hold of the plates with a carefully blank expression and tugged just enough for her to relinquish her hold on
them. Eddie couldn't have noticed, but the wess'har smelled of
seething anger. He wandered off and began rinsing the plates.
Shan gestured to Eddie to leave the table and sit down on the
sofa.

"Sorry," said Eddie. "When did he turn into Rochefoucauld?"

"Maybe I'm a bad influence," Shan said. "Me and my sunny
view of human nature, maybe."

"He's right, though, isn't he?"

He was. And something had changed that night, something
she had always known was fragile, but it was a cold moment
nonetheless. A chill spread from her lower gut and into her
thighs, a sensation she had felt before only when she was physically terrified. *A sheet of flame spreading down the transparent riot shield she held in front of her as petrol and glass
crashed and ignited in her face.* It couldn't touch her then, but
it scared her. And it couldn't touch her now, not even if it really
did burn her.

There were humans, and there were aliens, and she was

standing on an ice floe and drifting away from humanity. The gap opening up in front of her would now never close.

But there was work still to do. "I won't dress this up, Eddie," Shan said. "Are you prepared to provide something for me?"

"Information? Okay. I'll do my best."

"Bit more concrete than that."

A pause. "I ought to say no. But try me."

"I'll do a trade. Here's some information in exchange for material. I'll give you the wess'har war forecast for the next few months and you pick up a sample for me if you can."

"Sample of what?"

"Isenj DNA. You being so chummy and all that."

"Now why does that worry me?"

"Because you know what a clever and nasty bunch of bastards the wess'har are, and that they've got big sisters who are even worse."

"Oh, I need more facts than that, Shazza."

"Okay. They're going to seed Bezer'ej with a persistent artificial pathogen that's selective against humans. They used my DNA to create it. It's a bloody great keep-out sign."

Eddie still had his half glass of wine in his hand, and he was inspecting the contents with unnatural diligence. "And they want an isenj sample to do the same."

"Spot on."

"And what if the matriarchs decide to use it as an offensive weapon?"

"Well, Earth will be fucked anyway if we really piss them off, but look at it this way—they could have creamed Umeh ten times over, but the isenj didn't try to invade them, so they didn't attack them on their home ground. If humans show the same good sense, I don't think it's an issue."

"It's that word *think* that I don't like."

"Eddie, given time, they'll find how to extract it from my genome. I've got a dash or two of isenj in me. That's how I acquired a genetic memory, via Aras." She flashed her illuminated hands. "And a bit of bezeri too. So you might say we're family."

"How *did* you get *c'naatat?*"

"Aras gave me a transfusion of his blood when I was shot. It saved my life. So—are you going to do it or not?"

"You give me your word it won't be used as a weapon?"

"You'd trust me, would you?"

"Are we going to get a word in between us that isn't a bloody question?"

"Deal."

"You're an immensely persuasive woman."

"Seriously, Eddie. You've got a pretty good appreciation of what's a threat to these people and what isn't. Will you help?"

"I'll do what I can."

"Thanks. I mean it."

"Don't thank me. Like I said before, it's Falklands time."

"I didn't understand that."

"Twentieth century war history. You might want to read it sometime. I've seen accounts from British naval officers of how they sat on board warships in the Falkland Islands combat zone listening to the radio. There they were, in a place called San Carlos Water, just waiting for more Argentine air attacks, and the news was broadcasting information on what the British battle plans were. The government briefed reporters about everything. And there were these sailors, listening to this, knowing the plans were blown, and just waiting for incoming. Now, I don't know who was more to blame for making that information public, the politicians or the journalists, but that was the day reporters couldn't pretend we were neutral observers any longer." He scratched his cheek as if he were suddenly embarrassed by his impassioned speech. "It's hard to prove it changed events, and perhaps it didn't, but I always wondered what *I* would have put first. There are only so many times that you can stand back and say you were only doing your job."

Shan wondered if Eddie were acting. He seemed in his own private world, thinking aloud and wrestling with personal demons. The fact that he was inclined to wrestle at all endeared him to her. But if this was all part of his professional sleight of hand, she would kill him.

And she realized that she was being wess'har-literal when she thought that.

The wess'har were at the start of a siege, one potentially more serious than the last isenj war. So few of them, and so many humans and isenj waiting to take their place: but if Eddie needed that knowledge of their growing desperation to ensure his compliance and sympathy, she wasn't going to give it to him just yet.

"What do I need to do?" he said.

"Any biological material. Fluids—"

"We're not *that* chummy."

"—or anything they shed."

Eddie mouthed a silent *ah* as if he remembered something. "Why don't they ask the ussissi to do this? They're in and out of isenj space like a fiddler's elbow."

"Wess'har would never ask them to compromise their neutrality. They do their own dirty work."

"Explains why they need you so much."

"I wouldn't piss around with the ussissi either. I get the feeling it's like breaking up a pub fight involving soldiers. Take one on, and you've got to take them all on."

Eddie drained his glass. He studied the nonexistent dregs for a moment and then glanced over his shoulder to check where Aras was.

"They really are after your arse, you know," he said quietly. "I know you're not someone who likes hiding, but I'd keep my head down if I were you."

"I appreciate the concern."

"They've killed the story back home."

"What, me?"

"*C'naatat.* One minute I had News Desk screaming for a story and I tell them to shove it, the next I hear we don't talk about the subject. Commercial or government pressure. Sad day for journalism, even if I didn't want the story to run."

"Do you think they believe the threat's real, Eddie?"

"In what sense?"

"We're 150 trillion miles away. It must look like a movie to them. All the pictures, none of the problems. If the wess'har start on us—and I'm using the term *us* loosely—you know they won't stop, don't you?"

"Mjat made a big impression on me, Shan. I do know."

"You make sure they do, too," she said.

Eddie paused and then smiled knowingly. "You know, Shan, you're bloody good at this."

She smiled back. "You know, Eddie, I was being sincere for once."

His smile faded and so did hers. They both dropped their gaze. "I'll sleep out on the terrace tonight," he said. "Nice warm night. And I'd love to stare up at those stars." He nodded in Aras's direction. "Besides, I think you have some diplomatic relations to restore with your old man."

"I reckon," said Shan.

She waited for him to close the external door behind him. Then she allowed herself a grin.

Yes, she really was *bloody* good at it.

14

⟶   ⟵

If we believe a thing to be bad, and if we have a right to prevent it, it is our duty to try to prevent it and to damn the consequences.

Viscount Lord ALFRED MILNER, 1854–1925

"This is one of the hardest things I've ever had to do," said Shan.

No, it wasn't; it wasn't at all, not by a long chalk. The only hard thing about it was standing before the altar of St. Francis in the buried heart of Constantine colony. She could feel the exquisite light from the stained glass window at her back burning right through her. It wasn't the right place for a Pagan to be, not even a lapsed one like her.

She looked from face to worried face in the congregation, people she knew and who once trusted her.

"You have to leave Constantine," Shan said. "You have to move everybody out."

There wasn't so much as a murmur. She wasn't prepared for that. All her training and instinct was targeted towards meeting resistance. Right then she wasn't sure exactly what she was meeting, so she carried on. She could see Josh in her peripheral vision. She couldn't see Aras.

"The political situation is extremely tense," she said. "Earth's sent another vessel to this system without seeking permission from either the wess'har or the isenj. You know the wess'har even better than I do, probably. They're taking extreme action."

There was a sigh from somewhere near the front. And still there were no questions.

"They're going to block landings permanently by the only means they have. Basically, they're going to seed this planet with organisms that will kill humans and iṣenj. And that means you too, I'm afraid. The good news is that if you agree to leave, you can start again on Wess'ej. There'll be a habitat for you." Their faces were stricken. *Maybe I didn't express that very well.* "So, any questions?"

"How long do we have?" asked a woman in the front pew. It was Sabine Mesevy, the botanist from the *Thetis* mission who had found religion and opted to stay. Shan hadn't spotted her, and that was bad, because Shan was used to taking in every detail of a crowd.

"Two months, tops," Shan said. "There'll be plenty of help to get you packed up and shipped out. I'm sorry this had to happen."

Mesevy wasn't giving up. "Won't our biobarrier protect us?"

"They're shutting it down. They don't want to hand over a potential foothold to either side."

"They could land with full biohaz protection."

"Maybe, but it's one thing to work in a sealed lab and another to live in one. This planet would be no more use to them than Earth's moon."

"Is it just the planet that humans might be interested in?"

Shan hesitated. "I suspect not."

Nobody said anything further. Shan found herself irritated and wanting to get on with the evacuation. The silence continued and it had a sound of its own. She began counting a full minute.

When she glanced at the floor, there was a brilliant shaft of ruby and emerald light from the stained glass window slanting between her boots as she stood with her legs slightly apart. The light from Cavanagh's Star was somehow channeled down into the colony: every day, the image of St. Francis, surrounded by the creatures of Earth and Bezer'ej and Wess'ej, came to life at sunrise.

She wondered if they would try to dismantle the window and take it with them to their new refuge. She hoped they would.

Sixty seconds. She looked up, and it was as if the silent moment had become permanent.

"I'll leave you to talk, then," she said. "You'll have more questions. I'll be at Josh's house when you're ready to ask them."

It was a long walk down that aisle. It felt as long as the walk through the *Thetis* mission compound to tell the payload that Surendra Parekh had been executed for causing the death of a bezeri infant.

Parekh didn't mean to do it.

And I didn't plan to give the bastards a stronger incentive for coming here.

She was almost at the end of the aisle when a man she vaguely recognized stepped out in front of her. Her reflexes said *threat*. Her *c'naatat* said *no problem*.

"We're not going," said the man. "We're not leaving. This is our home. Don't you understand that?"

Shan was taller, harder, and armed. He didn't seem to care. "That's too bad," she said. "You have no choice."

"How can you side with them? You're human."

She'd heard that challenge before. He was an inch too close, and his fists were clenched. "What I do doesn't matter," she said quietly. "They'll do it with me or without me. This is your one chance to go."

"We can't leave all we've worked for. We were born here. We don't know anywhere else."

He moved, probably not intending violence, but it was enough for Shan to reach out and seize his forearm with a gloved grip that might have hurt. It certainly rooted him to the spot.

"You'll do it," she said. "Your forefathers did it, and so can you."

"You can't force us."

She let go of his arm. They were surrounded by crowded silence. "Look, love, one way or another, you're not going to be here in three months' time. You can start again, or you can end up like Mjat."

Shan stared at him, unblinking, arms at her sides, until he stepped back and sat down in the pew, shaking visibly. There were kids sitting next to him. They looked transfixed by her.

She looked back to the rest of the colonists. "Just don't do anything bloody stupid, okay? No heroics."

That was the trouble with people who thought they were going to heaven. They just didn't take death seriously enough.

The sight of smoke-blue grassland around the Temporary City was as emotional as a homecoming. Aras was glad to be out of F'nar: Shan might have enjoyed its urban intricacy, but he felt hemmed in by it even now that he could walk its terraces almost as a proper *jurej*.

The Temporary City itself was looking less temporary than ever. The reinforcement of the garrison was visible.

Will we listen to the bezeri if they say something we don't agree with? He watched a transport vessel landing, settling slowly on yielding legs. Wess'har were capable of trampling benignly over the wishes of others. Sometimes he felt that was right. Sometimes he wasn't so sure.

The bezeri had not forgotten their routine. He had only to stand for a while on the cliffs above the bay and ripple a sequence of lights from his lamp for a bezeri patrol pod to half surface. The patrols kept an eye on bezeri who might swim too near to the surface in curiosity and beach themselves. The constant military traffic across the region must have given them a great deal to be curious about.

The Mountain to the Dry Above? the lights asked.

I will visit Constantine later, Aras signaled back. *First I need to speak to you all.*

Constantine was set on an island. For the bezeri, it was one of a number of steep peaks rising out of their marine territories and into the Dry Above, as alien and hostile to them as space was to a human. He waded out into the water and eased himself into the open sac of the pod before suspending his respiration and letting the water flood in and engulf him. It was the price he had to pay for getting a lift. It wasn't pleasant, but he couldn't drown. He had the isenj to thank for that.

The pressure was uncomfortable in the depths of the bezeri

settlement. The local sea tasted of dead *pifanu* and mud. Light
danced everywhere, complex patterns and colors of conversations and songs between one bezeri and another. Aras could
recognize a few concept sequences, but without the signaling
lamp that interpreted for him, he was deaf and mute even after
so many years. He turned it over in his hands.

A group of massive fluid shapes eased out of an opening in a
carefully molded tower of shell and mud and came to a halt a
few meters from him, blue and lime points of brilliant light rippling across their mantles.

There is something wrong, the lights said.

More humans want to come here, said Aras.

If they came, would they prevent the isenj returning?

Their horizons might have been limited by the sea, but the
bezeri understood political alliances. Aras chose his next
signal-words carefully.

Do you doubt we can keep you safe?

The patterns of light now formed ornate orange and red con-
centric circles. *There are too few of you and you must put yourselves first. We must choose the option that keeps the isenj at
bay. If we could choose freely, we would like both humans and
isenj to stay away.*

Aras calculated again. *Do you understand the differences between the humans of the Mountain to the Dry Above and the
newcomers?*

Clouds of silt billowed as one of the bezeri jerked its tentacles up to its body. *What we understand is that the isenj fouled
our cities with their excretions and that if they come again, we
will all die.*

Aras paused to search for a neutral answer. He needed to
know what they wanted, not what they would agree to, whatever Mestin had ordered. He signaled carefully. *If more humans come to the Dry Above, they may find something here that
will be used to cause trouble to other people in other worlds.
We will create a barrier here that will stop both humans and*

*isenj settling. We will remove the humans from the Dry Above
and we will also remove the Temporary City in time.*

You will abandon us.

No. You won't need us here.

You fear you will lose control of this system.

Yes.

Then our only choice is to rely on your science.

The bezeri elders paused in the dark waters for a moment
and then swept away in a burst of green light. Aras steadied
himself against their expelled water by clutching an outcrop of
esken and waited, but nobody else came to talk to him. The pilot shimmered scarlet and amber.

I think you should go now.

On the trip back to the surface, Aras wondered if he now
contained the characteristics of so many life-forms that he had
forgotten what it meant to be any one of them. Why should the
bezeri care about what happened on dry land, let alone other
planets? All they could rely on was their memories. All they remembered that the isenj had once had settlements here and that
they had fouled the water. Asking them to address the problems
of other species that they would never see when they perceived
an immediate and very real threat to their daily lives was futile.

Maybe wess'har spent too much time now worrying about
their responsibilities. Perhaps they didn't have as many duties
as they thought. But that was human thinking: all rights, no responsibilities. He shook the idea off, disgusted.

What had they said? *If we could choose freely, we would like
both humans and isenj to stay away.* Mestin had given them
what they wanted. In hindsight, Shan had acted correctly in do-
nating her genes.

Aras was still trying to define what had disturbed him so
much about the sequence of events. Shan had not deceived him:
she had simply taken the straightest path through a complex situation to arrive at the correct result. Intent was irrelevant. Only
action mattered.

It was the action that worried him. Wess'har had not been ideologically pure enough to destroy that knowledge of bioweapons any more than they had declined the utility of *c'naatat* in a personal crisis.

And he hadn't had the will not to use it to save Shan's life, because his wants mattered more in those few minutes than his principles.

He headed up the beach and towards Constantine, wondering what had happened to his sense of right and wrong.

Josh ladled more soup into Aras's bowl than he thought he would ever be able to tackle. Huge butter beans broke the brilliant orange surface like fat white islands, and Aras prodded them with his spoon. There was a sense of relief about the Garrod family: the last time they had seen Aras was when Nevyan had arrested him. Excessive food was a substitute for expressing affection, so he accepted it as such. It was good to know they still welcomed him even if he brought bad news. Deborah and James simply smiled at him from time to time: Rachel, now six, studied him intently.

"I realize how terrible this must be for you," Aras said.

Josh shrugged. Nothing seemed to panic him. "I feel a certain sense of relief that this world will be quarantined. I've been worried about access to *c'naatat* since the day your people detected *Thetis* for the first time."

"They can't take it. They can't land here now. They will always focus on access to me, or to *Shan Chail*."

Josh hadn't mentioned Shan at all. The lack of reference to her was conspicuous, and Aras felt a pang of annoyance that the colonists might now resent or even hate his *isan*, but he knew she would say that she didn't *give a fuck*.

He tore off a chunk of bread and dipped it in the soup. The meal fell silent. Josh's home was a perfect haven, cut into the rock just like a wess'har home, with soft filtered sunlight streaming down through the roof-dome that doubled as a solar panel. The thought of this place being abandoned and erased by nanites saddened Aras. But the colonists had never intended to stay here forever, just long enough to wait out the dark days until Earth was ready to be restored again.

He suddenly thought they were insane to come here. The construction work had been backbreaking, and he had played his part. He'd looked very different in those days.

"You must find this very sad after investing so much labor," he said.

"Material things can be remade," said Josh. "And we will rebuild."

"If I can help, I will."

"I would rather you helped me tear down than build."

"I don't understand."

"There are things we can take and things we can't. I want to destroy everything in the church that we can't take with us."

So much for material things having no meaning, Aras thought. The more he discussed their beliefs with them, the less sense they made. But it wasn't the time to debate with them. Their faith would be the only thing that would keep them going through the crushing misery of being uprooted and having to start again on a world they didn't know.

"I know you have always told us to stay away from Christopher Island," Josh said carefully. It was another island in the chain that was home to Constantine. Once it had been called Ouzhari. It was all black grass in spring, a plant unique to the island. "And that's the only place *c'naatat* can be found, yes?"

"I didn't realize you knew," Aras said.

"I didn't," said Josh. "Not for sure."

It was the first time—the only time—that Josh had ever tricked him. The sensation was unpleasant. Josh was a decent man and Aras knew he had no reason to doubt his integrity. But it hurt. They sat in silence and busied themselves with the soup.

They had named the island after St. Christopher, another of these not-quite-gods that they made out of men and women. They had beatified all six islands in the chain: Constantine, Catherine, Charity, Clare, Chad, and Christopher. Aras had learned about saints. He still thought it might have been more appropriate for the *c'naatat* island to be named St. Charity, given the nature of her martyrdom. Saints needed to suffer. It was one of those dark needs of humankind.

The first robotic mission to Bezer'ej had landed on Christopher, and Aras had relocated it as far up the chain as possible with the help of wess'har comrades long since dead. The colonists knew exactly what *c'naatat* was. They had no interest in it, almost to the point of dread. Some of them regarded it as the *devil's temptation,* whatever that meant. The kind of eternal life they were looking for involved something called the bliss of God, not resistance to disease and injury until you lost everyone you ever cared for. No, they were no threat. They *pitied* him. He would never go to heaven.

Josh closed his eyes for a second. He might have been praying. Humans thought aloud to God, and Aras had never worked out how they expected their deity to pick its way between their billions of conflicting needs and desires.

He opened his eyes. "You'll hold on to the gene bank, of course."

"Whatever happens," said Aras, "I will ensure the species bank is preserved. Whether it will ever return to Earth, I can't say. But we won't hand over any of those people or plants to *Actaeon.*"

"Are you really removing the biobarrier?"

"You know why we have to."

"They really would wipe us out too, then."

"Yes."

Josh looked him in the eye for several long seconds. Aras could see his ancestor Ben in him. Aras felt sorrow and fear for them all, but he didn't feel guilty and he didn't feel repentent. For a moment he thought that Josh had finally seen him for the alien he truly was: neither a miracle nor a guardian nor anything sent by divine providence to help them carry out their task, but an alien with a radically different morality.

"I understand," Josh said, and Aras knew he didn't. A gulf

had opened up between them. It had always been there, paper-thin, but now it was a canyon and widening fast.

Aras stayed in Constantine for two more days. He made sure he visited the school and walked as many of the subterranean streets as he could. The spring crops were sprouting: two of the rats he had liberated from the *Thetis*'s pharmacologist had produced a litter because the colony's children hadn't quite worked out how to sex them, never having experienced live animals larger than insects before. It was all normal and full of unspecified hope.

Josh's son James was taking good care of Black and White, two of the lab rats that Aras had taken a particular liking to. Aras played hand-chasing games with them for a while, but they weren't as nimble as they had been. Rats aged fast. Shan had warned him they would die in another year or so, and that he shouldn't get upset because that was normal for rats.

Above ground, all that was visible of the settlement were the discreet domes of skylights and the carefully arranged patches of crops. The air was scented with damp green fertility.

He paid a visit to the church of St. Francis.

GOVERNMENT WORK IS GOD'S WORK.

The inscription had been one of his earliest memories of the colony. He had watched bots carve it years before any humans arrived on the planet. They had been *gethes* then. He had stopped them using other creatures for food and turned them into acceptable humans.

I had a choice. I was still the custodian of Bezer'ej. It would have been no trouble to kill them before they woke from chill-sleep.

But he hadn't. And he hadn't let Shan die either. He didn't regret either decision. Regret was pointless and human. It had nothing to do with reality.

Aras would have to turn the reclamation nanites loose in the tunnels and galleries. They would reduce all artefacts to dust as efficiently as they had wiped out all traces of the shattered isenj settlements on Bezer'ej. It was a pity about the window, though.

He walked up the aisle of the church and studied the stylized figure in a brown robe. He had assembled most of the image: he could take it apart again. The colonists would need something of this place to take with them, and it was as iconic and representative of their purpose as anything he could imagine.

Shan came up behind him. He caught a pleasant breath of her distinctive skin-scent, a smooth, mouth-filling smell of sawn wood underlaid by a human bittersweet musk.

"You okay?" she asked.

"I am."

"I'm sorry. I really am. Not for them, but for you."

He sized up the window, working out how he would dismantle the many leaded pieces of glass and record their positions so he might reassemble them in F'nar. "It will further help them get to their heaven," he said.

"Are you taking the piss?"

"Not at all. I mean it. The more they have to do things they find hard, the better their god loves them, it seems. I still don't understand the value of suffering."

"Yeah, it beats me too."

"I shall stay and help them depart. It's the right thing to do."

Shan slipped her arm through his and they stood looking at the stained glass saint who had loved all creation, and his entourage of animals, some of which might have eaten him had he fallen into their grasp. Aras suspected an *alyat* would have overlooked St. Francis's respect for it if there had been a lean hunting season.

Shan was looking intently at the window too. Aras didn't have to ask why. It was the areas of blue glass that spoke to her. When she first saw them, they had looked white: humans couldn't see the colors as wess'har did. Then she saw them for the color they were, and knew what he had done to save her. She'd been enraged and terrified.

"It's beautiful," she said. Clearly the association was no longer painful. "And I still don't know how the sunlight gets down here."

"I could show you."

"Later." Her eyes moved over the image. "You're going to save it, aren't you?"

"Yes."

"Good. I'm glad." She squeezed his arm. "I'll hang on here, then. If there's any dissent, I'll handle it."

"They're taking it hard." He was glad she would be around. She seemed to relish restoring compliance: he saw it only as a necessity. "It will make it easier having you here."

"I might have to do things that you'll find hard to accept. I don't want it to drive us apart."

"Shan, you're my *isan* and I'm bound to you, whatever you do or say."

He felt all her muscles tense. "You sound as if you wish you weren't."

"No. I'm perfectly content."

"Look, when the dust has settled, let's take a few days out of F'nar and get ourselves straight again. Perhaps we could visit Baral." She reached into her jacket, took out the small red cylinder of her swiss and pressed it into his hand. "No point my carrying this. Nevyan's given me a new communications thing. I don't think I'm ever going to get the hang of it somehow."

The antiquated swiss was no use to him either. And it was full of details of the demons that drove her, the terrible things that *gethes* did. But he knew how much it meant to her and that she was giving it to him as a gesture. He suspected she would never use the word *love,* but he understood nevertheless.

"I shall take good care of it," he said.

A pause. "I'd better be off, then." She gave him a brisk kiss on the cheek and strode back down the aisle, boots echoing.

Yes. A few days of quiet—without matriarchs and Eddie and all the tension that had accompanied them since the day they met—might be good for them both. Aras watched her go and marveled at how unconcerned she seemed. Then he walked to the bell tower and took hold of the long ropes of hemp and *efte* attached to the six glass bells.

Ben Garrod had never believed that bells could be made from glass. Humans had limited technology in that area. But he had been delighted by the sound they made when struck. It was a wavering note rather than a low metallic gong, but it carried for miles and it had an ethereal quality that the humans liked.

It was a sound that generations of colonists had grown up hearing. Aras had no idea why Josh insisted on destroying them now and not leaving them to the nanites.

Aras glanced up into the top of the tower that housed the bells. In daylight the brilliant blue was visible, and if he stood at the right position in the aisle he could look up and see the curved transparent shapes through the beams of the roof. He was still staring up, remembering the effort of making them, when he scented Josh coming through the church.

The man looked tired. "Let's do it," he said. "One last time."

"We could remove them," Aras said.

"No," said Josh. "No nanites, either. I want to see them gone now. No looking back."

Josh took one rope in both hands and gave it an all-out downward tug, tipping the bell back on itself and drawing a long, plaintive note from it. Then he stopped and placed another rope in Aras's hand.

"Just pull this when I indicate," he said.

Aras had never cared to learn the complex sequences of ringing that the colonists took great care to practice. He rang now because Josh wanted him to; that was the least he could do for him, even though their friendship was now feeling strained. Using only two bells, the ringing had none of the magnificent tonal complexity of what they called *plain hunt* or *rounds,* but perhaps the tolling of two bells was more apt than peals that were celebratory in tone.

The sound vibrated in Aras's throat. He felt he could taste it.

Josh paused for breath. "They used to use church bells as an alarm signal," he said. "There was a war in Europe when they stopped churches ringing their bells for the whole six years of the war, because if the bells rang, it was a warning that England had been invaded." He stared up the length of the thick beige rope, and Aras could have sworn he was in tears. "It's just material, Aras. We don't need these things to know God."

They rang solemnly for five more minutes. Then Josh brought his bell to a dead stop and showed Aras how to do the same.

"I've collected the items from the altar," Josh said. It was a strangely dispassionate way of describing the carved image of his tortured dead deity. Aras still found their fixation with redeeming physical agony a disturbing one. "I'll bar the door behind me so we don't have any accidents."

"Are you absolutely sure you want me to do this? It seems unnecessary. The nanites will—"

"I want them destroyed here, please."

"It makes no difference how they are eradicated."

"Yes, it does. We need a harsh reminder that we have burned our bridges. It makes us move forward."

Aras gave him time to clear the building. Then he climbed the fragile ladder that led to the top of the tower and squeezed into the gap between the vault of the roof and the headstock to which the bells were attached. He took out his *tilgir*.

It had been a pleasure and an education to make those bells. It was fitting that he should now be the last person to touch them.

It took a while to hack through the rope and composite pins that secured the crowns to the headstock. There was creaking. Then gaps began opening, and with a sudden lurch all six bells dropped in close sequence down the well of the tower in a brief, unnatural silence that ended in a cacophony of bouncing shards that churned in a glittering eruption of sapphire and cobalt fragments like a missile piecing the surface of a frozen sea.

The agonizing noise calmed in seconds into tinkling, then into nothing at all. The bells of St. Francis were finally silent.

The erasure of Constantine had begun.

15

Humans lie even to themselves. They promote the idea that all intelligent beings—intelligent by their narrow definition—are all the same within and will behave the same if exposed to the same environment. They fear to admit that there are varied characteristics that define each race and species. If they still have not managed to erase great differences within their own species, how can they believe they can achieve it with nonhumans? And yet they will labor on under the willingly shared lie that all beings will be reasonable and behave like humans if they are treated like humans. Logic and history tells us we will behave like isenj, or like wess'har, or like ussissi. We all behave as we are.

SIYYAS BUR, matriarch historian

Okurt wasn't unlikable. He wasn't as quietly impressive as the Royal Marines from *Thetis*, but neither was he the sarcastic buffoon that he seemed to have created as a defensive shell. Eddie thought the current situation was a lot to ask of a man who had never been properly trained for alien contact.

He expected to be debriefed as soon as he put one foot through the last of the inner hatches. But there was polite restraint from everyone. It was a full twelve hours before Okurt left a message inviting him to lunch in the wardroom with the senior staff.

Meals were the backbone of the day. Okurt believed that his staff should have one meal where they didn't have to operate a console with one hand and snatch a snack in the other. "We are not a grazing animal," he told Eddie. "Officers *dine*." There were disposable napkins and matching shatterproofs. The table itself looked like solid naval oak until you stood up too quickly and caught it with your leg to discover it was tough, feather-light blown composite with a convincing grain, and that it stowed up flat into a bulkhead. It was sweetly patriarchal. Okurt sat at the head of the table like a father waiting to carve the Sunday roast.

It would have been a nice ordinary lunch if Eddie hadn't had a long list of unpleasant news he needed to impart to *Actaeon* and her masters.

"You do seem to be getting on well with the isenj," said Okurt. "Still using an interpreter?"

"Not with Ual," Eddie said. "Very fluent. It's a struggle for him to make the sounds, but he knows exactly what he's saying."

"Shout."

"Eh?"

" 'If they fail to understand, shout: and do not dissemble, because God is your authority.' " Okurt laughed. "Old advice to those taking on the white man's burden in the colonies."

"Good if you're talking to people with pointed sticks. Bad if they have missiles."

"We could do with fostering some enthusiasm for the space program, seeing as it pays us." Okurt passed round sliced protein that might have been soy but could just as easily have been cell-culture chicken. The parallel of bountiful provision by the government's hand was not lost on Eddie. "I hear the views of F'nar raised approval a bit. Staggeringly pretty. Shame the inhabitants would rather blow our heads off than let us visit."

Lindsay picked at her chicken salad, or perhaps it was a soy salad after all, and looked preoccupied. Eddie thought it was time to put her out of her misery. It was a matter of things being best hidden in plain sight.

"Can I ask you a question, Malcolm?" Eddie liked to give his quarry a sporting hundred-meter start. "I hear from reliable defense sources back home that the *Hereward* has changed course."

Lindsay looked up at him. It was convincing shock. It was a shock that he had mentioned it, of course, but it did the job just fine. She hadn't told Okurt that Eddie knew about it. Maybe she hadn't even told him that *she* knew. Okurt made a commendable show of looking unperturbed.

"It's true the *Hereward* is being deployed to this sector, Eddie, yes. Your sources are correct. Might I ask how and when?"

"*Sources.* The only item in my professional code of honor. That's all you need to know."

"How widely have you discussed this?" Okurt asked.

"We haven't reported it yet." Eddie smiled. Well, that was true. Okurt would know that anyway. "Come on. You don't pay me."

"Do the isenj know?"

A sloppy admission, very sloppy. So he was more worried about the isenj than the wess'har, and that was a view Eddie couldn't share after the events of the last week. But then Okurt was just a field officer, not a politician. "Would you like me to ask them?"

Okurt managed a smile and pushed the jug of instant Chardonnay-flavored drink down the oak-alike table. Lindsay fielded it and poured, a study in displacement activity.

"It's only a support vessel," Okurt said at last. "And it won't be here for twenty-five years."

"A well cannoned-up support vessel, though. Never mind. Plenty of time to get back in everyone's good books." Eddie sliced his hydroponic tomato purely as stage timing. "Because the wess'har know about it, and they're mobilizing."

Okurt and Lindsay both stopped chewing for a split second at exactly the same time.

"I imagine you're going to tell us all about it," said Okurt.

"Yes, because I'd like to be out of here before they're ready to roll. I'm old-fashioned that way. I like to keep my entrails inside my body cavity."

Okurt was shunting bits of chicken around his plate with his fork. Despite being lightweight composite, the crockery still carried a gold rim and the ship's huntsman crest. Eddie couldn't help noticing that the huntsman was being ripped apart by his own hounds.

"They interpreted it as a hostile act, and it was bad timing after extracting all the human crew from *Thetis*," said Eddie.

"Why?"

"The ussissi have gone ballistic. The paranoid little buggers think we're shaping up to destroy the ship because of the opposition back home to bringing isenj to Earth."

Lindsay said nothing. She took another pull at the glass of not-wine that Eddie now wished were hundred-proof navy rum. He could have done with a real drink.

"Want to see my rushes?" said Eddie.

It wasn't quite the same game he had played before. He liked juggling with information, flushing out who knew what, as much as Shan clearly enjoyed the challenge of interrogation. But he just needed to be clear—in his heart of hearts—why he was playing.

He was helping to avert disaster. He was trying to stop humans making a big mistake and getting into a fight with another species that would actually win, and win well. He was saving the last of a civilization of intelligent squid.

He hadn't abandoned his professional standards at all.

"Yes, we would," said Okurt.

Eddie unrolled his screen and set it on the console table that ran down the length of the short bulkhead. The assembled senior staff watched the raw footage like they were staring at a road crash.

"I tried to get as close as I could," said Eddie modestly.

The bee-cam was staring down into the cockpit of a huge and enigmatic fighter craft. If he had sent the cam up its tailpipe it wouldn't have told a human the first thing about how it worked and what it could do. In fact, it didn't even appear to *have* a tailpipe.

"There are a thousand wess'har cities down there, and they've all got a box of kit like this," said Eddie. He was watching faces while they watched his shots: he had hit the spot, and hard. "And I don't want to worry you, but Wess'ej is just the outpost of a larger wess'har civilization about five light-years away. The ones on Wess'ej are the namby-pamby lefty liberals and hippies. The others are a lot less tolerant."

"What's that?" asked the weapons officer. He was looking at a brightly colored 3-D map of wilderness crisscrossed by regular lines and angles, giving the impression of plans for a rigidly designed road network that someone was hoping to build on a greenfield site. It was Olivier Champciaux's geophys data from Bezer'ej, the material that had made even Shan Frankland nervous and that Champciaux hadn't been willing to let him broadcast for copyright reasons. Eddie didn't give a stuff about copyright now.

"That's a geophys scan of part of Bezer'ej. It was an isenj city. A big one." Timing was part of the show. Eddie paused and spread butter on a bread roll. "And that's all that's left of it after a visit from the Wess'ej Liberal Party."

There was a collective murmur of unease. This propaganda business was *easy*. Eddie wondered why he hadn't made it his life's work.

"Do they know you spied on them?" said Okurt.

"They knew. They just didn't give a shit. You can be that confident when you've got an arsenal like theirs."

"I don't suppose I could ask you for this material to show to the joint chiefs before you broadcast it, could I?"

"If it keeps my entrails in place, you're welcome," said Eddie. He left the playback running. There was the usual jerk and blur as the recording changed to another session's shooting, and the cam rested on an idyllic wide shot of F'nar's shimmering terraces. Shan, back to camera, walked into frame and stood with hands on hips. Then she turned her head, appeared to notice she was in shot and stepped aside. The mike picked up a brief "Sorry."

Eddie saw Lindsay's reaction. She leaned forward a fraction, no more.

"Sorry, Lin," said Eddie.

"No problem," said Lindsay. "So she lives there, now, eh?"

"Yeah."

Okurt didn't appear interested in Shan, which was odd given his shopping list. "Is there anything else? Not that you haven't kept us absorbed so far."

"Yeah, the wess'har are about to plow in the salt." It was a neat line. Eddie got the attention he had planned, with eight heads all turned towards him in uniformed synchrony. "They've developed a biological agent that's specific against humans and they're about to spread it around Bezer'ej to make sure we're never going to land there. They're really very freaked about the risk to the bezeri. Oh, and they're kicking the colony off the planet. So they took the news about *Hereward* really well, all things considered."

"*You* told them."

"And I flushed out a lot about their capability. Better to find out now."

Okurt gave Eddie the sort of look that made him think he might check under his bunk before turning in each night for the foreseeable future.

"And what about this biotech?" said Lindsay.

"You'll never get it."

"I didn't think they'd hand it over."

"I mean that it's a natural organism from Bezer'ej, and you're never going to get there anyway now. A fluke. There's no tech to steal or buy or borrow. The only route to it is a chunk out of Shan or Aras, and I think you can calculate the odds of getting *that*."

Lindsay's expression didn't flicker. "We could offer to help evacuate the colony," she said. "Might give us some access."

"Don't bother," Eddie said. "Shan's doing it personally. You know what she's like for getting stuck in."

He thought he saw Lindsay's expression brighten, but he was mistaken. She drained her glass and went on picking at the remains of her salad. Eddie, satisfied that he had drawn a very accurate picture of the risks of provoking wess'har wrath, dubbed the footage across to a chip and handed it to Okurt.

"Knock yourself out, Commander," he said. "As long as my arse is out of firing range."

Eddie walked back to his cabin, feeling that he had done the right thing for once, albeit with a little more theater than the fearsomely wonderful Mestin might have thought decent. Shan would have appreciated it, though. They came from the same school of psyching out the opposition. He respected that.

He swung his legs up on his bunk and began wondering if his nerve would hold long enough to get a sample of DNA from an isenj.

"How much of this am I supposed to know I've heard?" asked Okurt.

Lindsay wasn't moving. She was leaning against his cabin hatch. If Okurt was going to leave before she'd had her say, he'd have to go through her.

"All you need to know is that I'm detaining a wanted person and that I've requested access to a shuttle. We have a very narrow window for this, and it might be the only one we ever get."

Okurt spun his coffee cup on the table, looking past it in defocus at the status board but not appearing to see that either. "And even if you can land, how do you plan to get off the planet? We can't retrieve you. You know that."

"Dr. Mesevy's still down there. We can merge in with the colonists when they're evacuated." She had the story ready. He had no way of checking it. "She'll help."

"There are only a thousand or so of them. Don't you think they'd spot a stranger or six, especially rather fit ones with very short hair and palm-bioscreens?"

"Depends how we embark. We can also get access to the original colony mission shuttles and fly out."

"Just like that, eh?"

"Have you ever worked with Royal Marines before, Malcolm?"

"No, I haven't."

"If it can be done, they'll do it."

"Your chances are still close to zero."

"We're prepared to take casualties. The priority is to get her."

"I still don't see how you're going to take her. She's effectively on home turf."

"We don't have to. We just need a good stash of tissue samples."

Okurt suddenly recovered his focus. "My orders said *alive*. You'll have to have a bloody good reason for bringing her back in kit form, if you get out at all. Unless, of course, Dr. Rayat has overriding orders."

"He does, but you don't need to know."

Okurt had his back to her now, refilling his cup. "Okay, next question. Suppose you do get to her and—God knows how—take a chunk. And you can't get the shuttles airborne. How are you going to get the material off Bezer'ej?"

"Remote sample collection bot. Six kilos, self-propelling." Waiting had paid off. She was cold and detached now, a million miles from the sobbing mother who had heard the news from Ade Bennett that they were going to exhume her baby. "You were looking at that to get a sample from David's body. You must have thought it was feasible too."

Okurt turned slowly to face her. "I know I should have told you. I'm sorry."

"But you didn't. Now I'm telling you how it's going to be. I'm landing at Constantine by Once-Onlies with the detachment and we're going to find Shan Frankland, neutralize her and get a sample off the planet. Either we lift clear and you can have a shuttle rendezvous with us at a safe distance, or you can intercept that sample. Job done."

"We can't extract you if it all goes tits up."

"I said we know that."

"The wess'har will go completely fucking crazy."

"They're cranking up to war anyway. We'll be out on our ear so we might as well use what time we have left to acquire that—

that parasite, bug, whatever—for our own use." She had to cover the armaments she wanted to take, hiding the real plan in plain sight. The only hard bit was showing the right side of the puzzle to the audience of the moment without an inconsistency alerting them to the fact that she was planning something else entirely. "Dr. Rayat has commandeered appropriate ordnance."

Okurt was spinning his cup in its saucer, first clockwise, then anti-clockwise: his hand slipped and it tumbled to the floor, bouncing a couple of times. Lindsay didn't field it. He left it where it rolled.

"God help us if you screw this up," he said. "I should stop you taking tactical weapons."

"The armory inventory is locked down."

"I still have my key-code and I can still count."

"Forget what you counted. It's just for insurance." Lindsay kept her face carefully blank and hoped a red flush at her throat wasn't giving the game away. She'd fastened her shirt to the top. "Just in case."

Okurt turned away and consulted his screen. "I'd better work out how we're going to get you near enough to the drop zone," he said. "And that's not a given."

It was very hard not to run down to the barracks, the small makeshift mess that the marines had set up in compartments vacated by building materials for the biodome on Umeh. They carried their Royal Marine-ness with them wherever they went.

Lindsay wanted to *sprint* down there. Instead she swung herself through hatches with controlled excitement.

All she had to do was monitor traffic movements around Bezer'ej to get a *when*. She was going to get Shan Frankland and her plague. It even made it worth working with Mohan Rayat again.

She leaned round the hatch and found Webster, Qureshi and Chahal sitting around the table having a contest to see who could eat a whole bar of nutty sideways in one go. They turned to her looking like startled hamsters.

"Stand to," she said. "It's time for postcards from Bezer'ej."

* * *

Lindsay spread the Once-Only suit on the hangar deck again. She wanted to see Rayat's face. It was worth it.

"You don't have to come."

He swallowed discreetly, but hard. "Oh yes I do."

Twelve square kilometers. Lindsay had kicked that figure around for days. That was the surface area of Christopher Island. Rayat, consulting his database, was confident that six ERDs would do the job, a combined six-kiloton blast and lethal rain of neutrons. She hoped they were right about the location.

"You're taking a marine's place," said Becken. He wasn't pleased that Lindsay had decided they had eight bodies and six suits, and that his and Webster's weren't going to be filling them. There were barely tolerable spooks and there were bad spooks, and Lindsay could see the detachment had decided with one mind that Rayat was the latter.

Rayat smiled politely. "I really do have a job to do, gentlemen. And ladies."

Qureshi looked studiously blank. "You don't have to operate it, Doctor. Webster can rig an emulator that'll take telemetry from my suit, and all you have to do is sit tight and not puke." She gave him an unnaturally controlled smile in return. "It'll mirror my suit's position but it'll be offset by ten meters to avoid collisions. You'd better hope I don't land on a cliff."

Lindsay had to hand it to Rayat. In the teeth of a gale of hatred and contempt, he looked wholly unruffled. It was something he had in common with Shan. "You land me on Constantine and get me to my location, and I'll solve the rest of our problems."

Twelve square kilometers.

They had a shuttle ready to eject them and the maiale at five thousand kay from the planet, provided that the wess'har didn't detect the vessel. The maiale would tow them to two hundred kay before they unhitched and began the descent. It all looked fine on paper.

"Retrieval bot?" Lindsay had to preserve the illusion.

"Check," said Rayat.

"ERDs?"

"Yeah, all with delay timers."

"That's comforting."

Qureshi watched Rayat and Lindsay wheel the big dull green tubes across the deck and heave them into the shuttle. The Once-Onlies, hanging from their deployment rail like some weird new fashion, sagged as the ERDs were loaded into them.

"Is that it?" asked Qureshi. Explosives were her speciality. She stood behind Rayat, peering into her appointed suit with its tiny, terrible payload. "I'd be happier if I knew what was going on in there."

"Just ERD," said Rayat, emphasizing each letter. "We detain our infected comrade Frankland, or useful parts thereof, and destroy the source of this organism. That mission objective is now ranked classification ten. Happy?"

"No," said Qureshi. "I reckon the whole ship knows about it by now."

Bennett's face was a grim study in betrayal. "Easy peasy," he said flatly, and Lindsay couldn't work out if his *you're dead* look was directed at her, or at Rayat, or both. "Home in time to watch the footie, I reckon." He'd liked Shan. He'd liked her too much. She wondered if she could rely on him.

It was hard enough juggling the various cover stories in her own mind: and she was struggling to ensure that she presented the right set of facts to the right audience. She had to look as if she planned to get a sample of *c'naatat* off the surface right up to the last minute.

And Ade Bennett still planned to get one of the colony's ancient shuttles into the air. He'd spent hours poring over manuals and working out a route and timings to the mothballed craft. She doubted anyone could manage it, but at least the marines could seek evacuation with the colonists. She wouldn't.

"You confirmed Frankland's still on Bezer'ej?" asked Rayat.

"Best intelligence we have is from the ussissi on Umeh, and they say she is." Lindsay thought there might have been the faintest hint of disbelief on Rayat's face. "They're not secretive, any of them. They don't think information matters. They seem to base everything on physical superiority and they think nobody can take on the wess'har."

"They're probably right," said Rayat.

Bennett checked the seals on his spacesuit and ran his glove across the visor of his helmet, tucked under one arm. He wasn't looking at Rayat: he was looking at Lindsay.

"You okay, Ade?" she asked.

"No, ma'am, I'm not," he said. "But I'm not paid to be okay about things. I'm paid to front up and earn it."

"You *can* refuse what you think is an unlawful order."

"You'd have to give me that order first, ma'am," said Bennett. "And then I'll have to decide if it's one step beyond that line. Won't I?"

16

BBChan 77896 "World in Focus" 0700
*The Alliance of the Americas today lodged a diplomatic protest
against FEU plans to allow a party of extraterrestrials to land
in Europe.*

*Following weeks of violent clashes between police and
demonstrators, the Sinostates are understood to be considering
withdrawing their support for the landing. AoA spokesman Luis
Carreira said today: "We're fully prepared to use military means
to prevent an unauthorized landing if the FEU doesn't heed the
very real concerns of governments worldwide."*

Ual was not returning calls. Eddie wasn't sure if that was because he simply wasn't available or because he was making a
point. So he kept calling. Every call meant a trip to the *Actaeon*'s comms suite—a grand name for a cabin the size of a
toilet, he thought—and obeisance to whichever junior officer
was on duty.

Eventually Ual responded. He responded personally, and that
was something Eddie had rarely experienced with a human
politician. He didn't even have embarrassing sexual material on
him to guarantee the call-back. For a moment he wondered what
might constitute sexual depravity for an isenj.

"I am unhappy with the news, Mr. Michallat," Ual said, all
sucks and wheezes. "It's most negative."

"I hope I haven't been."

"How can I tell? All I know is that I watch your channels and
I see angry people who already hate us before they have met us.
My colleagues who are still in sleep en route for your world will
have an unpleasant awakening if we can't establish a more am-
icable approach in the next few years."

Blame the news editor. But Eddie's material was so exclusive that almost nothing was left on the cutting room floor. It was all his doing; he had to put his hands up to it. "I've not tried to depict your people in any negative way."

"How can I tell? We have just begun to know humans and so we don't yet know if you calculated to appall your audience."

"Have I shown anything that's inaccurate or misleading?"

"Nothing. We are as you show us."

"Then I can only apologize. There are elements of your lifestyle that some humans find frightening."

"That there are so many of us?"

"Mainly."

"You have a fixation with vermin in your culture."

"It's not our nicest trait, I know. But I haven't set you up. My only option would be to not film your cities at all, and I don't think I can justify that."

"Because it panders to us, or because it panders to humans?"

"Because it's not how I've chosen to do my job."

Ual let out a long bubbling breath. Eddie had no idea what that meant, and no ussissi on hand to interpret it for him. "I understand," the minister said. "Then we will have to address the issue the next time we talk in front of your camera."

So there would be a next time. The only right answer to give, Eddie realized, was the honest one. It worked every time and you didn't have to remember any lies. He couldn't imagine why more people didn't try it.

Even the game he was playing with Okurt—and through him, with the government—was simply the truth.

The biosphere in Jejeno was still several months away from completion, and living there before the accommodation units were in place meant being bundled up in a sleeping bag in a freight container at night. It was a one-night novelty as far as Eddie was concerned, but it made a few nice shots. It also gave him a reason for being around isenj.

He sat on a narrow seat in the ussissi shuttle with his bag on his knees and one hand clutching the straps of webbing the pilot had strung all along the bulkheads of the tiny cargo area. The pilot said he was fed up with humans falling over and being sick when he came in to land.

"You're supposed to wish me a nice day," said Eddie with a grin, but the pilot just fixed him with a feral black stare and didn't offer him a hand down. He didn't thank him for flying Air Ussissi either. Eddie wanted to say that he understood why they didn't trust humans any more, but thought better of it. Whatever his good intentions, he still looked like a regular human to them. He adjusted his respirator.

Serrimissani met him at the entrance to the construction site, which didn't appear to have progressed much since his last visit. She was looking sullen. It was hard to describe a sullen-looking mongoose, but he knew which expression and body language went with her blacker moods: eyes slitted half shut, arms unnaturally straight at her sides, lips compressed. He tried to imagine her and a wess'har matriarch relaxing with a beer and telling *gethes* jokes. Somehow he couldn't see it.

"We have seen the news," she said.

"Ual's not very pleased either."

"I meant your threat to destroy the *Thetis*."

He'd missed something. He squatted down so as to placate Serrimissani, but not so close that she could sink her teeth in him. "What threat?"

She beckoned him to follow her and he walked up the path that was studded and rutted with building debris and vehicle tracks. There were two small knots of ussissi; one was standing ten meters from the main habitat entrance and the other was outside the site manager's hut. They stared at him and said nothing. He followed Serrimissani into the dome and she commandeered a hand-link from an isenj, tuned it with a few savage pokes of a claw, and thrust it under his nose.

"If you share a communications relay with people, you must expect them to hear what you say," she said.

Eddie didn't have to scroll far through the BBChan headlines. He got as far as *use military means to prevent an unauthorized landing* and stopped. His stomach was tumbling slowly but inexorably past his caudal vertebrae.

"Humans make a lot of threats they don't really intend to carry out," said Eddie.

"Fascinating," said Serrimissani. "But we do not."

It was quite a difficult morning after that. He almost forgot that he had a urine sample vial in his bag that needed filling, and not with anything that was likely to vent from his nervous bladder. He had blagged the vial from sickbay via the obliging Lieutenant Yun on the premise that he'd chanced across some yeast with a *very* high alcohol tolerance.

He sat on a dormant bot watching work continue. There were more accommodation cubes than before, and the vines had made an impressive job of covering the interior framework. The incongruously decorative fountain tinkled and splashed ahead of him. It could have been a chic and minimalist shopping mall under construction if it hadn't been so very, very far from home.

His BBChan ID badge—which had expired on December 31, 2324, he noted—wasn't going to be much use now.

There were countries where it was a token of immunity. There were others where they didn't like it much, but where they had a pragmatic attitude to letting a reporter from a respected news source operate largely unmolested, even if censored on transmission. There were a few where it didn't matter a damn and they would shoot you anyway, but that was because they were stupid and didn't realize that killing useful journos was a self-defeating pastime. If you got killed, it was largely bad luck on your part or political naiveté on the part of your attacker.

But wess'har, isenj and ussissi no longer had any use for him. They already knew what they needed to know. He was just another alien from a species they all had their doubts about.

One thing was for sure: even if he managed to get a piece of isenj tissue, he wasn't planning to rush back to *Actaeon* with it while the natives were so restless. It was an awfully big, shiny, illuminated target.

And it was—like him—awfully alone out here.

Aras was happy. When he was happy, distractedly happy, he made sporadic *urrrr* noises under his breath, like someone riffling through the pages of a crisp-paged book at high speed. It was also the sound he made when he was enjoying *oursan*.

Shan combed carefully through his hair and began braiding it, relieved at his temporary good mood. It didn't take much to keep him happy. On close inspection, it wasn't at all like human hair: instead of smooth shafts, it was more like threads of feather, with minute wispy vanes and barbs that curled down the length of each strand. She rolled it between her fingertips and admired the bronze highlights.

He stopped *urrrr*ing. "Two months is a very short time for them," he said quietly.

"I think that was based on matriarch packing time, not human." When she turned to pick up a length of hemp tape to tie the braid in place, her boots crunched on something. She stooped to look. "Where's all this bloody blue glass coming from?"

"I must have trodden it in from the bell tower," said Aras.

The fragments were beautiful, like vicious little high-grade sapphires. When Shan picked one up to examine the color, it cut her palm and left a small speck of blood that stopped flowing immediately. The blue light in her hands fluttered behind the shards as if trying to match the exact shade and then died down again.

"Did it upset you, smashing the bells like that?" she asked.

"I thought it an odd request. I don't understand why he felt the need to obliterate them with such violence. If he wanted to ensure they were never used again, the nanites would have done that. But he said they had to burn bridges."

"If he likes dramatic gestures, why didn't he do it himself?"

"I didn't ask."

"They're all as mad as fucking hatters anyway," Shan said, and finished the braid.

She wanted it over and done with. She would always love Bezer'ej in the way that you could when you were somewhere desolate for a day trip and you could go home to familiarity later. But it wasn't home, not even with Aras, and not even here in Josh's soothing, gold, buried house with its soft light and calming silence.

She wasn't sure what home was any more.

"A few of them are digging in to stay," Shan said. Aras stiffened. She smoothed down his hair and arranged the braid carefully down his back. "They didn't think we'd salt the planet. It was hard to tell them we'd already started."

"But you did."

"Of course."

There was no turning back now. On the four landmasses in the southern hemisphere, troops from the Temporary City were dropping units of the bioagent that would spread on the air and water, propagate, and then go into a dormant state on surfaces as soon as the optimum concentration had been reached. It would take about fifty or sixty days to complete. Then they would come north and begin seeding the remaining landmasses, including the continent that broke up into a chain of islands with saints' names.

The clock was ticking.

"Clever buggers," said Shan. "I spoke to the bloke who designed it. He said he studied some of Constantine's archive files on anthrax to achieve long-term dormancy. And I said to him, blimey, do you know how much you would be worth to the military back home? He wasn't amused."

"You think of us as *blokes* now. Is your assimilation that complete?"

"It must be. I've not lost any sleep knowing I'm a weapon. That's a pretty good indicator."

There was one more thing she had to do, one of many, but it was personal rather than part of the evacuation. Aras trailed a few paces after her as she walked down to the shore to the Place of Memory of the First and the Place of Memory of the Returned, shrines to the bezeri explorers who had beached their craft to explore the Dry Above. Some never made it back.

It meant a long walk through Constantine's fields. It meant walking through the scattered patches of crops in full leaf and flower, past people who had once learned to trust her and who were now probably wondering why they ever bothered.

She tried to imagine what it was like to have to leave behind everything—*everything*—you had ever known or worked for. Then she remembered that she had.

It was tough shit.

This was for the bezeri.

At the water's edge Aras handed her the signaling lamp that translated speech into the patterns of lights the bezeri used to communicate. "Reckon I need it?" she asked, flexing her fingers and sending a kaleidoscope of colors dancing under the skin. Aras had learned when she was joking and when she was not, and he simply cocked his head a little. She didn't want him to accompany her. It was only the second time she had ventured into the bezeri's submarine world.

The other time had been to return the body of a dead infant, killed because Surendra Parekh had ignored an order not to take specimens.

Shan didn't need breathing apparatus now. It would be unpleasant, but she knew she couldn't drown. The isenj had done her a favor even if they hadn't known it when they had tried a dozen and more ways to kill a *c'naatat*-infected wess'har.

She stripped off her uniform down to her briefs, not wanting to walk back in sodden clothing, and steeled herself for the coming moment of complete animal terror as water flooded her lungs.

She glanced over her shoulder first. Aras was sitting on the shore, elbows braced on his drawn-up knees, chin resting on his hands. She felt suddenly stupid. It was hard to maintain an image of silent menace in a pair of pale blue panties and a dog tag.

"Nothing to see here, folks," said Shan. "Move along. Break it up."

Aras didn't smile. He pointed past her. There was the faintest suggestion of lime-green light in the shallows. The bezeri patrol was watching. She walked towards it. And contrary to popular myth, she stepped clean through the surface of the water. She couldn't walk on the damn stuff at all.

The sea was achingly cold despite the balmy day. The cold stopped her breathing for a couple of seconds and then *c'naatat* overrode her weak human reflexes and forced her lungs into action. Currents tugged at her as she got in chest-deep. The pressure squeezed her ribs.

Just dive.

She plunged in. She couldn't stop herself taking a great gulp of air before going under; nor could she stop herself holding her breath until the need to surrender to the reflex overwhelmed her and she inhaled. She screamed for air but there was no sound, just the endless sucking gasp that didn't have a beginning or end. She couldn't stop her arms flailing.

I'm not dying I'm not dying I'm not dying I can't die I can't die I can't—

And then she felt something like cool water, separate from the sea, trickling over her from the top of her head and through the core of her. Her breathing stopped. *It stopped.* And she wasn't dead, not unless dead was a long way from what she expected it to be, which was black oblivion.

She let her eyes adjust to the low light and the distortion of the water. Then she realized she was flat on her back. She eased herself into a crouch, straightened up and looked around for the signaling lamp, which had settled into the sand a few meters away.

The water in front of her blackened and moved. Then it was as if someone had suddenly switched on the Christmas lights in a shopping center. There was a wall of color. She had forgotten how big the adult bezeri could grow.

Why are you here? they asked.

She fumbled with the lamp. Her voice vibrated in her ears, and wess'u seemed to translate a lot better than English ever had. *I once promised you I would maintain an exclusion zone around this world. It was the job I came to do.*

But the wess'har are withdrawing. How can you help?

They're leaving a weapon that will protect you, and it was made from my body.

There was a silent moment. The great gelatinous shapes, trailing tentacles that were striped with rippling gold and carmine, hung in front of her.

We know you would kill your own kind for us.

There was no tone in the translation and she wasn't sure if they were complimenting her on her solidarity with them or saying they didn't trust her an inch.

She picked her response carefully.

I'm sorry we've caused you so much grief.

They knew *sorry*. They'd seen the word from her before. She held out both hands and concentrated until the luminescence in them danced. *That* got a reaction. The bezeris' lights flared and the lamp spluttered a burst of what sounded like static. She wondered if it was the bezeri for *well, bugger me.*

She had to explain it. *I have something of you in me. I'm like Aras now.*

Silence. They just hung there, watching.

I just wanted to know how you felt.

Still nothing. Then one glided forward and stopped a meter short of her. It—he—loomed almost twice as high as Aras, tentacles trailing almost straight down. *If we had weapons like the wess'har, we would fight your kind, and the isenj. But we do not. Until then, we must rely on the courage of people we cannot see.*

It was an ambiguous answer. What was she expecting, absolution? Was any of it her fault? It felt like it. She felt ashamed to be human. It was time to go.

Goodbye.

Perhaps they didn't have a word for farewell. The lamp was silent. She backed off a few steps and then turned and walked back the way she had come, navigating by rocks and plant growth. She didn't look behind again. A little further up the slope, she struck out with her arms and legs and summoned up some primeval human instinct to swim that she had never used before.

When her head was clear of the surface, she choked on air again. She knelt on all fours on the beach, coughing and retching up water. She could feel that her briefs were halfway off one hip and she wondered what the lads from her relief at Western Central would have said if they could have seen her, if any of them had still been alive. They would have laughed themselves sick.

Aras's boots came into view. She retched again, coughing out mucus and seawater in long strings.

"It's sheer glamor that attracted you to me, isn't it?" she said, and tried to grin. But the remnant of the sea wanted out, and fast.

Aras put her jacket over her shoulders and sat with his arm round her back while she recovered her breath and her underwear dried.

"That wasn't as bad as you expected," he said, forestalling any comment from her that it had actually been bloody terrifying. "In time, you'll control it."

It was another tick on the list, another life-threatening event that her new body had treated as a learning opportunity. She had long known it, but this was the first time she had genuinely felt that she wasn't human.

And if she was no longer human, she had no need to be ashamed any more.

Eddie could sleep anywhere when he had to, and a pallet on the construction site at Jejeno provided a sounder night's sleep than a bunk on a vessel that was one big target roundel in his mind's eye. He didn't want to say as much. He worried that he made things happen just by saying them.

He got up and splashed his face in the fountain.

"Oi, don't you know there's a bleedin' shower over there?" said a worker in a hard hat and coverall. He jerked his thumb to help Eddie better locate the facilities.

"Ah, silly me," said Eddie. "Thank you so much."

It was hard doing laundry in the shower, but he managed to wash and rinse his change of shirt and smalls and left them draped over a bot to dry. It made him feel quite the correspondent again: news editors, anchored to their desks, had no idea about the messy logistics of being in the field. He entertained a brief fantasy about dumping Boy Editor in the middle of a war zone where the local food was beyond human digestion. It gave him a warm feeling. It was exactly where he was now.

"You look untidy," said Serrimissani when she collected him to escort him to see Ual.

Eddie checked his distorted reflection in a polished metal plate. He did his shirt up a little higher. It seemed to placate the ussissi, and she trotted ahead of him in silence. He opened his screen to check the news while he walked.

"Keep up," she said, not turning. She had a predator's hearing, the sort that listened for small things burrowing. Shan had told him about their taste in snacks. It didn't surprise him one bit.

The headlines didn't help. The diplomatic row—and Eddie normally found that an amusing mental image—was intensifying. It was all unspecific threat, typical of frightened people led by even more frightened politicians who wanted to look like they were Doing Something About It. Eddie wasn't sure if the Americas or the Rim states could actually take out *Thetis*. But even if they could, they had a long wait ahead before they could see the whites of her eyes.

Eddie tried to work out how long it would be before *Thetis* came within range of Earth vessels, trying to juggle seventy-five-year transit times against near light-speed, and gave up. There weren't that many deep space vessels about even now:

they cost money, and space was neither a popular tourist destination nor a vote-getter. It was the main reason why they were
using an old knacker like *Thetis* instead of saving twenty-five
years by sending a modern vessel to pick them up.

A group of isenj laborers walked across his path like a badly
adjusted film sequence, all jerks and twitches. His hard-wired
reaction to quick, staccato movement said *spider* and he tried to
think *person*. But he failed. Maybe they were failing to make
that conceptual leap on Earth, too.

They had left little dusty tracks across the Instaroad that had
been rolled out to stop the bots digging even deeper gouges into
the soil. Eddie paused and looked down. It looked like someone
had shattered a flowerpot and left some of the fragments of
black plastic behind.

Oh, he thought. *Oh.*

There was only one movement between involvement and
noninvolvement. Eddie paused before making it. They said
time wasn't linear and that all things really happened at once
but that you just saw it sequentially. Eddie knew that was bollocks. Once he had taken this step, there was no quantum state
that would untake it for him.

He uncapped the urine sampler and scooped up the black
fragments. He was pretty sure he knew what they were. He
hoped they would do.

Serrimissani had realized he wasn't keeping up and scuttled
back to chivvy him. She followed his wrist action with
scorpion-eater's eyes as he closed the cap on the vial and
popped it into the top pocket of his shirt.

"Don't hold us up," she said. "Minister Ual is waiting for
you."

"Sorry," he said.

She didn't say anything else. He walked behind her at double time like a Greenjacket. When they got into the ground car,
she stared out of the open door as if to avoid conversation.

The boundaries of the site were marked by no more than
chevron tape strung between waist-high poles, but the isenj

treated them like fortifications. The crush started right outside. As soon as the car was past the tape, it had to press slowly through the throng. Eddie remembered the isenj who he thought he had seen fall and wondered if he'd ever got up again.

They didn't seem to be a brutal or thoughtless people. But it was very hard to stop a crowd moving, even an orderly one that seemed to have its own unspoken rules of flow and speed.

Ual greeted Eddie at the door of his office, covering ground like a piece of badly designed furniture on castors.

"I'm sorry that things are still so tense back home," said Eddie.

"You're not responsible for your governments," said the minister, still sucking in and wheezing out the alien words through a hole in his throat somewhere.

They sat in his fine plain aquamarine office and sipped something that might have been coffee. It was too liquid for Eddie to choke on. But he thought he might, and he didn't feel clever and he didn't feel in control. He took an occasional but discreet glance at Ual's coat of projections strung with beads— red ones today—and wondered what perverse universe created a species with quills that was also doomed to live at very close quarters.

"We will be careful not to react," said Ual. "We are not the ussissi. And we truly want a mutually helpful relationship with humans."

Serrimissani wasn't in earshot but Eddie still winced. "Do your people know what's been on our news?"

"Yes, but it's not their preoccupation. It's a long way away and they have problems here and now to cope with."

"We really do have a lot in common." *Yes, and you're using it to kill them.* "If it's any comfort, we behave the same with members of our own species. We don't take kindly to strangers."

"It's a wise precaution."

"Are you in direct contact with the FEU foreign minister?"

"Not as directly as I am with you. He sends general messages, I send general replies. All encouraging words about technology and understanding. I don't believe he is ready for a real-time exchange, as you call it. I imagine he has people around him who I don't see but who want to check every word in and every word out."

"You're absolutely right."

"And yet you have no such problem."

"I'm a journalist. We're not here to make politicians happy. Quite the opposite, in fact."

If Ual was a two-faced weasel, it would make what Eddie had to do so much less painful. Eddie had no idea yet whether isenj were enough like humans to play nasty little games, or whether they were like the wess'har and the ussissi—aggressively frank and literal because they not only didn't know how to lie but felt sufficiently confident not to need to.

Weasels. Eddie decided he would see animals differently in future, if he ever got home. Maybe weasels had something to tell him.

"We understand your natural fear of overcrowding," said Ual. Now that was for the bee-cam, for sure. "I wish your people would be reassured that what we want is your help to learn your technologies, so we can address our own problems. Your planet is not our target. I do believe you should stop people reading those books by Mr. Wells."

Eddie laughed. "He was a journalist too. We're a lovable bunch."

"There is a predisposition among your trade to make trouble," said Ual, and made a gargling sound like a fast-emptying drain.

"I take it you wouldn't mind if I broadcast our conversation?"

Ual looked at him—he imagined—with amusement. Eddie had no idea, really: isenj had no discernible eyes.

" 'Every mike is a live mike,' " said Ual. "That is correct, is it not?"

It was always satisfying to play the game with a professional. The key to self-respect was self-awareness: as long as you knew the game was on, it didn't hurt at all. Ual had learned it rather well.

There was a small glassy *ping*, and one of Ual's decorative beads bounced and rolled on the smooth-polished floor. Eddie fielded it deftly.

It had a fragment of quill still attached.

"Split ends are a bugger," said Eddie, and held it out on his palm, willing Ual not to take it back.

"I have many," Ual said. "Do keep it. I think you call it corundum. We have mined a very great deal of it over the years."

"Rubies?" Eddie was briefly distracted: the stone was just tumbled, neither faceted nor polished into a cabochon. He'd never seen a plain stone. *And those green beads might have been emeralds.* "Thank you. But don't tell too many humans about these, eh? It plays to our most excessive fantasies."

He kept the bead and the quill in his palm until he was clear of the ministerial offices and waiting for the car outside with Serrimissani. Then he uncurled his fingers and breathed properly again. Serrimissani was looking the other way, but as he tightened the cap of the vial, she jerked round and stared.

"Look what Ual gave me," said Eddie, having no choice.

Serrimissani looked him over as if she was searching discreetly for evidence. She reminded him of Shan, who always kept watch on what was happening around her even if she was also looking you straight in the eye. Coppers could do that.

"Is that all he gave you?" asked Serrimissani, and got into the car before he could frame an answer. He was expecting her general irritability to erupt into a lecture on how he should not interfere with the affairs of other nations, but she just studied her text pad, with an occasional yawn that ended in a slight whine and a snap of jaws, much like a fox's.

She was not on anyone's side, and his actions were his own to take, and to justify.

"D'you know, I've never parachuted," said Rayat.

"Shut up," said Barencoin.

The Once-Only suits hung from a sliding rail in the shuttle bay, ready to be fired out into space by a pressure jet when the aft hatch opened. Lindsay felt like a silk cocoon waiting to be dropped into seething water. She debated whether to kill the suit-to-suit comms but they needed to be able to hear each other.

They had plain old radios too: no AI comms, automatic switching or multiples. It was back to basic radio procedure. She hoped she could remember it.

Barencoin appeared to have stopped Rayat's muttering. He was surprisingly discourteous for a Royal Marine. And he was goading Bennett mercilessly. She wondered if it was nerves.

"DZ IN THIRTY SECONDS," said the pilot over their headsets.

I'm going to die, thought Lindsay.

"DZ IN TWENTY SECONDS."

I'm not coming back. I didn't think about that.

"DZ IN FIFTEEN SECONDS."

I only thought about going. Sorry, Eddie.

"TEN."

At least . . .

"NINE."

. . . I'll be . . .

"EIGHT."

. . . near David.

"SEVEN."

"Ade, hold my hand. . . ." said Barencoin.

"SIX."

"Ade, I want to pee. . . ."

"FIVE."

"Cork it."

"FOUR."

"Ade, are we there yet?"

"THREE."

"Fuck you, Mart."

"TWO."

"Shut it," said Lindsay.

"ONE. DZ. GREEN LIGHT. AWAY."

And she thought she fell.

Foam exploded into the suit's inner skin and in seconds she was encased in a soft but insistent molded cradle of polysilicate. And she kept falling, but her brain said she should have landed by now. She could see the thin line that tethered her to the ma-iale; if she had been able to summon up the courage, she could have looked back and followed the other section of tether to see Bennett and the others, strung like beads from the tow-line.

Humans needed a floor. They needed it more than they needed a definite up and down. This was not flying; this was not banging out of an aircraft through the canopy; this was not an EVA with a safety line rigged to the hull. This was complete, unconnected, disembodied physical terror, made all the worse because she had no reassurance of gravity.

It was all she could do not to be sick. She shut her eyes. Her suit, like all of them, had its own autopilot, but it was very hard to trust that when you were in a foam-filled plastic bag that you hoped would withstand reentry temperatures. She could hear the quiet, almost casual chitchat between the marines. Baren-coin had stopped teasing Bennett. They were all business now.

"Sunray this is Labros Two, over," said Qureshi's voice in her ear.

"Uh . . . this is Sunray, over," said Lindsay.

"Just checking Sunray, out."

"I'm here too," said Rayat, but nobody responded.

"Sunray, focus on the planet until suit rotation," said Qureshi. "Not long to go, out."

Time seemed to pass in fits and starts. Two hundred kilometers was a bloody long way, and a bloody long time. She felt the sudden push as the suit detached from the tether and switched to its internal navigation: 150 kay. One moment she was look-ing at the one suit she could actually see—whose?—and the next Bezer'ej was filling her field of view and there wasn't much black left.

Then the suit flipped her over on her back.

That was good, because she now had the black heat-shield deployed where it was meant to be, but it was also bad, because she was staring back into a void and she couldn't see any reference point. She started to count. They were at fifty thousand meters, more or less.

"Sunray, this is Sunray Minor, here comes the tough bit, out," said Bennett, and Lindsay started feeling . . . warm. It might have been her imagination.

In the thin layer of elastomerics and softglass a matter of inches from her spine and vital organs, the core temperature was reaching 100C. On the surface the suit was meteor-hot. *Don't think about it.* She was prepared to nuke herself to destroy Shan Frankland, but the thought of burning up on reentry was one step too far. It was slow.

She couldn't touch the ERD or the bot stowed in her suit because the foam had embraced them as closely as it had her.

"Sunray Minor, this is Sunray," she said shakily. The vibration and g of reentry was beginning to become unbearable. She didn't care if they knew she was scared. The only people who wouldn't have been bricking it then were either mad or Shan Frankland. "I—I'm having telemetry issues here. How's the approach, over?"

"Sunray, this is Sunray Minor, we're on the nose, out," said Bennett, and she would never have guessed that he had once reached Mach 1 with just foam and liquid glass between him and incineration. "Not long now."

Lindsay had stopped looking out of her limited faceplate view and shut her eyes. She had contemplated death in her shuttered coffin of a bunk and now she was trying another shroud on for size. She wasn't thirty yet. It wasn't fair.

She was just thinking that Shan Frankland would have told her that there was nothing about life that was fucking fair, so she should buck up and get on with it, when she was jerked so hard that her teeth threatened to shatter. It was the chute deploying at ten thousand meters. She blinked. There were clouds. There were flashes of iridescence. *God, please let the landing zone be right, I don't fancy falling into the quicksand....*

In a minute or so she would be—

The wind was punched out of her lungs. She rolled, not because she had remembered her ejection training but because she hadn't been expecting to hit the ground right then. She struggled to breathe. It was solid ground, and the head-up display in her helmet said she was one kay from Constantine. As she rolled she felt a lot lighter. The heat-shield had detached.

"Sunray at target, over," she called at last.

"Sunray Minor at target, over."

"Sunray Minor, what's your location, over?" She couldn't look at her palm display until she was free of the suit.

"Sunray Minor, two south from target, no visuals yet, out."

"Labros Two, three south-south-west of Constantine, out," said Qureshi's voice.

"Labros Three, south-south-west of target also, I have visual of Labros Two, out," said Chahal.

There was a pause, more puffing, and then Barencoin's voice. "Labros Four at target, no visual of Sunray Minor. Wait one . . . Sunray, I'm right next to you, over."

"Labros Five, this is Sunray—where are you, Rayat? Over."

"Oh shit . . ." It was his voice all right, for all the shaking in it. So much for Webster's emulator. He wasn't near Qureshi at all.

"Sunray Minor, I have Labros Five, out," said Bennett's voice.

Then she lost him. There was a lull. There was a clamor of exertion in her earpiece, and Qureshi's voice. "Oh bollocks," she said, abandoning voice procedure. "Shit."

Then the puffing stopped dead as if the mike had been cut. Lindsay waited.

"Sunray here, I've lost voice—Labros Two, Labros Three, this is Sunray, respond, over."

Nothing. Chahal was gone too.

But at least they were all down. They were in one piece,

more or less. The elation was so great that she tried to leap to her feet, but the remains of the suit wouldn't let her, and there was the small matter that she and Barencoin were several kilometers from the rest of them.

It wasn't far under the circumstances, but time mattered. It would slow them a little, and the more time they spent on the radio, the greater their chance of being picked up.

It took a while to peel out of a Once-Only. It was like unpacking electronics: the foam was reluctant to part. Lindsay cracked the seal on her helmet and pushed up the visor to breathe Bezer'ej's thin air. She was still easing open the suit when she heard Barencoin, somewhere outside her field of vision, say, "Oh."

Oh wasn't a very marine-like word. But she understood why he said it. She was trying to get her other arm free through the horse-collar-shaped opening when the bright Bezer'ej sky was obscured by Josh Garrod.

He was aiming a very, *very* old rifle straight into her face. Firearms warranted respect regardless of antiquity.

Now she had a good idea of what Qureshi had decided was *bollocks*.

"Get up, Commander," he said. "I'm fully prepared to break the Sixth Commandment."

17

URGENT.

FIRE CONTROL PARTY MEET AT THE MAIN PUMPING STATION IM-
MEDIATELY. CRAFT INTERCEPTED IN EXCLUSION ZONE. IF ISENJ
CAN BREACH DEFNET, SO MAY OTHERS. COLLECT ARMS AND PA-
TROL ISLAND. DO NOT INFORM ARAS OF PATROL INTENTION. RE-
PEAT, DO NOT INFORM. HE SHOULD NOT BE EXPOSED TO RISK.
JOSH GARROD to council members,
via pager

It was an old rifle but it was very clean, and that meant it
probably worked.

Lindsay could see that just fine. Josh jerked the barrel in a
gesture to hurry up and she scrambled out of the Once-Only.

No. It doesn't end like this. Her plan had been defeated by
farm-hands. *No, we've come too far.*

"Okay, Josh," she said. "Take it easy."

Barencoin had a museum-piece rifle trained on him too. It
had to be a humbling experience for a commando of his caliber.
But paratroops had always been vulnerable in descent; and they
could get their arms free fast, unlike the detachment, who were
effectively shrink-wrapped. The Once-Only was designed to
save your life, not to be shed easily in combat situations.

Barencoin struggled out of the suffocating suit and stood
looking remarkably resigned. It took him several minutes.

"How the hell did you land in those?" Josh asked. "And what
have you come for?"

Martin Tyndale, a man Lindsay had always associated with
fretting about broad bean crops, was rummaging through one
charred, crumpled suit casing, making the foam crackle and

squeak. There were small wisps of smoke rising from what looked like shiny puddles of black oil. What remained of the detached portions of the heat-shields were still shedding heat.

"Lots of metal stuff in here that I don't feel too confident about," he called.

"Arms?"

Lindsay took her helmet off very slowly. She hadn't survived free-fall from space to get her head blown off by an antique, and she still might salvage the mission. Martin was fumbling with the retrieval bot.

"Don't," Lindsay said. "It might go off." The chances of his finding the right manual detonation sequence were remote but she had a feeling that bad luck was going to be the order of the day. "It's explosive."

"Have you come for Shan?" Josh asked.

"Yes," said Lindsay.

"You won't take her, or the parasite."

Lindsay gambled. Eddie had always said the truth had enormous shock value. "I haven't come to take her, I've come to destroy her and *c'naatat* so that it never gets into the human population."

Barencoin was a little behind her, so she didn't see his expression, but she knew that he would be concealing his opinion rather well. They'd all been suckered into her private mission. Succeeding didn't make her feel good.

Josh simply looked at her, without hatred and without fear.

"The organism's on Christopher, isn't it?" she said.

"Doesn't matter. You're not having it. It's an abomination. We should have destroyed it. We considered burning the island."

Lindsay saw the options flash up in front of her like numbered cards. "I think I can help with that."

"How?"

"We have a device that will destroy all life on the island in a controlled burn. At temperatures *you* can't create."

Josh's aim didn't waver. Lindsay wondered if he was hoping

to shoot her anyway for being a sinner, a fornicator, a paid killer. "You brought weapons here?"

"Frankland's a tough bitch to kill. You might have noticed."

"You hate her that much. God forgive you."

"I hate her, but this is about neutralizing a biohazard."

"Sounds like vengeance to me," said Josh. "And that's not for man to dispense."

"Sounds like a clean job. As long as she lives, someone will be after what she's got. They'll never risk chasing Aras, but they'll keep taking a crack at her, and they won't stay away from here forever."

Lindsay wondered how long Josh could hold that rifle steady. The barrel hadn't moved a hair. He looked as if he was physically digesting her words.

"And you, a soldier, want to destroy *c'naatat* even though you would have so many military uses for it," he said at last.

I'm not a soldier. I'm a naval officer. It was a silly thing to care about right then. "I know exactly how it'll be used, thanks. That's why I want all sources eradicated. And I know you have some regard for Frankland, but she doesn't want it getting loose any more than we do."

Barencoin cut in. "Those weren't our orders, ma'am. We're supposed to detain her alive."

"Shut up," she said without turning. "Josh, if you can get us to Christopher, we'll carry out a burn of the island. I've got three marines in the field anyway. You got lucky catching us, but you'll never take them, and you know it. This way we all get what we want. What's it to be?"

Josh had very unsettling pale eyes. He looked like a man who had a temper that he controlled with care, and his gaze reminded her all too much of Shan's. "You have one marine left, then, because we captured two a little way from here. Those suits really are a liability, aren't they?"

"Ah." She was running out of bargaining chips. "You're not as bucolic as you look, are you?"

"And you want Superintendent Frankland."

They stood absolutely still, absolutely silent. *Don't blink. Don't speak first.* Lindsay tried to play Eddie and Shan, praying their respective professional tactics would work for her. It was a bad time to discover prayer.

"These weapons of yours," said Josh. "These bombs. Are you certain they'll only burn the island?"

"They're enhanced radiation devices. I know that sounds shocking, but the radiation is the short-lived kind. The detonation will be confined to the island."

Josh stood unblinking but not focusing on her. He was taking his time.

"It's just one island against the future of many worlds," he said at last. "And it is *only* on Christopher, Commander, nowhere else. But it's all sinful destruction in the end." He let out a long breath. "I'll take you to Christopher. And I'll bring you back. How you retrieve Shan Frankland is a matter for you."

"Is she in Constantine?"

"No. Temporary City. Our transport is being organized from there."

"Thank you, Josh."

"I shall pay for this. I should have told Aras, but he would do something foolish, and I don't want his safety put at risk."

Barencoin was suddenly right on Lindsay's shoulder, and she realized she had never really noticed what a big man he was. "Ma'am, I want to remind you our orders were to detain her, nothing else," he said quietly.

"Marine, this is a direct order," she said. She wasn't at all sure he'd follow it. "You will rendezvous with Sergeant Bennett's party at the preagreed point, retrieve the remaining devices from Rayat, give them to me, and then you will capture and detain Superintendent Frankland."

"And then?"

"You let me worry about that."

She could do it herself. She could make sure Rayat set the

damn ERDs himself and then she would do what was needed with Shan. There was no point asking any of the marines to go beyond their rules of engagement.

Because you know they'll defy you. No, it was the right thing to do. If anyone was going to breach the regs, it would be her. It was an officer's responsibility.

Liar. They won't follow you and you know it.

"If you use your radios beyond this island, they might detect you," Josh said.

Barencoin was tapping his finger against his hand, eyes fixed on a point just past Lindsay. Then he looked intently at his palm. "Got Ade," he said. "He'll leave the devices for you at these coordinates in twenty minutes."

Lindsay tried to give Josh a reassuring and knowing smile. "Morse," she said. "Out of use for centuries. But not for us. As long as you've got something to make a sound or a light with, you're in business."

"We'll send a scoot to collect them," Josh said. "We won't attract as much attention."

"I need the other three devices. Six in all."

"Very well."

Lindsay paused and then cracked the remaining seals on her spacesuit and heaved herself out of it, leaving it in the scrubby blue grass of the wild sector of Constantine's island like a shed skin. No point declining Josh's help. As she looked at Barencoin, the only indication that he was deeply unhappy with the mission was his expression of intense concentration.

"You sure you know what you're doing with those ERDs, Boss?" asked Barencoin. "Let Izzy set the damn things."

"Of course I do," said Lindsay. "If infantry can set them, then Rayat can too."

The wess'har appeared to be occupied with loading colonists and their baggage. There were none around as they made their way through the crops and the wild grass down to the cove where Josh kept a couple of RIBs, ancient shallow-draft powerboats.

His son James stood guard with a rifle. The sight of a teenage boy with a weapon he clearly knew how to use was disturbing. Lindsay's view of the colonists as hand-wringing, passive eccentrics had been shattered.

"How did you know we were coming?" she asked James.

"You looked like shooting stars," he said. "We could see you for ages."

If the colonists had seen them coming, then maybe Shan had too. She hoped so.

Josh came back on a scoot with a man she didn't know, and one she knew too well. Rayat was balancing three meter-long cylinders on his scoot. They waded out into the shallows and piled them into the boat with the other devices. The boat settled alarmingly low in the water.

Five for Christopher. And one for Shan Frankland.

Lindsay looked at Rayat with as much contempt as she could muster. It wasn't up to one of Shan's cauterizing glances, but she felt it sincerely. They stared at each other for a moment and then scrambled to opposite ends of the vessel.

It was a bumpy, spray-sodden and uncomfortable journey to Christopher at forty knots: it took nearly two hours. The nine-meter RIB—the rigid inflatable whose design hadn't changed in three hundred years—had just enough room for the scoots, Josh, another colonist called Jonathan, Rayat, and herself. They traveled in silence.

It was a long time to spend thinking about how she would get to Shan, or not, and whether she was now going to die at all, something she had thought was inevitable.

What she wanted more than anything right then—apart from being dry—was to visit David's grave and sit by the beautiful stained glass headstone that Aras had made.

Rayat said they could set the device timers for up to twenty-four hours, but Lindsay wanted to be gone from here inside six. She wondered if she would have time to find David's grave. It was probably out of the question if they were going to find Shan.

But she had a feeling that Shan would come to find her when she found out what they had done.

Shan had two messages on her wess'har comms device that morning and she almost erased one by accident. She liked the swiss better. The *virin* was intuitive for a wess'har, but she was still fumbling with it.

It was like a bar of transparent glycerine soap with images that appeared both within it and on its surface. When Shan wasn't concentrating on her hands, the lights would flicker from them and shine confusingly through the *virin*, triggered by her subconscious desire to communicate. Operating the device required a full hand grip with as many finger positions as a three-dimensional guitar. It was exactly what she should have expected for a culture that wrote in fish-bone diagrams rather than a linear style.

She hated it. But it could access the wess'har archives, and the swiss could not.

One message was from a ussissi crew, reporting scan contact with one of *Actaeon*'s shuttles six thousand kilometers from Bezer'ej. They'd warned it off: the pilot had claimed navigation problems, and they followed it all the way back to *Actaeon* just to be certain. The other was from Nevyan, wishing her well and asking how things were with Aras.

Nevyan was a nice kid. Shan sat on a packing crate at the entrance to the Temporary City, watching the loading of Constantine's essential impedimenta and composing a reply with difficulty. *C'naatat* clearly thought that skill with a *virin* was low on its priority upgrades list.

A very young male, Litiat, came up to her, smelling submissive and agitated. He beckoned to her.

"The *gethes* want to speak with you," he said.

"Josh?"

"No, a *gethes*. Okurt."

"He knows I'm here, then." *Thanks, Eddie,* she thought. But that didn't matter: they couldn't touch her. She wondered what last-minute bargain Okurt was trying to strike, and rather relished the prospect of a verbal tussle. She didn't envy him his task.

Litiat led her to the screen in the lobby of the Temporary City and stood back at a respectful distance. Shan stood, arms folded, hands concealed, and waited for Okurt's image to resolve. He looked a lot thinner than she remembered from the last video link. She wondered if she looked very different to him.

"What can I do for you?" she asked.

"Good morning, Superintendent. You're evacuating Constantine?"

"You know we are."

"I'm formally offering assistance."

"Oh yeah. You would. Thanks, but we've got a lift."

Okurt paused. "I wondered if you might reconsider your position regarding returning home."

Shan paused too, just a couple of seconds longer. "Okay, I've considered it. I'm just fine here, thanks."

"I assure you no action will be taken against you if you cooperate. And the asset wouldn't be made available to commercial interests."

"And that's supposed to reassure me, is it?"

"We could make it worth your while. You would be able to free up your considerable personal assets on Earth as well."

"D'you know, son, it's been *years* since anyone tried to threaten me with losing my pension." He really didn't get it at all. "So they've frozen my funds. I'm on a planet 150 trillion miles from home and there's no shopping mall here. Try again."

"It doesn't have to be this way."

"Commander, nothing could induce me to turn myself in. And you can tell that to whoever put you up to asking me. Haven't you got the picture yet?"

Okurt was fidgeting: he was moving almost out of frame at times, shifting in his seat and leaning back. He was working up to saying something.

"Anything else?" said Shan. Okurt paused just one fraction

of a second too long. You could spot that sort of thing with ITX: there was no transmission delay. He looked grim. Shan felt he was trying to keep her talking, fishing for something else. Her copper's instinct was fine-tuned and she was proud of it. It had now started screaming in her ear. "Want to apologize for letting a shuttle stray a bit close?"

"Perhaps I should simply apologize and leave you to your task."

"No, hang on, you've got my interest now. I'd hazard a guess that you don't know something you need to know, and you're checking. Now, what could that be?" No response: if she'd been Okurt, she'd have been off the link by now, but he was desperate to know *something*. It was just like old times, an interrogation, and she was good at that. She let her instinct drive. "You're checking. What would you be checking? Something you can't verify by technology. So . . . let me see . . ." She dared not blink. She needed to see every muscle, every twitch of his face. "I reckon . . . ah, you want to know if something got through. Something you can't contact or verify. You tried to do something daft, didn't you? What was it?"

"The pilot was off course. He's got no nav beacons he can log into out here."

"Oh, please. Don't insult my fucking intelligence. Haven't I explained the wess'har mentality to you? Make a bloody good note of this—they don't have rules of engagement. It's total war or nothing with them. Just *go*. Go home. Whatever it is you're doing, just stop and leave *now*. You have no idea who you're provoking."

She punched the link closed and sat for a couple of moments with her forehead in her hands. Litiat hovered.

"Get Aras," she said quietly. "I think *Actaeon* is about to take us over the brink."

Christopher was the smallest and southernmost island in the chain. It was flat and black.

The wind had dropped a little but billowing storm clouds

were beginning to gather. As the boat drew closer to the shore, Lindsay could see that the blackness was actually grass, and the shoreline was pure white sand. Shafts of sunlight punched through the cloud, making the sand look almost illuminated. It was extraordinarily beautiful in its unnatural palette of monochromes. It looked like ideal landing terrain.

More detail emerged as the distance closed. There were small thickets of purple foliage now, looking funereal against the glossy black grass that was swaying like a crop in the breeze.

Twelve square kilometers.

Then a thought that should have been obvious struck her a little too late.

"If we land, are we going to be infected too?" she asked.

Rayat looked up from the text pad in his hand. "The only tests we have for this are going to be pretty conclusive."

"Sorry?"

"We'll shoot you. If you survive, you've caught it. Then we'll have to try something more permanent. We have six on board." He looked at Josh. "Ever been tempted, Mr. Garrod?"

"That's not the kind of eternal life we seek," said Josh, still with a white-knuckled grip on his elderly rifle even after several hours of being buffeted by waves. "We know what it does."

"And you knew about it, Rayat, didn't you?" said Lindsay. Maybe it was the prospect of imminent death that had clarified her thinking and sharpened her memory. "That's what you were always looking for off-camp."

Rayat, still unperturbed, said nothing and steadied himself on the plank athwart the boat. He was first out, picking his way through the surf and up the beach. Lindsay had every intention of following his every move even if Josh shot her. She didn't trust him then, and she didn't trust him now, whatever he said and whoever he was working for.

"Get back here and help get these scoots ashore," Josh yelled. "Now."

It took all four of them to lift the scoots and carry them to dry land. It was the sort of thing the Booties did well, but they were a hundred kay behind her, and she hoped they were ready to blend into the beige mass of colonists and get to safety.

"I'd suggest placing the devices in a three-by-two pattern, maximum two kay apart," said Rayat. "Purely for coverage."

"You've got five to play with," said Lindsay. "One's for insurance." She beckoned to Jonathan to help her lift one clear of the scoot's floor plate.

"I'll set them to ground-burst. On their legs, about a meter."

"You sure they'll burn hot enough?"

"Thousand meter fireball each, down to a depth of three meters. Charcoal." Rayat shrugged. "I would have preferred double the number for certainty, but believe me, this won't be a popular tourist destination for a while."

Josh and Jonathan had their heads bowed, both absorbed in their own worlds. Then Lindsay realized they were praying. She found it more uncomfortable to realize that than to contemplate detonating neutron devices. Josh looked up again.

"We do a terrible thing," he said. "It's to prevent something worse. But let's recognize the sin we're committing, shall we? We have to answer to God, and I also have to answer personally to Aras in this world. He will vent his rage."

"Let's get on with it," said Lindsay.

It was a small island, easily covered by two scoots in less than an hour. It was also exquisitely beautiful, and the knowledge that she was helping devastate it was starting to eat away at her. The two scoots stayed within visual range of each other. It would have been a pleasant excursion had the pillion riders not been carrying rifles.

The black grass flattened beneath them like dark sea, and Lindsay found herself holding her breath. It was pointless but instinctive: if she were going to be contaminated, it was too late to stop breathing. She didn't even know if the organism was airborne anyway.

"Josh," she said, uncomfortable at having him sitting close

up behind her. "I still think Rayat's planning to get a sample off the planet."

"And were your orders any different?"

"No. We were told to grab it for the military and stop commercial companies getting it."

"So you deceive your own comrades too."

"Yes, I do. Much as it sticks in my throat to admit it, Frankland was right. It's a plague."

"Be sure that's why you're doing this," said Josh, and they lapsed into silence.

It took under an hour to place and prime all the devices. Lindsay held onto hers. She had grenades, but she hadn't come this far to take chances. Shan had to be obliterated. They stopped the scoots on the beach and got their breath back.

It really was a lovely spot.

The four destroyers of Christopher stood on the idyllic white beach, taking in a magnificent pre-storm cloudscape as dramatic as any William Blake woodcut. Four was an apocalyptic number; and the shafts of sun piercing the cloud were so unnaturally sharp and bright that Lindsay feared seeing the hand of God reaching through in cartoon retribution. She glanced at Rayat.

I have to be right about this. "So this is what they mean by limited damage," she said.

"Yes, it's beautiful here. It's a terrible and necessary shame."

They walked down the perfection of Christopher's icing-sugar sand and pushed the boat back into the water.

She *was* sure why she was destroying Eden. Wasn't she?

18

There's risk inherent in trying to reverse-engineer the isenj ITX relay. If we examine it and make our own prototype, we'll be independent of them. If we screw up and damage it, they'll know all about it. Ripping off new allies is suicidal. Let's wait.

Professor S. D. GALLAGHER,
special adviser to Secretary of State for Technology

Shan was angry. She had been angry all the way back to Constantine from the Temporary City and she wasn't bothering to conceal her scent.

The boat journey hadn't helped her mood. Vijissi had insisted on coming with them: Mestin had ordered him to look after her, he said, and so he would.

It was rather touching. He moved closer and Aras thought for a second that he was going to rub against her legs like a flattering cat. He didn't. He just sat very close, looking in the same direction as her.

It was a gesture of solidarity. Ussissi mirrored each other, whole packs moving as one. Shan appeared to realize that, because she almost smiled and sat still for a few moments as well.

It was the only thing she would have to smile about for a while.

Aras couldn't imagine how any *gethes* could land. They were technically limited, even compared to the isenj. And the defense net was now set to destroy—not immobilize—any incoming craft that came in range and didn't transmit a friendly signal. "Why do you think they would target Constantine?"

"They're looking for me," she said. She was fidgeting, meshing her gloved fingers hard together and stretching the fabric taut. "They think I'm there."

He walked behind her through the fields and down the ramp into Constantine. There were small groups of men in beige and taupe work clothes carrying crates and studying pieces of hemp paper. The final check was being carried out before Constantine was abandoned forever.

But they couldn't find Josh. And nobody would tell them where he was.

"I don't like this," said Shan. Aras was surprised how very fast she could move now. "Where's Josh? Something's gone bloody wrong."

"I fear he might be trying to solve a problem without bothering us."

Shan stopped abruptly and he nearly collided with her. "Do you know something I don't?"

"Nothing, except Josh. He can be foolhardy."

"I'll give him foolhardy."

They reached Josh's house. Shan shoved the door open and went from hall to kitchen. They found Deborah, Rachel, and James packing. James flinched visibly. Deborah and the little girl just froze, bewildered.

Shan fixed on James immediately. There was something in his reaction that triggered the hardened police officer in her. Aras knew that persona was in there: he had simply never seen it. "Deborah, take Rachel and get in the bedroom."

"Shan, what—"

"Just fucking do it. *Now.*" Deborah snatched up Rachel and the door slammed behind her. Shan rounded on James. They had never seen her like this, and neither had Aras. "Where's your father?"

"He's not here."

"You've got three seconds to tell me." Shan was nose-to-nose with the boy, leaning over him, white-faced and terrifying. "What's happened?"

James stood his ground in silence. Shan grabbed his collar and slammed him to the wall, cracking the back of his head against it. "You tell me and you tell me *now.*"

"No."

She drew back her arm and backhanded James so hard across the face that he fell. No, Aras had never, *ever* seen her like this. She dragged the boy to his feet again and pressed him to the wall. His nose was bleeding. Aras wondered if he should intervene before she killed him.

"*Now,*" she said. She had her forearm pressed across his throat. There was blood on her gloves. "Plenty more where that came from."

James struggled to speak. "Dad's trying to protect you."

"I don't need protection."

"They landed soldiers." He could hardly get the words out. "They landed. We saw them."

Shan slackened her lock a second before Aras would have pulled her off James. "You tell me everything you know."

"They landed the soldiers from *Thetis*, and Miss Neville. The soldiers are here. Dad's taken Miss Neville and Dr. Rayat."

"You've disarmed *marines*?"

"They came on parachutes in these cocoons. We tracked them all the way down."

Shan was all cold fury. "Fucking idiot. That's just *great*. We've got bloody Royal Marine commandos on site plus my biggest fan and that little shit Rayat. Why?"

"They're trying to stop anyone getting hold of *c'naatat*."

"Where's Josh taken them?"

"To Christopher Island."

"*Shit*. Aras, let the Temporary City know we've got a breach on Christopher."

Aras could hear Shan but he was instantly not quite there, not quite hearing. Josh had gone to the only environment where the *c'naatat* organism existed naturally. He had taken two *gethes* with him. Aras couldn't imagine what game he was playing. James's chin was trembling.

"Why?" Shan asked.

James seemed on the edge of tears. He was just a child. "To destroy it for good."

Shan marched James to the door by the scruff of his neck. "Take me to the marines."

"You're on your own now," said Josh.

Lindsay stumbled into the shallows and lost her footing. If Barencoin hadn't stepped in and hauled her to her feet again, she felt she would never have had the strength to stand upright. Bennett stood on the shore, rifle clutched across his chest, with an expression that said he was rapidly losing what little enthusiasm he had for the mission.

Rayat tumbled out after her. Nobody made a move to help him but Barencoin watched him carefully. Lindsay checked the seal on her rifle, making sure the water hadn't seeped in to the targeting mechanism. Josh stood in the bobbing vessel as if he was looking for a reason not to leave.

"What are you going to do now?" Lindsay asked.

"When your bombs detonate, I'll go and answer to Aras."

"And you trust him, do you?"

"He was my great-great-great-grandfather's friend," said Josh. "I suspect he merely tolerates me." He paused and pulled his messaging device from his pocket. He frowned at the small screen and let out a long breath. "My wife says Shan has paid us a visit. She's on her way to question your soldiers."

That was just fine. Lindsay looked at her watch and then at the bioscreen in her palm: even if Shan got any information out of Qureshi or Chahal, it was too late for her to do anything about it. And they could pass on a message for her, at just the perfect time.

Come and get me.

Aras's instinct to defer to a large, angry female had kicked in completely. He trailed behind Shan and the stumbling, terrified James, knowing he would find it hard to intervene now. They reached the drying barn. Inside, two soldiers he knew as Qureshi and Chahal were sitting on the dusty floor, cross-legged, looking unconcerned while Martin Tyndale stood over them with a rifle.

In the corner was a mound of glossy white fabric streaked and smeared with black charring.

"What's that?" asked Aras.

"Landing craft," said Martin. "One-man suits." His expression said he was thinking the same as Aras. It was unbelievable. "You got to hand it to them. They've got guts to attempt that."

Aras was shocked. He had no idea that humans were that reckless for their own safety. *That* was why they hadn't detected them.

Shan dropped James and shoved him over to Aras, then took her gun out of her waistband and held it on the two marines. "Have you searched them?" she asked.

"We've got their rifles," said Martin.

"Sweetheart, these are Royals. Booties." She stopped two meters from them. Her tone was incongruously kind. "Come on, fellers. You know the drill. Face down, on the floor, hands behind your heads, and don't piss me about." The marines obeyed without a word. She beckoned Martin forward. "If they move, shoot. Got that?"

"Got it," he said.

Shan handed her *virin* to Aras and then body-searched both the marines, gun still in one hand. It took a little time. She retrieved knives, lengths of sharp-edged wire, ammunition, flares and tubes of plastic explosive. She handed the haul item by item to Martin.

"Hands behind your back now," she said quietly, and handcuffed and hobbled them with reactive tape that would contract further with movement. Then she pulled them into a sitting position. "And that," she said to nobody in particular, "is why you *always* do a proper body search."

Shan suddenly reacted to Chahal. He was just looking at her hands. No, he was looking at her *watch,* or trying to. She squatted down in front of him.

"What is it, Chaz?" she said. "Late for tea?"

"Marine Balwant Singh Chahal, Three-seven Commando, number five nine oblique eight seven seven six alpha."

"Okay, I get the idea. I know it'll take me a lot longer to get an answer out of you than Jimmy here, but I *will* get there in the end."

Silence. She was staring into Chahal's face, no malevolence or anger visible at all, just sorrow. Qureshi was staring straight ahead and past her. Aras wondered how far Shan would go. He knew all too well how far she had been prepared to go in the past.

But that was with criminals. These were elite soldiers. She respected them.

"Where's the rest of the detachment?"

"Marine Balwant—"

"Give it a rest. What's so important about the time? What are Lin and Rayat up to?" Now Qureshi was staring at her hands. It was the lights: violet shimmered across her fingers as they curled round the 9mm weapon. Shan flicked a glance at Qureshi.

She didn't miss a thing, Aras thought. She was still a *good copper*. "Yeah, I light up too, just like you do. Is that bioscreen still working? If I take a look, will I pick up Lin's signal?"

She moved behind Chahal and jerked his arms up, twisting his wrist so she could see the illuminated screen grown into the cells of his palm. It was hurting him; Aras could smell it. The marine didn't react.

"Ah," said Shan. "No readout from Webster or Becken. Well, that's two we don't have to worry about. And we've got Bennett and Barencoin still on the loose, I see. Lin's pumping, though. Look at that heart rate. What's she up to?"

Qureshi shifted a little. "It's 1600 or thereabouts. You're too late."

Chahal let out a hiss under his breath but Shan didn't move. She glanced at Qureshi. "What's Lin done, Izzy?"

"You'll see soon enough," said Qureshi. "I'm really sorry. And we did come to take you."

"Fair enough," said Shan. "Nothing personal."

The *virin* that Aras was holding for her burst into light and color. The message was from the Temporary City. In the transparent layers of the device, Aras saw reconnaissance shots. A ussissi auxiliary unit was searching the seas around the southernmost islands.

The marines exchanged glances, and Shan was watching them. She seemed obsessed with the element of time. She walked slowly round the two marines and Aras wondered if she was going to kick one of them, *putting the boot in* as she called it. He had many half-formed memories from her, and that was a common one.

"So, you're trying to work something out," said Shan. "Did Lin get there or not? So I'm guessing time matters to you because there's an extraction planned, which means she's taking a sample, or something is going to happen later, and I reckon that means a device of some sort." She stopped in front of Chahal and pressed the muzzle of the gun carefully against his forehead, right between his eyebrows. She *would* shoot him: Aras was sure of it. The humans might not have been aware of her state of mind, but even without a scent to guide him, he could see the tension in her muscles and the blood absent from her face.

"Commander Neville had bombs," said James suddenly. Evidently he also believed she would fire her weapon.

Chahal was simply looking down into his lap now, jaw muscles twitching every so often. "What sort?" said Shan.

"Radiation bombs," said James. "They're going to burn the island. And then she's coming for you."

"Nukes? She's got nukes with her? Oh, *fuck*." Aras had expected Shan to erupt at that point, but she was still all white-faced control. "Izzy, I've got a terrific memory for detail. Ade once told me you were EOD trained. Well, you don't get ordnance that's much more explosive than this, so you can come and help us dispose of them."

Chahal looked up. "That contravenes the—"

"Chaz, shut up," said Shan gently. "You can report me to the Hague when you get back." She still had her gun to his head. "Are you in voice contact with Lin?"

Chahal's eyes flickered. "I have audio implants."

Shan straightened up and stepped back. Then she walked round behind him, gun still targeted at his head, and released the tape round his wrists. "Give her a bell. Tell her Shan wants to see her. Go on. Call the bitch."

Chahal paused and then pressed points on his wrist and palm. He was muttering under his breath: Aras could hardly hear him. Whatever implants these soldiers had, they were sensitive. Shan had once joked—or maybe not joked, perhaps—that she would never copulate with Sergeant Bennett because the whole detachment would hear. Aras finally understood exactly what she meant.

Chahal then went silent, as if listening. He looked up not at Shan, but at her gun.

"Commander Neville says she'll meet you."

Shan looked grim. She had stopped blinking completely. It was an unnerving thing to watch. "Tell me what she really said."

"She said, 'Come and get me.' "

Small wonder Chahal had tried to paraphrase it. Aras watched Shan's jaw clench and lock. He interrupted.

"She's trying to provoke you, *isan,*" he said.

"She's doing a fucking good job of it."

"You can't afford anger."

"I'll settle for some rough justice, then."

Aras caught Shan's arm carefully. "The ussissi will carry out the search for the weapons. But you stay here."

She almost shook him off, then appeared to relent and put her hand on top of his. But she still had her gun in the other. And it was still held on Chahal.

"I never sent a junior officer in to do the dirty work," she said. "And I'm not going to start now."

"I will accompany Qureshi."

"No. It might be a booby-trap for me."

"I will have my way on this, *isan.* Once the ussissi have located the devices from the air, I'll ensure she deals with them. No risks."

"You're very confident of that."

"You forget what I was." He was a soldier. He had been a fine one, too. He had forgotten none of it. "You stay here."

"And you forget what *I* was. EnHaz. Environmental crimes unit. I'm going to have that stupid little cow because she's prepared to trash the environment to get me. Now let me get on with my job."

"Listen to me. This is not necessary."

"Like the time you listened to me when I told you not to go after the isenj?"

"And you nearly died because you insisted on coming with me."

"I learned a lesson or two. I'll fire first this time."

Aras knew he could never force Shan to do anything. And he was running out of time arguing with her. "Promise me you'll be prudent."

"Okay. Prudence it is." Shan turned back to Chahal. "Tell her I'll see her at Constantine. Remind her that I know the tunnels, and she doesn't, and I'm in a fucking bad mood. And warn Bennett and Barencoin to stay out of it."

Chahal's lips moved and Shan appeared to be listening intently to him. She turned his palm over with one hand and said, "Show me where they are." She was checking the location coordinates to verify that Lindsay and the others were actually on the island and not just decoying her. Then she retaped his hands and called Martin over.

"Give me one of their rifles," she said.

Aras had rarely experienced indecision, but he was experiencing it now.

Shan *could* wait. She could wait until he got back, and then they could tackle Lindsay and her marines together, or—better still—they could leave them and wait for the pathogen to dispatch them. It would take a week or two, but the result would be the same.

No, Shan would never wait. Nobody could make her. He wanted to protect his *isan,* his *isanket,* his comrade-in-arms. But he was Bezer'ej's custodian, and he still had his ancient duty.

"Let Vijissi go with you," he said at last. "Please?"

"Okay. If it makes you happy." She turned to Martin. "Make that two rifles."

Qureshi did a credible job of matching their pace all the way down to the beached boats on the shore. Aras had his fingers tight around her upper arm just in case she tried to make a run for it, although he had no idea why flight would solve any problems. All he knew was that Shan had told him marines were supposed to escape if they could and harass the enemy. He didn't enjoy thinking of them as enemies.

"What are you going to do with Josh when you find him?" said Shan.

It was a question he hoped she wouldn't ask because he didn't want to ask it himself. Josh had betrayed him. Josh had helped *gethes* who were intent on—on what? Securing *c'naatat* or destroying it? They didn't seem to have a single purpose. But either way they were a threat to Shan and to Bezer'ej.

"I have no idea."

Shan strode on. "I know you're upset about James. I'm sorry I had to do that."

"He's a child. Did you have to hit him?"

"You're going soft."

"I don't shy away from necessary force."

"Anyone can bomb strangers. But sometimes you have to hurt your friends."

It was savage, and it was true: and he feared she despised him. Sometimes she was more wess'har than he was. But the drive to protect and nurture the young was powerful and he couldn't completely override it. "He's still a child."

Shan stood on the shingle, hands on hips, looking out to sea. There were no lights visible from shallow-swimming bezeri. "I'm an equal opportunities bastard," she said. "I don't care how old they are, how disabled they are, or what sex, culture or religion they are. I'll get answers out of them. I'm very fair that way."

She gave him an unconvincing smile in the way that she did when she wanted him to believe everything was all right when it wasn't.

Aras dragged one of the shallow-draft rigid inflatables down to the beach. Its engine started easily, as if it were warm from recent use. He climbed into the boat and pulled Qureshi in after him. She was heavier than her slight frame suggested, but she was still a very small female compared to his *isan*.

Aras looked back at Shan. "Be careful," he said. "They're still marines first, friends second."

"You be careful of Josh," Shan said. "He's stiffed you once. He'll do it again."

"I've known six generations of his family," Aras said. "I know his beliefs. Why would he do this?"

"Because, sweetheart, deep down he's a shit-house like every human," she said, and held her hand up in a parting gesture. Then, almost as if she had thought of something, she pulled the *virin* from her pocket and lobbed it into the boat. "You'll need this. See you back at the Temporary City."

There was a following wind. They would make good time. The boat bounced over the surface, whipping spray into the air, creating a sense of a storm that wasn't there.

Qureshi was uneasy. She was scanning the horizon with an increasingly furrowed brow.

"What's wrong?" Aras said. "Looking for something?"

"I wouldn't go charging in if I were you, sir," said Qureshi. "How close are we to Christopher now?"

"Fifty kilometers. If you know when the bombs will explode, you must tell me."

"You're already too late," said Qureshi, and leaned back against the gunwale with her handcuffed wrists between her legs, eyes closed.

Aras was leaning on the wheel and keeping an eye out for craft from the Temporary City when three rapid flashes of brilliant, burning, blue-white light caught his peripheral vision.

"What's that?" he asked.

Qureshi jerked her head round. She registered shock, instant acidic shock. "Oh shit," she said quietly. "Turn around, sir. It's too late."

A solid column like a gray *efte* tree had grown suddenly out of the sea to the south. The head of it blossomed into a canopy. Aras had never seen anything like it, except in *gethes* books. Qureshi had scrambled on to her knees to stare at the spectacle.

"Oh, my bezeri," Aras said. It was his first thought: he thought of the beautiful black-grass island and he thought of the massive shock wave transmitting itself through the sea. "My poor bezeri. I promised them. I *promised* them."

Qureshi looked utterly defeated. He half hoped that she would give him an acceptable explanation that wouldn't confirm his worst fears. He wanted her to say that it was okay, that humans he had watched over and protected for generations hadn't betrayed his foolish trust and that it could all be put right again.

Wess'har were brutally pragmatic. His hope lasted less than a second.

The billowing canopy was flattening and spreading.

Aras had not experienced helplessness for five hundred years. He was the guardian of Bezer'ej, of the bezeri, and of the island the humans called Christopher. And he'd failed. He didn't even know how.

He grabbed the marine's face in his hands and jerked it up to make her look at him. Qureshi's eyes said that she didn't expect to survive the next few minutes, but she maintained her composure.

"Do you know what you've done? Do you?" His wess'har instinct that told him to freeze and evaluate before reacting to a threat suddenly couldn't override a growing pressure in his chest and throat that felt remarkably like reliving one of Shan's rages. Aras wanted to lash out. It was an alien emotion in every sense but it almost consumed him until he let the sensible wess'har numbing reflex kick in. "You've poisoned the island. You've poisoned the water."

He loosened his grip so suddenly and completely that Qureshi almost tipped over the gunwale of the shallow craft. He grabbed her before she fell. She wouldn't have survived long in the water with her wrists bound.

She hadn't actually done anything. She had just landed in hostile territory, serving her nation, as he had once done. It was wrong to punish her.

Aras took out the *virin* and looked for the latest reconnaissance images. The high aerial view was from a patrol craft. Aras couldn't see the island at all; it was a mass of flame and plumed tumbling smoke and filth. The cloud of debris sucked up from the blast was drifting south over the sea.

He could feel the swell building as the shock wave pushed out from the island.

"It's neutron bombs, sir. I know it's terrible, but they're designed for minimal long-term fallout."

Aras couldn't take his eyes off the cube of images. "Is this supposed to comfort the bezeri?"

"It might not be as bad as you think, sir. I'm really sorry."

EVACUATE said the *virin*.

Aras stood at the wheel again, swung the boat to starboard and opened the throttle. He felt the first spots of heavy rain on his face. It was the promise of a downpour.

The fallout would drop into the sea in the embrace of rain. In the short term, Qureshi need not have worried too much about contamination.

The bezeri, sensitive to pollution, slow breeding, a fragile population at best, would feel it first.

He hoped—no, he *prayed,* in case the *gethes* thing called God could hear, and act—that they would flee.

20

RECONNAISSANCE REPORT, USSISSI PATROL

Ouzhari no longer exists. The landmass has been obliterated almost to the waterline.

We are also detecting high levels of cobalt in the fallout from the detonations. It has entered the sea and spread north with the currents to other island coastal areas. You must expect great loss of life among marine species.

The gethes lied to you. The poison from the bombs will linger for years.

Lindsay looked at her watch and checked the bioscreen in her palm.

"It's done," she said. "Christopher's neutralized."

She had imagined they would have to crawl commando-style through passages to infiltrate the underground colony.

But Josh must have called ahead. The ancient shuttle had been prepared: Bennett looked over the cockpit and shrugged, apparently satisfied at its readiness. When they came through the main thoroughfare, there were a couple of men dragging a crate between them, and they simply glanced at Lindsay, the marines and Rayat, and went about their business.

Bennett and Barencoin, rifles ready, overlapped and covered each other, checking entrances, looking up at the galleries, still as wary as their training in urban warfare made them.

"Would they booby-trap the place?" asked Rayat. Lindsay wouldn't give him a rifle and he was edgy. He was carrying the last ERD in a bergen across his back. It was quite a feat of endurance; and he didn't look especially robust. "You never know with these types."

"We'll find out the hard way," said Bennett. "Want to walk ahead?"

It wasn't at all like Bennett to be insolent. Barencoin was silent. Lindsay didn't trust Rayat enough to have him armed with the shuttle a long sprint away. She had no idea what an intelligence officer's skills might be. She wasn't going to test them.

And she hadn't visited David's grave. She wouldn't have time now. She'd never see it again; and that hurt. But the pain was good, because it kept her motivated.

From time to time the sound of falling soil stopped them in their tracks but it was just the walls crumbling. Lindsay stared at the trickle of gold granules.

"I think they've started with the nanites," said Rayat. "Let's hope the whole place doesn't fall in on us."

"It won't if you shut up," said Barencoin.

They stopped at St. Francis. The magnificent stained glass was gone, leaving a clean window-shaped hole. Lindsay adjusted her ballistic jacket, thinking that it felt insubstantial, and checked her rifle. She could feel Bennett's gaze boring into her.

"You ever been hit by a round, ma'am?" he asked.

"No," she said. "You know damn well I haven't. But I can give as good as I get."

"Ma'am, it'll still bloody hurt even with the jacket."

"She'll have a 9mm pistol, not an elephant rifle."

"She'll have whatever she took off Izzy and Chaz." He gestured with his own rifle. "If she uses one of these buggers on you, you'll know it. And if she gets a head-shot in, no jacket is going to save you. This is all about timing now." He held up four candle-sized sticks of dark green metal. He'd made his own private plans, then. "Stun grenades. One's enough to immobilize a room. I think it might take two to slow her down. Once we get her on the deck, we restrain her and get to the shuttle."

"We need her down and disoriented for at least ten seconds," said Barencoin. "Look." He demonstrated the titanium composite straps he'd borrowed from engineering. *Snap, snap, snap*:

they locked in place automatically. They were what you used to secure odd-shaped loads in the cargo bay. "This all depends on getting her in a confined space. If you're too close to her when it happens, you'll be on your back for a while too."

"And if we can't get her positioned right?"

"We'll shoot."

"Right. That'll be about as effective as a chocolate teapot."

"It'll slow her down. That's all we need."

"And you make damn sure you're gloved. She's a biohazard."

Barencoin tapped one gloved hand on his helmet with a carefully blank expression. Bennett was looking at him as if he had said something out of turn. Lindsay could read him too easily now; he didn't like the idea of hurting Shan. He'd definitely go soft. She'd have to watch him.

"Problem, Ade?"

He shook his head. "Just remember that Shan's used to using a gun and she's trained to avoid situations where she might be jumped. Don't get too confident."

She wouldn't. If she had to walk up to her and detonate the ERD on the spot, she'd do it. Barencoin had almost certainly told Bennett that she planned to kill Shan.

Or he might have thought it was a ploy to convince Josh she was serious. Either way, she still wasn't sure she could rely on either marine to help her do it when push came to shove.

She swallowed hard and lowered her voice. She really hated deceiving them. They deserved better. "And if anything goes wrong, you get the hell out, okay? Even if that means evacuating with the civvies. Just run. Promise me that."

They waited.

The interesting thing about a colony of galleries and tunnels, especially one that was now empty of people and sound-deadening materials, was how far sound carried. Lindsay stood in the center of the main passage, looking up and round her, now with a clear plan to run into the church when Shan found her. It was a warren of rooms but she knew her way in and out. And Bennett had his stun grenades.

She thought she heard boots. She held her breath.

Then the sound stopped. Maybe it was a colonist. It was a good way to get your head blown off, but it was too late to yell at them to keep clear. Then the footsteps got louder and resolved into two sets, one heavy, one light, and Lindsay raised her rifle a second after the two marines did.

It was a woman in colony-standard beige overalls leading a small redheaded boy. They looked surprised but not shocked.

"You need to clear this area, ma'am," said Barencoin, dipping his barrel a little. "It's not safe."

The woman shrugged. "We're staying." She took a tighter grip on the boy's hand. "The wess'har aren't going to get rid of us and neither are you."

And she walked on, the child gazing back wide-eyed over his shoulder at the intruders. Barencoin shook his head. "Silly cow. They'll all be dead in a month."

Lindsay thought of the ERD. They'd be dead sooner than that. She wanted to go after the woman and tell her to save her son, to run, to join the others and get off the planet. But she drew on the kind numbness of Sandhu's medication and concentrated on her rifle.

Shan had to be coming

She *had* to.

Lindsay glanced over her shoulder, first one way, then the other, to check that Bennett and Barencoin were still in alcoves on either side of the passage. Then she moved into the center of the main route through the colony, defying her, presenting a target.

Come and get me, bitch. I don't need to live through this.

If she was out there. No, Shan couldn't resist it.

Lindsay wasn't entirely sure what happened next. One second she was on her feet, looking up and around at the empty galleries, rifle ready, and the next, something hit her hard at knee height from nowhere and she was on her back. Her rifle went flying. Something landed hard on her chest and pinned her down. She was looking into a mouthful of needle teeth and then she saw the rest of the ussissi and its weapon.

"Give me a clear shot, Vijissi," said Shan's voice. "Get off her."

And Shan was suddenly standing over her with a rifle—an FEU issue rifle—pointed into her face. Lindsay couldn't work out where she had come from. Shan didn't say a word: and Lindsay had expected an awful lot of words from her. Shan just looked into her eyes with that soulless, unbreakable gray stare, pressed the barrel to her forehead—and then there were shots, and a shriek, and *it wasn't her own.*

Lindsay thought Shan had fired. She was hammered into the ground and for a moment she thought she was dying because she couldn't breathe. Her ears rang.

The moment was both forever and instantly over.

Lindsay couldn't get up. She floundered on the paving and tried to reach for her rifle but could do nothing but watch. She watched Bennett empty his magazine into Shan, and she watched her drop next to her, facing away.

Then there was silence except for the aftershock of the rifles' report in her ears.

"Shit," said Lindsay. She got up far enough on one arm to see the ussissi crumpled on the ground. They'd dropped them both.

Then Shan moved. She rolled over onto her stomach and reached into her belt and returned five shots.

Nothing came back at her. Shan got to her feet, unsteady, stumbling, but she was still moving, gun raised, and that was when Barencoin came out firing.

And Shan was still standing.

She was standing right up to the point when she fired again and Barencoin fell. Bennett rugby-tackled her to the ground and almost had her pinned flat when she head-butted him and sent him sprawling backwards.

Barencoin scrambled over to them and threw his weight on her. Between them, they managed to flip her face down and get the straps on. There was a lot of swearing and grunting.

"Fuck me," said Barencoin. He sat back and nursed his knee. His pants were soaked with blood and he fumbled in his belt, pulled out a primed needle-pack and slammed it into his thigh. Then he let out a long sigh and took the dressing that Bennett was holding out to him. "Fuck me, Ade, she should be dead. You all right?"

"So much for using the stun grenades," Bennett panted. There was blood streaming from his nose and spattered across his face. His helmet hadn't been much use against Shan's low-tech approach to self-defense.

Lindsay managed to stand up and retrieve her rifle. She limped over to the three of them, feeling as if her ribs had been smashed. Shan was still struggling weakly, face contorted with pain, also bloodied, and struggling for breath. Her trousers, waist to knee, were peppered with holes, and there were a few in her jacket. Bennett had obviously assumed she was wearing her ballistic vest.

"Is that hers?" Lindsay demanded. "Is that blood from her? Show me."

Bennett was crouched over Shan, all concern. He looked up at Lindsay and his expression was one she hadn't seen before—absolute loathing. He looked very different, not like good old Ade at all, and it wasn't just the mess across his face.

"No, it's *my* fucking blood," he said. He wiped the back of his glove across his nose and succeeded in smearing the blood still further. "She nutted me. She's not even bleeding from wounds. Look." He indicated the ground and the near wall. "Just the initial spatter. Are you clear? You were pretty near her."

"Nothing on me, and I haven't got any open wounds anyway." Lindsay tried to turn Shan over with her boot, but Bennett raised his arm to block her. She really wasn't in command any more. She wondered if she ever had been.

"You leave her, okay?" he snapped. He turned back to Shan again and put his hand under her head. "Easy, ma'am. You'll be okay. I'm sorry. I'm really sorry."

"You arsehole," Shan hissed at him. "You frigging idiot. Don't you see what you've done?"

Lindsay thought that Bennett had finally realized, and was now ashamed. It didn't matter. They had her. *She* had her.

Barencoin was silent, adjusting the dressing on his leg but watching her with clear distaste. Rayat emerged from the passage. He looked down at Shan, wide-eyed. "How many rounds did it take to stop her?" he asked. "My God. Think of what—"

"And you can fuck off, too," Shan said. For a woman with an awful lot of holes in her, she was remarkably vocal. "You shot Vijissi, you fucking bastards." But she had to be in agony. Lindsay took a roll of gaffer tape from her leg pocket and ripped a length off.

"He's still alive," said Bennett. "He'll be okay."

"You shit—"

"I'm going to shut you up once and for all," Lindsay said. "Hold her head, Mart."

"No, she won't be able to—" Bennett began, but Barencoin cut him off.

"She'll bring the whole bloody wess'har cavalry down on us, mate," said Barencoin. "We'll take it off later."

For a moment Lindsay thought Shan would sink her teeth in Barencoin's arm, but she was seriously weakened despite her stream of vigorous invective. The tape cut off her last expletive, which began with c.

Now that she was immobilized and silenced, Lindsay took out a first-aid wipe and scrubbed at Shan's face. It wasn't concern. She was looking for a wound, any abrasion at all, but there wasn't a mark on her and it *was* Bennett's blood after all.

Shan's expression was murderous. It wasn't cowed, and that both bothered Lindsay and gratified her, because there was no honor in defeating a weak enemy.

But Shan could still give her that look, and it made her remember how much of a disappointment she had been to her mother.

Bennett was fiddling with the fracture dressing that he had placed across the bridge of his nose to stop the bleeding and reduce the inevitable swelling. Shan had given him one hell of a crack.

Rayat crouched down next to Shan and started assembling a sample vial. "Let's get some tissue samples off her now just in case."

He put one hand flat on the floor for a second. Lindsay stamped down hard on it, heel first. He bit back a cry and glared up at her. Barencoin swung his rifle on him and looked rather keen to see if it still worked.

"Let's not," said Lindsay. "Let's get the shuttle going instead."

Barencoin started limping down the passage, herding Rayat ahead. Bennett hung back. Barencoin and Rayat stopped too.

"Go on, Ade," she said. "Get moving, all of you."

"I'll help you carry her," said Bennett. "You won't be able to do it on your own."

There was no point continuing the charade any longer. Lindsay took out the grenades from her belt-pack. She would have preferred the remaining ERD to be certain, but that woman and her son had disappeared into the warren around them. The grenades would do just fine. She started setting the timers. "Get out of here, Ade. Now."

"What are you doing, ma'am?"

"We can't hand her over. Surely you can see that." Lindsay didn't want to meet Shan's eyes again. It was one step too far. She had never killed anyone face-to-face: she'd given orders to *launch*, to *take*, to *open fire*, but she had never done a soldier's job, never this close up. "We'll all end up like her. Get shot up, then back in the fight. Over and over. And that's just the start. She has to die, Ade. She went to a lot of trouble to keep *c'naatat* out of our hands, and for once I agree with her."

"That's government property," said Rayat. "You can't. You've got orders."

"I couldn't give a toss," Lindsay said. "Come on, Ade. Get back to the shuttle. I'll be with you right away."

Bennett looked remarkably calm. He was a man who had always grappled with physical fear, and overcame it anew each time. It was one of the things Shan had said she liked about him. He had guts.

Now he raised his rifle and aimed at Lindsay. She looked just past the barrel and into his eyes, because he wasn't a big man, and all she could see was dried and drying blood from his eyebrows down to his chin. The dressing across his nose looked almost comical, a racoon's mask: his determination didn't.

"Disarm the grenades, please, ma'am."

"That's an order, Sergeant. Leave us."

"No ma'am. You put the grenades down and you put your rifle down on the ground and back away. Or I'll fire."

"Bennett, don't be stupid. Back off. It's an order. Last chance." Lindsay tried to stare him out. It wasn't working. The grenades felt uncomfortable in her hands. "I have to do this."

"Ma'am, I won't let you murder an unarmed civilian. Not even if it was Rayat." There was an ominous whirr from his rifle as the automatic targeting tried to accommodate the close range, and he showed no sign whatsoever of lowering it. "You can't order me to breach the convention. So help me, I'll slot you right now if you don't put those bloody things down and step away from her."

"I don't think he's joking," said Rayat. "And we don't have all day."

"Piss off, sir," said Bennett without breaking his gaze. But Rayat was right. The sergeant wasn't backing down. It struck Lindsay that they might just have been waiting for an excuse to shoot her. And then Shan would be free.

Lindsay thought briefly of pulling the pins anyway, right now. She had factored that into her plans too. It was a sacrifice worth making.

She looked at the small, dull metal levers and thought, *yes, now, on the count of three.*

But she didn't.

She tried to move her hands, but she just stared at the grenades.

She had visualized it so many times. But when it came to it, she couldn't do it, not even for David. She wanted to *live*.

"Okay," she said, and lowered both devices to the floor. Barencoin limped forward and picked them up. For an ill-advised moment, Lindsay let herself look at Shan; and her expression, even with a length of tape over her mouth, said it all.

You don't have the guts.

Shan would have pulled the pins. Lindsay knew that. But she wasn't Shan, and now she knew she never would be, not even when it really, really mattered. It was a moment of self-revelation that she would never forget however hard she tried.

"Let's get her in the shuttle and put some distance between us and the wess'har," Lindsay said, trying to sound brisk and efficient. "Because when they find out, they're going to be furious."

"More furious than they'll be for torching Christopher?" asked Barencoin, without using the word *ma'am*.

It wasn't working out as she planned.

She would have to come up with something else, and fast.

Ussissi were like journalists. They had osmotic communication. If something was happening, they knew all about it at a cellular level, and they seemed to know about it all at once. If there was any more instant form of communication than entangled photons, it was the collective consciousness of ussissi—and journalists.

Eddie suspected the ussissi knew something now.

He watched them as they huddled by the site manager's office at Umeh Station. The office was another pastel green cube that you could snap together anywhere, anytime. The ussissi—about ten of them—were agitated, bobbing their heads and darting in and out of the little pack. Eddie decided to ask them outright. That was his job: he didn't have to apologize for it. But he'd keep clear of the teeth. He stood up slowly from his relatively comfortable perch in the cab of an idle forklift and walked towards them with deliberate strides so they wouldn't feel he was stalking them.

He hoped that being a lot taller than them didn't bring out their defensive instincts. Crouching near to them always seemed to be asking for trouble. "I hate to fall back on cliché, lads, but what's going on?"

A female with the same cheerful demeanor as Serrimissani rounded on him. "We hear you have used bombs on Bezer'ej. Are we your next target?"

"Shit," said Eddie. This wasn't an interview. This was diplomatic contact. He didn't think he was equipped for that. "This is the first I've heard of it. Do you want to tell me what happened?"

"Your troops invaded Bezer'ej and set bombs to destroy an island."

Constantine. The stupid bastards had tried to take Constantine. He couldn't imagine why: it was a stupid way to get a foothold on a planet that was going to be made uninhabitable by humans anyway.

"Anyone killed?"

"We have no numbers. It is serious, *gethes*. The wess'har will have those who did this."

"What else?"

"Why did you use weapons that poison the world?"

"Chemical weapons?" Christ, that was over the top. Maybe he should have returned to *Actaeon,* and then he wouldn't have been caught on the hop like this. "That's banned under—"

"Radiation."

"Nukes?"

"The whole island of Ouzhari is devastated. We hear you did it to destroy *c'naatat.*"

Eddie was suddenly lost in a maze of references. He was also very, very scared. Nuking a militarily superior nation—or its buddies—seemed a good way to end up as charcoal. "Ouzhari is what you call Constantine?"

"No, Ouzhari is the island to the very south, the one where none may land. And you will die for that."

Eddie spread his hands. "I haven't got a clue what you're talking about." He wished he did. One part of his brain was chattering *great story, great story, great story* in an insistent reflex, and another part was saying *run, run like hell.*

"The wess'har are searching for your Commander Neville."

Oh God. Lindsay.

"I think we've really fucked up this time," said Eddie. "I'm sorry. Really I am. Are Shan and Aras okay?"

"Aras is looking for bezeri to see how badly affected they might be. I know nothing of Shan Frankland."

Eddie stood back, utterly helpless and ashamed. The ussissi bared their teeth and then scattered, glancing back at him as if they might change their minds and fall on him like a pack after all, acting out the *Actaeon* myth.

He was caught or the wrong side of a border crossing, and he could see it closing before his eyes like the doors of an elevator he had just missed. He would never be going back to *Actaeon* again. His stomach was churning and he could feel the pulse in his temples through his teeth.

But he wasn't so sure he was on the wrong side of the line.

Actaeon definitely wasn't the safest place to be right now.

21

There ought to be a room in every house to swear in. Under certain circumstances, profanity provides a relief denied even to prayer.

MARK TWAIN

The first bezeri to be washed up on Chad Island—to the north of Christopher—was a juvenile female.

The cobalt in the *gethes'* bombs had poisoned the air and the land—and the sea. It was an especially filthy weapon. It was designed to poison for many years to come, a grotesque twist on the sleeping pathogen that his wess'har comrades were spreading. It killed indiscriminately.

Aras knelt down and laid his hand on the gelatinous mantle of the bezeri. There were already tiny *keteya* swarming over it, seizing the chance of a meal. And his heart broke.

He had never understood what humans had meant by that, but he knew now. There was a definite sensation of pain deep in his chest, a pressure that made breathing unpleasant, and it ran all the way up the back of his throat into his mouth.

Why did they do this?

He stood up and looked out across the bay. The cloud cover meant that he should have been able to see some light from bezeri near the surface, but there was nothing. He had walked into the water several times and used the signaling lamp, but they didn't come.

Aras knew how vulnerable they were to poisons in the water. Their settlements were clustered near landmasses. The slightest chemical changes were dangerous: isenj pollution had nearly destroyed them. It was very easy to kill bezeri without planning to.

Aras battled with the pressure of sorrow that threatened to crush his chest and thought of all the years he had spent watching the bezeri recover their numbers, never as great as before the isenj arrived, but a recovery nonetheless. The isenj hadn't planned to kill bezeri any more than the *gethes* had.

Surendra Parekh hadn't set out to kill bezeri either.

He had balanced that crime with two shots from Shan's old but efficient hand-weapon. He wondered what it would take to balance this crime, and he began to see it would take a great deal of balancing indeed, and more than he could carry out alone.

And then there was Josh. Aras was staring at the water but not seeing it.

Why did he betray me?

Josh was another *gethes* who probably hadn't planned to kill bezeri. He never *meant* to do it. Aras could almost hear him now. He would *repent*. He would seek *forgiveness* from God. But it was none of his god's business to forgive this.

Aras wasn't minded to leave Josh's punishment to his god. He'd do it himself. He had forbidden the ussissi and the Cetekas clan to touch him.

Find him. Hold him. Wait for me to get back.

After nearly two hundred years of living alongside them, Aras had finally understood a fundamental aspect of humans. For a moment he feared it had become clear because the Shan-parts of him had clarified it.

Difference made others invisible to *gethes*.

Was *she* like that? No. She behaved differently, whatever went on in her mind.

The sea was still dark gray and lightless. There were no bezeri to be seen.

Aras recalled a game he used to play with little Rachel Garrod. She called it hide and seek. Sometimes he would find her huddled in a corner with a garment over her head, and she was astonished that he could see and find her, because she could not see him. Adult *gethes* behaved similarly. They believed other species had no individuality, no sense of self, simply because they couldn't see it, measure it, or experience it; and if they could not conceive of it, it could not exist. Perhaps wess'har, used to feeling fleetingly what another felt through *oursan,* could stretch their imaginations a little further.

Aras knew that the bezeri female who now lay rotting at his feet had felt and feared, because that was what all life did in one way or another. And even if she had neither complex language nor the ability to conjure up abstract concepts—and she did, he *knew* she did—then her life would be no less valid because of that. *That* was what separated his kind from *gethes.*

Gethes thought their imaginary god had made them unique, both as individuals and as a species, even if they no longer believed in him.

The *keteya* were leaving visible holes in the bezeri's mantle now. Aras wondered what would happen to them, too.

For a moment he wished the *gethes* had succeeded in grabbing *c'naatat* for themselves. He would have delighted in seeing them reach extinction in their own filth and excess.

But many others would have died with them, and he shook the vengeance away. It was a uselessly violent thought, and he hadn't lavished one like that even upon the isenj. The thought felt like Shan's. He understood her various angers a lot better now.

He stood over the bezeri until she started to fall apart under the small but persistent assaults of the *keteya.* It was getting dark. He had been there on the shore for hours, and it occurred to him that Shan would be worrying about him. She would be back by now. She would have found Lindsay Neville and killed her. The marines wouldn't touch her. He was sure of that.

Shan could always imagine what it was like to be behind someone else's eyes. He thought of the gorilla, and was glad that she could still feel pain for the being, and for all things that were even less like her than the ape. He hadn't misjudged her at all, not from the very first time he had met her. He would go back to Constantine and find her, and then he would seek some comfort from the one human who had ever justified his affection and loyalty.

A light caught his eye.

It was faint, and green. He had never seen that single, unchanging color before: it defied the signal lamp's translation. The device stayed silent. Then the light was joined by others.

Aras scrambled back up the cliff as fast as he could to get a better vantage point. When he turned and looked down onto the darkening water, he could see light upon light, all green, all unchanging, but growing in intensity and number

His signal lamp started to crackle. He couldn't make out any words.

The lights flared. They were brighter than he had ever seen now, even brighter than the communal songs that rippled through the water for weeks at a time; and still he didn't understand them.

The sea was on fire with green light. He stared at it, lost, remembering the wess'har who saw the lights many years before and who first understood when the bezeri were calling out *help us*.

The signal lamp spat out a stream of loud static, and his own moment of revelation was terrible. The bezeri weren't calling for help this time.

They were screaming.

22

We have had no contact from Shan Frankland or Vijissi. They might be keeping radio silence because they still seek the human invaders. We would also ask for confirmation of the identity of an unidentified vessel that has left Constantine and is heading for Wess'ej. It is not on our schedule even though it responded with nonhostile code.

(Operations overseer, Temporary City)

In zero g, the shattered rounds that were easing out of Shan's body simply drifted in front of her. It was like watching a film of yourself being shot, run backwards. Eddie would have been amazed by it.

Shan had wondered if she would ever get used to *c'naatat*'s thorough healing procedures and now she knew she would never have the chance to.

She couldn't.

Vijissi was curled up in a ball beside her, panting. He was badly hurt. Shan nudged him with her shoulder, making him drift back against the bulkhead, and he opened his black hunter's eyes and focused on her. She hoped he'd make it. To his right, just in her peripheral vision, Ade Bennett was still fussing with the tape over his broken nose, checking carefully with the mirror of his camo compact held very close to his face. Shan had never taken him for a vain man. He looked upset.

Then he noticed she was looking his way. He snapped the compact shut. "How you feeling?" he said. He swung as close to her as he dared. "You still in pain?"

She stared at him. It was all she could do while gagged but she knew she could always convey a command without opening her mouth. He shot a few nervous glances in Lindsay's direction and then began easing the tape off.

"Leave that," said Lindsay, looking up from the tracking screen.

Bennett took no notice whatsoever and peeled the last of the tape clear. It hurt. He winced as if he could tell. Shan looked into his earnest hazel eyes and the grubby dressing that separated them. They were almost nose-to-nose.

"Piss off," she said.

If she'd head-butted him again, he couldn't have looked more wounded. He cared what she thought of him. He probably thought he'd done the honorable thing and faced down his superior officer to save her life. Under normal circumstances, it would have been an heroic act. But he really should have let Lindsay fragment her. It just made things a whole lot messier now.

"I'm really sorry, Boss," he said to her. "Really I am. But I'll make damn sure they treat you right."

"I bet," said Shan, and she could have sworn his eyes looked a little glassy.

"Here we go," said Barencoin. The shuttle was tiny: one main compartment forward, propulsion section midships, and two aft service compartments leading on to a small open cargo bay. Shan could hear everything. "Isenj codes, ussissi pilot. That's our escort. Twenty-eight minutes to intercept once we break course. On your mark."

"Okay. Get us out of Wess'ej space."

"Very good, ma'am."

Shan pushed herself away from the bulkhead with her feet and rolled slowly to get a better look. Lindsay was leaning over Barencoin, looking at the readouts.

"I need a pee," Shan said. She kept thinking about the grenades. Barencoin had them: she could see them tucked neatly into pockets on his webbing. It would be a damn shame to blow them on this fragile ship and take two good men with

her, but she had run out of options. She just needed to get her
hands and legs free, and she had less than twenty-eight minutes
to do it. She tried not to think of Aras but it was impossible.
"Does this thing have heads?"

Lindsay drifted over to her. Shan expected a boot in the face
or something equally eloquent. It never came.

"You shot me point-blank," said Lindsay. "Aren't you supposed to shout something like, 'Stop—armed police'?"

"No, I was trying to kill you," said Shan. "And I don't normally miss at that range. Not unless some bastard shoots me
first, of course."

"How many people *have* you killed?"

Shan paused to count. "Eight."

"Including Parekh?"

"Maybe. I forget."

Lindsay had never believed that. And now she looked
scared. Shan thought she might be scared of her. Then it became clear. *Oh, it's not about revenge. Not entirely, anyway.*

"Can't you wait half an hour?" Lindsay asked. Her tone was
quiet, her expression seeking something.

"When a girl's got to go, she's got to go."

"Not going to try anything stupid, are you? You know I need
to hand you over."

Lindsay had always found it hard to meet her gaze. Shan had
spent a professional lifetime cultivating that gorgon's stare and
she knew it worked, especially on Lindsay. But she was looking
into Lindsay's eyes now, and it was very clear she was thinking
something she wanted Shan to realize.

Ah.

Lindsay might have been gutless when it came to it, but she
knew Shan wasn't.

"You know you can trust me to be sensible," said Shan. *Go
on, Lin, do something right for once.* "I know how much I'm
worth."

Lindsay almost looked relieved. "I'll take you aft."

"I can do that," said Bennett, who clearly didn't trust Lindsay any further than he could spit. "I—"

"Sod off," said Shan. "I still have my dignity."

They didn't even have to take her alive to get a tissue sample. She had to be *gone,* really gone. And there were ways to be gone forever out here.

For exactly five vivid and painful seconds, she thought of Aras again and it was unbearable. Then she switched off, as she always had.

"I come too," said Vijissi suddenly. He heaved himself straight and pulled himself hand over hand to the hatch. "She is not to be trusted."

Shan gave Lindsay an imperceptible nod. Lindsay shrugged, clearly playing along. "If you bite, I'll shoot you, you little bastard," she said. She fumbled with the locking straps and released Shan's legs. For a second Shan thought of putting the boot in, but it would only have satisfied her temper, not achieve her objective. She behaved.

Vijissi looked like it would take all his effort to accompany them a few meters. He trailed the two women through the propulsion section, through a barely hip-wide passage, and into the aft section that opened onto the cargo bay with its loading hatches on deck, deckhead, and three bulkheads. They were all closed. Through the pressure hatch, it was a black void.

Lindsay hit the hatch lock behind her. "What are you planning?" she asked.

"You know damn well or you wouldn't have secured that hatch," said Shan. She turned slightly and gestured with her bound hands. "They'll never find a small cold object in space. It's about as dead as anyone can get. And it's quick. They reckon less than twelve seconds." But twelve seconds sounded like a long time right then. *Where's my last noble thought? Why am I just walking through this? Where's my fear and regret and panic?* "Get this off me."

"No."

"If I go, I go with dignity, not fucking trussed up like some chicken."

"I'm sorry."

Vijissi struggled into animation. It seemed to have dawned on him a little late that Shan was planning an exit through the air lock.

"No!" He settled beside her. Zero g made his panic slow and undramatic. "No, I promised Mestin I would always look after you—"

"It's too late, mate."

No, no, no, I don't want to die, and I want to see Aras again, and it's not the way I wanted to end it, and—

Then the other Shan took over, the one who always knew what to do in a crisis. "Free my hands," she ordered.

Lindsay hesitated.

Then she relented and reached for Shan's wrists. Shan thought a final punch might have been satisfying, but there was no adequate amount of revenge she could ever exact for detonating ERDs on Christopher.

Lindsay seemed confident that the ERDs had detonated. Shan hoped Aras had been a long way from the explosions, but if he had survived, he'd be alone, and she knew he dreaded loneliness more than death. *My poor bloody Aras.* It wasn't fair to him.

The comms panel beside them lit up. Bennett was on the squawk box.

"Hey, what's happening back there?" he demanded. He must have seen the lock status show up on the panel. And they'd taken longer than he'd allowed for. "Commander? Come on, bloody well—"

"Stay out of this Ade," said Shan. "Do me a favor and tell Aras I'm sorry and I didn't abandon him."

"Christ, you—"

Lindsay shut off the sound. Shan wondered if Bennett had heard her, and if he could still hear her now. And then she looked round at the locked hatch behind them, and she could see his face pressed to the plate, all horror. She really wished she hadn't. She turned quickly back to the cargo bay.

"I've never doubted your integrity," Lindsay said, and moved like a swimmer to the manual controls that would open both the aft hatch and all the cargo bay doors.

It was the compliment that hurt, not the hatred. Shan almost weakened. She had one last weapon. It was personal and it was vengeful. It struck her as very telling that in her last moments she still wanted to lash out and wound.

So that's what I am, then, she thought. *And here's something to remember me by.*

"Now *this* is how you do it, girlie," Shan said, and stood as tall as she could manage. "Next time you lose your bottle and you can't pull that pin, think of me. Because you'd give anything to be just like me, wouldn't you? And you never will. I'm all the guts and conviction you'll never have."

Lindsay said nothing, not with her mouth anyway. Her face crumpled for a second.

Gotcha, thought Shan. Lindsay would have plenty of time to think on that until she died old and disappointed by her own inadequacies. It was better than a punch. Bruises healed.

I would have been dead by now anyway. Old age back home, or here with an isenj round in my skull. Borrowed time. And it's run out. Quit whining.

Then Shan stopped thinking. It was down to her brain-stem now, the lungfish-lemur-monkey within, and she let it do the panicking rush to destruction for her, because every second she examined the situation was a second closer to turning back and surrendering. The bezeri had died for this. Her life didn't matter a damn, except to her.

And to Aras.

Stop it.

The cargo bay hatch opened and Shan stepped over the coaming. The opening in the bulkhead was closing in two sections, top to bottom, like a pair of scissors.

Vijissi shot through after her.

"For Chrissakes, Vijissi, get back *now*," Shan yelled.

But Vijissi tried to look after Shan to the very last, and as the deckhead opened and the escaping atmosphere whipped her hair, her lungs began struggling and he grabbed her hand hard in his oddly soft paw.

So this it, Shan thought. She really was dying. It didn't feel that momentous, just disappointing. She gripped Vijissi, not wanting to look into his face.

It was agonizingly cold. Her chest hurt. She had seconds.

She pushed out from the open hatch and let go of Vijissi and didn't see where he went, because she had screwed her eyes up tight to shut out the bottomless, distanceless, silent void that had no up or down or near or far.

She was holding out in vacuum longer than any human. That was something. It felt like walking under the sea to apologize to the bezeri for the last time, only much, much colder.

Her last thought before her lungs gave up straining for one final breath and the final blackness engulfed her was that she had never told Aras that she loved him.

I think I do.

Maybe he knows anyway.

Maybe—

23

*I can assure you I had no idea what Commander Neville was
planning. Her orders were only to detain one of our own citizens,
Superintendent Frankland. I greatly regret the events on Bezer'ej
and I fully appreciate the likelihood that this will be viewed as
an outright act of war by the wess'har authorities. Your offer of
asylum for those members of the* Actaeon *crew who want it is a
generous one and we will evacuate to Jejeno any personnel who
wish to leave.*

Message from the FEU foreign minister
to Minister Par Paral Ual

"He lies," said Ual.

Eddie thought of the urine vial in his inside pocket and the
way the ruby bead and the fragment of quill rattled, pricking
his conscience. He hadn't let the container out of his sight. He
wasn't sure if he'd ever be able to hand it over to Shan now.

He was stranded on Umeh. But it was still a safer haven than
Actaeon.

"Why do you think that?" he asked.

Ual shimmered with emerald beads. "How did he expect to
take this Frankland off Bezer'ej if they landed by dropping in
cloth suits?"

"You know a lot."

"There are no restricted frequencies on what you call ITX.
That concept is one we have to learn from you, I think. Unless
you speak in that odd code some of you employ, all hear everything if they choose to listen."

"And you do." Eddie was still finding it hard to come to
terms with the fact that enemies could share an open ITX relay.
Humans wouldn't. But then if there was a serious threat of the
wess'har trashing the thing in a fit of pique, and the isenj

couldn't nip out to repair it . . . no, he was starting to grasp how they thought. Nobody poisoned a shared water supply. "I would like to broadcast a story on this. Can you confirm how serious the situation is?"

There was a cup of coffee and a bowl of some isenj beverage on the polished cube of a table between them. Ual didn't seem to be in a drinking mood. Even without a facial expression to guide him, Eddie knew the minister was scared.

"The ussissi are saying the environmental damage to that area of Bezer'ej is severe and that the bezeri are dying in very large numbers," said Ual. "You will recall what happened when we did the same thing unintentionally. Your kind appear to have used a very unpleasant device indeed, one containing cobalt, a persistent poison to add to the initial destruction."

Eddie didn't know much about physics, although he had an extensive mental catalog of things that people could use to kill each other. He checked his database. Salted bombs, especially cobalt, were at the far unethical end of ordnance, a terrorist's weapon. They were ultra-dirty.

"They weren't leaving anything to chance, then," said Eddie quietly, ashamed beyond belief. He could hardly believe it of Lindsay. He still found it hard to accept how ruthless women could be. "I have to tell this story, Ual. People on Earth need to know what we've done."

"Humans have no difficulty saying negative things about their own kind, then."

"I certainly don't. But sometimes the likes of me are the only ones who will tell hard truths."

"And why are you asking me for help?"

"For facts I might not know."

"Your masters might not broadcast them."

Eddie was caught off guard. He had grown up in a world where information couldn't be suppressed easily. There were simply too many routes and too many connections between people and nations for anyone to control it, except . . . except if you were isolated on one end of a line 150 trillion miles from home.

They could cut him off.

He couldn't call anyone except via that ITX line, and the FEU was controlling the Earth end of that. There was no chance of placing the story elsewhere or slipping a note to someone down the pub. If he had a story, it went through BBChan, and BBChan was reliant on the FEU relay. The station could make all the brave stands it wanted, but if it didn't receive the information, he was stuffed.

"I took my eye off the ball," he said. "But I'll find a way through."

"I think you might not need to," said Ual. He leaned forward, rattling musically like fine crystal, and pushed the now tepid coffee towards Eddie. "And I assume you will stay. I enjoy our chats. This isn't a sensible time to return to *Actaeon*."

"Thanks," said Eddie. "I know."

The ground car was waiting outside the ministry, parked so close to the entrance that when he opened the front door he could step straight into its open side without walking on pavement. Serrimissani was waiting inside the vehicle, absorbed by moving images on her text pad.

"You exceed even the isenj's crimes," she said. She wasn't her usual impatient, stroppy self: she seemed very subdued indeed. "What have you started, *gethes?*"

Eddie bristled. "Don't lump me in with them," he snapped. "I am *not* crew. I am *not* military. I'm an independent civilian and I'm as disgusted as you are."

She stared at him. And then, overtaken by an impulse, he squeezed past her, the back of his hand brushing against that odd stiffly ridged coat for the first time, and stumbled out through the car's other side opening onto the street and into the tight-packed crowds of isenj.

He almost fell, but the press of bodies held him up and he regained his balance. So many isenj stopped in their tracks that the river came to a halt at his point in the stream. He heard a chattering commotion from a distance where the flow had not stopped as fast, a motorway pile-up in the making. He wondered if any isenj had been crushed or trampled. But there was nothing he could do except move or not move with them.

For the first time, he walked the roads of Jejeno. He had no choice. This was not a crowd. It was a current and he drifted on it. The scent of wet wood and leaves, incongruously sylvan for a world with no forests or open land to speak of, filled his mouth. He couldn't speak their language and he had no idea where he was going. He looked down on the top of thousands of spider heads.

The chattering and rasping was rising in volume. "Anyone here speak English?" he shouted. *Oh, you tourist. You swore you'd never say that.* He was near the ministry. There might be government staff in the throng. They might speak—

"Why you do this attack?" rasped a voice behind him.

Eddie tried to turn his head. The isenj sounded about three or four meters away. "I don't know. They're afraid of *c'naatat.* Lots of humans would want it."

"Fool," said the voice.

"Don't you want it?"

"Look around you," said the isenj. "*Fool.*"

It was a great moment in television, but Eddie couldn't get his arm free to release the bee-cam from his pocket. He accepted it as a lesson in reality. This moment was about him, and not an event to be filtered through a lens into distant entertainment.

And how was he going to get out of the crowd?

"Michallat," called Serrimissani. There was an exchange of chittering. He craned his neck as far as he could. Serrimissani was clambering over the mass of isenj like a sheepdog running across the tiled backs of a tight-packed flock. "Move diagonally. Swing round."

He tried. He changed direction. It was like being a container ship. He could turn, and he could stop, but it was a big U-turn and a long time stopping. Serrimissani caught up with him, the angry mongoose again, and seized his sleeve to steer him. The cacophony around him was deafening now.

The ussissi held onto him until they had eased around a full arc and the car and the ministry building were in sight again. She shoved him the last meter and he fell into the open car.

As he was scrambling to his knees, Serrimissani cuffed him hard across the back of the head and he felt hot needles plunge into his shoulder. He yelled out.

She had bitten him. She was enraged.

Eddie rolled over and hoisted himself backwards onto the seat by his triceps. He hurt all over, especially his head and shoulder.

"Next time it will be your throat," she hissed. "*Never* do that again. You cause chaos. You cause injury. Your kind will never learn to control your impulses."

"I'm sorry," he said. He felt his shoulder: it was wet with something he suspected was his own blood rather than her saliva. He wondered what you could catch from a ussissi bite.

"Take me back to Umeh Station," he said. "I want to hear what you all have to say. I want to show humans back on Earth what you think of us, in case it helps bring us to our senses."

Serrimissani gave him her scorpion-snack look and stared deliberately out of the opening. Then she turned back to him.

"I am afraid for you," she said. "And you should fear us too."

"Will your people talk to me on camera?"

"Let us hope you continue to be useful to the isenj, or there will be no *gethes* left alive in this system by the end of the season."

Eddie took that as a yes.

The ussissi were one now: they prowled around the quiet disorder of Constantine's evacuation, oddly synchronized in their movements, sniffing through the final ranks of colonists who were waiting to embark from the Temporary City. High-pitched chattering filled the air but the humans were silent.

Aras stood and watched from a distance. All he wanted was Josh Garrod and Dr. Mohan Rayat, but he wanted Josh more. He had never felt quite like this. Wess'har were not vengeful. They would balance, and do the job without hesitation as he had done at Mjat, but they didn't invest emotion in the act. Now Aras not only wanted to hurt Josh: he *needed* to.

He wasn't proud of it. It was a human legacy. But he felt no guilt either.

And where was Shan? She still hadn't called in. He would have to search for her. He was beginning to worry, even though she was the one person other than himself who had least to fear from violence.

The ussissi were still searching, staring up into faces, comparing features to the images in their *virin've*. Aras was reminded of pictures from Constantine's history archive, of dogs set to guard humans. He didn't want to dwell on the parallels. He was responsible for the humans being here and he was ultimately responsible for Shan becoming a magnet for human greed. He hadn't set the bombs, but his actions had led to this point. He had to clear up the mess he had made.

No, Josh betrayed me. He betrayed the bezeri. He could have chosen otherwise.

Aras had been watching the search of the line for a while when someone new joined it and approached one of the ussissi.

It was Josh Garrod.

He wasn't making any attempt to slip unnoticed into the queue. The ussissis' single, constant, chittering voice stopped abruptly and they all stared as one at Josh.

For a moment Aras thought they were going to disobey him and rip the man apart where he stood. They were certainly agitated enough to do it. But they didn't, and simply surrounded him as if he might make a run for it. The other colonists made a sudden and large space around them. Josh spotted Aras and moved towards him, one arm outstretched as if in plea.

When Aras saw Josh's face—stricken, anguished, drained of blood—something in him welled up and took him over in a way it hadn't when he destroyed Mjat. This was a man he had held as a newborn, whose father and grandfather and ancestors right back to Ben Garrod had been his friends. They had almost been his family. He had come as close to loving them as kin as a wess'har ever could. And now in an instant they had smashed everything he had struggled to restore for five hundred years.

He grabbed Josh by his collar. His eyes hurt, as if there was an unbearable pressure building inside them, and he had never felt that before. He tried to shake the sensation aside. It was constricting his throat.

"Why did you betray me? Why did you do this?" Motive didn't matter, but a part of him needed an answer. "Tell me. I thought we shared the same purpose. I thought you were my friend."

Josh's voice was almost a sob. "We didn't know what was in the bomb, Aras. We didn't know."

"You took the *gethes* there to carry out their desecration. You *knew.* How could you do this?"

"But we didn't know they were going to use such a persistent poison." Josh's breath was coming fast, scented with the sourness of an empty stomach that was almost more pungent than the acrid scent of panic. "They told us it would dissipate in days, or we'd never have helped them. We'd never have risked the bezeri like that. We thought that burning the island was better than allowing *c'naatat* to be exploited. Tell us what we can do now to help. Anything. Just tell us."

Josh sagged against Aras's grip. Aras believed every word of his repentance.

But words weren't enough to soothe his pain. He envied Shan her profanities. A ussissi seized his other sleeve, trying to pull him away from Josh.

"We will do this," she said. "This will distress you. Just go."

Aras shook the ussissi off. He let go of Josh and stood looking at him and almost drowning in the pain that was threatening to overwhelm him. And he felt Josh's anguish and regret too, because Josh was a good man who had never wavered from a path of respect and noninterference until the *gethes* drove him to it.

"I'm sorry, my friend." Josh appeared to be weeping. He put his hand out to touch Aras, something he had always avoided for fear of contamination. Aras stepped back. It was too late for that now. "We never meant this to happen. God forgive us."

Aras knew that and it made no difference. His human side wanted to comfort Josh but his wess'har mind—and he was still wess'har, however altered—said that the man's apologies and tears and true intent counted for nothing.

Aras felt himself reach for his *tilgir* and pull it from its sheath as if he was going to do some harmless pruning. "I truly cared for your community, and I truly cared for you." He should have let him pray first, he knew, but prolonging the agony wasn't the wess'har way. "Now I have to balance. I'm sorry. I am so very, very sorry."

Josh opened his lips as if to speak and Aras swung the blade two-handed, right to left. Josh fell and the only sound was two thuds as he hit the ground.

The silence around Aras was complete and lasted three seconds.

Then it dissolved into small cries, and then screams, and the ussissi turned as one and rushed at the huddle of colonists, scattering them.

They were simply holding them back. But it all fell into chaos, children crying and screaming, men running. Aras stood looking down at Josh's body, only half aware of the panic and noise around him. He wasn't about to repent and he felt no guilt.

He was wess'har. He had done what he should have done many, many years ago.

But it hurt him in a way that shooting Surendra Parekh never had. He could feel shaking starting in the pit of his stomach and the pain in his eyes had grown from prickling to stabbing.

The ussissi female trotted up to him, head lowered in appeasement.

"Go," she said. "We will deal with this."

This time he accepted her help. "Be careful of the blood," he said. He noticed he had a great spray of it down his tunic and he could smell it. "He has been to Ouzhari. Or I might have caught him with my claws." He doubted that even *c'naatat* could survive decapitation, but Aras was taking no chances. "Burn his body."

Fire was a prudent move. But Aras also remembered all that Ben Garrod had told him about Hell, and the image distressed him.

Aras walked down to the cliffs again and searched for the lights. His *tilgir* dangled from his hand. He'd clean it later.

It wasn't unknown for the bezeri to go deep at times of threat and crisis. He hoped that was what they had done, but he doubted it in that core of him that understood and accepted reality. He'd watched the single, unbroken mass of green light fade and die, and that was what he knew had happened to the bezeri.

Those were the ones who had died quickly, closest to the fallout from *Actaeon*'s bombs. There were other bezeri settlements further from the chain, but in time the contamination would travel further and drop silently into the sea with each rainstorm. It would seal the fate of the remaining bezeri population and the other life on which they fed and depended. They were tied to place. They could never flee.

Now there was Rayat to hunt down.

Aras would *have a go,* as Shan called it. He would also *have a go* at that little female, the one Shan called Lin, if Shan had not already killed her. It had been her doing as well. Perhaps he would turn Rayat over to the ussissi. It would appease their rage for a while.

And where was Shan? *Isan* or not, he would give her a piece of his mind for worrying him so.

He was still contemplating how much he needed her to tell him it would all be fine when one of the young Cetekas males approached him, reeking of anxiety. He thought for a moment that the boy had heard—or seen—that he had balanced the crimes of Josh Garrod.

The boy stopped three meters short of him.

"What is it?" asked Aras. It would be more dead bezeri, he knew. They would congregate around stricken comrades rather than flee, just like the ussissi, but quite unlike humans or even wess'har. They would come to the source of the pollution. "How many this time?"

The boy looked puzzled. "I was told to let you know the ussissi are talking about a ship."

"What ship?"

"A small vessel that left here some hours ago. One of their Umeh-based pilots has been asked to rendezvous with it and transfer passengers. His destination is *Actaeon*. He is hesitant."

Aras was silenced by how wrong his expectation had been. He knew at that moment that his carefully reconstructed world of relative normality had been fleeting and was now crumbling apart. He knew what the boy was going to say before he said it. He could feel his freeze instinct gripping him even before the words emerged.

"They have a prisoner," said the boy.

Aras wanted to scream. He tried to form a sound. But nothing came out.

Had he known, he would not have given Josh such a quick end.

Lindsay sat in the aft section with her head in her hands for at least ten minutes before unlocking the inner hatch and hauling herself back down the passage into the forward compartment.

She was shaking. Her mind was completely empty, unable to grasp anything. She hoped it would stay that way for a while.

She tried to think of David for a moment and found she couldn't recall his face or his smell. She wished she had kept the clothing he had been buried in.

Aras had interred him, and now Aras would know what it felt like to lose someone you loved.

Bennett and Barencoin were talking very quietly, head-to-head in the two cockpit seats. Rayat was staring at the port bulkhead, turning his text pad over and over in his hands.

They stopped instantly as if someone had thrown a switch.

"So it was all for bloody nothing," said Rayat. "You have no idea what you've thrown away."

"I do," said Lindsay. "And it wasn't." Neither marine said a word. That was frightening. "How long to rendezvous?"

"Eleven minutes," said Barencoin, not looking up from the steeple of his fingers.

"You killed her," said Bennett.

He seemed remarkably subdued for a man who had seen the object of his affections step calmly to her death. He was fingering the bridge of his nose, still covered with the pressure dressing. He hadn't cleaned his face: the blood had dried into flaky streaks from nostrils to chin. Perhaps he was making a point.

"It was her choice," said Lin. "If you'd let me set the bloody grenades, she'd have been spared this."

Bennett didn't answer. He turned away and took out his camo compact again and seemed to be checking his nose. For some reason it was really bothering him. Lindsay was starting to realize the intensity of his crush on the late superintendent. She'd butted him with every scrap of force and venom she could muster. It wasn't quite the romantic memory a man could hang on to in the dark days ahead.

"I wish the sodding pilot would get on the voice channel," said Barencoin, and not to her. "I think he's shitting himself and waiting for incoming. I expect the wess'har know we're off-planet by now. There's a hell of a lot of chat from them on the ITX but I can't understand a word of it."

Lindsay leaned back on the bulkhead out of habit, because nobody needed to lean anywhere in zero g. It was hard to find you were hated even more than Mohan Rayat.

She could hear Bennett and Barencoin talking in very low voices. She caught the words *bloody hero*. They might have been saying that they weren't going to play the *bloody hero* to save her arse, but she doubted it.

She knew damn well who they were talking about.

"*Gethes* shuttle," said a voice from the ancient console. "We are from Umeh. I am Litasi."

"Shuttle Charlie five niner echo, Umeh shuttle this is Shuttle Charlie five niner echo," said Barencoin. "About time, over."

The ussissi wasn't any better at radio procedure than Rayat. "I have a problem, *gethes*," said the little reedy voice. "What have you done?"

"Umeh shuttle, I've got a 9mm round in my right quad and I want to go home," said Barencoin. He looked at Lindsay: it was her job to do the diplomacy. "Want to talk to our boss, over?" There was no response, just the vague background sounds of cockpit activity. He eased himself out of his seat with some difficulty. The medication was wearing off. "Over to you, ma'am." He pronounced the *ma'am* with the clear meaning of *arsehole*. "Don't forget to ask what's happened to Izzy and Chaz."

It was coming her way. She never thought it was going to be easy. What was really bothering her was that she almost felt regret that Shan was gone. She didn't want to feel that at all.

"This is Commander Lindsay Neville, European Federal Navy. What's your problem, pilot?"

"We are neutral, perhaps in a way you cannot comprehend."

"I know that."

"But we are not fools."

"Spit it out."

"What?"

"Come to the point of this conversation."

"You have used cobalt weapons and there is talk that your prisoners are *Shan Chail* and Vijissi."

Lindsay paused. And this was the point at which she knew hell was about to shrug its shoulders and wander out for a spot of bother. She heard the word *cobalt*. For some reason it was more insistent than *prisoners*.

"We have no prisoners," she said at last. "They're dead. What did you say about cobalt?"

"You destroyed Ouzhari with a poisoned bomb. The bezeri

are dying in great numbers. Now repeat what you said about prisoners."

There was a very long silence. It was what Eddie called *dead air.* Lindsay felt her face become numb but her lips moved and she heard her own voice above the pounding in her temples.

"We used neutron devices. That's to confine the damage to the island. The area should be pretty well clear in a couple of days."

"You lie. And I ask again, where are your prisoners?"

"They're dead." It slipped out. She was more fixed on the word *cobalt.* "They're gone."

The line went almost completely silent save for a slight crackling sound. "*Gethes,* I cannot receive you. You ask too much."

Lindsay turned and looked at Rayat. It was all tumbling out of control too fast. "You heap of shit," she said. "*That* was your straight ERD? What the hell have you got us into?" And before she knew what she was doing, she had spun to aim a roundhouse punch at him, a touch too fast in zero g. Barencoin caught her as her fist cracked against Rayat's face with half the force she had wished for. He grabbed her arm. "You bastard. You *lied,* you bastard."

Rayat looked unconcerned. "You're naive, Commander. Never take vague assurances about technology. Remember how Frankland insisted on checking the camp defense cannon herself?" He pushed himself further away, as if reassured that Barencoin would stop her reaching for a weapon next. "And you punch *straight* for power, not round. You're confusing it with a *slap.* I would have thought you'd seen Frankland do *that* properly, too."

I don't need reminding.

Lindsay held her free hand away in concession. Barencoin still had a tight grip on Lindsay's other forearm: a small cockpit was a dangerous place for a brawl.

"Cobalt? Fucking floor-cleaners?" he said. It was their tag for BNOs. He let go of her arm. "Oh boy. Are we in the shit now."

Litasi's voice interrupted. "I suggest you set a course for your mother-ship now. Or perhaps the isenj will accept you on Umeh."

Lindsay struggled to stop her voice cracking. "You work for the isenj."

"And you have killed a ussissi. You make your way there alone."

"We didn't kill him. He . . ."

"What, *gethes*?"

"He chose to stay with Shan Frankland."

There was more dead air, dead *dead* air. Lindsay wished more than ever that she'd had the balls to pull those pins and blow her and Shan and anyone nearby to pieces. She'd been duped into using salted nuclear weapons. She'd unleashed an environmental catastrophe. She had all kinds of questions but right then the sheer enormity of the disaster overwhelmed her. The fact that she'd denied *c'naatat* to humanity was lost, buried under the tumbling rocks of realization.

"Will you accept a surrender?" said Bennett suddenly.

"Ade?" said Lindsay. Even Barencoin looked shocked. "What the hell are you doing?"

"Not you," said Bennett. "*Me.* Pilot, I want to surrender to the wess'har authorities. Will you take me inboard?"

"Why?"

"I want to be tried for involvement in the death of two civilian prisoners."

"Ade, for fuck's sake," said Barencoin. "It was that stupid cow, not you. We stay together and we find Izzy and Chaz."

Bennett pulled his bottle-green beret from his jacket. "Sorry, mate." He shaped it on his head and hauled himself over to the hatch. He turned to look at Lindsay. "You going to stop me, ma'am?"

She had no idea what he was playing at. It wasn't a generous gesture to save them. She knew what he felt for Shan. This was revenge. She just didn't know how or why.

"They'll cut your bloody throat the minute you land," she said. "We nuked Bezer'ej."

"Fine by me, ma'am," said Bennett.

Barencoin let go of her. "If we wait any longer, we'll have a wess'har patrol up our chuff. Let's thin out. *Now.*"

It was just Bennett. He could go, for whatever stupid sentimental reason he had to sacrifice himself. They could make it back to *Actaeon* under their own steam now. She knew it. One fewer pair of lungs to exhaust the oxygen. Fine. She had to concentrate on something.

"We accept his surrender," said the child's voice that Lindsay knew belonged to a creature that could tear out her throat. "We will transfer him to the appropriate authority."

Lindsay turned to Bennett. "Sod off, then." He didn't matter. It was Rayat she needed to fix. She couldn't even begin to imagine what to do with him now, or what his objective really was. "Get a move on."

Bennett saluted her mechanically. "You can't even swear like her," he said. He adjusted his beret and pulled back the handle that opened the hatch to the lobby. Then he stepped in and closed it behind him. He appeared to be fumbling with it and there was a hiss of air on the intercom.

Lindsay stared through the softglass at him, uneasy.

"Bastard," she said.

The next minute was a very, very long one. Eventually there was a faint scraping along the hull: the ussissi shuttle was docking, forming a temporary seal with the top hatch. Bennett began wiping his face clean of dried blood with the antiseptic pad from his medical kit, checking in the mirror of his camo compact like a girl.

"Ready," said the ussissi pilot. "Pressure equalized."

Lindsay wondered why Bennett was so preoccupied with his face. Then he peeled off the dressing from the bridge of his nose, starting carefully at his left cheekbone. And he raised two fingers to her in the gesture of defiance that had been Albion's way of saying *fuck you* since Agincourt nearly a thousand years before.

There wasn't a mark on him: no hint of swelling eyes or deviated septum or even a split lip to show that he'd been smashed in the face.

And the dressings weren't *that* effective.

She'd missed something. Shan had been cut, or Shan had healed instantly, but Lindsay had missed a critical break in her skin.

"Oh no," said Lindsay. "You bastard."

"You'll pay for Shan," said Bennett. "Don't you worry about that, ma'am. You'll pay, one way or another."

She tried to force the hatch manually. He watched her for a couple of seconds and then held a cigar-sized tube to the glass: foam sealant. He'd jammed the wheel.

"I'm a regular gadget shop," he said. All she could do was watch him as he climbed the ladder and disappeared with something she wanted to destroy more than anything else in creation.

Rayat turned to look. Lindsay bit her lip so hard that she could taste hot, wet saltiness. She didn't want him to know what she'd just seen, ever. It would all start again.

"What a complete balls-up," Rayat hissed, and turned away again. "I *told* you we should have taken samples."

Bennett was right, though. They couldn't even swear like Shan Frankland.

24

*Be not afraid of them that kill the body, and after that have no
more that they can do.*

Luke 12:4

Mestin had been thinking about the outrage for half a day.
People came and went in the Exchange of Surplus Things and
glanced at her briefly. They were more distracted by the terrible
images of Ouzhari on the public screen that spread the full
width of the end wall.

The island had always been black. The unique grass there
made it so. But the land was a different black now, the dull dirty
charcoal aftermath of a huge fiery explosion. The sky looked
hazy and overcast.

"Destroy them," she said at last, more to herself than the matriarchs beside her.

It wasn't a huge task. The *gethes* had one ship: but it was in
orbit around Umeh, and that meant ignoring an ancient courtesy. Wess'har had never breached the isenj homeworld. The
isenj had been in the Ceret system before wess'har arrived, and
for a very long time.

Fersanye and Chayyas waited with Mestin, but every so often they glanced at Nevyan. She was all acid agitation, tugging
at her *dhren* occasionally, more like a nervous *gethes*. She was
examining a pannier of ripe *jay* but appearing not to see them.

"What about those in the ship who are *not* responsible for
this attack?" said Fersanye.

"It's a warship," said Mestin. "But we will give them warning to disembark the uninvolved."

"But *Actaeon* is orbiting Umeh."

"Then we shall ask them to withdraw from orbit to a safe distance first."

Nevyan turned very slowly from the *jay* and stood over her mother. "You simply don't understand *gethes*. They won't be polite and move themselves to be killed more tidily."

Her scent had started to shift. It made Mestin uneasy, and Fersanye sat utterly still.

"If *Actaeon* is destroyed that close to Umeh, there will be debris," said Mestin. "This is not the doing of the isenj."

"That is irrelevant," said Nevyan. "I say they should take the consequences of their ill-chosen alliance."

The silence around the matriarchs—and Nevyan, formally or otherwise, had entered that cadre—was total. Those wess'har bringing in produce and taking it away were halted in their tracks. Matriarchs seldom wrangled: rapid consensus was embedded in their genes.

But Mestin stood up. Nevyan was shorter, smaller. She was still her *isanket* in many ways.

"It's wrong to punish the isenj, even by accident," she said.

Nevyan stood her ground. "You never spend enough time learning from *Shan Chail*. We can't defend ourselves with our hands bound. This is a *gethes* trick—a *human shield,* they call it. Like *hostages.* A reliance on the niceness and *decency* of your enemy, their fear of what will happen to the innocent." And suddenly her rasping sour-leaf scent was swamped by a massive, throat-closing burst of dominance. Mestin stepped back.

It was over. She was no longer senior matriarch of F'nar. It had been a brief duty.

Nevyan jiggled her head, realizing what she had done, but she was now fully dominant and didn't seem uncomfortable with it. Mestin saw a stranger for the first time. "I have to contact Shan," she said. "We have heard nothing from her for many hours."

"Vijissi was supposed to look after her," said Mestin. "If there had been problems, he would have let us know."

"I still need to talk with her. I need *her* knowledge."

A *gethes* mother might have taken offense, but Mestin was

proud that her daughter was pragmatic enough to take her lessons where she could. She had long suspected the girl would be a better matriarch than she could. It was sad to know she couldn't teach her enough for the changing times, but Shan could fill the gaps, and she resented the human not one bit.

They returned to Nevyan's home to sit in the main room and wait for news.

And it came.

They heard a ussissi running down the terrace outside, a rapid scrabbling over stones, and when he burst into the room Mestin watched Nevyan freeze for a brief moment. Then she stood. The ussissi came to a halt at her feet, looking up.

"*Shan Chail* is dead," he said. "And Vijissi too. The *gethes* took them." His lips were pulled back and all his teeth were visible. "We want balance. We want revenge."

Nevyan took the news in silence and walked out slowly to stand on the terrace, Mestin a little behind her. The new matriarch of F'nar looked down on her new responsibility and let out a piercing territorial cry that rang round the caldera, note over note, for a count of ten. The sound echoed off the walls of the basin: the disembodied voice continued for a while after Nevyan closed her mouth and lowered her head.

Then she turned round, looking past Mestin, and beckoned the ussissi forward with one gesture of her arm. Even without that heavy, overwhelming scent, she was suddenly the most extreme, most dominant female her mother had ever seen.

"Make contact with the World Before," said Nevyan Tan Mestin.

25

This is a dreadful place. They call it Mar'an'cas *and it's no more than a rock. We'll have to rely heavily on the hydroponics to grow enough food. It's an island: Mum says it's like Alcatraz was, to keep up away from everyone on Wess'ej. I don't even know if we'll have food to spare for Black and White.*

I can't believe what happened to Dad. I can't believe Aras did it. The world's ending, and God isn't answering my prayers.

JAMES GARROD,
in his private journal

"They will pay for this," said Nevyan.

Mestin said nothing. In the past three seasons, the blockade of Bezer'ej had fallen to the isenj, and a *gethes*—no, an *isan*—she thought of as invincible had made the greatest error of all.

It didn't surprise her that *Shan Chail* had sacrificed herself to thwart the *gethes*. Right or wrong, she always liked to have the last word.

And it broke Mestin's heart, as she knew it had broken Nevyan's. That was another English phrase that was worthy of acceptance into wess'u because it was perfect in its description of agony.

The Exchange of Surplus Things, the largest single room in F'nar, was packed with utterly silent matriarchs and ussissi from at least half the city states of Wess'ej. Nevyan walked to the front of the hall. Mestin remained where she was with Fersanye, Chayyas, Siyyas and Prelit.

Nevyan trailed a scent of pungent dominance through the crowd. It was what Vijissi had called *mangoes*. Mestin would miss him more than she could say.

"We have no choice now," said Nevyan. "Will you commit

your males with ours?" She was standing on a crate so she could be seen; despite her great courage and drive, Nevyan was shorter than the average female. She was Shan's height. "I have work for them to do. And I have called on the World Before to help us deal with this threat once and for all."

Wess'har didn't respond as a mob even though they were communal. There was a quiet murmur. A ussissi scrambled onto a crate to peer through the forest of tall females.

"Think carefully before you call for assistance," she said.

"We can't deal with *gethes* alone," said Nevyan. "Not while they have allies in the isenj."

"We know the World Before through our kin there. You don't. They are very different to you."

"They are still wess'har."

"Indeed they are, but they're far stronger even than Wess'ej, and if you're wrong, and if they don't behave as you would, you may end up paying a high price for their aid."

Nevyan did appear to consider the ussissi's words carefully. "Have you an alternative?"

"No."

"And neither have I."

And the room began to empty.

Shan would have said that they didn't do it that way on Earth. There would have been intrigue, skirmishes, riots, angry mobs, and headlines in the news.

But it had taken only a few moments earlier in the day for Nevyan Tan Mestin to depose her mother as senior matriarch of F'nar. She had now launched the first assault on the *gethes* and broken millennia of isolation from the World Before.

There was no pain in it for Mestin. She was proud. It was the only warm thing in her at that moment to ease her mourning and fear. Nevyan stepped down off the crate as if she were embarrassed at having needed it. But her scent of dominance was stronger than ever.

"I told Aras," she said.

Mestin felt relief and dread simultaneously. The two *isan've* stood in the center of the empty hall and silently accepted everything that had happened.

"I would have found that hard," said Mestin.

"As did I," said Nevyan. "You can't imagine his grief."

Mestin followed her from the hall and into a late summer evening that was perfectly beautiful and scented with the fragrance of *aumul've*. The *tem* flies were swarming on the last warm stones left after Ceret's setting: they would be moving further south now to follow the warm weather.

The deaths of tens of thousands of bezeri and *Shan Chail* and Vijissi would take a great deal of balancing. Mestin wondered if Nevyan would start with the displaced colony or even the human base on Umeh.

No. She would begin with *Actaeon*.

The isenj would learn to pick their friends more carefully.

It was an old long-range fighter, but it was serviceable. Nevyan had watched it climb into the clear sky the day before and now she was tracking its advance towards the gethes ship *Actaeon*.

The pilot was one of her *jurej've*, Cidemnet. Mestin didn't think it was kind to send one of her new family into battle so soon after accepting them, but Nevyan said it was important that she demonstrated she would commit her own males to the war. She sat down in front of the screen and Lisik brought them bowls of *tea*. It was unpleasantly bitter, and Mestin couldn't understand what Shan had found so desirable about it. She would still have drunk it gladly if Shan had been there to share it. She missed her already.

"We could have sent a drone missile and destroyed the ship by now," said Mestin.

"And we would have lost the opportunity to add an important message," said Nevyan. "Besides, they have had time to disembark more *noncombatants and civilians*, whatever that distinction might mean. We'll deal with them in due course."

Unlike *gethes,* whose wars were fought in secret, any

wess'har could access the channel and follow Nevyan's conduct of the mission. They could watch what Nevyan was seeing; they could hear her conversations with the fighter. They would also be able to hear any exchange with the *gethes*. They had nothing to hide.

Mestin knew they were as baffled by her tactics as she was. It didn't matter. Nevyan seemed grimly confident of the lessons she had learned from *Shan Chail*.

She touched the console. The screen showed Cidemnet's forward view from his cockpit, just the ochre disk of Umeh. The *gethes* ship in orbit around it wasn't even a speck but the display in front of Cidemnet across his field of view showed a moving constellation of lights, ussissi and isenj vessels and the larger target that was CSV *Actaeon*.

"Contact *Actaeon*," she said. "Let me speak to the commander."

It took a while. When Malcolm Okurt's voice crackled into the chamber, it sounded surprised. There was no image. The disembodied voice was disturbing. Then it was joined by a shimmering image of a *gethes* with a thin face and every fidgeting sign of agitation.

"Am I speaking to the wess'har chief of staff?" he asked. He was expecting a soldier.

"I am Nevyan Tan Mestin, matriarch of F'nar. Shan Frankland was my friend."

Mestin thought it was an odd way to identify yourself. Okurt paused too. "Ma'am, we're genuinely sorry for the events of the last forty-eight hours. I can assure you we had no knowledge of the intent to use such extreme measures."

"But you brought them here, so you must have considered it."

"Purely defensive, ma'am. If there's anything we can do to help deal with the contamination, we're at your disposal."

"Are you *taking the piss?*" Nevyan asked.

Okurt looked completely stunned by her sudden command of colloquial English. "Sorry?"

"Don't lie to me. You sent troops to Bezer'ej with aggressive intent. The bezeri are dying in great numbers. Two of my friends are dead. And you talk of helping us to clean up."

"Our mission was to detain Frankland, not to kill her, and certainly not to cause devastation to the environment. My colleague exceeded her orders. I believe we can come to some understanding if we can meet and talk this through."

Nevyan cocked her head in amazement and shot Mestin a glance. The *gethes* really hadn't understood them at all. "No discussion," said Nevyan. "Who's responsible?"

Okurt paused again. "As commanding officer, I am."

"Responsibility is personal."

"The individuals who carried out the attack will be disciplined when they return to this ship, but the buck stops with me. You understand that phrase, I take it."

"I do."

"I'm really very sorry about Superintendent Frankland."

"And so are we. But only actions matter, and I regret what I must do just as you regret what you have done, and the end will not be altered by either."

Mestin was getting agitated too. Why was Nevyan spending so long talking with this creature? Cidemnet didn't need time to maneuver. His missiles were aimed and locked: this was entirely superfluous. It was a game. Wess'har didn't play games.

Okurt's face stopped moving and his voice sounded a little higher in pitch although it was steady. It was a sign of nervousness.

"I know you have a small vessel on station observing us, ma'am."

"Yes, a single fighter. It's more than five thousand years old. It still works."

Clearly he didn't think one ancient, distant fighter was more than a gesture, but he was confused, that was clear. "Ma'am, are you threatening us?"

"No. I'm targeting you. This is the act of balance for your crimes. *Launch.*"

Cidemnet let loose three warheads. Okurt's transmission cut off halfway through words that sounded like *stand to* and Mestin saw the three trails of light spread in the sudden image of Cidemnet's viewplate. *Actaeon* now had less than the time it took to boil two cups of water to make that strange, bitter *tea*.

Nevyan had not only launched an attack on the *gethes*, but had also sent them a message that she could do so with the least of her arsenal. Mestin now understood the game her daughter had learned to play, taught by Shan Frankland and Eddie Michallat.

A tiny pinpoint of white light flared briefly against the disk of Umeh, then another, and another.

"You can come home now, Cidemnet," said Nevyan.

26

STAND TO—VESSEL CONTACT.
  OPS ROOM, BRIDGE: VESSEL ON SCREEN VISUAL,
RED 300, MOVING LEFT TO RIGHT: PWO, OFFICER OF
THE WATCH, THREE CONTACTS INCOMING, UP THE
CHUFF, RANGE 450 KAY, SPEED THIRD LIGHT. BRACE
BRACE BRACE.
  SECOND CONTACT INCOMING.
  BRACE BRACE BRACE
  STAND TO.
                      Voice traffic downlinked to FEU Fleet Command
                 from CSV Actaeon. *No further transmission received.*

There were so many fragments from the shattered hull of
Actaeon that isenj actually froze their constant river of movement to watch the fireballs streaking across the sky above Jejeno even during daylight.

A couple had crashed into the suburbs of Tivsk on the next
landmass. There were a lot of casualties, the sort of numbers you
couldn't avoid in crowded places. If *Actaeon* hadn't been easing
out of orbit, running up her engines after the last emergency
evacuation to Umeh, it would have been far worse.

It was quite a display. Eddie watched it too. It continued into
the dusk. If you dissociated it from the circumstances, it was
spectacularly beautiful. But he couldn't do that sort of mind-
trick, not any more.

He kept wondering if what he had told Malcolm Okurt about
c'naatat had been the root cause of this. He had been so sure he
was doing the right thing. But he had told him—and Lindsay
Neville—where it was, and where Shan might be found. It was
an agonizing thought. He didn't want it in his head.

Umeh Station boiled with angry ussissi. Shan had summed it

up succinctly, as she always did: take on one ussissi, and you took on all of them.

Eddie hadn't realized he had made such an impact on them. Apparently they admired his pluck for facing them after the destruction of Ouzhari.

So they had sought him out first to tell him that Shan Frankland and Vijissi were dead.

They had become a pack. They roamed among the workers and military personnel in the biodome, sniffing and darting away. Eddie had never seen that before. It made them look like hunting animals, like mongooses on to a cobra. It seemed only a matter of time before they attacked.

Even Serrimissani joined then for a while, weaving around and becoming one part of a single, increasingly angry creature.

Eddie sat on a trestle made up of a sheet of greenhouse composite and two stacks of pallets that would eventually become composting bins if Umeh Station was ever completed. He should have been very glad that he had decided against returning to *Actaeon*: but all he could think about was Shan.

"Jesus Christ. *Jesus Christ.*" Eddie said it so many times that the words didn't sound like English any more, just a mantra, a sound, a song in a foreign language. "Shan. *Shan.*"

Serrimissani had gathered her belongings in a sack. She lowered her head as if something was raining down on it. "This is the last place I would want to be at this moment."

"You're leaving?"

"The *gethes* have killed *Shan Chail* and Vijissi. There may be more retribution, and they may target every human here." She took Eddie's arm. "If you have sense, you will come with me. I am returning to Wess'ej. Come with me and beg forgiveness of the matriarchs, and perhaps they will spare you. You have done a favor for them." She looked up anxiously. "And you have been honest. Come on."

"The humans didn't kill them. Not actual murder."

"And would they still be alive had they not been captured?"

"Yes."

"Then spare me your sophistry."

Eddie reached for the urine vial in his pocket and pressed it against his chest to make sure it was still there with its single ruby-beaded quill. He'd hand it over. He wouldn't have the slightest trouble doing that now.

Eddie had run for his life a few times. It was always several hours after everyone else had come up with the idea first. There was something about seeing a world through a camera lens that made you feel less vulnerable: added to the detachment of being a reporter, it made for a poor sense of mortality. Journalists in danger zones got killed with depressing frequency. Eddie didn't plan on joining them, not because he was scared—and he was, oh God yes he *was*—but because he hadn't told his story yet.

He owed Shan that much. He wanted to know everything. He hoped they wouldn't execute Ade Bennett before he could talk to him.

"Okay," he said. "When we get the evacuation warning, I'll come."

"Warning? They will not warn you. You didn't warn them. The vengeance will come, and soon."

Eddie pulled out the bee-cam. "Tight on me until further notice, divert for explosive and sudden movement," he told it. "And upload every five minutes." He didn't want to die with an unfiled story in the system. He hoped the isenj link would relay his material now that *Actaeon* was no more than a spectacular shower of false meteors.

He quickened his pace behind Serrimissani. At least she had come back for him; he'd had native guides abandon him in the middle of riots. As they walked, they saw ground cars trundling materials towards the Jejeno sphere. One slowed down and an orange-suited foreman leaned out of the cab.

"Want a lift?" he asked.

"I'm leaving," Eddie said. "But thanks. Have you had a security alert yet?"

"No. Why?"

"I don't think Jejeno is going to be the safest place to be after what happened earlier."

"What?"

"Doesn't matter. There's a war starting. Don't be here when it does."

The foreman shrugged and heaved himself back into the seat. Eddie and Serrimissani walked on, quickening their pace. Isenj were obviously starting to work out who would be next after *Actaeon*: there was a definite thinning out of the crowds in the neighborhoods closest to the sphere, and some isenj were carrying bundles on their flat heads, children trailing behind them in orderly lines. They knew the wess'har well enough to have come to the same conclusion as Serrimissani.

"And where will your humans go now that *Actaeon* is destroyed?" Serrimissani asked. They flagged down an isenj vehicle and she chattered at the driver. "They are stranded here."

"Is Lin back yet? Where's the shuttle?"

"I would not waste concern on her."

"I was thinking of Mart Barencoin, actually." Shan liked the marines. She would have wanted them kept out of the aftermath. "How can I check what's happened—"

"Think of your own safety." Serrimissani reached down and pulled Eddie up into the seat, and they sat in silence until they came to the outskirts of the airport. The driver was anxious to get as far away from Jejeno as he could, and taking them to the terminal seemed to be asking for more time than he was willing to spare. They began a brisk walk up the main approach road, dodging isenj workers who seemed simply to be going about their tasks.

Eddie motioned the bee-cam to get shots of them. "How many of them will still be alive next week?" he asked.

"If the wess'har attack, they will only target the sphere. If the isenj stay clear of it, very few will die. There will be substantial disruption, though." It sounded like a few traffic jams: but Eddie imagined water pipes spurting and power lines cut and fires raging and food shortages. And very high casualties.

There was no room in this tight-packed infrastructure to have any sort of emergency without the isenj suffering too. Ual would be busy in his serene aquamarine offices.

He thought again of Shan and wondered if anyone had broken the news to Aras. His grief would be terrible.

"Jesus, I still can't believe she's gone," he said, not caring if the bee-cam picked it up. It shot back to concentrate on his face, intruding into his own grief, a fitting punishment for his calling. "Oh God. *Oh God.*"

"She was a good wess'har," Serrimissani said. "She accepted Targassat. To die to preserve the balance of life is a commendable act."

It seemed that every ussissi on Umeh had the same premonition of war as they did. Anxious little faces and chattering teeth greeted them as they pushed through the lobby and out onto the apron nearest the ussissi shuttle. One had already left, packed to just above safe lading weight. They were loyal creatures if they had a personal charge to care for, but they weren't stupid.

"I have to make some calls," said Eddie.

"We must go."

"I need to ask Ual for a few favors. The ministry is at least fifteen kay from here. Even if they start bombing now—"

"You have until this evening. I will stay with you, in case you become foolish and try to get more stories that end up killing you."

"You're a doll," Eddie said, and meant it. Yes, they were loyal, dog-loyal. But Serrimissani didn't understand, and nor did it appear that she was interested in doing so. She stared at the vessel filling up with ussissi. So did Eddie.

"Sinking ship," he said.

"It will fly," said Serrimissani.

"I meant—never mind. Rats leaving sinking ships—they're supposed to be the first to know when a ship is in trouble." He was gibbering. He always did that when fighting down emotions that threatened to overwhelm him. "Doesn't matter."

"What are rats?" she asked.

Eddie thought hard. "Another kind of people."

His mind was a mess of fragments, personal fears, professional worries, loss, confusion. But he centered on what he was at his core—a reporter. It anchored him again and he felt calmer. If Ual's link was denied to him, he could ask the matriarchs of F'nar to hack into the ITX link. He had to get that story filed: it was the least he owed Shan Frankland.

He had once made a mistake and thought she was like everyone else, available at the right price, but he'd been wrong. And he was glad he had the chance to tell her so.

Everyone needed heroes. He still had his, intact and immutable, and now he always would.

Aras suddenly realized he was kneeling on the floor, and he had no idea how long he had been there. His forehead was on his knees, his hands tucked in under his chest.

It hurt too much to move. It certainly hurt to think.

"*Actaeon* has been destroyed," said Nevyan gently. "I made certain of it."

He knew he was back on Wess'ej. He heard her but the pressure in his throat had taken over. He had forgotten about Josh and he had forgotten about the bezeri and he had forgotten about his failure to protect Bezer'ej after so many, many years of standing sentinel.

They had taken his *isan*. Shan was gone. He couldn't move for grief.

He tried to focus on the pain. It was a trick he had learned when he was a prisoner of the isenj, when he couldn't die but wanted to very badly, when every second was infinite. He found that if he concentrated on the pain, on the moment, the enormity of the unspecified void ahead of him was pushed to one side.

"Can he hear us?" It was Mestin's voice.

"I think so. Leave us. I'll stay with him for the while."

Aras tried not to think of Shan and failed. She consumed him. And he thought of Askiniyas, and he hadn't seen her or held her for centuries. There had been a time when he couldn't summon up her face or scent despite his perfect wess'har recall, but now she was vivid—and astonishingly alien. But he wanted Shan. He wanted to hold her.

They had even denied him the comfort of cradling her body one last time.

Wess'har males who lost their *isan* remated or else they died. He could do neither. And he didn't want to. He never wanted to move beyond this grief even though it was burning him alive.

"You can come and stay with us," said Nevyan.

He couldn't form any words. Even breathing was an effort.

"Or we can bring you whatever you need. You need not see anyone until you want to." Nevyan moved, sending a cloud of very dominant scent into the air, and knelt down beside him. The smell triggered a primeval urge to placate her, but he felt as if he would fall apart, limb from limb, if he tried to move. "We have had messages from their leaders. They want to talk and apologize. But I have sent word to the World Before. I await their reply."

Nevyan waited an uncharacteristically long time for a senior matriarch. She waited, kneeling, but Aras was frozen.

She's gone. She's dead.

"Eddie has asked to live in F'nar. He'll be alone here. I doubt he will ever get home."

Aras struggled to think. His mind was trapped in a loop of reliving the first realization that Shan was gone. He could not imagine the pain ever stopping. It kept rolling over him again and again.

"I think you and Eddie could be a great comfort to each other," Nevyan persisted. "Shall I tell him he's welcome?"

Aras wanted oblivion. If he could have moved, he would have gone and taken the grenades Shan kept as bizarre souvenirs and laid upon them and *died*.

He forced his head up.

"She's *c'naatat*," said Nevyan. "You must not lose hope. We have no idea what the parasite's limits are."

Aras hated Nevyan suddenly for that suggestion. *C'naatat*

was remarkable: but it could not bring back the dead. That was a conjuring trick for the humans' god. He managed to pound his fists on the stone floor. He felt the skin tear and the blood flow, albeit briefly. The pain helped.

They always seemed to think a *c'naatat* couldn't feel pain. They were wrong.

"We'll bring her body home," Nevyan said. "We'll find her. Every wess'har has the right to return home to the cycle. She'll be taken back into the world, however long we have to search."

Aras thought how much it would have meant to Shan to be spoken of as a wess'har. He wanted to see her body. He wanted to hold her one last time. He didn't give a damn about the cycle. He wanted his *isan*.

Nevyan was still staring at Shan's few personal items on a shelf that was rapidly taking on the appearance of a human shrine. She put her hand out towards an imperfect emerald glass bowl but stopped short of touching it.

"I would like something of her," she said. "She made this, yes?"

Aras couldn't form the words, but he didn't feel the urge to stop her. He still had more of Shan than anyone would ever touch. He had her memories, the very fabric of her, genetic material he had not even begun to see expressed yet.

Nevyan placed the bowl in the folds of her *dhren* and clutched it to her like a child. "She shaped me, Aras. She was my friend. She taught me that you can't withdraw from the world and you can't run from threats. You must engage them and not spend your life in dread of their coming. And this view will guide me now that I have succeeded Mestin."

What will I do without her? How will I carry on?

"Aras, I know you can hear me," said Nevyan. "I shall send Eddie to you. And then there are the other humans. There's the soldier, Bennett. He asks to talk to you."

Bennett would never have harmed Shan. Whatever he claimed, he would never have killed her. Aras knew it. He needed to talk to him. But it would have to wait.

He sat back on his heels. It was the most effort he had managed to muster in days. It was a primeval survival reflex gone haywire, from the tunnel-dwelling past when keeping still when faced with an unseen threat might be the difference between living and dying for the proto-wess'har. Aras was always surprised when it caught him out like this. The last time had been when Askiniyas took her own life.

He now had two *isan've* who had been suicides in extreme circumstances. It was too much to ask of a wess'har male.

"Bring them here," he said.

Bennett was a soldier. Eddie was a soldier too, except he could fight with words, and *gethes* were very vulnerable to those.

He would need them both if he was going to exact his own balance for the death of Shan Frankland.

27

A spokesman for the FEU Foreign Office said they regretted the incident and would revise the guidelines for future missions. But the spokesman declined to comment on whether any formal protest would be lodged over the fate of CSV Actaeon.

Meanwhile protests continued against the planned landing of isenj delegates from the EFS Thetis. *The veteran ship is still more than seventy years away from the solar system but the Sino-European Space Commission admits it has carried out a feasibility study into whether a mission can be launched to retrieve the vessel and speed its journey home with modern propulsion systems.*

"We have so much to learn from the isenj, and bridges to build," said technology minister Francois Teilhard. "We would rather that happened as quickly as possible."

BBCHan bulletin.

"Come on," said Eddie "You can patch me through to my News Desk, can't you?"

He had drilled down as far as the Defense Ministry comms control desk, and he suspected he'd only made it that far because he was on Minister Ual's private link. Ual was proving to be a reliable and valuable friend. Eddie was laboring under no illusions that it was his witty repartee ensuring the minister's cooperation.

"Mr. Michallat, this is a military communications channel," said the woman on the other end of his precious and fragile lifeline. She was very chic and dark, a little too exotic for the drab uniform of an army major. She reminded him of Marine Ismat Qureshi. "We don't feed into the entertainment networks from here."

"You did all the time it suited you, though."

"I appreciate your frustration."

"I need to let my people know I'm alive. They think I was on—in—*Actaeon* when she was hit."

"And it's clear you're still on Umeh."

"It's clear to you, but not to them. Maybe you could *make* it clear."

"Wait one."

The screen flicked to the holding menu of warnings about confidentiality, federal security and dire penalties if any one of a thousand rules and regulations was breached.

Eddie didn't want to be polite at all. He wanted to scream that the news they were currently broadcasting was bollocks, less than half a story because it didn't mention why the wess'har had fired on *Actaeon* with three massive missiles that shattered her backbone and broke her into fragments in minutes.

He knew that because the wess'har had provided the information via Serrimissani. He also knew the Defense Ministry didn't have all the data because there were no survivors from *Actaeon* to file a sitrep or take part in a wash-up. All they had were the last transmissions from the ship and reports from the surface of Umeh about the magnificent fireworks display that meant all hands were lost.

That meant 106 out of nearly 500 men and women, civilians and service personnel. Everyone else had been evacuated to Umeh Station during what the military delicately called the *period of tension*, as if the threat of war was some sort of minor back pain.

Someone back at BBChan had to be asking why the wess'har attacked. He knew they wouldn't swallow whatever pat answer they had been fed. But one thing reassured him. The news about *Actaeon* had leaked fast, in hours rather than days or months. It was the price of ITX. Once the routine of instant messages and telemetry between remote stations and Earth had become established, a lot of people in dull support jobs noticed when they suddenly stopped. And those people talked, both to their contacts at Umeh Station and to their chums back on Earth.

Eddie had been afraid that ITX's exclusivity would mean all news would be suppressed. He should never have underestimated the power of the human mouth.

The warning menu dissolved and the glamorous but inflexible major was back in frame again.

"Mr. Michallat, I can certainly pass on a message to your employers. You'll appreciate that we have quite a bit on our hands at the moment."

Eddie's brain started scrambling for a message that would let News Desk know that the information the Defense Ministry spokesweasels were pumping out was incomplete. Okay, they knew that anyway. It was part of the game. But they didn't know exactly what they were omitting and—unlike on Earth—the opposing forces' view from the Cavanagh system would be channeled through the Cerberuslike DM liaison desk. They couldn't just call the wess'har for a comment.

He hadn't been this cut off even during the Greek war. He had been able to buy the protection of a militia minder, complete with armored car, and drive the damn story over the nearest safe border.

Now that was a thought. He'd have to work on that as a backup plan.

"Thank you," said Eddie. Inspiration suddenly struck him so hard that he had to squeeze his nails into his palm to stay deadpan. "Can you tell them I have a Belgrano to file?"

"Spell that."

"Bravo Echo Lima Golf Romeo Alpha November Oscar." Eddie hoped his gambling wasn't visible. He was banking on nobody being familiar with three-hundred-year-old incidents during a war even the military had forgotten. But News Desk would look it up. Think. *Think.* "Bloody Expensive Living, Gratuities, Research And Nobbling Officials. I'm out of barter items, love. I want to file my expenses to replace them for when I get home."

There was a pause. Major Gorgeous was making notes, lips moving slightly as she keyed in the acronym. Then she smiled coldly. "You journalists," she said. "You really are callous bastards, aren't you?"

Eddie managed a convincingly guilty shrug. "Not the first war I've been in," he said. "How about you?"

"I'll see this is relayed immediately and get back to you. Good day, Mr. Michallat."

Eddie held his aw-don't-be-hard-on-me expression until he was sure the connection was cut. Then he punched the air in brief triumph. That was one fucking *amazing* God-given stroke of genius. He had no idea that he could bluff that well or lie that fast. *Belgrano*? *Jesus*. It was as if everything he had ever done, however minor, had been designed to lead up to that point in time.

Serrimissani was at his shoulder immediately. "We have to go."

"One more hour."

"We can return when the wess'har have finished with Umeh Station."

"What if they don't attack?"

"Then we come back and find it intact."

"I need to know if News Desk got the message."

"What is *Belgrano*?"

"It was a ship, but I made up the acronym on the spot. Nothing to do with my expenses." Oh, he was *pleased* with himself. "Provided the teenage morons running News Desk spot that I've sent a spoof message, they'll know something's wrong."

"More wrong than one of their warships being destroyed?"

"Spare me the sarcasm. This is journalist maths. If they spot the problem, they'll look up *Belgrano*. I'm just hoping the Defense Ministry is sufficiently ignorant, badly educated, and European enough not to have any knowledge of an event in an obscure British war."

"Which is?"

"An Argentine warship that was sunk by a British submarine, HMS *Conqueror*, and there was a big row over whether or not it represented a threat to the British forces. That's irrelevant. What matters is that it started a major bust-up between the military, the government and the media of the day about what really happened. If my colleagues make the connection, that ought to be enough to let them know there's an even bigger fucking story behind this one."

He was going to wait until the walls came crashing down, even if that meant making Serrimissani leave without him. For foul-tempered ferrets, they had an unshakable sense of devotion. He liked them. Right then, he liked every species except *Homo sapiens.*

Just like Shan.

The thought caught him unawares and his spirit sank briefly before he dragged it back up by its collar again, assuring it he was going to do right by her. He owed it to her to fight.

The Defense Ministry was cutting it fine.

Serrimissani had already started circling him like an impatient sheepdog when the FEU menu screen appeared and paged him. He waited three seconds and hit the control.

It was Major Gorgeous.

"Mr. Michallat," she said, "I have a message from a Mr. Chetwynd at BBChan Foreign Desk. He says your expenses claim gives them some cause for concern and he wants to know if you're trying to claim for . . ." She looked down, apparently at a screen. ". . . more *Conqueror* brand whisky, given the argument you had over it last time. He'll be back in touch when he can, but in the meantime not to hand out too many more bribes."

Eddie felt relief wash over him like a warm shower.

"What a tight-fisted bastard," he said grimly, and convincingly.

"As are you all," said the major, and the menu screen replaced her lovely but unlovable face.

Serrimissani was at eye-level with him. "We go now," she said. "Do you have your answer?"

"Oh, I do," he said, and began cramming his text pad and editing screen in his bag. "Thank God for BBChan researchers."

Yes, they now knew damn well what he had meant.

Conqueror.

Round about now, fellow journalists he had neither known nor worked with would be calling contacts and harassing media spokespersons and challenging ministers.

They would be asking what the hell they *hadn't* been told about how CSV *Actaeon* came to be blown to kingdom come while in apparently friendly space. And they wouldn't rest until they had heard from the BBChan man on the scene. *Him.*

"Ready when you are, doll," said Eddie.

Nevyan was settling comfortably into the role of senior matriarch. Mestin watched the expression on Eddie Michallat's face as he came into the large kitchen and looked expectantly at her, only to be waved towards Nevyan.

"Don't be embarrassed, Mr. Michallat," said Mestin. "Political power here is not the same commodity as it is for *gethes*. My daughter has precedence now, and we're all content with that."

"You really ought to invade Earth sometime," said Eddie. She knew enough of humans now to realize he was being flippant. "It would make our life a hell of a lot simpler."

Nevyan had Giyadas with her. *Isanket've* needed to learn how to conduct themselves, and there was no reason not to start early. The child sat patiently on the floor at Nevyan's side with her head against her legs, watching Eddie with unblinking eyes. He was trying not to watch the child, and not succeeding.

"You have asked for *asylum* here," said Nevyan. "Is that the correct word?"

"Yes. I don't want to live among the human community, either here or on Umeh."

"Are you going to find it difficult living among us and remaining on good terms with the isenj?"

"I'm a journalist. I'm professionally neutral. But if you're asking if I'm going to be a spy in your camp, try this for size." He put his hand inside his garment and took out a small transparent container. He held it at the level of his ear and rattled it. "A quill. Ironically, from the seat of government."

He held it out and Nevyan took it.

"It's too late for the bezeri," she said.

"I know, and I'm sorry. But it's not too late for the rest of Bezer'ej. The vast majority of life will survive. This is for them."

Right answer, thought Mestin. Giyadas craned her neck to peer at the container as Nevyan turned it over in her hands.

"What is the bead?" she asked.

"Ruby," he said. "Corundum. Valuable, where I come from. Keep it. It's not my color."

Nevyan trilled to summon Lisik and handed the vial to him. "Take this to Sevaor," she said. Then she concentrated on Eddie again. "If you stay here, I would appreciate it if you would provide company for Aras."

"How is he?"

"Grieving."

"Sorry. Stupid question. Is he going to want me around?"

"It will be easier for him to be with a human than with a family here that reminds him of his loss."

"Suppose he wants to be alone?"

"He has spent too long alone. He needs friendship now, even if he doesn't see that." She paused. "He has executed Joshua Garrod. I believe that is troubling him too."

Mestin, keeping a silent watch on the exchange, couldn't interpret Eddie's mood until that point. He was too much of a jumble of emotions and agitation to detect any scent clearly. Then overwhelming panic roiled off him, pungent as human sweat. He swallowed hard and the knobbly lump at the front of his neck moved visibly.

He seemed to be chewing on unspoken words. His jaw moved. It was a few seconds before sound emerged.

"Oh," he said.

"The soldier called Bennett is here too. He surrendered. He'll be useful."

"I can't imagine him surrendering."

"He claims to have caused Shan's death. He saw her die."

"Ade? Never. He had a big crush on her. He might have screwed up, but—look, can I talk to him?"

"Ask Aras. You should go to him now. You know where his home is."

"Thank you." Eddie still seemed shaken. "I appreciate your kindness."

"And we appreciate your willingness to help."

"There's one more thing I want to ask of you. I need to send back reports. I can't let that garbage about *Actaeon* go unchallenged, and I reckon people back home are asking questions now about what really started the conflict. When they let me tell the story, I want to have the stuff ready to file. I owe it to Shan, especially if Ade will talk to me about it."

"Professionally neutral," said Nevyan. "Wasn't that your claim?"

"I was lying," said Eddie. "Sometimes neutrality is just an excuse for being spineless."

Eddie had clearly scored highly with Nevyan. She patted his arm. Mestin sent Serrimissani with Eddie, just to make sure he reached Aras's home in one piece. Humans had poor memories, and she couldn't rely on him to remember the way. She was also worried he might not cope with the steps and terraces with their sheer drops into nothing. Humans didn't have good balance, either.

Giyadas was trilling *spineless, spineless, spineless* under her breath, trying out the word with overtones and then trying to limit herself to one note. The weight of the last few days settled on the adults while the child delighted in the novelty of new alien words.

"What a strange language English can be," said Nevyan. "He'll never learn wess'u. He'll never be able to pronounce it, anyway."

"It's English you most need him to speak," said Mestin. "Because it's the humans who need to listen."

Eddie hesitated before knocking on the lovely pearl door. He knew it was shit, but it didn't make it any less magical. And knowing Aras well didn't make it any easier to work out what to say to him.

The door opened. Aras, grim and huge, filled the opening. He didn't look any different, but then Eddie wasn't sure he would show signs of not eating or sleeping.

And he knew wess'har couldn't weep.

"I don't know what to say to you," Eddie said. "I'm truly sorry, and I miss her too, and I won't presume to tell you I know how you must feel, because I don't."

Aras said nothing, but held out his arm in a gesture to invite Eddie inside.

Eddie stood in the center of the Spartan room, afraid to sit down in case he was taking a seat that had been Shan's. He waited for Aras to indicate a place on the incongruously human sofa.

"Thanks for taking me in," he said.

"Shan was very fond of you."

It was painfully touching. Eddie knew she enjoyed their verbal sparring but he had no idea that the relationship generated any degree of warmth at her end. She was good at holding people at arm's length. "It's all my fault," he said. "If you want to kill me, I wouldn't blame you."

"As always, you confuse knowledge with action," said Aras.

"If I had kept my mouth shut, they wouldn't have known she had the damn thing. I even told them where to find her. And *it*."

"No. If you had kept those things to yourself, they would still have found out in time, and pursued us, but you would have been long dead, and so oblivious of the events."

Aras had an accidental talent for making Eddie feel better. Eddie hoped he could return the favor. But he had a feeling that the questions he needed to ask Aras would simply scrape at wounds so fresh and raw that the pain would overwhelm him.

They didn't talk much for the rest of the day. Aras busied himself cooking, which Eddie took as displacement activity, but he was glad of it because it was good food. Aras didn't eat anything. He just gave Eddie a pile of *sek* blankets, showed him the sofa and went out.

Eddie thought he might be going into the center of the city on some errand or other, but as he watched from the terrace, taking in a vista that had still not yet palled for him, he saw a figure walking out into the dry plain.

He hoped Aras wasn't going to do anything stupid.

But Aras was *c'naatat*, and that made killing yourself a very tall order. Eddie still decided he would keep an eye on him.

The room was stark despite the odd touches of human upholstery—a bed against one wall, the sofa, a padded stool. Eddie looked around. There was almost no storage. It was like being back in the cabins at *Thetis* camp. He rummaged in the one cupboard and found some glass bowls, Shan's carefully folded formal uniform jacket, thin-woven hand towels, and two hand grenades. It didn't really surprise him. She liked to be ready for emergencies.

It was painful to realize that she wouldn't come striding through the door and give him a stream of inventive and good-natured abuse. He thought of how she'd taken a laser cutter to Rayat's desk when he'd argued about some trivia, and he smiled, and it hurt. He'd miss her.

Aras was going to have a very hard time of it.

Eddie picked up the grenades, prayed that they were disarmed, and put them in his bag. Fragmentation was the one thing he knew that could kill *c'naatat* troops. There was no point taking chances.

He spent the rest of the afternoon playing with the insubstantial-looking translucent console at the far end of the room. He worked out how to get images, sound, and data from the wess'har archives, but the tuning defeated him.

He was still fiddling around when Aras, silent and unexpected, walked up behind him and showed him where the data streams from Earth could be found.

"Thanks," said Eddie. "Are you okay? Want to talk?"

"No."

At least Eddie could watch the news. He wasn't sure he wanted to. There was nothing worse than being spitting mad and 150 trillion miles away from being able to do anything about it.

He watched the news anyway, curled up on the eccentric white sofa while Aras disappeared onto the terrace.

"I can listen," Eddie called. "And I don't mean an interview."

Aras grunted noncommittally from a distance. Eddie turned back to the screen to wander through his favorite news channels.

He was glad he did. The European Federal Union's junior defense secretary was having a hard time. His boss had gone to ground, leaving him to deal with reporters covering a space war for the very first time. Eddie could sense their excitement.

People always tut-tutted about journalists being pushy and rude and disrespectful. But Eddie thought there was nothing finer than the sight of a minister being doorstepped and harried all the way from his shiny office door to his overpriced privilege of a chauffeur-driven limo by a pack of reporters.

It was democracy. He loved it. He could take all the abuse and slammed doors in the world because, when it came down to it, *this* was what the job was really about.

It was about being one of the last ordinary people left with enough clout to put those in power on the spot and make them account for themselves.

Shan would have loved it too.

Serrimissani had slotted into the gap left by Vijissi without asking or being asked. She wanted to be useful. She sat on the steps of the terrace beside Mestin and Nevyan without comment as they waited for a response from the World Before.

The wess'har populations no longer spoke the same language, but the ussissi moved between the worlds and could make contact and translate. Shan had found it hard to work out how the ussissi could work with such differing cultures without being a conduit for any of them. Mestin would have sent her out with them to learn and understand, but it was too late now.

"They're wess'har, like us," said Nevyan. "However differently they live, they will share our basic drive for cooperation. And they will not be *gethes*."

"What do you want them to do if they accept our approach?" asked Mestin.

"To tell us what's possible in confining the *gethes* to their own system, and what support they will give us to achieve that."

"So we're back to the *policing* that Targassat so despised?"

"She felt we sought out cultures for interference because we believed we were morally superior, and that it would over-stretch us and cost us our own civilization. *This* is a response to outright aggression."

"Outcomes, *isanket,* not motives. And perhaps she was just wrong."

"And perhaps she was right for the times, but not for now."

"You don't need to comfort yourself about betraying a dead woman's ideals." It seemed they were being driven by respect for opinionated and exceptional matriarchs who were no longer around to enforce their own philosophies. "You make your own judgments. The will of Wess'ej supports you. It's time to act."

And if it wasn't, it was too late to step back.

Nijassi, a member of Vijissi's pack, came scrambling up the steps. "There is a message," he said. "It has taken time to find the right people to ask the questions, but we have an answer."

"And?" Nevyan stood up and shook down her *dhren* as if she were heading somewhere to receive a visit.

"They will arrange a conference by screen as soon as they have spoken to the various cities."

"This isn't an answer. What did they actually say? What were the words?"

Nijassi sat back on his haunches as if he had forgotten to note the most important part of the message. He seemed to have taken it as understood.

"They said that what threatens us threatens them. And threat is now. They will come."

28

When our defense personnel die in action, we want to hear the truth. We can handle it. We might even think their lives were worth sacrificing. But what we can't handle is lies.

CSV Actaeon *was the first vessel to be sunk—if that word can apply—in a war in space. Before we rush to condemn the alien forces that destroyed her, we need to ask what made them attack after living peacefully with humans for nearly two hundred years. Why won't the government let us hear from the one independent observer who can talk openly to all the parties in this tragic conflict? We challenge the FEU president to let us talk to Eddie Michallat, unedited and unrestricted. If we're going to live with aliens, we need to understand them before it's too late.*

Editorial comment, "Europe Now"

Aras wondered how long it would be before even a *c'naatat* succumbed to lack of nourishment.

He really didn't feel like eating. It was more than simply being off his food. Food was communal: he had cooked for Shan, and Shan was no longer there to enjoy it. She had not been there for nearly seven days now and she would never be there again.

There were no stages of grieving for wess'har, no denial or bargaining. First they were paralyzed by grief and shock, and then they accepted it. Males remated and the pain was soothed, but not wholly forgotten. So did females. Aras had to find his own solution, and for a second time.

But he was mired in human anger.

He spent the morning wondering how many scores he would feel obliged to settle before his life was too miserable to be faced.

"Aras," said Eddie. He stood at the door to the terrace and called him. He seemed scared to come within Aras's reach, as if he would receive a blow. It was a shame. The human was doing his best to support him, misguided though it was. "Aras, Nevyan's at the door. She's brought someone to talk to you."

It was Sergeant Bennett in his camouflage battle dress, even though there was no longer any point in concealment, and he was wearing that odd flat green fabric headdress that he called a *beret*. Nevyan gestured the soldier forward silently. He saluted Aras.

"Sir," he said. It sounded like *sah*. "I need to talk to you urgently."

Aras stood back and let them walk in. Bennett simply stood in the center of the room with his hands clasped behind his back, legs a little apart. They called it *standing easy*. It certainly didn't look like there was any ease about it.

This man had shot his *isan*.

He had also stopped Lindsay Neville from killing her. Aras didn't know what to make of him, but he had once liked him a lot more than he had liked Josh, and he needed his skills and knowledge.

"Go on," said Aras. He didn't sit down either.

Bennett put his hand in the expandable pocket on his trouser leg and took out Shan's gun. He handed it to Aras on the flat of his palm. "She would have wanted you to have it, sir."

Aras took it and turned it over in his hands. He'd used the weapon before. He had executed Surendra Parekh with it. It hadn't done Shan much good. Pain, the real physical pain of grief, gripped at his chest.

"She asked me to tell you that she was sorry and that she hadn't abandoned you," said Bennett. "You would have been very proud of her, sir."

Aras wanted to hear it and yet he didn't. "Tell me what happened," he said. "Everything." He turned to Eddie. "And you need to hear it too. Because you will tell the *gethes*, and I know you will tell the truth."

It was a hard story to hear. Bennett kept stopping. He related it like a report, but he was struggling to keep his voice steady.

"And you shot her," said Aras.

"It took nearly the whole magazine to bring her down," he said. "She wouldn't give up. It took two of us to restrain her and even then she head-butted me. Hard."

"Do you expect sympathy? She admired you. She *trusted* you."

"I mention it simply because she was so bloody brave, sir."

"And she—" Aras stopped. He couldn't say it. He needed to sit. Eddie stepped in smartly.

"I think we want to know if she really . . . jettisoned herself of her own free will, Ade."

Bennett's jaw worked silently for a few seconds. "She did, but not that she had much of a choice. She told Commander Neville what she thought of her, and just stepped out into space, and the ussissi wouldn't leave her." He swallowed and his whole throat seemed to move. "It was horrible but I'm glad I was there. Some people disappoint you. They're all mouth. Shan wasn't. She got on and did it. I just wanted you to know that."

There was a silence. It went on for a while, and Nevyan seemed to be having the most difficulty with it. She was almost billowing acid agitation. She stood up and peered into Bennett's face.

"Can you give me any location?" she said. "We want to retrieve her body. And Vijissi. They deserve to come home."

Bennett held out his hand. The palm was illuminated green, showing flat lines and numbers. "It records a lot. There'll be a month's worth of location data in there. You'll have a job on your hands, though, even with the coordinates."

"Then it's a job I should be getting on with," said Nevyan.

"I still don't understand why you surrendered," said Eddie. "You didn't kill Shan. You didn't help her much, but you know it wasn't your doing. Had enough of the FEU shunting you around to nursemaid corporations or something?"

Bennett hadn't taken his eyes off Aras. He held his hand out to him, palm up, fist clenched. He nodded towards the *tilgir* on Aras's belt.

"Want to take a slice out of me, sir?"

"That won't bring her back."

"That's not quite what I meant. Please. Just cut me."

Eddie looked completely stunned. *No,* thought Aras. *No, not that.* But he took his knife and he caught Bennett's arm and drew the blade down from the inside of his elbow to the faint blue vessels on his wrist. It was a shallow cut. It was all it needed.

Blood welled for a moment and stopped. Then the cut settled into a red line, and then a pink one, and then it was as if he had never been cut.

"Oh shit," said Eddie. "Here we go again."

"See, I told you she nutted me," said Bennett. "I mean *hard,* too. Blood everywhere, right across my face and hers, and I thought it was all mine because there wasn't a mark on her when we looked. It was an accident. She didn't know she'd infected me."

Aras stared. It was one more difficulty he didn't need. It was the sort of problem Shan would have made him feel better about had she been here to advise him.

He needed her. And he didn't need a human *c'naatat* soldier to worry about.

"Sir, I thought it might be best for everyone if I went deep for a bit," Bennett said, looking rather modest for a man who had kept his nerve under unthinkable circumstances. "And I did tell Commander Neville I took a piss-poor view of what happened to Shan, but it was probably bloody daft of me to let her know I was infected. Anyway, here I am, sir. Can you tell me if the rest of the detachment are okay?"

Eddie interrupted. "I'll find out," he said. "In the meantime, take a seat. I'm sure you'll come in very handy."

The pearl icing of F'nar looked perfectly wonderful in heavy rain.

Eddie stood at the door to the terrace, watching the downpour wash in great waves down the walls of the caldera. The glass conduits were almost singing. At some points the city looked like a designer water feature, the torrent rolling across the iridescence in swirls and channels and creating an abstract animation. Eddie had sent the bee-cam in, fully weather-jacketed, to capture footage while he waited.

It was now five days since he had become the most sought-after interviewee on four planets. It wasn't a position a journalist ever expected to find himself in. He watched angry debates and call-ins with people demanding that he be allowed to speak, and still the call didn't come.

He had interviewed Bennett. It was one of the best he'd ever done, and he reckoned so himself. Bennett had an endearingly frank quality and a matter-of-fact manner that made the telling of Shan Frankland's last grand gesture something of a showstopper. She would have liked that.

But Eddie couldn't use it. The whole story hinged on *c'naatat*. If he ran the line on Shan's death before he conveyed the enormity of the attack on Christopher—on Ouzhari—then nobody would hear the detail. They would be working out how feasible immortality might be for them. Once again one of Shan Frankland's moral stands would have to remain a secret.

She hadn't been able to admit even to him that she had once sacrificed her career and reputation to protect a bunch of ecoterrorists with whom she sympathized. He knew anyway. Whether anyone agreed with her or not, there was something heart-stoppingly admirable about a woman who would put everything on the line—her life included—for a principle.

Eddie was going to make sure she had prime-time if it was the last thing he ever did. He'd just wait a while.

There was no interview with Lindsay Neville or Mohan Rayat, of course. He wanted that most of all. But he could wait for that too.

Eddie walked back into the house and stood in front of the screen, now sliced into five different news channels. Then he hit the message key: still nothing. No incoming calls from Earth. *Call me, you tossers.* Eddie wondered what Ual made of the FEU's poor handling of the row. He needed the diplomatic channels to stay open, at least until he had filed.

Maybe it didn't matter. By not being able to speak, Eddie had become a silent nod to growing speculation that humans had started the war. Yes, they were using the word *war* on every channel. The legal niceties of declaration had gone by the board, even on BBChan bulletins. If your loved ones had died, you needed to hear that it was a war. Nobody wanted to hear that they'd been killed in a diplomatic misunderstanding.

Eddie went back to the door and watched the rain punching through ever-changing rainbows for a long time.

"Does it piss down like this all the time?" asked Bennett. Eddie hadn't even heard him come up behind him. "Been walking round F'nar, getting accustomed to the layout. Pretty. Very pretty."

"Heard from the others yet?"

"Izzy and Chaz are on Mar'an'cas, but Izzy's bioscreen packed up so I'm messaging Chaz. I think they quite like setting up the colonists' camp there. Something good they can do. And Sue, Jon and Barkers are on Umeh."

"And Lindsay's okay?"

"Not interested in her," said Bennett. "Maybe you could ask Nevyan if we could get them all over here. They wouldn't do anything stupid, I'd see to that. When things calm down a bit, of course."

"As POWs?"

"Why?"

"You want to be deserters? Even this far from a court-martial? Otherwise we have to explain why you've cut loose."

"Come on, they'd never try to take me here."

"It's not about that, really. If the *c'naatat* story goes fully public, then who's going to give a shit about a few dead squid?"

"Or Shan," said Bennett.

They stood and shared a homebrew beer. It hadn't fermented

long enough but it was more a symbol than an expression of the brewer's art. Bennett was politely tactful.

"Interesting," he said.

"You can't get drunk any more anyway," said Eddie. "So Shan said."

The front door opened and let in a blast of damp air. Aras had come back from the fields with a basket of muddy vegetables. He dumped them in the bowl under the spigot, rinsed them, and then went to the lavatory and locked the door.

"That's not good," said Eddie. He wanted Aras to talk, at least to Bennett if not to him. He walked up to the door and tapped very gently with his knuckles.

"How are you feeling, mate?" he asked.

There was no answer.

"Aras, come and have something to eat."

"Later," said Aras.

Eddie went out onto the terrace again and began working out how he might get a story off Wess'ej. He couldn't think of any route that didn't involve ITX and bribery. Bennett busied himself cleaning his rifle.

Eddie was still coming up with nothing and feeling increasingly frustrated when he heard Aras moving around inside the house. There was the sound of a container easing open and then a sharp slam as something else was opened and closed.

The sounds of rummaging became more rapid and frantic. Eventually they stopped and Aras came slowly out onto the terrace.

"You have taken something of mine, Eddie."

It hadn't been a bad premonition. There wasn't much of anything to take from Aras, being wess'har: just the grenades.

"It's no good looking for them," Eddie said. He was suddenly scared. Aras could have torn him apart with little effort, and in his current state of mind there was every chance he would. Bennett stood back, watching them carefully. "You won't find them."

"Eddie, how can you do this to me?"

"Because I care what happens to you."

"I can't stand another day like this. I have lived long enough and I have nothing left now. If you had any respect for me you'd stop this stupid game, so give me the grenades."

Eddie had nowhere to run. He stood with his arms held away from his sides, thinking where he'd left his bag. It was stowed under the sofa. He edged between Aras and the door. His stomach was churning. Aras twitched and Eddie almost leaped back, but he stood his ground. "I'm not going to let you kill yourself."

Aras was still for a moment. Then he seized Eddie by his collar and thrust him so hard against the wall that it hammered the breath out of him and he thought Aras was finally going to kill him.

"Let me *go*, Eddie. Let me die."

Eddie gasped for breath. "Fuck you, no. *No.* You want to do it—you do it alone."

"Give them to me. Sergeant Bennett, will *you* give them to me?"

Bennett walked slowly forward, one careful pace at a time. "I'm not helping you, mate."

"Why? What's it to either of you?"

Eddie choked. "She wouldn't have wanted you to do it. And you're the last bit of her left."

Bennett finally came close enough to lay both hands on Aras's arm, very slowly, very gently. "Come on," he said. "Eddie's right. I know what you're going through, remember. I know better than Eddie, anyway. You help me through it and I'll help you. Okay?"

My fault, Eddie thought. *My fault.* Aras didn't let go. He didn't even look at Bennett.

"I failed the bezeri," said Aras. "I killed Josh Garrod. And now I've lost her. How can I carry on?"

"Because it's not finished. It's just starting. She's not here to sort it. But you are."

Bennett's hands tightened on Aras's arm. "Aras, just let it go. Come on. I know it's hard. Come on."

Aras was pressing so hard on his chest that Eddie thought he would black out. Then he let him go, and Eddie slid down the damp pearl wall. Aras sat down slowly beside him.

"I need to lay her to rest," he said.

"You leave that to Nevyan. She's got the ussissi searching."

"Is there more than this life, Eddie?"

"No, mate. Only what we do. That's why it's important that *you* hang on."

"You have your focus, Eddie. You want to tell the story and shame your government, and you'll always find one to shame. I'm not sure of my purpose beyond vengeance."

"Then do it for Shan. Even if it's only revenge, the end result is the same."

"I shouldn't have hurt you," Aras said. "I apologize."

"It's okay," said Eddie. He gave Bennett a *go away* look. *I'm fine. We need to talk.* Bennett shrugged and went back in the house.

They sat in the puddles on the terrace for a long time. Eddie didn't want to leave him sitting there alone. After a while he looked at his exotic, man-beast face and saw something he knew couldn't be, but was.

There were definite tears in Aras's eyes.

C'naatat had relented and handed him one new adaptation that he had wanted so badly for so long. He wept for his *isan*.

Eddie joined him.

29

*I see no case against coming to the aid of Wess'ej. They have
been provoked. Their allies have been invaded and slaughtered.
The ussissi are calling on us to intervene to save their kin as
well. It will be a long-term commitment but now we all know
what is at stake, the end is inevitable. Now or later is meaning-
less: the gethes will invade again. And if they do not, then they
still commit acts on their own world that we cannot tolerate.*

*The word gethes is from our distant past. If we forget what it
means, then we forget what we are at our core. It's the antithesis
of all things that are wess'har.*

SARMATAKIAN VE,
adviser to the council of matriarchs of Eqbas Vorhi,
commonly known as the World Before

Minister Ual called Eddie in the early hours with the best
news he had heard in recent weeks.

Aras shook his shoulder to wake him. He stumbled to the console and tried not to think what would happen to this odd friendship if Ual found out about the quill. Eddie suspected the wily
statesman would think it was fair game, nothing personal at all.

"Pressure from one direction can be deflected," Ual said,
wheezing and sucking. "But pressure from two sides can crush.
I have your link."

"Thank you," said Eddie. He motioned to Aras to find
BBChan 56930, the current primary news feed. He had to
nudge him: Aras was fixed on Ual's image, unblinking. "How
did you manage that?"

"I told your Foreign Office that I was most disappointed that
humans were taking a dim view of a race who would help them
establish instant communications across galaxies. I also said it

would ease my own electorate's fear of aliens if humans were seen to admit their failings."

"A stylish threat, sir."

"No threat," said Ual. "You have a full hour, and I think the phrase is *live to air.*" He made that rattling bubble that Eddie liked to think was a giggle but could as easily have been a curse. "And I do *not* care for your news editor."

"I'll buy you a beer one day, Minister. Thank you."

Eddie had a half-hour package ready to run. It opened with the patrol craft recce footage of Ouzhari burning. It ended with Ade Bennett's eyewitness account.

"Shall I leave you to it?" asked Aras.

"No, you stay right here." Eddie pulled on a fresh shirt and hoped his stubble would make him look authentically warry rather than a man who'd been dragged out of bed and caught on the hop. He set the bee-cam on the console and pulled two stools into place. "Because when this lot finishes running, you're on. I'm interviewing you."

"What do you want me to do?"

"I'll ask you questions and you answer them as you see fit. They might not sound like kind questions, but don't get angry on air. You can punch me later."

"This sounds very negative."

"You know when you tore into me at dinner that time?"

"I was very rude. I meant to be."

"And it would have been great TV. Just say what you think."

"What game is this, then?"

"Showing them what they're taking on. Conveniently running back-to-back with scenes of destruction caused by gung-ho humans."

"Is this a substitute for drama, Eddie, or have you become a propagandist for us?"

"I'm treading a fine line. But all I'm doing is showing people things that they're not here to see for themselves. How they process it is down to them."

Eddie keyed in his code and found that it still worked. He

could begin his transmission at any time with a sixty second
stand-by so the current anchor could get the bulletin out of the
segment and manage a reasonable throw to a live OB from 150
trillion miles away. He could see the output from the split feed
from Umeh Station.

He didn't even have to talk to News Desk.

"Thirty seconds," he said to nobody in particular, and
smoothed down his shirt.

Lindsay Neville walked through the crowded biodome of Umeh
Station and found a path had cleared for her.

It wasn't the sort of leeway granted to Shan Frankland by
dint of her commanding presence. The evacuees just didn't
look like they wanted close contact with the woman who had
carried out an act of war against a militarily superior neighbor.

And Okurt and his senior officers had died in *Actaeon*. She
was now the ranking officer in a ship of chaos.

She had the feeling she wasn't going to be popular. It was
hard to be loved and respected when you had stranded nearly
four hundred people a long way from home without the
prospect of rescue.

"There's Jon," said Barencoin. He put his thumb and forefinger between his lips and whistled so loudly that Lindsay
jumped. "Oi, Jon! Over here!" He grinned, but not at her. "And
there's Sue. The old firm again, eh?"

"I want you lot to keep Rayat on a leash for the time being,"
said Lindsay.

Barencoin inhaled slowly. "He's your problem now,
ma'am," he said. "He's not going anywhere. None of us are
ever again, I reckon. If you'll excuse me, I'm going to find a
doctor to get this bloody round out of my leg before the meds
wear off."

He limped off into the milling crowd to be reunited with his
two comrades. If Lindsay thought she'd have marine backup,
she was mistaken. She wandered into one of the construction
huts and asked for the duty foreman. It was time to make a start

on creating some order and purpose. She was going to be here a long time.

"Well, that was fucking clever." The young engineer sitting behind the makeshift desk just glanced up at her once. He was checking inventories. "You're the military genius who nearly got us all fried, eh?"

"I'm not even going to discuss that," said Lindsay wearily. "We need some organization here."

"We've got nearly four hundred people in a half-finished habitat. It's enough water, lavatories, and food facilities that we need. You offering?"

There was no point pulling rank. Civilians didn't jump for her. "Okay," she said. "You get on with the logistics and I'll round up my personnel. Then we can sit down and talk sensibly later."

"And bring a shovel," said the engineer. He jabbed his thumb over his shoulder without looking up. "Have a look at the news. You're on. Or at least your handiwork is."

Lindsay cast around and found the small screen obscured by piles of insulation sheeting. She was going to leave: she didn't have time for this. But she didn't. She watched. She watched because she heard Eddie's familiar voice over images that she should have recognized but didn't.

Lindsay watched Eddie's news special with detached horror. She had lived these events. They looked much worse on screen. Stripped of the emotion of experiencing them, she saw only what history would see: destruction, anger, panic and a huge gamble taken on what humans might have done had they got hold of an organism called *c'naatat*.

Viewed cold, it seemed a very slim risk.

What have I done?

It gave her an unpleasant feeling in her mouth, the sensation that the sides of her palate just above her teeth were closing together like Scylla and Charybdis. She wasn't sure if it was adrenaline or nausea.

Eddie was now interviewing Aras.

"Who do you see as the greater threat now—isenj or human?"

"The isenj managed to destroy almost the entire bezeri population. Humans—gethes—finished the job, as you would say. I have no great love for either species."

"Do you feel the alliance between the two has increased tension here on Wess'ej?"

"Of course it has. The isenj are native to this system, but you're not, and you have no right to be here. As long as you have a base within striking distance of us, we will not rest easy. We have seen what a handful of you can do."

"And your people have a reputation for all-encompassing military solutions."

"If you're referring to the cleansing of Bezer'ej, yes, we act decisively."

It was extraordinary. There was no mention of Shan. There was no mention of *c'naatat*. Eddie had skirted neatly, round it but the question hung there: why bomb the bloody place? Lindsay wondered what game he was playing. Maybe his bosses had warned him off. She was angry. It named her and it named Rayat and made them both look like war criminals.

"It wasn't like that at all," she said angrily at the screen. "Eddie, you bastard. Tell them why I did it."

"Yeah, *I'd* love to know," muttered the engineer.

Lindsay turned and walked out. She'd done the right thing, but the wrong way. She'd wiped out—no, she had *almost* wiped out—a dangerous organism that humans simply couldn't be trusted to handle. And she couldn't tell anyone right then, or maybe ever. All they saw was her crime and her stupidity.

It was just like Eddie had said about Shan and that business with Green Rage. It was Rochefoucauld's classic example of perfect courage, a massive private sacrifice that won you no worshipers.

For the first time, Lindsay knew exactly how it felt to be Shan Frankland.

*   *   *

Ceret was rising. The *tem* flies, swarming before moving south to hotter climates for the winter season, battled for position on the first sun-warmed stones.

"It's still the prettiest damn thing I've ever seen," said Eddie. "It's not a bad place to be marooned."

Eddie had more of a choice than he had realized. F'nar was not the only city of pearl, just one of a chain of settlements and cliffs and other convenient surfaces that stood on the *tems'* migration path. Aras said he regretted not showing all of them to Shan.

The *tem* flies were on the move now, great black clouds of smoke across the face of Ceret. If you looked at them long enough, you could pick out images that resembled animals or plants or landscapes.

Children enjoyed the game of recognition. Nevyan waited with Giyadas for an especially large cloud of flies to sweep across the setting red disk of the sun.

"Great shot," said Eddie, like a fond uncle. The bee-cam was diligently recording it all. He'd use that the next time he got an uplink.

Giyadas, absorbing English at an alarming rate, watched him intently.

"Great shot," she said, accentless.

Mestin had promised to send Serrimissani to fetch them when the message came through from the World Before. She was waiting by the screen, an unusual act of patience for her. There was a vague promise of help in the recognition of a common threat, but Eddie had heard that before on Earth. Had it been the matriarchs of F'nar who had said it, he would have believed it.

But not even the ussissi knew how the World Before would really react to a plea for help from a band of outcasts who had cut themselves off thousands of years ago because they didn't want to get involved.

There was always the chance they would come back and tell them to piss off.

"Have you seen pictures of them?" asked Eddie.

Nevyan jiggled her head like an Indian dancer. "No."

"You're pretty short on curiosity for a clever species."

"Curiosity leads to exploration, and we never planned to go back. But I *am* curious, Eddie."

"You'll find out soon enough."

They all would.

Bennett had persuaded Aras to come out and see the swarming. Aras was sitting with his head bowed, absorbed in the contents of a small red cylinder whose fragile screen was strung between filaments. It was Shan's swiss. He never put it down now. Bennett simply sat and watched him. They had a lot in common. If Aras was going to survive his grief, it would be Bennett who would be most help to him.

A bloody shame, thought Eddie. *Poor sods.*

Serrimissani was suddenly among them, agitated, urgent. "They are responding," she said. "Right now. Come."

Eddie wasn't the last inside. Aras was reluctant to watch and shook his head. Bennett waited with him.

"Call me when I can do something useful," he said, and held the swiss in both hands as if it would break. When it did, there would be nobody left who knew how to repair it or where to find the parts.

The rest of them—Nevyan and Mestin's families and Eddie—stood and watched the image from a city that was well-proportioned and softened by planting, but very, very urban.

For once Eddie was not alone in his bewilderment and wonder.

The whole of F'nar had ground to a halt. The signal had been made available to everybody: there were no secrets among wess'har. The usual backdrop of domestic noise, of scraping glass utensils and caterwauling matriarchs, had ceased. For the first time Eddie could hear the trickling water from thousands of glass conduits around the caldera. It was as heart-stopping as a total eclipse.

They were all looking at their screens, wherever they were, because that was what he was doing too. They were looking for the first time at kin they hadn't seen in ten thousand years.

And the face in the image was almost wholly alien.

The wess'har genome was as flexible as thread, alw adapting, reshaping. It was what made them such a perfect h for *c'naatat*. And in ten thousand years, both branches of family had gone their own distinctive ways.

"That's a wess'har?" Eddie asked.

"Yes," said Serrimissani. "A matriarch."

The scarcely recognizable creature had a ussissi interpre and that much they could all identify. It was the ussissi v spoke after a stream of double-voiced but unintelligible sov emerged from the female who looked little like the *isan've* die had now started to see as normal.

"Tell the *gethes* we are coming," said the ussissi, repeat the words of his matriarch. "Tell them that we too believe balancing, and that the bezeri will have justice, even if no are left to witness it. What threatens you threatens us."

Nevyan had her long arms crossed over her chest in that c nervous gesture the females seemed to have. "So it's done," said. And she simply turned and walked out on to the terra again. Eddie went after her.

"Is that it?" he said. "What next?"

"We will arrange liaison now. It will take a little time. A you have much to do."

"Yeah, I've got some stories to broadcast, when the tim right. You've seen the news. Earth's boiling. So I'm busy. W will you do?"

Nevyan pulled her *dhren* up around her neck. "I have imp tant work to occupy me."

"What exactly?"

Nevyan cocked her head, taking in Aras and Bennett, w were just sitting on a low wall and not talking.

"I'm going to find my friend," said Nevyan. "And I'm go to bring her home."

Look for the third volume in The Wess'har Wars, co ing soon.